The Abandoned Isles

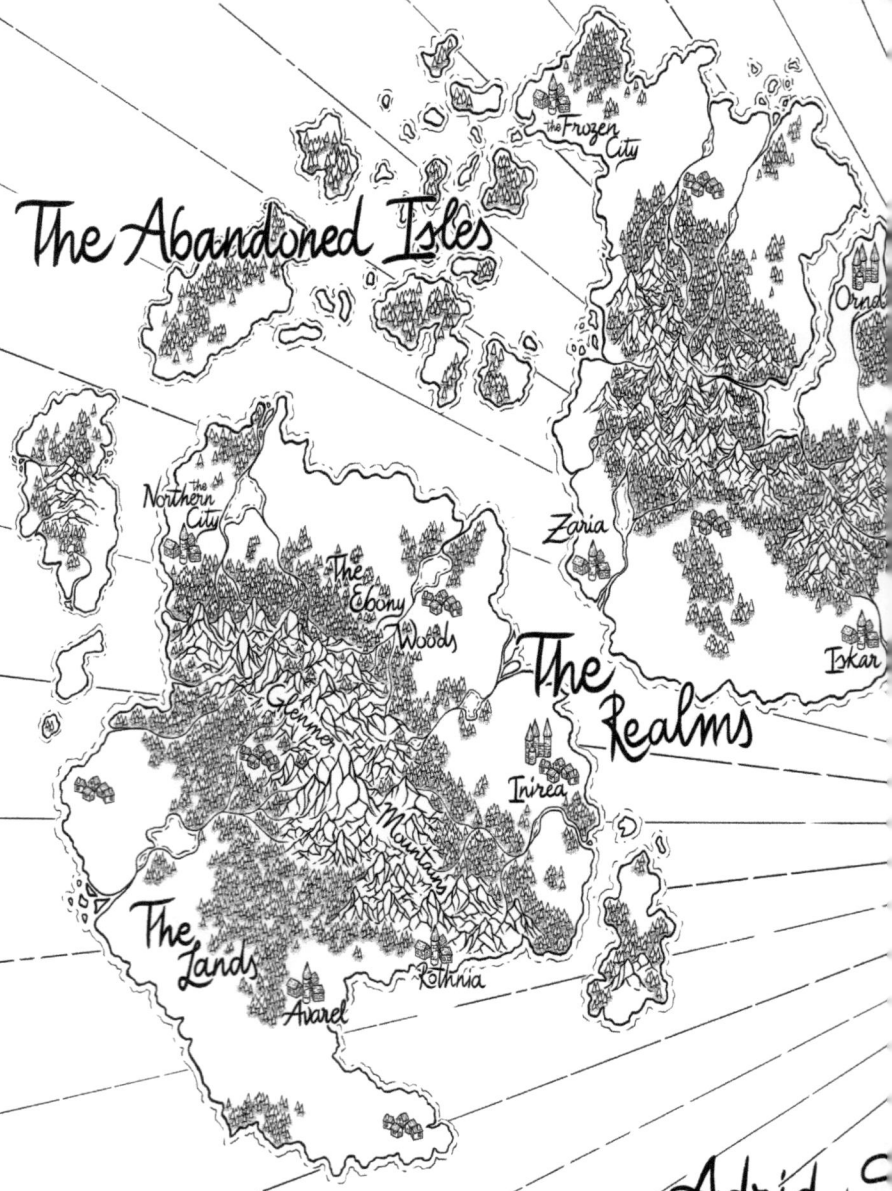

the Frozen City

Ornd

Northern City

Zaria

The Ebony Woods

The Realms

Iskar

Glenna

Inirea

Mountains

The Lands

Kothnia

Avarel

Adrid

Aeris

Nanadral

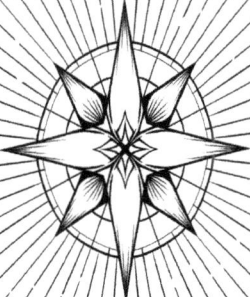

Duval Sea

Kelna

Elliner

Telford

Curse of Lies and Darkness

PLAYLIST

In no particular order

-MIDDLE OF THE NIGHT

Elley Duhe

-EXPERIENCE

Ludovico Einaudi, Daniel Hope

-IN THE NAME OF LOVE

David Guetta, Bebe Rexha

-CALL YOU MINE

The Chainsmokers, Bebe Rexha

-MIDDLE OF THE NIGHT (VIOLIN)

Joel Sunny

-MAY IT BE

Enya

-I'M YOURS

Isabel LaRosa

CURSE
OF
LIES
AND
DARKNESS

THE LOST FAE
BOOK ONE

V.A. HAUGEN

Mom, you've been there from day one.
Thank you for all that you've done.

THE PROPHECY

"A PRINCESS BORN OF SKY AND EARTH,
THE STARS WITHIN HER VEINS.
TIED TO THE LAND SHE IS,
A SAVIOR SHE WILL BE.
HOWEVER THE PATH MAY LEAD HER,
ITS DARKNESS SHE COULD CLAIM.
AS A CURSE IS CAST UPON THE LAND,
THE WICKEDNESS MOVES FREE.

TAKEN FROM THE LAND SHE LIVES,
TO GROW AMONG THE TREES.
A WISH MADE IN ANGUISH AND
THE MEMORIES SHE MUST RETRIEVE.
RETURNED TO INIREA SHE'LL BE,
A SINGLE TASK SHE MUST COMPLETE.
A YEAR SHE HAS TO BREAK THE CURSE,
OR ALL HER EFFORTS ARE IN VAIN."

--THE HARUSPEX. DURING THE RULE OF
KING ELIAS THE FIRST, INIREA, 1463

Prologue

Inirea, 1792

THE KING SAT MOTIONLESS ON his throne, surrounded by the deafening echoes of steel and shouts reverberating through the corridors. The gravity of the situation was not lost on him; it had all come down to this final moment. His failure weighed heavily upon him, crushing him under the weight of his own inadequacy.

He'd failed.

He had failed his people, his kingdom, and most of all, his family. When he received word that the Lord of the Dark Fae was preparing to attack, and that a legion was rising up against him, questioning his rule, he had begun preparing his city and its inhabitants. But he had believed he had more time, and as a result, he had failed to act sooner.

The siege had begun early that morning, abruptly interrupting his peaceful slumber and forcing him and his family to flee their beds. He had reluctantly entrusted his wife and children to the Keepers, members of his trusted guard who he knew would protect them with their lives.

The words of the prophecy echoed through his mind once more, a constant reminder of the potential savior that his firstborn daughter could have been. She was the one born with the Power of Stars, a gift from the Immortal Gods, and he could only hope that she had managed to escape the invading danger.

As he clutched his sword tightly in his lap, he couldn't help but reminisce about a time when he could have watched his family grow and flourish, without the looming threat of danger always present. But now, his only goal was to protect those he loved, even if it meant sacrificing his own life.

The legion had reached the castle walls, and they were quickly making their way towards the main castle. The King had no other options but to accept his fate; he would not run, he could not run. He hoped that his sacrifice would buy his loved ones the time they needed to escape. However, his heart sank at the sound of his daughter's voice, filling him with fear for her safety.

"Papa!"

The muffled cries of his daughter echoed behind a door. She should not be here. Calling for him again, the terror in her voice.

"Papa!"

As if on cue, the door to his left burst open, revealing his daughter Astraea. Her hair was disheveled and her dark green dress was stained, her eyes wide with terror. Without hesitation, the King leaped from his throne, his sword forgotten as it clattered to the stone floor behind him.

"Astraea, what are you doing here?" he asked, catching her in his arms. She wept openly as he scanned the dark hallway from which she had emerged, finding no sign of anyone else. Holding her close, he could feel the fear coursing through her body.

Kissing the side of her head, he gently lowered her to her feet, brushing her hair from her face and wiping the tears from her cheeks. "Astraea, where are Aden and your mother?" he asked, his heart pounding in his chest.

"They're gone," she whispered, clutching her stuffed bear tightly.

The King's heart sank as he realized the gravity of the situation. The sound of steel-on-steel grew louder in the outer corridor, signaling the approach of the enemy forces. He knew that he had to get his daughter somewhere safe, and quickly.

Leading her behind the throne, he brushed aside a tapestry on the wall and pushed open a trap door. Urging her inside, he kissed her forehead and whispered, "Be brave."

Nodding once she wiped her tears from her cheeks. He knew this was going to be the last time he would ever see her again. This would be the last time he ever saw her big beautiful eyes, deep down, the magic was telling him that she was going to right this. The wrong would be corrected one day. The king smiled weakly at her, whispering softly, "I love you."

She stared up at him, fear in her eyes. Signaling her to keep quiet, he shut her inside. Checking to be sure the door was shut tight, the tapestry fell back over, concealing her inside. Murmuring a displacement spell, in hopes it would hide her from Him. The guilt he carried, the sadness and heartache at the outcome of these events, weighed on him. She never should have been put in the middle of it. She was innocent, whatever fate had planned for her, he hoped it would give her mercy. Picking up his sword from the stone floor, the shouts in the corridor outside the throne room set his nerves on edge again.

A moment later the large wood doors flew open.

Ezra.

"Where is she?" he demanded. His sword in hand, the blade red with blood. If this was how he wanted to do things, then so be it.

The king gripped his sword tighter, "Gone."

Ezra bared his teeth. "You lie, Elias. Where is she?!"

A cruel smile spread across Elias' lips, "She is safe. From you and everyone who wishes her harm, Brother."

The darkness in his eyes flared, "I will find her, and when I do, everything you fought for will end with her."

Elias laughed, "If she dies, the whole realm dies. You know this."

A roar escapes from Ezra as he throws himself forward. His sword poised to kill. The force strong enough to slice through him. In one movement, Elias parries Ezra's attack, sending his sword flying from his hand and to the floor. Elias had always been the better swordsman, his skill with a blade far outranking Ezra's. But the momentum of his parry sent his brother off balance and crashing into the stone steps of the dais.

"Give up Ezra, stop all of this madness." Elias pleaded, the tip of his sword pointed at his brother's throat, at the soft spot where his pulse thrummed in his veins.

As he stared at his twin brother, Elias was overcome with conflicting emotions. They had been born as two halves of the same whole, inseparable from the moment they took their first breath. But as he looked into Ezra's eyes, he saw that something had changed. The bright green that had once shone so brilliantly now held a darkness that made Elias uneasy.

Despite this, he could not bring himself to harm his own flesh and blood. They had grown up together, shared everything, and he couldn't bear the thought of turning his sword against his twin. But as much as it pained him, Elias knew that he had to put his family's safety first. They were his only concern, and he would do whatever it took to protect them, even if it meant fighting against his own brother.

Lowering his sword, his eyes pleaded with him. "Please."

"No. All of this should have been mine. Father made the wrong choice." Ezra spat at him, getting up to his feet. Ezra was not going to back down.

"By your actions, I believe he made the best choice for our realm."

Another roar erupted from Ezra as he launched himself at Elias. The king didn't see the dagger in Ezra's hand as he moved, before it plunged into his chest. Eyes wide, shock on his face as Ezra pulls him closer, the blade burying itself deeper in his chest.

"I know the secret, *brother.*" Ezra whispered in his ear twisting the blade, a final killing blow. The blood oozed from the wound. "You cannot protect her forever, hide her away but I will find her. She will come to me. The land has been cursed; the entire realm will be mine."

A wet laugh- turned cough escapes from the King's lips, blood spilling from the corner, "All of this trouble, and you still haven't won Ezra. What have you gained from this..." Mockingly, "Lord of the Dark Fae?"

Ezra scoffs before pulling the knife and stepping away. Watching the king fumble for the throne clutching at his chest, his sword lay forgotten beside him. He watched his brother die before him, the light leaving his eyes as he slumped down. A regiment of Fae knights in black armor rushed in through the doors.

"Find her." Ezra barked.

PART I

BROKEN HEARTS, BROKEN MEMORIES

--

CHAPTER
One

Rothnia, 1810

Serra

I'VE LIVED IN THIS VILLAGE for most of my life, and for the most part that's fine by me. But in late fall when the sky fills with birds migrating to the continent in the south for the winter-traveling thousands of miles to get there- I get homesick for places I've never been. Places like in my dreams.

Enchanted forests, forbidden lakes, lush green gardens surrounding a large stone castle ravaged over time by war. A world of fairies, Fae, goblins and immortals. A world occupied far beyond the confines of Rothnia and the Mortal Lands. A realm that only existed in my dreams. A realm so unrealistic that my mind reprimanded me each morning for the falseness that it was. However, as I watched the birds fly home, I cannot help but wonder if I was meant for greater things.

As if I could grow my own pair of wings and fly away with them.

We had made it through another winter and spring was almost in full bloom. The migratory birds make their voices known by the songs in the trees. The burrow animals coming out from hibernation, the world was waking up again. A familiar sound and smell. The wet earth is full of life and ever-changing. The trees in bloom and the harmony of existence carries on.

With the changing of the season came the changes of the Lands. In a few short weeks, the Lands would be alive again with mundane daily life. As mortals, we were merely inhabitants. Insignificant to the life around us, to the binding of time. It came and went, never stopping. No matter how you tried.

But winter slows everything down, being so close to the mountains on one side and the ocean on the other, it causes trade routes to close. The snow off the mountain caps often caused avalanches in the pass and the winter winds on the water sent more to their watery grave every year.

With Spring, Sailors could set out safely for work again, men and women would come together in the village square to sell a wide variety of things. Pastries, jewelry, even stones and gems from far off places. The children ran the streets, laughing and singing, reciting old nursery rhymes, and kites raised in the spring breeze. The merchants made port and the pass opened up again to trade.

Rothnia wasn't large, but it was a port city- technically. One of many for those who stopped after crossing the Adrid Seas. I wish all of it was so appealing to me. The joy and happiness Spring brought. The preparations for the Spring Festival.

But not this year.

This year was different.

A calm breeze had picked up around me, lifting the shawl around my shoulders. The chilled air sent a shudder down my spine. My dark hair was braided back to keep it out of my face, a few tendrils falling loose, left blowing gently as the breeze caressed my face. The linen fabric of my skirts moved softly, the hems covered in crusted dirt and mud. I didn't own much, but I was cared for.

Or at least I had been.

I didn't have a lot to my name.

Just this plot of land outside the village and the cottage next to the garden. The building was small- constructed of rock and limestone mortar. A thatched roof kept the rain out. The interior was warm, made up of a single open room with a large fireplace and table. A couple chairs, a few cabinets to make up a kitchenette and a small bedroom at the back with a loft above. It wasn't large by today's standards, but it was home.

My home.

While it was tucked up off the main road, it was still nestled a few feet from the forest edge at the base of a smaller mountain. The stream running along the edge of the property wound its way along before disappearing into the Ebony Woods.

The black barked trees and the white leaves kept many from entering its depths, but as a little girl I often played next to it- my imagination traveled rapidly and wild. I never quite wandered in though, even as it called to me. It beckoned me to step just one foot inside.

The dark magic pulled me. It wasn't from here, the feeling that it was from another realm wore on my senses. The whispers on the wind that whipped through the trees. Caressing me as I stood on the edge. A sad murmur, *Come home.*

"Coooome hooome."

The trance over my senses broke every time. The trepidation of the woods and its hold on me doing just that. But it was the creatures hidden from sight and the cackles in the low brush that would keep me at bay. I wouldn't step inside it. The dark, I wasn't afraid of the dark. But I was afraid of the Ebony Wood. Eyeing it now, I kept moving along the paths in the garden. Checking each row before moving to the next, my basket in hand. It wasn't quite planting season, but the ground was ready.

Crouching down to check the dirt, I noted I could begin planting soon. Mentally mapping out where each seed was going to be sowed. Over the next couple of months, I would faithfully tend to them. Allow them to grow and flourish before harvesting and storing what I could in the fall. During the other days of the month, I worked at the local tavern- our sole income. I wouldn't call it a glamorous job, being the dish maid. But it brought in coins.

And we needed it, I needed it.

A breath escapes as I stand, making my way to the flower patch on the far edge. Most evenings, I collected the flowers that grew along the stone wall at the back of the garden. While they brought a little bit of happiness and joy, these flowers were for someone else. Every chance I had; I made the trek to the other side of the village. A stop at the cemetery, to lay the flowers on a set of graves.

My father, my mother and my little brother. These flowers were not only for the family I lost. Not this time. There was one extra grave for me to visit. One extra grave to tend. One extra heartbreak to add to the pain I already harbored.

My Nona Luna's.

Snipping the flowers at the base of the stem, balanced on the balls of my feet. A sad smile spreads across my lips. Her memory would not die with her. I would not let it. Nona was a force to be reckoned with. She was something else. The townspeople used to say she was crazy.

With her stories and her beliefs. All things she passed down to me. Nona Luna was my guardian. And I loved her to bits. She had left me everything- the land, the cottage, the garden.

All of it was mine.

A sad tear escapes from the corner of my eye and rolls down my cheek as I add a bundle of flowers to my basket. Forget-Me-Nots, fitting for now. Unfortunately, with her passing it has left me alone. Again. Even when my family died, Nona Luna was there. I was almost seven when it happened, my little brother was just a babe. It's hard to remember any of it, just the flames and the shouts. A dark cloaked figure, really is all I can recall.

It's like there's a block on that part of my memories. It's hazy and every time I tried to reach for it, to remember- it relinquishes its hold on me. I often feel drained and exhausted trying to remember my life before. The memories of those I lost. I barely remember their faces. The kind eyes of my mother, the fire within my father. My brother's toothless happy smile and blonde curls. Other than that, I don't remember much from before I was put in her care.

Just that she was already old then.

Now eighteen years later, she was gone, taken from me by the sickness. No one knows when it started or where or how it showed up, but every year someone is taken by it. There was talk that it comes from a place lost to us, that its punishment for things done wrong in the past. I don't know, Nona wouldn't divulge any knowledge she had on it. Just that it was spreading, and I should be wary.

Nona was eccentric. Not crazy.

Sure, she mumbled to herself when she thought no one was listening, or I was out of earshot. But I chalked that up to her just being cautious. She guarded much of herself and of me from the world. She trusted very few. And in turn, neither did I. Her ramblings made little sense but while she cared for me, and she made sure I had what I needed, she also made sure I would be able to care for myself.

She showed me how to patch my dresses, sew new pieces when we had the fabric to do so. How to mend my shoes to get me through another season, how to cook. Taught me everything I needed to know in the garden and the use of every herb and flower before me. How to care for those who were sick and dying, care for the animals who would come and go, many of them searching for help- everything.

She taught me that everything was a gift, life is a gift. The world around us was gifted to us by the Immortal Gods and we must not take it for granted. We must cherish it, nourish it and allow it to grow. Or we lose it entirely. We would laugh together, sing together, and she always let me cry when it felt like the world around me was against us. She told me stories. The stories of the Lost Fae and Inirea, the City of Immortals. Stories of goblins and fairies, dragons, and beasts.

She told stories of him.

The Goblin King.

A murderous and ruthless being, the ruler of Inirea and its people. Nobody knows where the stories of the Goblin King originated. How the tales came to be. But they were a part of the village and its people.

Nona Luna would tell the stories of the missing children. The ones taken from their homes in the dead of night. A new child is taken every year, at the beginning of Spring. Never to be seen again. I asked once when I was thirteen how it was possible. She'd stated that he'd come into the village in a rush of wings and wind, and then disappear again with them before anyone knew he had been there.

No one has ever seen him and those who claim to have vastly different descriptions of him. Some say he was tall with gangly limbs and straw like hair, others say he was short and round with bark for skin. I heard from a traveling merchant once that he only comes when wished for. Never will he reveal his true self to those who summon him. The tales say that only the one who is worthy will see through his glamour. Whatever that means. I don't pretend to get caught up in the village folklore. Nona's stories were more than enough to entertain me.

Hearing her stories though of the Goblin King a question always remained. What did he do with the children he stole away, and why did he do it? Nona once said that the children were turned into goblins and resided in a city outside the castle gates. Left to live out their lives while the wishes that brought them there were granted. I used to make wishes to the Goblin King, foolish as I was.

They were never granted.

Only recently in the last year had I again made a foolish wish to him. I had spoken rashly looking back on it now. I wished that a boy would be whisked away for breaking my heart. Whispered in the darkness as I cried over him. The boy I had once wished *for*.

The first boy I had fallen in love with.

Kaston Conwell.

Kaston was not only my first love, but he was my first everything. He was my first kiss, my first partner. My first heartbreak. I had crushes but Kaston was more.

So much more to me at the time.

The sting of what he left me with still hurt. His cruel words, his snide sneer after he fractured me in two. It did not help that he came from one of the more prominent families. One with huge amounts of wealth. Not only did the Conwell's hold a large portion of Rothnia's wealth, but their charities also benefited greatly from them.

And while Lord Conwell operated the shipping part of their wealth, the sons: Torian, Caine, and Kaston, walked around Rothnia with such arrogance. I often wondered what their mother thought, if she cared. Even so the dallying of young men in Rothnia was far less frowned upon than those of women. Unless you were a Lady of the Night you were to stay pure and intact until marriage.

Any who did not well, we were demeaned. . . tainted.

I truly had thought myself in love with Kaston once. I truly had thought that he was there for me, that he was the one. The boy I dreamed of, the knight to liberate me. I wanted so badly to believe he had been my chance at true happiness and love, at a family, that I had been blinded by his true intentions. And he sure did let his intentions be known, more than once. What happened when I confessed my feelings, I confessed my heart and love to him?

He'd thrown it back in my face.

He broke every part of me, every part I had given him. I was his secret. I still remember the look on his face, the look of triumph and satisfaction. I begged. I had pleaded. Despite it all, despite begging him to court me in public, he still used me.

He got what he wanted from me, he got what he was after, over and over. The thought of him having touched me caused a shiver to run down my spine. He had left me in tears, he had left me alone by myself to find my way back. That night the Ebony Woods cradled me as if I were part of it.

Kaston Conwell had no rules, was free to do as he pleased with whomever he pleased. I had been swept up in the romantic notion that he was there to save me. But in the end, he tossed me aside like a used pair of riding boots. He had said it was fun and while he enjoyed my company, I wasn't more than a fling. A conquest. The amusement in his eyes as he said it crushed every last part of me. Leaving me empty and forlorn. And because I had no dowry, I was no one. I was worthless.

I'm improper.

I'm different. Now I was worthless to any man. So, Nona's stories became my friends. They became my company. And now, that's all that I have left.

Of her, of my family and of me.

If I never woke up again, it would be a blessing.

It felt like yesterday that I said goodbye, the days blending in together. Today was the first real day I was able to get out of bed and go to her. She'd been buried under a large oak tree. It overlooked everything. She would have loved it. The dirt was still fresh but settling and the flowers from the day of her burial had dried up and blown around the grass. She would be my first stop before going to the spot where my family rested.

She deserved more honestly but I couldn't give it to her. The oak tree spot had been lucky, otherwise I wasn't sure what I would have done. It was only thanks to her friend Bern that she had found such a beautiful stop to rest. She'd given so much and asked for little in return. And for that I will forever be grateful, she meant so much to me.

A soft cry escaped from my lungs, the weight of her passing sitting heavily on my shoulders. Remembering how quickly it had happened. It started with a nasty cough, but as the night wore on, she deteriorated. Finally letting go only days after the first signs. Saying goodbye to her, knowing that never again would she be waiting for me inside the cottage. Never again would she scold me for my adventures or tell me stories.

"Nona, why did you leave me? Why did you leave me here alone? I cannot do this." The breeze fluttered about me as I buried my face in my arm, the tears rolling down my cheeks. My voice a soft whisper, thick with the sadness in my heart, "I'm not strong enough to do this on my own."

A peaceful silence settled itself around me, as if to say, it's okay. For the first time since this morning, I welcome it. The silence had been deafening. Waking up to the kitchen quiet of all noise and the lack of Nona's mumbles had really started to feel empty. Unfortunately, silence afforded me the comfort to dream or make up nightmares. Whichever you prefer. And because I had no real friends I was often left alone.

To let those nightmares run its course through my vivid imagination. The Goblin King was always the subject of my games. Wishing myself away to him, enraptured by him and the Lost Fae. Fancying myself his bride; that kind of nonsense. When I'd wake up or return from my daydreams, I would talk of my adventures. After telling Nona all about the things I imagined I'd get scolded for it. Nona would mumble about goblins and Fae making up such a foolish game.

"Hush, child!" Nona Luna chastised after I told her that I asked to be taken away, "It is not wise to wish for the Goblin King. He has no remorse; he knows no mercy."

She ushered me back inside and shut the door, baring it tight to keep those who are not welcome in, out. "The Goblin King will take whatever it is you offer him and not think twice of taking it."

I catch sight of the setting sun, my wish lingering on my lips as I whisper to myself, "I wish. . . I wish. . . I wish. . ."

I hesitate. Maybe this was a bad idea. Maybe I was going crazy with grief. Or I was just plain stupid and needed a mental evaluation. But before I even realized what I was saying it was out. "I wish to be free of this attachment, of this torment. I wish to live without this grief."

In the distance, the sound of a raven startles me, bringing me back to this moment- the basket next to me filled with flowers, the world around me, the chilled spring air that now promises rain. The horror of what I had just said aloud.

'That's quite enough for today.'

The sun was making its way down toward the horizon, the shadows stretching as the darkness moved in.

And all my life, for as long as I could remember, I wasn't permitted out after the sun went down. The reason being far more chilling. This time of year was not safe, for anyone. Because who knew what was going to take you. Children were not the only things taken at night.

While it was rare, it happened.

There are creatures, many who liked to roam these lands. Many with no master, no boundary to stop them. No one quite knows where they came from or how they got here. It was instilled into us from such a young age, that the forest behind my home was where they resided. It was home to more than one unknown species than the stories warned against.

And if you were caught out roaming, or hiking within the Ebony Woods, especially after dark, then you were at their mercy. Sometimes, late at night, I heard their cries. Their footsteps would sound outside my window, the crunch of the leaves or rustle of the grass. I wondered if it was him if he was there for me. Having heard my calls, having come to finally answer. Whatever it was, I was not about to find out. What lurks around my home can stay in the dark.

As I stood, my knees aching from the prolonged crouch, a flurry of movement in the distance caught my eye. The raven had flown off from a branch along the forest's edge, causing me to pause as my heart pounded in my chest.

"Stupid bird." I uttered softly.

For a second, it soared high above the trees. But its path changed quickly as it dove back down. Its wings stretched wide, gliding across the air current. If I took my eyes from it now, who knew what it would do. But I hoped, *hoped* it would continue flying on. That it was out for another reason. But it's the gust of wind that picks up along the grass I see next. Rushing towards me, the large black bird at its center. A swirl of dead leaves, debris, and flower petals in its wake. I knew then what was about to happen.

Nona's warnings rang in my ears.

I should run. My legs should be moving.

Instead, a cruel laugh echoes around me, bouncing off the trees, the ground, and the stone as it rings in my ears. A laugh malicious enough to send a shiver down your spine. I could not stop my instincts to shield my face, not as the debris rushed at me, swirling around the garden. As the wind slows, the leaves and dust settle to the ground. Apprehension and trepidation had a firm grip on my nerves. I certainly was not sure I wanted to look, but his laugh echoed again. I dropped my arm anyway and looked up- my senses adjusting to the change in the air, to the magic that lingered on my tongue. A man was standing there, one who certainly was not there before. One with pointed ears and a cruel smile on his lips.

"Hello, Serra." he drawls.

The viciousness and malice in his voice set every part of me on edge. This is not where I wanted to be. This was not someone who you wanted to be in the presence of. I need to run. Oh, do I need to run. Everything, every voice, every sense, they were all screaming at me to run.

But I can't.

I'm rooted here amongst the flowers of this garden as if I were a plant myself. One fleeting thought, a feeling that this was not the first time I have met him. This isn't the only thing that screamed at me.

How does he know my name?

CHAPTER
Two

Serra

THIS BEING, THIS MAN, had come out of nowhere. Appearing in a whirl of smoke, wind, and shadow. The darkness around him shimmering as he stood before me. The hairs along my arms and neck prickled as unease coursed through my veins. The grass and trees around me had gone quiet, as if they too could sense something was wrong.

What had I done?

At first glance I noticed that he was tall. Far taller than any of the gentlemen back in the village, with long silver blond hair, so pale it appeared white. He'd left it loose, allowing it to blow softly in the breeze. Several strands had blown across his face, drawing my attention to his eyes.

His eyes.

They were calculating.

Watching my every movement, I was sure he could see my breaths coming in short gasps as my heart pounded violently in my chest. The smell of fear rolling off me in waves. But something was different about them. Remarkably, each iris was a different color.

Curious.

One was of the lightest blue, so pale it was like ice. The other was a shade of green so brilliant it made my stomach flutter. His face was slim with high cheekbones, his strong jaw line was well defined and his nose so straight, it would make a god jealous. If they weren't already. His lips were full, and his ears arched in a tapered point. Fae.

He was definitely Fae.

No mistakes.

He wore a velvet doublet of the darkest blue that you could mistake for black at first glance. The gold embroidery that ran along the front was so finely done that it would have taken an experienced seamstress weeks to do if not months. It ran from the hem to his collar in a set of vines and leaves.

A set of brilliant gold buttons accentuated the filigree design. His fitted trousers were the color of coal made of soft suede, which he had tucked into the top of dark knee-high boots. Polished to such a shine I could see my reflection in them. He was very well dressed for a man of his station. The thick black cloak around his shoulders moved with the breeze that surrounded him in his wake, before settling back down amongst the leaves, petals, and smoke- remnants of his arrival.

But it was his scent, the smell of citrus, smoke and evergreen that assaulted my nose. A smell I found comforting, familiar.

A smell my mind knew from once upon a time.

My brows furrowed in confusion before my mind finally caught on. My throat constricts, acutely aware of who he was. Still, like the fool I am, thoughtless, stubborn and mental I stammer hoarsely. "Who are you? Why have you come?"

His smile widens at my questions, the cruelness of his sneer making me cower. The sharp canines on display. I was sure he could sense my fear and foolishness. As if it drifted on the wind, his keen Fae sense of smell detecting it.

"You know who I am."

His voice was like honey, thick and sensual- caressing every fiber in my body. Causing a thrill to run through me, up and down my spine. Making my toes curl in my worn brown leather boots. A shiver forces itself through me. Nauseated at myself for my response to him and his presence.

Gods, I am such a fool.

His laugh echoes through the trees sending another chill down my arms, along my spine and into my toes, right into the ground that held me hostage. His words that follow, force me to go still. My chest inflated with air, my lungs screaming for it.

"I have been watching you for a long while, did you think that your wishes went unanswered? That I did not hear them?" He folded his arms across his chest and adjusted his stance. "That I was not biding my time?"

My heart dropped.

Nona was right, and I had just made a grave mistake.

Panic overcame me as my breath came in quick bursts, my lungs gasping for air. I shouldn't be out here. I quickly turned to look behind me, measuring the distance back to the cottage. It was possible, maybe I could make it. But then again, I didn't know how quick he was or if he could catch me before I even made it to the garden wall and through the gate. After all, he was Fae, known for their quickness, intelligence, elegance, and most of all, cruelty.

As if he could read my thoughts and body language, his eyes tracked my movements as I felt a twitch in my hand, preparing to run and waiting for the challenge to chase.

A hunter upon his prey.

"There is nowhere you can run that I will not find you. I would think twice if I were you," he warned

Another shudder ran down my spine, but I couldn't shake off the feeling that I needed to face him. I took a moment to observe every inch of him, calculating and scrutinizing, unsure if it was trepidation disguised as curiosity overtaking the panic I had felt. I knew I was taking a risk, but recognition and hostility urged me, forcing the words out before I could stop myself. The loathing was evident on my face as I spoke.

"I know who you are," I said, and his eyes flashed brightly in response. I chose my next words carefully, from fear of his retaliation. "You're him, aren't you? The Goblin King."

His reaction was subtle, a mere lifting of his chin, yet it conveyed satisfaction and delight at my affirmation, at my recognition. A smirk gradually spreads across his lips. A flood of emotions surged within me- terror, curiosity, uncertainty, and even hate. But for some reason, awe took over.

The being in front of me was a complete contrast to how he had been described. Instead of a grotesque and straw-haired creature, he appeared to be the most beautiful being I had ever seen. His fingers, although long, had a delicate fluidity to them and were not knobby as I had expected them to be. It was hard to believe that he was as normal-looking as any other living and breathing creature of our world. My mouth gaped open in bewilderment as I blurted out, "But you appear entirely human."

I noticed a shift in his eyes, but I couldn't quite put my finger on what it meant. It was like a switch had been flipped and his entire body had stiffened for a moment. I had clearly hit a nerve. Not my brightest move, especially considering he was a good head taller than me and far more intimidating than any Rothnian soldier. I had just set myself up to fail, digging a hole that I wasn't sure I could climb out of.

The sound that escapes his lips was a mix of irritation and vexation. "Far more than just a human," he spat, his voice dripping with contempt. A stray breeze sent a few strands of his hair across his face before hitting me, causing a cold chill to run through my bones.

As I pulled my shawl tighter around myself, the curiosity within me demanded more answers. "I don't understand, how is this possible? The Fae don't exist, they haven't for decades," I questioned, unable to contain my disbelief.

Curiosity was a strong trait in me, one Nona noted time and time again. It was going to get me in trouble one day. He's quiet for a moment, contemplating before he finally says, "The stories told to you, are false. The Fae live, just not *here*."

"I'm afraid I don't understand."

The Goblin King's eyes narrow briefly before he sighs, a sound so unadulterated it makes my heart race. "You've heard of Inirea, yes?"

I nod, my mind flashing back to the many tales I've heard about the barren landscape in the northeast of Rothnia. The other side of the mountains was a forbidden territory where no one was allowed to venture. But curiosity had always gnawed at me, urging me to know more. I had heard the stories, each narrated with varying details, but they all had one thing in common - no one ever returned from that desolate land. The rumors said that it was dying, but all of it was only hearsay. How are we to know if it was true or not if no one had ever returned to tell the tale?

"It's not as the tales have been told." He says, I could just make out the despondency in his voice before it was masked over again by animosity. "It's a very real place, Serra."

"Inirea? Isn't it the land of goblins and demons, of nymphs and fairies. It's not a safe place."

The sun was setting on the horizon and in the distance the wind whips the tops of the trees. I could hear the cackles in the low brush. The creatures hidden from sight; ones who did not want to be seen.

"It is not safe for many of my kind." I whispered. The gleam in his eyes would have me think otherwise, that it was perfectly safe for us. But that was how he played his game. I knew the truth. Every story Nona would tell came with a warning.

'Beware of Inirea, of the Goblin King. Wickedness is his game. The land is tricky. And trickery leads mortals astray.'

My heart was pounding so hard that it felt like it would burst out of my chest. The warnings about this Fae male echoed in my head, but I couldn't bring myself to move. He was dangerous, and I knew that, but I couldn't decide if I was truly afraid of him. It was a fear unlike anything I had ever experienced before. It reminded me of the time when I was eight and stumbled upon a boar.

I had spotted the boar from a distance, digging at the base of a tree just outside the forest's edge. Every fiber in my body was telling me to run, but my feet wouldn't budge. I was paralyzed with fear, unable to move or even scream. The terror I felt was indescribable. When the boar finally lifted its head, I saw its bright red eyes staring directly at me. I knew in that moment that I was in serious danger. It was like something out of a nightmare.

My nightmares.

As if it had stepped straight out of my nightmares, the boar's tusks were decayed, its skin dry and scaly. The stench of rot and foam emanating from its mouth was putrid, like a mixture of swamp water and death. Even now, the smell remains etched in my memory. It stomped once before charging for me, the sound of its hooves hitting the ground echoed through the trees. All I could do was scream and cover my eyes. Resigned to my fate, I waited for it to attack me. But it never came. When I was able to look again it was gone.

It was like it never existed.

I never told anyone, convinced I had imagined the whole thing. I felt far more afraid then than I felt now. Because none of this was real, none of this was happening. Convinced this whole thing was my imagination. The Goblin King wasn't here in front of me.

"Serra, you owe me something of value to you." The Goblin King said, this time his voice was thick with impatience. "For the wish that I was summoned here, by you, to grant."

Pulling me from my thoughts, "What?"

His annoyance at my response could be felt from where I stood. While he only stood all but ten feet away from me, the air around us remained charged, heavy and lethal. He was tired of waiting, and he was getting irritated. However, the threat of him and what he was, *who* he was, did not deter me.

"I have nothing to give you. I own very little. This was a mistake. I didn't mean it."

"Oh, you didn't?"

"No, I spoke rashly."

"Regardless, I was brought here. You cannot unsay it."

I stared up at him, he was going to grant my wish. None of them, not one I had ever asked of him had been in the past.

"Why now?"

He sneered, his lip lifting as he uncrossed his arms. "I have my reasons."

I couldn't help myself, not as the boldness I felt took over and inquired, "And what would that be?"

"That is not any of your business. Are you going to give me what I seek for granting your wish or not Serra?"

"I do not have anything, I already told you that."

The Goblin King pointed a long delicate finger at the cottage, at the last remaining piece I had of Nona Luna. "You have that."

It was easy to decline. "No."

"I expect something, Serra."

"I said no."

"Hmm." He smiles at me, his lips pulling across his teeth. My gaze snags on his canines as he steps towards me. I should yield, step away from him, but I don't. I would not cower before him.

"Luckily for you dear Serra, I don't want your run-down *farm*." he says, circling around me. His closeness makes me shrink away. But he takes a moment to stop behind me, lifting a piece of hair that had fallen out of my braid from the wind. Twirling it in his fingers before setting it back down. Wiping his hand on his jacket, like touching any part of me was beneath him.

I knew he was testing me, seeing what I would offer up. I had truly nothing. My wish was nothing but a mistake, I didn't think it would be heard. None of my wishes had ever been granted. Folding his hands behind his back, head high as he walks to the other side of me. He was comfortable. Of course, I was no threat to him. I wasn't underfed by any means, but we didn't have the extra money to indulge either.

Occasionally, on my birthday Nona would surprise me with a small box of sweets, the tiny tin full of as many different kinds as she could get for me. And I would savor each piece, trying to stretch them as long as I could.

We had survived mostly on what we could grow.

The meat on our plates was never the prime cut, not even close. The juicy steaks and succulent roasts went to the wealthy, who could afford to pay top coin for their meals. We made do with the scraps and off-cuts - tough sinews, gristle, and bone. But even those were a luxury, traded for with whatever we could barter or beg. It was the way of things in our corner of the world, a brutal hierarchy that left many hungry and sick.

As for me, I couldn't stomach the thought of killing an animal, let alone butchering it. My thin frame was a testament to my lack of meat in my diet. My arms and legs were long and lean, but toned from endless hours of work in the garden. My face was not something to be admired either, with my jawline and chin standing out because of my poor diet- except for my piercing green eyes that shone like emeralds against my tan skin. The color was so unique that it drew attention and compliments from everyone I met. They were captivating and I had grown tired of hearing the same comments over and over again.

It was a blessing and a curse, drawing attention to me wherever I went. I looked up at him, the Fae male who stood before me, and felt a shiver run down my spine. His expression was unreadable, inscrutable. His piercing gaze locked onto mine, and for a moment, I forgot all about the hardships of our world. All I could focus on were his eyes, which were equally captivating but in an entirely different way. I couldn't tell if he saw me as a threat or simply as prey. All I knew was that I was at his mercy, and my heart raced with fear and uncertainty.

"I don't have anything to give you." I said, my voice quivered slightly but I remained in control of the tremor that ran through me.

He turns on me, a ruthless smile crosses his lips. "You do."

"What could I possibly have that would be of any value? At least enough to give to you? I am of low status, undesired, and soiled. I have nothing!"

"Do you want to rid yourself of this anguish or not Serra? You made the wish mistake or no mistake. I am merely here to grant it."

I thought to myself for a moment- did I really want to let go of this? I'd lost everyone, my mother and father, my baby brother. And now Nona Luna. I had no one left, not really. Kaston made it perfectly clear that I wasn't anything but a tumble in the sheets. I'd been deflowered, tainted and unsuitable to be married to any other. I suppose I could live alone and become an old maid. But lifelong solitude and the torment of everyone I lost to keep me company?

It did cause some hesitation.

Did I want to care what the townspeople thought of me? The whispers I heard every time I came and left Rothnia. The things they said behind my back, I heard them. They hadn't truly stopped. They just hadn't the nerve to utter a word when Nona was around. They found her ways to be unnatural.

Trollop.

It's no wonder no one wants her.

It's her own fault that she defiled herself.

Her whole family was killed in a fire.

Heard she caused it; it was her fault.

The sickness plaguing us, it's her fault.

I heard she cast a spell on the sailors, lost at sea.

She's been seeking retribution.

It's her fault.

It's her fault!

HER FAULT!

The world around me spun as the voices echoed inside my head. Crashing into me. Spiraling down, down, down...

My fault. . .

Was everything really my fault?

Did I cause the sickness?

Did Nona die because of me?

My family? I had no magic; I did not know spells. I wasn't an enchantress. Magic had left the Lands decades ago. I was just a heartbroken girl. Before I knew what I was saying the words had slipped from my lips. "Yes, take it please. Whatever it is you want, just take it."

Satisfaction crossed his face.

"Please." I begged.

He nodded, "There is but one thing that I want from you, nothing else. If you agree to this bargain, then I will rid you of what causes your pain, what taunts you."

"What is it? Whatever it is, yes."

I should have hesitated, I should have considered what it was, but I did not. My mind was haunted by the aching pain of loss.

His smile grew, his wickedness showed there. He was a master at deception and I knew this, I *knew* this but it did not deter me. Nona's warnings were forgotten amongst my insanity.

"I want your memories. Serra. Give them to me and I will free you from what is plaguing you. Think of what that means for you."

"My- my memories?"

"Your memories are sufficient enough for payment." He paced before me. "I want every memory you cherish. Every dream you've ever had." His grin turned wicked as he said. "That is what I require from you."

My dreams? My memories.?

What were they to me if not the heartache and nightmares that I suffered from daily. Surely, they were not that valuable, not to me. If giving the Goblin King my memories removed all this dark and pain that wreaked havoc on my heart~ and allowed me to live a peaceful life~ it was worth the risk.

Was it not?

"Done."

The gleam in his eyes was frightening as he accepted my deal. His callous laugh echoed off the trees and around me as light flared up where he'd been standing. Covering my eyes, his voice echoed in my head.

"I'll be seeing you again, Princess."

As the light dimmed, my eyes tried to recover in the darkness. The crickets' familiar chirps grounded me. A raven calls in the distance. Drawing my eyebrows together, I stood alone in the garden, a basket full of flowers. The confusion washes over me, the last thing I could remember was walking home from the tavern.

The sun had yet to set then, but now. . . I was unable to grasp the time. What was I doing? Why was I standing here? Glancing upon the horizon, fear washed over me~ the sun had set in my distraction.

Now was not a time to be out in the dark. Creatures roamed and people went missing. But for the life of me, I could not recall the last hour. How quickly the sun had set. I must have been dreaming again but there were no thoughts or ideas left. My mind was utterly blank, calm. It was as if time had escaped, and I couldn't retain the remembrance of it.

CHAPTER
Three

Serra

THE SOUND OF THE morning songbirds and the rays from the sun shining through the cracked window of my bedroom roused me from sleep. The nightmare I had the night before was making it difficult to open my eyes. I tossed and turned all night, rest never coming easily. It felt like I had lost something, something was taken and missing. The feeling left me empty and incomplete. The never-ending nagging that someone was gone. Something just wasn't right.

I'd lived with this feeling for far too long now. And truthfully, it was really starting to irritate me. Week after week this feeling hung over me. Day after day I chased after it, trying to figure out what it was. What was eating away at me.

As much as I wanted to grasp why it was there, why it bothered me so, I could not neglect my duties. I was due at the Tavern this afternoon and I still had work to do in the garden. The beds had been planted and the seeds would soon sprout. Another day, another set of tasks to be done. Sleep, tend the farm, work the Tavern.

Every day.

I yawned and stretched, my feet finding their way to the worn wooden floorboards of my cottage. Each step produced a familiar creak, the sound echoing through the silent room. I made my way over to the fireplace where the dying embers were still glowing faintly. I picked up a log and carefully placed it on top, watching as the flames leapt up hungrily.

The heat was welcome against my skin, chasing away the chill of the night. I reached for the old copper kettle- its handle worn smooth from years of use. As I lifted it, I could feel the weight of sleep still clinging to my head, my movements slow and deliberate. With a soft clink, I hung the kettle on the hook above the flames, listening as it began to hiss and steam.

It was only quiet this morning, too quiet. Glancing about the room, everything was in its place. The cups on the shelves, the chair by the fireplace, the mirror by the door. Nothing was missing, nothing had been moved. But something was still lacking.

A heaviness sat upon the place.

And no matter how hard I tried, I could not figure out what it was. The whistle from the kettle drew me from my stupor. Pulling a mug from the shelf and adding a small satchel of tea leaves to it before pouring in the hot water, a list of today's tasks sat on the counter next to me. I read over it again, committing it to memory.

The words across the small piece of parchment muddled together for a moment as my mind refocused. My own script staring back at me. It took another moment for the fog of last night's sleep to finally clear my head.

> *Plant tomato sprouts*
> *Install Trellis for green beans*
> *Move lavender and dillweed*
> *Fertilize and till soil for carrots, garlic,*
> *onion and potatoes, to be planted*

I'd read over it one more time as I brought the mug to my lips, the steam from the brewing tea assaulted my nose. I could not afford the beans of the koffie plant from Elliner, the continent to the south. Its warm waters and tropical climate were perfect for growing the plant. With its recent demand, it's been all the rage for the Nobles of Rothnia and the Lands. So much so that the merchants had trouble keeping shipments on a constant delivery schedule. The most recent header talked that a ship had gone down in a winter storm a few months ago, and with it all its crew and stores.

The crates of beans are lost to the sea forever.

It was a stretch, getting it during those cold frigid months. However, the price on the precious beans made it next to impossible for anyone but the Nobility to obtain. So those, like me, relied on brewed tea leaves. Taking a sip, the brew burned my tongue. Still too hot, the shock and sharp intake of breath had the tea spilling all over my list.

A sigh of defeat forces itself out as I set the mug down and reach for a cloth off the water basin to dab up the spilled amber colored liquid. I'd been so focused on the mess I'd made that I didn't notice at first.

A flutter of movement caught my attention. My peripheral vision caught it as I tossed the cloth back into the water basin. Although the grime on the window made it difficult to see, I had to check again. Unsure what I saw was real. While it wasn't the dirt or the smudges that had caught my attention, it was the animal outside. On the stone wall out front, a black raven sat, watching me from its perch. As it cocked its head to the side, another movement down the lane pulled my eyes away from it. It took off before they stopped outside my gate. The four of them were hesitant as they watched the raven fly away.

I pulled a blanket off the armchair by the fire and wrapped it around my shoulders. My reflection in the mirror by the door was a sight to behold. My hair was untamed, and I wore dark circles under my eyes. But I yanked the door open anyway, I was not going to hide. While I probably looked like a right mess to them, they looked uneasy to me as I approached them.

"Serra Harlowe?"

A man in gilded metal armor stepped forward. His hand braced on the hilt of his sword, his helm tucked away under his arm. He wasn't unremarkable but he was decent looking. His dark features and curly hair stood out. His skin tanned from hours out in the sun on patrol, causing his hazel eyes to stand out. I'd seen him before. He was the Captain of the Rothnian Guard. He often patrolled around the Conwell Manor when on duty.

"Yes?"

"We have a summons for you." His voice was deep, not unkind but sharp. Years of service hardening it.

"From where?"

"Conwell Manor."

Another guard stepped forward and handed me a rolled

parchment with the Conwell wax seal. I quickly broke it and unrolled the parchment. Reading the contents inside.

"This has to be a joke." I stammered. My eyes flicked back up to the guards. Landing on the swords at each of their waists. They could very easily take me out, no question.

"I'm afraid not." the Captain said. His frown caused the wrinkles at the corners of his eyes to turn down. "You've been summoned at once."

"Now?"

"Yes, we've been asked to escort you back to the Manor. It was requested."

Looking down at myself, still dressed in my night dress, I pulled the blanket tighter around my shoulders. Embarrassment stained my cheeks pink as they flushed, "A moment?"

A soft nod. The Captain was a gentleman, keeping his eyes above my neck. The same could not have been said for those under his employ. The snickers of the men behind him reached my ears.

Glaring at them, I turned to head back into the house, the rolled parchment crumpling in my fist. I tossed the blanket on the floor as I slammed the door shut. Causing the dishes and pictures to rattle. Dressing quickly, I donned my nicest dress and shoes. Wrapping my worn stained apron around my waist. I quickly glanced in the cracked and bubbled mirror of my bureau. The dark circles under my eyes had grown. The lack of sleep the last few nights was starting to show.

Sighing, I grabbed my hairbrush and quickly brushed it through my hair, taming what I could. My usually straight locks had gone wild in the night as I tossed and turned, causing a small knot at the back of my head. Finally, having wrangled the knot out I set the brush down and checked my reflection again. A small touch of rouge and a little bit of powder were all that I could do. There was not much that really could be done with my appearance anyway, so with heavy footsteps I heaved the door open. The parchment clutched in my hand again.

The Captain dipped his head at my approach, he did not bow. I was not nobility and certainly not royalty. Only out of respect did he do so, his companions however did not. He did not speak another word, a stern look to his company, and they had gone back into formation. Lips sealed and eyes alert.

I did not ask questions as they escorted me down the lane and into town, my heart thundering away the whole way there- sandwiched between the three men behind me and the Captain in front. The curious glances and casual looks of those around us as we walked through the town square drew my attention, my ears turning red with embarrassment.

I preferred to live without being noticed. I was not one for spectacle or amusement. So, when I became the spotlight, I became clumsy. I tripped over a loose cobblestone as we approached the manor. The man to my right was quick, his hand at my elbow to catch me. "Steady there."

His voice was deep, lethal, familiar. It unnerved me, throwing me off. Almost causing me to trip again as I glanced up into his face. But it was hidden by the helm. His cloak fluttered in the salty breeze.

My heart jumped, I thought. . .

No. . .

I could just make out his eyes, two different colors. Or at least I thought they had been. I blinked, and they had gone back to blue. My mind was playing tricks on me. I stared at him for a moment, as he shuffled on his feet, uneasy under my gaze.

I'd been so sure. . .

A loud crash in the square drew everyone's attention. The guards immediately rushed off; they'd done their job. This matter was of more importance, off to see to the noise and the exchange between two villagers. Their argument grew louder and louder as they blamed each other for the mess. From the sound of it, one had knocked over the table of the other.

A fit of jealousy?

A gust of wind?

Who knew, it would be sorted, and the culprit fined for the disruption. Turning back to the manor doors. The guards had left me at the doorstep of Conwell Manor.

My nerves took over as I approached.

CHAPTER
Four

Serra

THE KNOCKER ON THE large mahogany manor doors was enormous. Shaped curiously like a goblin head, with a ring in its mouth. I fully expected it to open its eyes and speak to me. Ask me about my purpose.

Intimidating.

I reached for it, lifting the heavy brass ring twice, the sound bounced back at me as it echoed through my surroundings.

A moment later the door swung open, "Yes?"

The man who opened the door stood tall and straight, his posture almost military-like in its precision. His uniform was immaculate, tailored to fit his lean and muscular frame perfectly. The black and white color scheme of his attire added to his air of formality and professionalism.

His waistcoat was tightly fitted and accentuated his trim waist, while his jacket hung just right on his broad shoulders. The creases in his slacks were razor-sharp, and his shoes gleamed with a high shine. His dark hair flecked with age in a strip of silver, was combed back, giving him a distinguished and refined look. His face was angular, with high cheekbones and a sharp jawline with eyes in a piercing shade of gray- were set deep within their sockets, their calculating gaze never leaving my form as I stood before him.

The butler's overall demeanor was one of authority and control, his movements efficient and purposeful. It was clear that he was a man who took pride in his appearance and his work, and he exuded an air of confidence and competence.

"Hello." My voice had come out with the slightest squeak. Clearing my throat I tried again, "Hello, I'm here to see Lady Conwell, I am to-"

He stepped aside for me as I walked past him, I couldn't help but feel a sense of unease. His face was expressionless and his eyes seemed to be scanning me up and down. I took a deep breath and stepped into the foyer, my eyes widening in awe as I took in the grandeur of Conwell Manor. The space was expansive, with soaring ceilings that seemed to reach for the sky. The walls were adorned with intricate moldings and ornate wall scences on the walls, cast a warm glow over the space.

I couldn't help but feel small in comparison to the vastness of the foyer. The marble floors shone underfoot, and I could see my reflection in the polished surface. As I looked up, my gaze was drawn to the grand staircase that led to the upper levels of the manor. The banister was carved from dark wood and adorned with intricate carvings of vines and leaves, making it seem as though it had grown naturally in place. The stairs were cushioned with plush dark red carpet that muffled the sound of footsteps. The black marble floors shone under the sunlight that streamed through the windows on either side of the doors.

The windows that graced the front of the manor were indeed as impressive as I had heard. They were enormous and seemed to stretch from floor to ceiling, with wrought iron frames that added to the overall grandeur of the space. The sunlight streamed through the glass, casting dancing shadows across the floor. A crystal chandelier that hung high above, its tiny crystals sparkling and casting an array of rainbows upon the walls. Everything was perfectly arranged, not a single object out of place, and not a speck of dust to be seen.

As I stood there, taking in the magnificence of Conwell Manor, I couldn't help but feel a sense of awe and wonder. The white limestone blocks that formed the exterior of the building were smooth and cool to the touch. Towering stone columns, each one wider than a man's outstretched arms, rose up from the ground and stretched towards the sky, holding up the roof of the building like a Parthenon. The roof itself was a magnificent sight, with its sloping sides and triangular pediments, making it clear that no expense had been spared in its construction. The overall effect was one of grandeur and elegance, befitting a structure of such magnificence.

The two-story manor was truly a sight to behold, and it was easy to see why it had dominated the center of Rothnia for as long as it had existed.

Forever large and imposing.

Although the exterior of Conwell Manor was familiar to Rothnians, it was the interior that captured my imagination. The grandeur of the exterior was matched by the opulence of the interior. The sheer scale of everything was overwhelming. It was hard to believe that people lived in such extravagance and luxury. As I looked around, I couldn't help but feel the stark contrast between their world and mine, so out of touch with the reality I knew.

"This way please, Miss Harlowe," the butler said irritably. Leading me down a corridor to the right after closing the door behind me. "Lady Conwell is meeting you in her sitting room."

"Thank you." I replied as he opened a large white door with gold gilding.

"She will be with you momentarily."

I offered him a slight nod and a small smile in gratitude as he closed the door behind me. The sitting room I stood in took my breath away almost instantly. If the foyer was magnificent, this room was lavishly ornate White marble floors- more white wood panels, gold gild trim, wall sconces made of crystal and bright gold. Another large crystal chandelier hung from the ceiling above me, its crystals sparkling as they danced. The golden drapes shining in the morning sun that was coming through. The fireplace to my right was large- done in marble and white stained oak.

The whole room was designed to impress.

But it had been the wall of windows across the room that caught my attention- that drew me in. Large, floor to ceiling windows, ones that looked out onto a large labyrinth of a garden. Spring flowers almost in full bloom- birds fluttered about the trees, back and forth between them and the large birdbath fountain in the center. Their songs echo through the window as I close my eyes.

Tranquility.

Familiarity.

That's what the garden had invoked in me. A semblance of peace and longing. I yearned to wander the paths- the hedges taller than I- wanting to get lost in the labyrinth. The beauty of it, the calm peaceful air that radiated off the space. The birds chatter as they flutter, the sun's warmth on my skin. The laughter of a woman, a babe in her arms as she called to me. The image shattered almost instantly- bringing me back to the present.

As the image flashed before my eyes, it felt like a distant memory that didn't belong to me. The feeling lingered, leaving me disoriented and confused. I stumbled towards the settee in the middle of the room, noticing two chairs placed opposite it. Despite feeling drawn to sit down, a wave of anxiety washed over me, making me hesitant to ruin the pristine furniture. The image of the woman in white continued to haunt me, intensifying my unease and discomfort.

I'd resigned myself to stand and wait as the doorknob turned. The large door I had come through opened to reveal a lady dressed impeccably for her station. My eyes lingered a moment as Lady Conwell swept through the doorway, her neatly coiffed auburn hair bouncing slightly with each step. Her golden eyes sparkled with life, and her every movement exuded natural grace and elegance.

She was a true vision of beauty in her pale green satin dress, with no wrinkles marring the perfection of her skirt or the unruffled bustle. The fitted bodice accentuated her full bosom, and a string of pearls around her neck matched those dangling from her ears.

As I watched her approach, I couldn't help but feel discontented at her flawless beauty. She had been blessed with alabaster skin, radiant golden eyes, and beautiful auburn hair, making her the epitome of elegance and grace. Yet, despite her enchanting appearance, I couldn't shake the feeling of unease that lingered within me as she summoned me to this meeting.

Because I, Serra Harlowe, wore an old brown dress that had been repaired one too many times. My once white apron stained. The sleeves of my chemise peeking out, showing signs of wear, long ago needing to be replaced. My basic canvas shoes are worn and dirty.

Here I stood, in a room of such elegance, in the presence of a higher Noblewoman that it didn't feel right.

None of this made any sense.

"Please, sit." Her voice was sweet- too sweet, as she sat in one of the chairs.

But I did as she asked and sat, the settee cushion sinking slightly under my weight. The fabric felt luxurious, soft on my skin. The blush pink velvet and satin pillows felt like sitting on a cloud.

"Well Miss Harlowe. I am sure you are curious as to why I summoned you here," She beamed. "I know I would be."

I gave her a slight nod of my head. "Yes ma'am."

"Well, every year I send out invites for my spring ball. And every year I have one extra." Her eyes followed the housemaid that entered carrying a tray in her hands. Scrutinizing her as she set it on the low table between us before departing with a curtsy.

A delicately painted porcelain teapot and two teacups with saucers, a tower of sweet desserts and confections sat before me.

"Tea?" Lady Conwell offered. "I'm afraid we ran out of koffie earlier this month. It's been hard keeping it here."

Her chuckle left little to be desired as I offered a light shake of my head before she went on. Pouring herself a cup and dressing it with cream and sugar. I watched her as she sipped it with delicate fingers and dignity.

She carried on, finishing her statement. "An invite, for a fortunate young lady to join us. And this year, that young lady is you."

I stared at her blankly. Shocked at what she'd said. It wasn't unheard of; everyone was aware that this is what she did. Girls dreamed of being the one to attend. Gossiped about it, actually. In fact, the only daughter of the village butcher was invited last year.

And she was able to secure quite the match from it. But I never imagined I would be summoned, let alone invited.

Something didn't seem right.

"My annual Spring Ball will be the talk of the town, as it always is. It's a masquerade this year. I do aim to outdo myself with this one." She went on, her voice carrying.

I watched as she set her cup down on the plate, her hands were so clean. The nail beds were neatly trimmed, not a speck of dirt under her nails. The sapphire ring on her left ring finger was far too large for her slender fingers. Absently, I buried my own fingers in my apron, to hide the dirt I knew was under them.

I cleared my throat, feeling a slight hoarseness as I spoke, "Yes, I've heard of your whimsical balls, and this year's event sounds truly exquisite and splendid."

A fake smile spread across my face, the compliment had her beaming once more. I learned a long time ago that flattery was always the key to the Nobles. The gleam in her eyes at my praise, satisfaction was the kindest way to put it.

"Oh dear, yes, well it's just a small gathering of friends and family. Nothing too grand," she said, feigning humbleness. "It'll be a special one after all."

I saw through her though.

She fancied herself as a matchmaker. Plucking young ladies up out of the dirt, brushing them off and flaunting them, a charity case. But she was like all the others. Bored and disconnected with reality outside her glass bubble.

A glass bubble.

An interesting thought ran through my head at the idea of it. My mind sparked with fascination at the mere thought of being encased in a swirling globe of magic and enchantments. The idea of it was so intriguing that I couldn't help but wonder if I had ever dreamed of something like that before. However, I couldn't recall the last time I had a dream, let alone one as unique as this. The thought alone left me feeling both curious and slightly unsettled, uncertain even.

I could hear Lady Conwell's voice in the background, but it felt distant, as if I was listening from underwater. Her words were just noise to my ears, and I struggled to focus on what she was saying. My mind spun and swirled with confusion and uncertainty, like a tornado tearing through my thoughts. In that moment, a strange hollowness in my heart, the one that had been plaguing me for weeks, fractured. A crack forming across the glass of my own globe.

The idea that had come caused another crack to spread, and I felt my world shatter around me. Was this all a mistake? Was anything real? I couldn't understand why I was feeling this way or why the emptiness within me was so profound, why it had lingered for so long. Why it festered and withered in my chest. The feeling of emptiness in my head caused it to become light and for a moment I felt weightless, like I was floating. It was as if I was no longer anchored to reality, and everything around me had become a blur.

None of this was real. . .

All of this had to be a strange dream and I would certainly wake up in my bed covered in a sweat, trying my best to calm down after this nightmare. But would it truly be so bad if this was true?

If this was *not* another nightmare?

"Mother?" A voice echoed in the hallway. "Are you in here?"

My heart sank, and my body tensed as a voice echoed in my mind. A voice that I had long forgotten, a voice that brought back feelings of dread, unease, and terror. I knew that voice, remembered it. Memories flooded back and I couldn't shake the feeling that something bad was about to happen.

Suddenly, the door opened and a young man walked in.

He was tall and lean, with a chiseled physique that spoke of strength and athleticism. His emerald green doublet was perfectly tailored to his form, and his dark trousers hugged his legs tightly. But it was his hair that caught my attention, his shoulder-length auburn locks tied back neatly with a ribbon. As he looked at me with his piercing golden brown eyes, I couldn't help but feel a shiver run down my spine. The way he looked at me, as if he knew everything about me, made me feel exposed and vulnerable. I tried to shake off the feeling, but it lingered, like a dark cloud hovering over me.

Her voice broke my trance. "Kas, darling, there you are. Come meet this year's invitee."

The memory hit me like a punch to the gut. It was his face. His face, twisted in a cruel sneer. The image of him buttoning up his shirt. He'd had my heart and broken it into pieces. How had I forgotten? This man was one I had wished for. The one I had wanted to take me away from the life I had been living. I had confessed to him my heart and my love after a midnight stroll and then had given myself fully to him.

The fracture widened. Cleaving whatever had held it back in two. Crumbling as a host of memories flooded in. As if the lock on them had been broken, the barrier wide open. The hold weakened at each ticking second in this man's presence.

Our first meeting over a year ago.

The one next to the fountain in the city center. He'd offered to help as I picked up the flowers that had been blown over by the gust of wind. The petals danced around us as our eyes locked. I remembered him, his eyes had been intense and molten. Smoldering, I had felt myself fall then. Our shy introductions, my cheeks had turned bright red.

I remembered he'd sneak out to the farm and throw pebbles at my window, beckoning me to come outside. Tiptoeing past Nona's bed, trying to avoid the squeaky floorboards. We would run off in the dark for a quiet stroll.

Our first kiss.

Shared under the light of a full moon. I remembered the way the stars twinkled above as he leaned in. His lips were so soft, the way a lover tenderly kissed their partner. The way his eyes held mine that night, sparkling with longing. Before placing a firmer, demanding kiss on my lips. Causing every fiber of me to melt into him. To want him.

To want more.

To *wish* for more.

I remembered every heated exchange between us as we met in the dark of night. Moreover, I remembered the first time, the pain from it, the hope that he would be my prince. The first and last man. Allowing him to take my maidenhead in terms of love. I hadn't said it yet. Those three words, even after months of sneaking off with him. But I had given myself to him. He was everything a gentleman should be. Waiting for me to signal I was okay after pushing in. Allowing me the time I needed to expand around him. Kissing me softly as he took me slowly. giving me all the comfort I needed as a first time.

When he was close, and I was about to shatter at my climax he held me, steadily increasing his speed and as I reached my peak and shuttered beneath him as my pleasure washed over me. He came seconds behind me before pulling out and spilling before me.

I remembered the conversation I had with him.

The one asking him to court me properly. To introduce me to his family. To ask for my hand. The proper way of things. The way he said that he could not. Not yet. Brushing me off and ignoring my requests. The days after flooded by into weeks and weeks into months. The days I would see him, and he would not make eye contact were the hardest. But he always came that night. The nights were his, and sometimes it left me feeling dirty. But I was enamored with him, wrapped up in the pleasure we shared.

I was his secret.

That last night surfaced; the night had been warm. The moon was full, lighting our way as we walked along the stream and toward the Ebony Wood. I hesitated at first, my fear taking over my body, but it was his kind words that convinced me to follow him. The forest closed in around us as we stood below one of the trees. I remembered the way he held me close to him, his lip on my forehead then a soft kiss on my lips. That was the night I finally told him, the night I said those three words.

"*I love you*" I whispered.

His lips crashed onto mine with such force that my head spun. I felt his hands roaming over my body, leaving a trail of heat in their wake. He moved his lips down to my neck, leaving kisses that made my body feel electric. My breasts were heavy with arousal, and I couldn't wait for him to touch me there. I remembered the feeling of wanting him, of wanting to give myself to him over and over again. I wanted him to claim me as his own, because I loved him. I felt his hand pull at my skirt, lifting it to reveal the slickness between my legs. His smirk told me he knew how much I wanted him.

Before I knew it, our tops were gone, ripped away in a moment of passion. His lips were fierce as he reclaimed mine, his bare chest pressing against my skin as he dropped his pants. I felt his hands on my thighs, lifting me up and pushing my skirt back.

My core throbbed with need as my legs wrapped around his waist, my hands gripping his shoulders for support. He teased me for a moment before pushing into me, filling me completely. A breathy gasp escaped my lips as he slowly sheathed himself to the base. I allowed myself to adjust to his size before he took me against a nearby tree, my head thrown back in ecstasy.

The bark biting into the skin on my back.

His hot breath tickled my ear as his teeth grazed the lobe, causing me to shudder with desire. I couldn't help but let out a moan as he took my breast in his mouth, his tongue flicking and teasing my nipple. He lifted his head to kiss me, and I could taste myself on his lips. He lowered me back down to the soft earth, his eyes locked on mine as he entered me again. I gasped at the feeling of him filling me up once more, and he silenced my moans with a tender kiss. The only sounds had been our labored breaths and the rustling of leaves as he thrust into me, our bodies moving in perfect harmony.

The moon above us cast a soft glow on our entwined figures as we gave in to our desires. He let out a guttural groan as he pulled out and slammed back in, the sensation building inside me. I tangled my fingers in his hair, pulling him closer as he pounded into me relentlessly. His lips crashed onto mine once more as we both reached the peak of ecstasy, our bodies shaking with pleasure.

As our bodies move together in a dance of desire, my moans filled the night air, a symphony of pleasure. I felt him deep inside me, filling me completely, igniting every nerve ending in my body. His lips on my neck, his teeth grazing my skin, marking me as his. I cling to him, my legs wrapped tightly around his waist, pulling him closer.

The trees and the stars bear witness to our passion, and I was lost in the moment, lost in him. I whispered his name like a prayer as he drives into me with a force that leaves me breathless. Our love, once so pure and true, now reduced to this primal need, this hunger for each other. I knew then it wouldn't last, but for now, it had been enough.

All that mattered was the way his body moved with mine, the way we had fit together perfectly.

And then it came, that moment of pure ecstasy as we both reached the peak of our climax, our bodies exploding with the intensity of it all. I arched my back and cried out, my body shuddering with the force of my release.

I remember the weight of his body lifting off me as he stood up, leaving me alone on the forest floor. The cold ground beneath me, my body still buzzing with my release, but my heart shattered into a million pieces. The sound of his belt being done up, the rustle of his clothes as he dressed himself. I watched him, silently begging him to stay, to hold me, to love me. But he didn't. He turned his back on me, his eyes cold and calculating.

The man I thought I knew had disappeared, replaced by a stranger full of disdain. He spoke harshly, his voice laced with contempt, telling me that it was nothing, that he had never loved me. *"I think you and I both know this was not going any further than this. It's been fun, Serra. Making you fall in love and then taking you."*

He looked down at me, his eyes raking over my naked chest, my disheveled hair, the pinkness to my cheeks. My swollen lips, like he was cataloging me, storing it away for the future. Before his eyes landed on my skirts and my folds, the wetness that remained there from him.

His lips pulled back in a sneer, *"Each and every time."*

The tear had started to fall, rolling down my cheeks and into my hair as he walked away into the darkness, leaving me alone in the forest feeling used, broken, and utterly alone. Leaving me half naked and soiled. The wetness he'd left running down my leg from his climax. The awful truth of what we had just done, what he had just done. The consequences and fear of it flooded me with dread. I'd re-dressed myself quickly and rushed back to the cottage, my face stained with tears as I encountered Nona waiting. The moon and stars watched as my world fell apart.

Nona. . .

The fissures that had been hiding my pain finally break apart and scatter, revealing the truth of what had happened between us. The enchantment that had kept me blind to the reality of our relationship shatters, and every moment we spent together floods back into my mind. I remember every touch, every kiss, every promise that he made me. But I also remember the pain, the betrayal, and the contempt in his eyes.

It was as if the world had flushed all of the memories back to me at once. The sweet and the sour. The moments of love and passion, and the moments of hate and anger. I realize now that everything we had shared was nothing more than a bet between his friends, a cruel game of woo and conquer.

And I was his prize, a conquest to be won and then discarded.

I had been degraded, defiled, and left as an unmarried woman taken by another man. A man who refused to take responsibility for his actions, and who refused to honor me by making me his wife. The memories of our time together now feel tainted and cheapened, as if they were never real to begin with. The pain in my heart grows with each passing moment, and I know that I will never be the same again.

I wanted to flee, to run from this place, from this man before me. From his mother who knew nothing about me. I wanted to escape the feeling of being laid bare, everything that had happened laid out before me. The dreams that I had wished for with him.

I wanted to go.

"This is Serra. She will be my special guest this year." Lady Conwell spoke, pulling me back from the horrible realization that I had forgotten everything between her youngest son and me.

He bowed slightly at the waist, no hint of recognition or realization in his gaze. His eyes were utterly blank, schooled. He'd been good at hiding his feelings. His true intentions. "It's a pleasure to meet your acquaintance, Serra."

The way he said my name sent a shiver down my spine. He knew. He had to know who I was, right? I couldn't breathe, the crushing weight of someone sitting on my chest. I had to get out of here. I had to end this meeting and get out.

"Isn't she lovely?" Lady Conwell cooed.

"Absolutely, Mother." Kaston appeased. His eyes flicking away from me. "May I speak with you please?"

"Sure dear, what is it?"

"Privately?" His eyes darkened as he glanced back at me- before returning to his mothers. "It's about. . ."

"Yes, yes, just a minute Kas." She waved him away. "I will be with you in a moment, and we may talk. But I am sure Serra is unbothered by your need to speak to me about Cressida."

My heart sank.

Cressida Finkley. A politician's daughter.

I've only seen her a handful of times. It was rumored she wasn't allowed out much, too busy with her studies and her father's desires to be governor. Kaston's eyes brush over my face, a glimpse of glee in them at his mother's slip of tongue. Of course, Cressida would be the right choice, a lady bred for this, for nobility. The right lady for marriage. He'd wooed her, he'd courted her properly and then very likely would request for her hand from her father.

Because that is how it is done.

I was just a fling; I was used then tossed aside by this man. But it was okay for the men to mess around before marriage, take what they wanted with no consequences, it was what they did. And no one batted an eye at them. Except. . . *Nona*. . .

Nona.

My sweet loving Nona. I'd forgotten about her. A pang of guilt and regret hit me like a wall of water. I remembered now. I fought back the tears that threatened to fall as I felt the love and care she had given me all my life. The anger and loathing she had for the man in this room. The man that had soiled me. Left me alone in the Ebony Woods. She'd gone on a rampage after I had arrived back at the cottage. My bed had been empty with no sign of me.

She later told me she had feared I'd been stolen away. Stolen away to where and by whom, I did not know. And when I showed up with my eyes red and face streaked with tears she had relaxed, knowing I was safe. But she had demanded answers even when I could not give them. All I could say was I was used and when I refused to give her his name, she had gone off on a tirade mumbling some nonsense about curses and wicked boys.

Nona had cleaned me up, gave me the tonic to prevent pregnancy and then sent me to bed. Never once shunning me or my actions. The same could not have been said about the townspeople. The jabs and sneers as Nona and I walked past days later were distasteful. I had caught her mumbling once about heirs and princesses. How the whole place was ungrateful and would see the truth someday.

The look on her face when she had caught me staring was alarming. I knew then that there was more that she wasn't telling me. And when pressed she changed the subject, warning me to stop making wishes and speaking of those who should not be spoken about. Nona had gone out of her way to reassure them that everything was okay, that it was all hearsay. I remembered now that she was gone. No longer a part of my life, no longer there to pick me up. An ache bloomed in my chest.

"Mother." Kaston's voice echoed in my head. His hand tightened on the back of her chair, a warning that this meeting was over.

"Yes, alright Kaston." Lady Conwell signed, turning towards me. "I will have a coach sent to you on the eve of the ball. I do look forward to your attendance Serra. It'll be marvelous."

I nodded, keeping my eyes on her and offering her a shy smile. Never once glancing back at Kaston. "That would be lovely."

She beamed. "Perfect!"

"Bastion will see you out, Serra." Kaston said, cutting her off. The tight line of his smile signaled I was done here. Dismissing me before his mother could, but his eyes gave him away. The danger there. Even with the relief I felt to get away, to be done with this and go home. To process everything that I had just recalled.

Without hesitation I rose and skirted around him- avoiding him and any contact. At the door outside, Bastion, waited. I could hear Lady Conwell and Kaston talking, not entirely concerned that I was still within earshot. "Kas darling, I do not understand why you are so worried? Just ask Lord Finkley already. Why would you not? She's divine, a perfect match."

"Mother, it is not that simple-"

I could not hear the rest of what Kaston had said as the door closed behind me and I followed Bastion to the foyer again. My thoughts turned back to him, what was he up to? I only paused for a moment watching Bastion open the door for me and usher me out. My feet carried me quickly down the front steps as the large mahogany doors boomed closed behind me.

The fact that Lady Conwell was unaware or unbothered by her son's tryst with me was baffling. Either she ignored the rumors, or she was so disconnected from everything and so caught up in her own schemes that she truly had no idea.

Still reeling from the encounter, the invitation and the forgotten memories. I hurried home- haunted by the lady in white and the forgotten memories with Kaston.

I did not notice the black raven escorting me.

CHAPTER
Five

The Goblin King

I SOARED ABOVE THE shipping port village of Rothnia, my wings propelling me higher into the sky. From above, I could see the hustle and bustle of the market below. The salty sea air mixed with the aroma of spices and fish from the merchant stalls that lined the streets. The colors of the various stalls and banners were vibrant and inviting, even from up here.

The wooden docks were teeming with activity as crew members loaded and unloaded cargo onto the vessels. The sails of the ships were varied and colorful, each bearing a unique emblem or design. The harbor was alive with the sound of creaking ships, bustling sailors, and barking dogs. The sea itself shimmered under the sunlight, beckoning to all who dared to venture out.

I could see the people of Rothnia going about their daily lives. Children played in the streets while their parents bartered with merchants. Stray dogs and cats roamed freely, searching for scraps of food. The stretch of my wings felt wonderful as I soared above in the open skies of the Mortal Lands. In my raven form I felt free, freer than I ever had. I watched as she hurried down the village streets, past the fountain, past stalls in the market and squeezed by the townspeople that lingered in the square.

As I continued to fly above everything, I couldn't help but feel drawn to Serra. It was as if there was an invisible force that kept pulling me towards her, urging me to follow her every move. I watched as she weaved her way through the bustling crowd, her long hair swaying behind her with each step she took. Her movements were fluid and graceful, almost as if she were dancing.

I couldn't help but be entranced by her beauty. Her ethereal aura and the shimmering stars within her veins were a testament to her divine nature. And yet, there was a vulnerability about her that drew me in even further. I felt the pull between us, a magnetic force that drew me closer and closer to her with each passing moment. Even after I'd finally answered her call.

Her wishes and dreams summoned me.

She hadn't truly been afraid for some reason.

However, everything was by design.

Everything was carefully planned; every detail of this web had been thought out. Except one. I knew that if something didn't change, and change soon, everything was going to come undone. She only looked back once. Flinching away as a group of young men bolstered past her on their way to the tavern.

She was on edge.

I couldn't chance the glamour again, not with her around. Not after this morning. It took far more than I'd intended to use to cover up the slip. Thankfully the goblins intervened because if I'd lingered any longer, she would have caught on. And I would not have been able to pull away. She saw past whatever magic I had been able to spin together. She saw my true form. And I could not hide it from her. It was easier to fool those with weak minds and even weaker hearts.

But not her.

Even in the garden, next to her home, she had seen me for who I was, all of me. Every detail. She'd seen right through my carefully planned disguise. It was not like I'd really been trying very hard either. But to anyone who had happened by her home, even all those weeks ago, they would not have seen me as she did. In truth, the glamour would fool the mortals, they would have seen her talking to an old, ragged beggar woman. Not the Fae male that I truly was.

The Goblin King, I guess. . . so to speak. A title given to me so many years ago. A title I had not really wanted at the time. Despite the magic that had come forward that day. Despite asking the goblins to pick someone else.

But it was her request, it had been so easy to displace her memories. Such a simple thing, easy magic. And while I had a basic grasp on the power that ran in my veins, there was still so much more I could not access. Still so much power that I could not reach, could not tap into.

Even now.

It simmered under the surface waiting to be called upon. It danced away from my touch each time I reached for it.

As I reflect on the events that have transpired, I could feel the weight of my exhaustion dragging me down. Suppressing the memories of an entire village was no small feat, but it had to be done. And I had paid the price for it. The wound on my arm was still raw, a constant reminder of what I had sacrificed to achieve this. I had always known that the spells would eventually unravel.

The threads had already begun to break, and it was only a matter of time before the entire thing came undone. But I had hoped that my own strength would be enough to contain it. Unfortunately, that was not the case. The lock on my magic was starting to weaken, and I could feel it slipping away from me.

She was stronger.

A girl with power beyond her understanding. If she knew what she was capable of, if she knew of the power that lay in her blood, the Realms would come undone. A power strong enough to either hold it together, or completely shatter it. Breaking it apart.

Light vs dark.

Shadows vs starlight.

But I needed her. I needed her to break what was holding me back. And I was willing to play this game with her to get what I wanted. I knew that I was taking a risk. If she failed, the consequences could be disastrous. But I had no choice. This was necessary. And if she got hurt in the process, so be it. She meant nothing to me.

The gaps were already there.

This was necessary.

Use her, gain what I was after. And the time had finally come. Forced to put the plans into motion. She was alone, and I was free to gain access to her. I'd been watching and waiting for her long enough. And while I only pushed the scale in my favor, to undo the block on this curse. She so *freely* offered to me the only thing I wanted, the only thing I needed. She had been trusting, and what a foolish thing she could have done too. I hadn't hesitated either, hadn't thought twice. Took the necessary steps to get her to remember what was forgotten. To free what was contained inside her. If it meant freeing myself as well.

To open up the locks.

Her memories were a key, and I was poised to unlock each and every one of them. The more she remembered, the more power was released.

The curse would break.

Caught up in my own thoughts, caught up in watching her, as I followed her back to her home. Gliding along the air currents, free from the leash that held me. Neither of us managed to notice the man with auburn red hair exit the manor and follow her down the street. Slipping past those in his way.

CHAPTER
Six

Serra

I'D RUSHED AS QUICKLY as I could out of town, weary of those around me. The young men that had blocked my path had paid me no attention. Too intent on their drinks and cards at the local Tavern. They were frequent patrons. I'd seen them come in frequently, their mugs piled up on the table throughout their visit. The village was alive today with the first warmer days of spring. The fountain square filled with stalls for market day, and the commotion from this morning had been handled as the sellers voiced their wares. I wanted no part in its festivities, not at the moment.

The summons to Conwell Manor and the invitation from Lady Conwell were more than enough to set me on edge. Nothing made sense, nothing explained why I had forgotten any of that. No sooner had I reached the cottage and gone inside, a knock at the door stopped me in my tracks. I hesitated behind the door for a second before turning to crack it open. Curious to see who was outside. But my heart dropped once I saw who stood there.

Kaston.

He was waiting on the stoop, hand resting on the frame of the door. His eyes trained to find me as I pulled the wood door open. My brows furrowed as I stared at him. When had he left the Manor? How had I not noticed him behind me before?

Was I that lost in thought I had not seen him?

"What do you want?" I asked, doing my best to block the door and prevent his entry.

It was of no use.

"To talk to you." he said, easily pushing past me and through the doorway into the main room of my home. The fire in the hearth cracked and spit as he walked around. The copper kettle left abandoned on the counter and the iron poker far outside my reach.

I was unarmed.

He paced around the space, taking everything in as he did so. His polished boots *thunked* on the floorboards, the sound grinding on my bones. His muscled arms behind his back as he glanced at the door to my bedroom before looking down at my cold mug of tea. The space was modest, small and while I had not noticed his size before, now it was perfectly clear. He had gotten larger since the last time I had been with him, and he dominated most of the space. My voice quivered slightly but I held my ground.

"Get out."

"Serra, do you really think that's the best way to speak to me right now?"

Kaston's voice caused me to pause, the underlying threat that was laced between them. I watched him with weary eyes as he picked up my forgotten mug from the counter and set it back down. Turning toward me with a grin on his lips. Kaston never would have dared come inside, let alone be seen here if Nona were still alive. He'd been just as afraid of her as everyone else.

"You need to leave; I have nothing to say to you."

"Yes, but I have something to say to you."

"I don't want to hear it." I managed to muster up as much venom into my voice as I could. Holding the door open for him, hopefully he would understand that his time here was over. That I did not want him here. "Leave."

Bad idea.

Unfortunately, I'd positioned myself in the wrong spot. Kaston approached me then, towering over me- forcing me to step back. He certainly had gotten bigger. The door closed shut as my hand let go, the soft snick as the knob clicked into place made me flinch. I was trapped. He advanced again, cornering me. I had nowhere to run. With as much spite as I could force out, even while my body was shaking with fear.

"Get out."

His hand found my throat, forcing me to look up at him. Squeezing just enough to block my air supply. "I warned you. Do not speak to me like that."

I couldn't help but stare at him in terror. The malice in his voice, the look in his eyes. I had never seen this side of him, I had heard the rumors but never experienced them for myself. His hand relaxed again, holding his grip on my throat, allowing precious air into my lungs. A squeak escaped me as he sighed, his expression was one of vexation.

"It bothers me that you were in my home today. I cannot talk my mother out of this. She would not see reason. She has her mind made up that *you* will be her next debutant." His hand flexed on my throat, squeezing enough again to block my air supply.

"Now, if I had it my way, and had I known beforehand this could have been prevented. She would never have met with you. How she even knew you *existed* and where you lived is beyond me. Why she's chosen you will be. . . troublesome for me. Unfortunately, for some reason, you slipped from my mind. Seeing you again opened a well of memories I'd forgotten. And those memories are. . ." he paused, his lips twisting into a smile, "delicious."

His hand remained on my throat, constricting my air flow as he went on. "However, it is vexing. Considering the circumstances- if you say anything, best believe me Serra when I say that I can and will ruin whatever future you have if you get in my way. You will keep your mouth shut about us or I will let every man, woman and child in the world know that you are a whore. Have I made myself clear?"

His eyes roamed my face before settling on my lips. His smile turned cruel, "It's really too bad you were raised by a witch. You're too beautiful. How had I forgotten? It's most unfortunate. Your pretty face will forever be ingrained in my mind. Especially the one you make when you come. Now. . . Had we met and you were of some kind of wealth this probably would have ended differently for us."

His thumb caressed the column of my neck, the pressure releasing slightly as it allowed me to gulp down some precious air. His eyes flashed, darkening with hidden desire. "But maybe it doesn't have to."

I knew that look.

"Now don't look at me like that. I could have you."

His other hand brushed the hair from my face, the stray tear that made its way down my cheek. "I would have you know, taken you as my wife. It would have made sense. No one in this shipping port village is as stunning as you are, not really."

He went on, his hand grazed my side, my hip poised to pull me closer, "Truly a shame if I were to be honest. But. . . lineage Serra. How would that look, hmm? I certainly could not marry someone who has a reputation such as yours. Your pleas before did not fall on deaf ears. Yet. . ."

I felt it then, the bulge in his pants as he stepped even closer. Pulling at his hand on my throat, pleading, I had to get away. "Kaston please."

His face softened slightly with a mocking smile, "I remember those words. What I wouldn't do to hear them again while buried deep inside you."

I shook my head, my heart pounding violently in my chest as his hand on my neck tightened its hold. It was definitely going to bruise. Eyes roved my face as he ground against me. A click of his tongue had me cowering, "I could you know."

He was larger than I was, his broad shoulders blocked out the sun that filtered in through the window, but I still felt his arousal. It wouldn't take much for him to overpower me. We were less than a few paces from my bed. Another fear ran through me. A tremble raced down my spine as he whispered in my ear, his warm breath tickling the exposed skin.

"Right here, in your own home and no one would know. Just like before and we wouldn't have to tell anyone."

I felt his other hand graze my hip again and move up along my side, pausing under my breast, the skin there prickled under his touch. His hand splayed across it as his thumb rubbed against the fabric of my bodice. The sensation caused me to recoil. A nip at my ear lobe forced an unwelcome shudder to run its course down my spine before another squeeze of his hand on my neck.

This was a game.

He was enjoying this. Watching me struggle and fight him, desire danced on his face and in his eyes.

"Please." I managed to choke out. "Please don't do this."

I did not recognize my own voice, the unshed tears behind my eyes before another one fell. I had tried to move on, tried to be okay with what he had done. But I could not live with this. This would undo me if he followed through with it.

Kaston's eyebrow arched, his gaze fixated on my lips as a tear trickled down my cheek. A low hum in his throat as he watched the tear rolled down off the edge of my jaw. Before I could process what was happening, his lips crushed against mine. I struggled to keep up with the force of his kiss, but he demanded more, his tongue pushing past my lips.

Tears continued to stream down my face as he pressed me against the wall, his hand slipping down to my hip and tugging at the fabric of my skirt. I winced as he lifted it, the rough material chafing against my skin. His palm burned against my bare thigh as he lifted it higher, trapping me in place.

Forcing himself even closer.

I felt his fingers dig into my thigh as his hand tightened on my throat, completely cutting off my air supply this time. The force of his lips on mine hurt. His tongue sweeping and claiming. Reminding me that he owned me. That he had taken it before and would again. Whether I wanted to give it to him or not this time. The flash of his teeth on my neck from the last time burned into my head. His hand slid up my leg, the trail it left behind was hot. The sensation left behind an unwelcome fire.

My vision blurred.

I could not breathe.

I could not fight him.

Lack of sleep had left me weak. All I could do was push against his chest as he forced himself on me. A guttural sob lodged in the back of my throat.

And just as quickly as it happened, he'd stopped. Biting my bottom lip and pulling away from me. His fingers squeezed my neck one last time, forcing me to look up into his face.

Waiting until my eyes met his.

"I'll see you again Serra and keep that pretty mouth of yours shut. I'd hate to have to put it to use if you decide to speak to *anyone* about this."

The last of his words settled into my chest as he let go of me. The sound of his boots on the wood floor thundered in my ears. I didn't see him leave, didn't see him yank the door open. The force of his grip hard enough that the knob broke. not as I crumpled and sunk to the floor with my arms wrapped around myself, trying desperately to hold myself together. The numbness he'd left me with as my body shook with sobs. The sound of him exiting through the gate rang through the interior of my cottage.

He'd be back.

If I knew anything about him, anything at all, I knew he was determined and relentless.

K ASTON DID NOT COME back that day. Nor did he come back the next day, or the day after that. In fact, I didn't see him at all. But it did not stop the bruise around my neck from appearing. It was angry, dark purple and sore. I touched the tender surface and hissed, carefully applying a cream of aloe and peppermint to the darkened skin. Anything to help relieve the pain. But the fear he left me with, the fear that he would come back and finish what he had started, hung over me like a heavy weight.

The knob on the door had been completely broken of with the

spindle snapped in two. It would require repair- a skill far outside my capabilities. For the time being, the deadbolt would have to do. And while it would keep out smaller creatures, I feared it would not keep him out should he return. He would find a way, no matter what. The fire in the hearth crackled and flickered, continuing its angry dance along the logs as I sat there. My mind wandering with the possibilities. I'd settled in after a day of work outside in the garden, my body no longer able to take anymore.

The sun had not set on the horizon when I'd finally stopped but my stomach had growled demanding to be fed. I'd dined on a small dinner of greens, vegetable soup and a chunk of stale bread- not worthwhile or grand but would have to do. As I watched the fire crackle and dance, my mug of warm tea in my hands. The lure of sleep called to me, my eyes growing heavier by the second.

A sharp knock at the door startled me awake just as I was about to fall asleep causing my mug to almost slip from my fingers. I paused, fear washing over every fiber of my being. Was it Kaston? Had he finally decided to come back?

I couldn't chance it, I grabbed the iron poker from next to the fireplace before placing my mug on the table. My steps were slow and deliberate as I walked to the door and leaned against it, the poker poised to defend should I need it. "Who is it?"

A quiet voice replied meekly with such softness I nearly missed it, "Miss, I have a gift here for you from Conwell Manor."

A gift?

From whom? My brows furrowed in confusion as I undid the deadbolt and pulled at the door. The loud creak it made as it opened echoed through the room. On the stoop stood the young girl that had brought us tea in Lady Conwell's sitting room a large box in her hands. Emerald green and wrapped with a black satin ribbon. I caught the carriage that waited for her outside as I stepped aside so she could come in.

"Please, come in, you can set it on the table there."

She did just that, setting it carefully on the table before backing away, bowing slightly at the waist. Noticing the iron poker in my hand. "He hoped you would wear it to Lady Conwell's Spring Ball ma'am. A gift and an apology."

My heart stopped, he? "I'm sorry, who sent this?"

"Lord Kaston, ma'am." She dipped her head.

She kept her eyes cast down, playing the part of a demure and obedient servant. As expected, she remained quiet, avoiding any unnecessary attention. It was clear that the servants were mere reflections of those who held their leash, with any deviance from the norm resulting in severe consequences. The thought of the injustice they endured on a daily basis was unfathomable. The wealthy and powerful were cruel and loathsome, and it was evident in every interaction.

That's when she saw it though, the envelope placed under the ribbon and bow that held the box closed. It had my name scribbled elegantly across the front in fine script. My heart sank but a wave anxiety rose up in my chest. I did my best to remain as calm and composed as I could, not wanting to draw any unwanted attention to myself.

"Thank you. I appreciate you bringing this to me."

She curtsied this time but didn't leave. Hesitating before saying, "He asked that I relay a message."

I glanced at her, the weariness in her eyes before snagging on the iron poker again, the bruise on my neck.

"He asked if you meet him. In your spot, tonight." she looked back up at me.

She was pretty, in her own way. I could see the chestnut-colored hair she had under her cap, the few loose curls. Her eyes were brown, but her face was sharp. The angles of her jaw and her cheekbones defined. Her nose was petite, but it was the small bruise on the side of her face hidden by the curls and fabric of the cap that drew my attention.

I wondered if Kaston was as rough with her as he had been with me. She was trembling. It took everything in me not to go to her, to ask her to stay. To be sure she was safe. She was so young and had been dealt cards worse than mine in life. Setting the poker down on the table, showing her I meant her no harm, my voice was soft. "Thank you~"

"Imogen."

Smiling at her, "Thank you, Imogen."

She dipped her head one last time and fled out the door. Hurried down the path to the carriage and climbed back inside. It lurched forward and took off down the lane headed toward the main streets of Rothnia and Conwell Manor at its center. I couldn't stop the worry that formed in my chest, for her.

For me.

Kaston wanted to meet me.

I knew what doing so would result in. And I had absolutely no intention of going out there. I've done enough foolish things in my life, I was not going to put myself through this.

Instead, I slammed the door closed and locked the deadbolt. It would not be much, it certainly wouldn't stop someone from forcing their way in, but as I pushed the table in front of the door as an extra security measure, my eyes snagged on the envelope again. I grabbed the poker and sat in my chair, ignoring the weight of the box and the envelope.

I would sit here all night if I had to. He was not catching me alone and unarmed again. But the lull of sleep called to me again as my eyes became heavy, drifting off into another nightmare.

CHAPTER
Seven

The Goblin King

OBSERVING THE MORTAL FROM afar, hidden beneath the shadows of the trees my blood boiled. This man was sneaky. Not only had he slipped past my watch, but he had gone into her home. I had not missed the bruise around her neck. How it angered me when I saw it. An irrational thought had presented itself to me shortly after I'd spotted it.

A thought that perturbed me more than anything.

How it would feel to repay him in kind. How I could crush his neck under my own strength and grip. The thoughts receded shortly there after. But because of this mortal man, I was not going to risk anything. I'd sent my companion to track her whereabouts the very next day, surveillance on her always. I could not risk serious harm coming to the girl before I could act.

She was still vital to my plans.

The goblins in my employ had so willingly followed him, kept out of sight, and reported back. And while they watched, they had learned more about him than he probably knew about himself. Their surveillance of him the last couple of weeks was fruitful, indeed. I was impressed really, I would have to give the goblins a raise for the work they had done.

Not only had I learned more about him than I needed to, but I had learned a bit more about his family. His brothers, his parents, even the girl he was currently courting. And with the knowledge I altered my plans to fit around him. While this man was a menace, he would be a nice pawn in this game.

However, I'd far underestimated the strength the memory spell would do on this mortal. When I planted the seed in his mother's head amongst the weaving of my other spells, I hadn't anticipated how quickly it'd come undone.

Fate had an interesting way of thwarting me.

Of interfering with every plan and every ambition I had. With everything it seemed, it was if it was mocking me as I tried to spin my web. One meeting, one moment, and it had all shattered. Not only was this thread completely broken, but his connection, this tie to Serra was stronger than I'd originally realized. I had not known how intimate their relationship had been. I had not known how much in love with him she had thought herself to be.

That spell. . . well. . . that was a fun one. Sending him to her.

I remember that day. I'd lingered in the shadows as I watched them meet. Watched it unfolded for a time before being forced back to the Fae Realms. Unaware that it had gone sour so quickly.

For now though, I would let Fate do its own thing, let it travel its course. Even if I had not accounted for how quickly things would escalate. How involved it would be. But this could work. It could play into my hand of cards so easily. This man's infatuation with her would be useful indeed. She had regained his attention, but it could be to my advantage. Certainly I'll use this unfortunate turn of events and I was more than happy to adjust to see it done. If I could use him to convince her to come with me and manipulate it all in a way that benefited myself, it would force her from the Mortal Lands.

Right into my ruse.

If it meant I would get wanted in the end, all that I cared about. I'd see it done because that was all that mattered.

But even while I stood there and watched this man, I could feel the forest round me. It was on edge as I stood here amongst the trees and the brush. They were silent, waiting for something. As if it knew what I was about to do. The cackles from the low brush had ceased upon my arrival and the air had gone still.

Quiet.

Shifting back into the darkness of the shadows, I waited. My eyes on the man hiding in the brush as he watched her door. But I was not here for the man, no. I was not here for him at all. I saw the carriage drop him off at the forest edge- taking off again as he slipped between the trees- before stopping outside her house. The maid was timid, scared. The large box in her hands as she made her way to the door.

A twig snapped under my foot, causing the mortal man to look up. His hand went to his hip, a dagger hidden from sight. He looked around the wood, the brush, before he settled in again, weariness on his face as he turned back to the cottage.

"He really shouldn't be playing in the forest."

"Sir, let us play with him?"

The hobgoblin's skin was a sickly green color, with deep furrows and ridges running across its forehead and cheeks. Its eyes were large and bulging, taking up most of its face, and they gleamed with a mischievous intelligence. The creature's nose although small and flat could sniff out anything and its mouth. . . it was full of razor-sharp teeth that glinted in the moonlight. Its ears were pointed and slightly askew, and they twitched as it listened intently to the world around it.

Each that had followed me this evening wore a suit of battered leather armor, with frayed edges and rusted buckles. Many carrying a mace strapped across their backs. Despite this ones scrappy appearance, there was a fierce determination in it's gaze, and I knew it would do whatever it took to complete the task I had set before it.

"In good time. . ." I responded, *"you know what must be done first."*

My eyes snapped back up at the creak of her door as it rang in my ears. I watched the maid scurry from the cottage and climb back into the carriage before lurched forward and barreled back down the lane toward the village, toward the building she lived in. For the home she had known these last years. For what it was worth, this was my favorite part, terrorizing the mortals of this world. My eyes went back to the man in front of me.

And this would be fun indeed.

The mortal man hiding in front of me, he would not see the Fae male, no. This mortal man who had roused a hidden emotion in me, who had laid his hands on her, his mind was weak and his heart even weaker. He was easily fooled, easily manipulated to believe what I wanted him to.

No, this man would see the beast.

The beast this Realm thought me to be.

"Whatever it is he plans to do, he'll find the forest has other ideas. It's honestly too bad he'll be collateral damage."

An echo of chatter, laughter and mirth went up around me as the brush shook and danced. The goblins had a job, and they would do it well. They always did. I watched as they spread out, past that man and down the lane. The look in the man's eyes as I stepped from the brush and prowled toward him, his nightmares come to life.

It really was unfortunate, what I was about to do. As much as I wanted to, as much as I really wanted to mess with this man more, I had to stick to the plan.

CHAPTER

Eight

Serra

I SAW THE FIRST missing person's poster two days after her visit.
The paper had been pinned to the town bulletin by the city hall
building. Another to add to the many that were already missing. The
page front and center amongst the many other pieces of paper, those
that advertised rooms for rent, auctions, jobs, sales, and other services.
But it was *her* face that caught my attention.

Her face was familiar.

Sad but kind, the sharpness of her cheek bones, the shape of her
jaw, her small nose. The curls that framed her face. And while I had only
seen her face twice. I knew who it was.

It was Imogen.

She'd gone missing and no one had seen her. Not a single trace of her was left. Not a single word to her family or friends, to the people she knew, and certainly not to the Conwell's. It was as if she had run away. Simply just. . . disappeared. The note at the bottom had mentioned a reward for information. That the guards were looking into her disappearance and sought anyone who knew something.

Do I tell them?

Should I mention anything I had seen?

My apprehension about any mention of her visit kept me from speaking. What if I had been the last one to see her? What if she never made it back to Conwell manor after being with me? I did not want them thinking I had anything to do with it. And I certainly could not mention anything about Kaston. I knew he had left the bruise on her face. The way she eyed the fire poker as if I would swing it at her and her unease told me all I needed to know. If I were to become a whistleblower, it would cause another problem I did not need.

Not right now.

I just hoped she was safe and living a happy life, hopefully with someone she had fallen in love with. And not. . . dead somewhere.

One could only hope.

I turned to head down the road toward the tavern. The briny sea breeze off the docks and the smell of freshly baked bread and cakes hung in the air as I meandered down the cobblestone street. The aroma from the apothecary shop and the smell of essential oils and creams drifted out the door as I passed.

Past the modiste with the yards and yards of brightly colored, jewel toned fabrics and laces. Even by Rothnia's sole bookshop, longing to step inside one day and just smell the pages. Feel the books in my hands. It's been so long since I had gotten a new one to read, and I missed it. I loved to read; Nona used to bring me books when I was a young girl, when we could afford it. But such luxuries were a dream now.

I wasn't openly friendly with most of the shop owners on this block, but Nona taught me to be courteous, even with the nasty things they would say as I passed. As I weaved through the shoppers and owners- the buildings towering above me, the smiles, and nods of those who passed by, I saw them. Kaston was ahead of me, making his way up the street toward where I was. I would recognize his auburn hair anywhere, very few in Rothnia had such hair. It was a family trait passed down by his mother.

But it was the young woman on his arm who snagged my attention. She was petite with blonde curls coiled up, an ostentatious hat atop her head, which blocked the sun from her face. Her dress of soft pink satin, lace ruffles, white hand gloves and rose velvet caplet marked her as a noble. Her hand was nestled into his arm, a beaming smile on her face as they went from shop window to shop window.

The bags he held and the boxes their escort carried, indicated they were here to spend. My heart ached. It had been rare that Kaston spent anything on me. Occasionally, showing at the cottage with a rose or two. But never like this.

Never so open.

The heavy weight of the emerald green box with the black satin ribbon haunted me. The apology, I could not bring myself to open it, to see what was inside. Feeling as though by doing so it would secure myself to him. I had left it on the table in the cottage; a stark reminder of him and what he was asking.

Of course, I could choose not to wear the dress, hoping I had enough to scrape together to get my own. But I knew in the end, I would have no choice. There was no way I would be able to get my own in such a short time. The coin I would earn tonight would pay the taxes that were owed for the year.

Hurrying past them as quickly as I could, keeping my face down, I felt his eyes land on me. A quirk of his lips caused my skin to flush and my head to pound in trepidation. Praying that he would not say anything. Praying that he would leave me alone and escort his companion back to her home. Praying he would not find me working at the tavern tonight. I could not keep living in fear of this man, but he made it so difficult. The ball was in four days, and I prayed I would not see him again before then.

THE TAVERN WAS CROWDED tonight. A new ship had docked in the harbor this morning and the sailors had found their way to one of the many taverns in Rothnia. My tavern, The Rusty Goat, which sat a block from the docks, was full. The rooms above booked out for the night.

The loud and boisterous patrons ordered round after round of ale and mead. The dishes piled up next to me through out the night. It would take hours to get everything cleaned up before my shift ended. But staying late would be no bother, not for me.

The owner had taken off for the evening, which left me, the barkeep Corey, and our cook Bern to run everything until his return later.

Tonight's menu offered steamed crawfish and seasoned potatoes as a main choice, but the usual stewed vegetable soup and bread, minced meat pies and mashed potatoes with ale gravy still found its way to the tables- a favorite for most. I glimpsed an occasional plate of apple pie leaving the kitchens.

My stomach grumbled as Bern sent out dish after dish. I had not eaten before leaving the cottage, I'd gotten stuck in the garden tending the new sprouts and had lost track of time. A loud laugh echoed as the door opened and Corey set down another tray of used mugs, bowls, and silverware. Before taking the ones I had just cleaned back out again.

"Serra, take a break. You've been working hard since you got here. The dishes will not go anywhere," Bern said, having peaked his head around the corner. We shared the space but with the way the tavern was laid out, the washing basins were nestled under the stairs that went to the rooms above. The kitchen stoves and ovens around a corner, giving him the most space.

"Thanks Bern, but I'm okay." My sleeves were rolled back, the front of my skirt soaked from the water. I blew the stray hair from my face as I glanced over at him.

"Serra, please, let me insist. You cannot tell me you aren't hungry. Take this bowl of potatoes and ale gravy and go sit in the back alley to eat. It's already past dinner time," Bern urged me with a kind tone. The steam rising from the bowl made my stomach growl, which he found amusing as he handed it to me.

"Go ahead," he said with a chuckle.

Grateful for his offer, I wiped my hands and accepted the bowl before making my way to the back door. As I stepped outside, the cool air brushed against my face, providing a brief moment of solitude. I found an empty crate to sit on and savored the delicious aroma emanating from my food. Bern was a trustworthy man, aside from Nona, he was the only person I could confide in.

He'd often looked out for me, giving me his advice. Bern had two daughters at home, his wife having succumbed to the sickness years ago. He worked hard to care for them, cooking at the tavern all day, serving at night, and throwing cargo onto ships at the docks when he could. Bern was as close to a father figure as I had. Having taken me under his wing at sixteen, at Nona's request. He'd been the one I had gone to when she passed. Helping me sort out her arrangements and personal affairs. But there were still secrets Nona kept, even ones Bern did not know.

A heavy sigh pushed itself past my lips as I looked up into the night sky and the stars twinkling above. They offered me peace, a sense of serenity. They called to me; the feeling of refuge was always there within them. I felt at home in the dark, despite Nona Luna's warnings. Like the dark was the other half of me. Even when I was not allowed outside after sundown. I felt safe, at peace amongst them.

A sadness washed over me as I took a bite from my bowl.

Things have been strange lately, very strange. I just could not put my finger on what it was. For weeks, I had the feeling of missed company, an odd emptiness. And in one moment, I remembered, as if I had amnesia during that time

It was odd.

Seeing Kaston's face, his eyes, the memories? It broke whatever had plagued me, the rift opening wide. But the feeling had not quite gone away. It hovered, waiting. As if there was more that had gone. Everything was a mess. I was a mess. A flutter of wings above caught my attention. High above on the rooftop of the next building, I could just barely make out a bird. It was dark against the night sky, but its eyes shone as it watched. The moon reflected off its feathers as the clouds moved. Unease washed over me, its presence unwelcome.

An omen in many homes within Rothnia.

A laugh echoed down the alley as a group of men rushed past on the street; causing me to jump and the bird to fly off. I ate my food quickly before allowing it to cool off any more than it already had. I had just slipped back inside and set the dish in the water basin when I heard Bern.

"Serra, can you do me a favor and take this tray to the front? I need to fill up another one and Corey is swamped," Bern requested while he busied himself with filling plates and bowls. "We just received a large food order from a new group of sailors; another ship has docked for the night."

"Sure thing, Bern. Do you need any help with the remaining servings?" I asked, peeking my head around the corner to watch him move from pot to pot.

"No, my dear. You'll be enough help just taking the tray to the front for me," he replied with a nod.

Taking the tray from the kitchen bench, I made my way into the main tavern. The weight of it making it hard to balance. The noise level was higher out here as I navigated through the drunken sailors and the women entertaining them, being careful not to spill or drop anything on anyone. As I approached the bar counter where Corey was, I overheard him and a group of off-duty guards talking about Imogen. They were asking if anyone had seen her, if she had been there, or if anyone had any information about her whereabouts.

Corey denied knowing anything.

While I knew very little about him, I knew he mostly kept to himself, he came in and did his job before going home. Or I assumed he did. He had only just started a couple of weeks ago. Never really talked to anyone other than those who sat at the bar. Occasionally he'd smile, but usually he did his job and then took off.

I had to admit, he was rather pleasing to look at. I remembered the day he first started. His dark brown hair was tousled from the breeze outside and his hazel eyes tracked my every move as I wiped down the tables. It caused my stomach to twist and flip with butterflies. The muscle in his arms would ripple as he wiped out cups and filled them with ale. I had only seen him smile at me once, but I was so tongue-tied that I slipped into the back as quickly as I could without looking back.

Since then, I'd kept my eyes cast down around him, fully aware when his eyes followed me, watching what I was doing. The way it left me feeling was unsettling, the butterflies fluttering about in my abdomen. It wasn't unpleasant, just. . . different. Unlike how I felt at the moment. Right now, I felt incredibly uneasy. A lingering feeling like someone was watching.

As I placed the tray behind the counter, I sensed someone's eyes on me. Worried that it might be someone I didn't want to see, I quickly scanned the room. But I didn't spot the auburn-haired man I was avoiding among the crowd of sailors. Instead, my gaze was met with the unsettling gaze of a man with two mismatched eyes. He 'd watched me intently as I had made my way towards the bar through the tables. Although my back had been turned to him, I could feel the electric current emanating from him.

It made me feel uneasy.

The man's face was mostly concealed by his hood and the dark cloak draped around his shoulders. Despite his efforts to blend into the shadows, his sparkling eyes caught my attention. It was the expression on his face that made me pause, though. His lips were pulled back in a tight smile, revealing unnaturally sharp canines.

Unlike the rest of the tavern patrons, who were boisterous and busy, he kept to himself in the far corner of the room, occupying an entire table. The air around him was heavy with danger, and people avoided him like the plague, avoiding all eye contact. It was as though he could strike out at any moment, slicing anyone who crossed his path with a blade.

"And what about you?"

I'd heard the question, but it did not register until I pulled my gaze away from him. Looking at the group of off duty guards in front of me. "I'm sorry, could you repeat that?"

"What about you? Do you have any information about the missing girl?" he eyed me cautiously. I'd seen him before, he had been one of the guards to escort me to Conwell Manor a couple of weeks ago.

I shook my head. "No. I only just saw the poster this morning. I'm sorry. I do hope she's alright."

He tipped his glass back before downing it and stood up. "Well, if you hear anything let me know. I'm heading the investigation into her disappearance. This time of year everything gets dangerous."

"Oh? How so?" Corey asked as he took the mug from the soldier.

The guard cocked his head, brows furrowed. "Do you not know?"

"I'm afraid not. I just moved here."

The guard looked at me before returning his gaze to Corey, apprehension on his face. Slowly he explained, "Every spring we get a visit from the Goblin King, and every spring someone goes missing. It has been happening more lately but this one was sudden. Her carriage had been ripped to pieces. The driver refuses to speak, says he cannot remember, and the horses are gone."

Corey stiffen beside me, the tension emanated from him. The Goblin King? Now where had I heard about him before?

The nagging feeling was back. I looked up to where the stranger was, but the seat was empty. Left abandoned. He was gone. I readjusted my gaze, "Of course, if we hear anything we will let you know." I offered a smile, as he dipped his head and left.

"SERRA IT'S LATE. I'LL walk you home."

"Thanks Bern but I think I can manage." I replied, following him through the door to the main room of the Rusty Goat. With the last of the dishes washed, we were ready to call it a night. My back ached and I was beyond ready for sleep. The fire in the hearth popped as my eyes scanned the room. Corey had already left, leaving the owner to tend to any stragglers that may come in overnight. As I approached the bar, I noticed a pile of coins sitting on the counter- one for each of us.

"I don't want to come in tomorrow and find out that you've disappeared too," Bern said as he tucked his coin away into a pouch. "Too many have vanished, and I'm not taking any chances."

I stuffed my own pile of coins into my pocket and looked up at him. "I wouldn't mind the company. It's been pretty lonely around here lately."

Bern smiled as we bid goodnight before making our way out of the tavern and up the street. He walked beside me as we passed by the closed shops, their owners having long since left for the night. Drunken sailors lay passed out in the gutters, and a few stragglers stumbled past us on their way back to their rooms, arm in arm with a lady. It was well past midnight as we left town, heading off into the darkness together and down the road that would take me to my home. Bern's voice broke the silence as we walked.

"How are you doing though, Serra?"

I hesitated before answering, it was not a question I was expecting from him. But it made me feel loved knowing he cared "I'm okay. Things have been. . . weird."

"How so?"

I had no intention of telling him about Kaston's visit or my visit to Conwell Manor. Those details I'd keep to myself. He didn't need to know I was in trouble or that Kaston had threatened me. Fidgeting with my shawl, I glanced over at him. Bern was handsome enough. He was not overly tall, but he wasn't short either. His dark hair was starting to turn white at the temples, the short strands sheered close to his head- allowing him the freedom from tying it back.

Working as hard as he did kept him in shape. The work he did down at the docks aided in his muscle tone, but his broad shoulders were enough to make you think twice before crossing him. In his younger years, I imagined him to be a very handsome person. However as time went on, his dark eyes started to frame with age and his movements grew slower. I could tell he was sad. Though the stress of his wife's death and raising his girls alone would take its toll on anyone in his position.

"Just weird." I offered, "I don't know how else to put it other than I've forgotten things. . . only to remember them later. Moments of my life just vanishing then reappearing when I see something, hear something or in some cases smell them."

We walked in silence, the only sound coming from the crunching of our boots on the gravel road. The gentle rustling of leaves from the swaying trees accompanied us as the night breeze brushed against our skin. The sounds of nocturnal animals filled the air, serenading us with their songs of the night.

A lullaby I knew.

"Ah, yes. Grief will do that. It tends to be temporary, but it can last a lot longer than you would think. I went through it for a while after my wife Malassa died." he said, his lips stretching into a sad smile. "The doc said after she died, grief tends to cause cognitive impairments and memory loss in many individuals. Many who have experienced significant trauma in their lives. Your Nona's passing was not easy for you. But it'll pass Serra. Just give it time."

I smiled at him as we approached the cottage, the familiar sight of it. The smoke that swirled from the chimney. It was home, Bern followed me through the gate and watched as I was able to push the door open with ease.

"What happened to the knob?" He asked, there was a note of

concern in his voice. He studied it closely, testing it between his fingers. His eyes found mine again, his brows pulled together in confusion.

"Oh, it's nothing. I yanked it open too hard the other day and it broke," I lied, setting my shawl on the chair.

"Why don't you come and stay with me and the girls. They would love to have you. They adore you."

"Thank you, but I'm okay here. The garden is starting to sprout, and I'd like to stay close by. Besides, I have the iron fire poker." I grinned.

His laugh bounced off the stone walls, "Okay. But I'll investigate getting it fixed for you, with everything going on, and the girl going missing, it would set my mind at ease knowing it was fixed."

"Thank you but you really don't have to do that. I have been saving up to get it replaced."

"Nonsense," He paused, his eyes roving over the place before landing on the table. "What's that?"

He'd noticed the emerald green box. I'd left it sitting out on the table. I'd been so busy with everything that I hadn't thought to put it away. My face flushed as I glanced at it too, "Oh, it's nothing. A gift from someone."

"Oh? A boy?"

I glared at him a smile spreading across my face. My mind wandered again, Bern had made sense. Grief does weird things to many of us but his comment still concerned me, "Good night, Bern."

He laughed again as he left, "Good night, Serra. Lock the deadbolt."

I closed the door quietly behind him, double-checking that the deadbolt was securely in place. I couldn't shake the feeling that something wasn't right, that there was more to my memory loss than what Bern had told me. But what was it? I tried to push the thoughts out of my mind, focusing instead on the box that sat on the table. The sight of it sent a shiver down my spine, and I couldn't help but stare at it, feeling a sense of dread that seemed to wash over me in waves. I knew what was inside- But the thought of opening it filled me with an overwhelming sense of fear.

As I stood there, paralyzed by doubt, I couldn't help but wonder if the memories I had lost were worth the risk. What if I uncovered something that I didn't want to remember? But at the same time, the curiosity was overwhelming. I had to know what had happened, and why I had lost those memories in the first place. There was a constant reminder that time was running out.

Four days.

I had four days before the ball.

CHAPTER
Nine

Serra

THE ROOM WAS GLITTERING.

The moment I stepped into the room, my eyes widened in awe and my breath caught in my throat. The opulence of the space was overwhelming, almost too much to take in at once. Crystal candelabras adorned the walls, while an enormous chandelier hung from the ceiling, casting a sparkling glow over everything below. The polished floor reflected the flickering flames of the candles, adding to the glittering effect. This was no ordinary room; it was a grand ballroom, decked out in shades of ivory and gold, shimmering in the light.

The lively chatter of the guests filled the air, as they mingled about in their finest attire. Champagne flowed freely and the guests greeted each other with familiar warmth and joy. The conversations buzzed with talk of trades, business, and upcoming events, as I made my way through the crowd. It was a place of excitement and anticipation, with the promise of future dances and festivities adding to the already palpable energy in the air. And while I could feel the excitement and merriment around me, it left me drained.

Four days had not been long enough.

They had come and gone quicker than I had time to comprehend. The feeling of it all had left me anxious. Especially after my last encounter with Kaston. It brought me little piece of mind. Avoiding him was going to wear on me, it had worn on me so much already. Each trip into town was a plethora of worry and anxiety, so much dread had hung over me that I'd encounter him again. I knew I couldn't keep avoiding him forever.

His sudden reappearance in my life had thrown everything into disarray and it had stirred up old emotions that I had tried so hard to bury. But this morning when I awoke and saw the box sitting there with my name on the envelope I knew I had no other choice. I'd resigned myself to wearing the dress he had left for me- my brown linen skirt and bodice simply would not suffice in a crowd as elegant as this one.

My gaze swept over the people before me as I stood there in the ballroom. The guests that Lady Conwell invited were dressed in a dazzling array of outfits- every color, style, and fabric imaginable. There were lace gowns and satin suits, gilded masks and silk flowers adorning hair and lapels. The air was thick with the fragrance of expensive perfumes and the sound of chatter and laughter. I felt a pang of self-consciousness, wondering if I had made a mistake in coming here.

As I wove my way through the crowd, I couldn't help but feel a twinge of envy at the effortless grace with which some of the other women moved. They seemed to glide through the room with practiced ease, their skirts rustling gently as they passed. In contrast, I felt clumsy and out of place, my own dress feeling stiff and unfamiliar. But I forced the thought aside, determined not to let my insecurities show.

I caught a glimpses of myself in one of the gilded mirrors that adorned the walls. My own mask, a work of art in itself- covered half of my face, leaving only my lips visible to those around me. The jewels that encrusted it sparkled in the light, drawing attention to my eyes. My dress flowed behind me as I walked, the soft blue satin swishing with each step. The silk chiffon organza added a delicate touch to the outfit, making me feel elegant and refined. It was the most beautiful gown I had ever worn.

My hair, which I had left down, was being swept away by the light breeze that drifted through the ballroom. I had given up trying to style it and let it fall in its natural straight locks. It added a touch of simplicity to my otherwise elegant outfit.

The dress Kasten had given me was a stunning piece of art, carefully crafted to leave a lasting impression. The neckline was low but still managed to maintain a modest air, thanks to the cowl of the dress that rested atop my breasts. The material was a soft, silky fabric that draped beautifully, and the cut of the dress was expertly designed to accentuate my curves.

As I turned to see the back of the dress, I gasped. It dipped low, far lower than I had ever felt comfortable wearing before. The sheer gossamer sleeves added a delicate touch to the dress, the detail that left me in awe. The sleeves were constructed in a bishop style that buttoned at the wrist in a cuff, adding a classic elegance.

The dress was beautiful, designed to make me feel ravishing and confident, but I couldn't shake the feeling that it was too revealing. I couldn't help but feel a sense of unease at the way the dress hugged my hips and chest, putting them on full display for all those in attendance. The fabric was soft and silky, and it felt like a second skin against my body. I tried to maintain my composure, but the feeling of being watched and judged lingered, making me feel uncomfortable and out of place. Judged by every person in the room.

But Lady Conwell truly had outdone herself.

The ball was a feast for the senses. A coach had arrived just after dusk to pick me up, pulled by large draft horses. It was not the same one Imogen had climbed into. The one that the guards said was smashed to pieces. This one was far more ornate, with mother-of-pearl inlay and black lacquered sides. The interior was lush and covered in rich purple velvets. It traveled down the streets, making its way to the Manor and the party inside, jostling me about slightly. The clop of the horses' hooves hitting the cobblestone steadied my nerves, the rhythmic, *clop, clop, clop* drowned out the thoughts in my head. But only for a moment.

Lady Conwell had extended an invitation to me, but she had not given me any specific instructions about what to do, if I were to meet anyone. As the carriage pulled up to the house- behind the line that was coming and going- I felt uneasy as my eyes scanned the large imposing Manor. My footsteps on the stone steps leading up to the large mahogany doors were drowned out by my own pulsing veins. My heart thundered in my chest as I looked up at the goblin knocker, felt as though it was staring back at me as I stepped into the foyer.

In spite of it all, between the fear and the anxiety I had felt an inexplicable pull to attend. The feeling tugged at my gut, urging me to be here, and I could not resist my curiosity. So here I was, standing in the grand ballroom of the family manor of a man I had once loved, despite his unfathomable treatment of me during his last visit to my home.

As I weaved my way through the crowd, my gaze caught a glimpse of a table adorned with various refreshments. Trays of delectable-looking food were stacked high, while waiters bustled about, offering guests glasses of champagne. Plates of cakes, sweet desserts, breads, and cheeses were carried past me, their aromas lingered in my nose. My stomach growled, reminding me that I should have eaten before coming. But my mind had been preoccupied with worries, causing me to forget.

Lost in my own thoughts I hadn't noticed the young man with auburn hair standing at the table with his back to me. My heart skipped a beat, and my stomach churned at the memory of the man I had once loved and the events of the past few days. However, as he turned around, I noticed that his face was more mature than Kaston's, and a wave of relief washed over me.

Like so many others in attendance, he too wore a mask and it was a striking sight to behold. Crafted from dark metal, it was adorned with intricate scrollwork and studded with emeralds and pearls that caught the light in a mesmerizing display. As I looked closer, I noticed that his jawline was more defined than Kaston's. And from what I could see of his eyes behind the mask's mischievous expression, they were the same color that had once enchanted me.

The man's outfit was just as impressive as his mask. He wore a silver jacket and white trousers that made his dark mask and hair stand out even more. But it was the embroidery on his vest that truly caught my attention. A network of delicate scrolls, vines, and flowers in rich shades of purple, blue, and pink, brought the entire ensemble to life.

"Hello." His voice was soft and welcoming, causing me to jump. I hadn't expected him to address me or speak to me at all. The beating of my heart was deafening in my ears as I looked to see him watching me intently. His eyes were fixed on my face before dipping down to my chest as we stood there.

"Hello," I managed to reply, my voice barely above a whisper.

"She's really out done herself this time, has she not?" He asked.

I hesitated briefly, did he think me one of them? My identity was a mystery to all but for some reason I felt bold enough to ask. "I don't think we've met before, do I know you?"

He chuckled, a sound that made my knees go weak. "Perhaps not formally, but I do believe we've crossed paths before," he said, his tone playful.

I couldn't help but feel drawn to him, despite the fact that I didn't know who he was. "I'm sorry, I don't think I caught your name."

He bowed his head slightly, the emeralds and pearls on his mask catching the light. "Forgive me, how rude of me not to introduce myself. Caine Conwell," he said, his voice smooth and velvety.

Kaston's older brother.

My heart raced as I stood face to face with Caine, the middle son of Lord and Lady Conwell. Fear held me fast as my mind raced, my heartbeat increasing with every passing moment. I couldn't help but wonder if he was anything like his brother Kaston, cruel and malicious, or if he was different.

Should I talk to him?

Should I tell him my name?

Did he know who I was, what I was once to his brother?

The silence between us stretched on, and I battled an ongoing war within myself. Part of me wanted to run, to escape this uncomfortable situation, while another part of me was curious. What would happen if I talked to him? Would he be kind, or would he be just like Kaston?

Suddenly, he cleared his throat, and the sound broke my trance, pulling me back to reality. "What's your name?" he asked.

"Serra."

The blood leached from my face. His voice caused every nerve to scream, the dread of his presence. Caine looked up; Kaston had wandered over. Of course, he would know it was me, he would recognize the dress. I questioned if he had picked it out for his own pleasure, his own reasons. Probably to use it as a guiding beacon, a way for him to keep me in his sights this evening.

Caine smiled at his brother. "Kas."

"Caine." His greeting made my skin crawl. Kaston's scent washed over me as he stepped closer. His proximity made me nauseous and while I battled the internal war to keep the contents of my stomach down, his voice echoed in the outer recesses of my mind. Grating on my resolve.

"I see you've found our mother's guest. Thank you for doing so. She has been looking for her."

I couldn't tell if it was a lie or if he was being genuine. But my stomach flipped as his hand grazed my lower back.

"Ah. Well. . . Serra, t'was lovely to meet you. I do hope I'll see you again this evening. Save a dance for me?" He took my hand and placed a kiss atop it.

"Doubtful, Caine." The disdain on Kaston's face had his brother retreating. A dark smile on his lips as he left. This would not be the end of this interaction.

The grip on my upper arm pulled my attention to Kaston. His eyes were dark, dangerous. He was angry as he yanked me away from the table, away from the crowd. I had no choice but to follow. He pulled me alone out to the hallway, before shoving me against the wall. My head whipped back, hitting it hard.

My vision blurred slightly at the impact.

"Stay away from Caine. This is my only warning, Serra." He glanced down, running a hand along the cowl of my dress, his knuckles grazing the skin atop my breasts before his eyes flicked back up. "Do you like the dress? I had it made for you. It pleases me to see you in it."

Pain pulsed through my head- the intense throb of it caused me my vision to blur as I struggled to focus on Kaston's words. I knew I had to tread carefully around him, to avoid arousing his anger or suspicion. The touch of his hand on my dress made my skin crawl, and the way his knuckles grazed the top of my breasts made me feel sick with disgust. I wanted nothing more than to be free of him, to run far away and never look back.

But I was trapped, with no escape from his presence. Kaston's arm blocked my way out, and his menacing gaze held me in place. I avoided his gaze, trying to distract myself by looking back at the door to the ballroom, where the other guests were mingling. Suddenly, Kaston's hand gripped my face, forcing me to look back at him. His fingers dug into my skin, and I winced at the pain.

"I'm rather disappointed in you right now," he sneered. "What do you have to say for yourself?"

My mind raced, trying to come up with the right words to placate him. "I- I don't know what you mean," I stammered.

But Kaston was not fooled. His rage washed over him, darkening his eyes even further. "You can't even say thank you," he spat. "Express any kind of gratitude for my generosity?"

I felt a surge of defiance rising in me as I pulled my face away from his grip. "Thank you," I ground out. It was all I could do to avoid his wrath, to keep myself safe for another moment.

To my surprise, he let go but then his grip found my waist, his fingers digging into my flesh. The pain that ran through me caused me to wince away from him as he leaned in. His breath was hot on my skin as he spoke- "You ignored my request," his voice was dark as he whispered in my ear, "And because of that, I was alone. Do you know what lurks inside the Ebony Wood, Serra?"

I should have known better, I should have listened to the voice in my head but part me wanted to believe the man I had loved was still in there. That the person before me was not the real Kaston.

"It is not my fault you went inside. You're the one to blame, Kaston. Not me." I retorted, my anger fueling my response. How dare he blame me for his own actions?

The sting of his palm on my cheek took me by surprise. I could feel the heat spreading across my skin and the tears welling up in my eyes. My hand flew to my cheek, trying to alleviate the pain. Kaston's face twisted in anger once again.

He'd just slapped me.

"I asked you to meet me, you will do as you are told. Have I made myself clear?" he demanded, his voice cold and unforgiving.

I could not stop the bitter words that came out next, "Why? What do you want from me, Kaston?"

His laugh was low, deep, quiet enough not to draw attention. "You, Serra. I thought I had made that perfectly clear the other day."

"So, what am I to be? Your whore? Your mistress? Certainly not your *wife*, you made *that* very clear."

The smile that spread across his face was undeniable.

I'd spoken the truth. That was what he wanted from me. Not only would he not marry me, but he would not let me be with anyone else. His finger traced the spot he had marked, the bite he had left. While it had healed and disappeared it was the memory of it that lingered.

"You are *mine*." He towered over me, his body pushing against my own. His heat caused my stomach to turn, it was stifling and suffocating. "Understand this, if I wish it, you will comply. You will not belong to anyone else. This whole thing my mother has planned will end tonight. Do you understand me, Serra? No. One. Else."

Of all the things that could have happened, this was not what I had expected. He had taken me, used me, threw me aside and then wanted to come back? And he fully expected me to comply with his wishes, indulge in his whims, be his mistress, his whore. The word was out before I could stop it.

"No."

"What?"

The shock and disbelief on his features had me standing up straighter. I would not cower, I would not bow down to this man. "I said, *no*."

"You are treading dangerous ground right now."

"I will not be your whore. I will not be your secret. You made your bed, now you will lie in it." I moved to slip away and to head back toward the ballroom, back to the crowd of people- if only I was strong enough to fight him off.

His hand flew out and grabbed me by the arm again. His face turned red with violence and burning desire as he yanked me down the dark hallway and through a door. The force behind his shove had caused me to stumble into the room, trying my best to catch my balance as he shut the door behind him. The terror that ran through me at that point was unmistakable and I prayed that he'd come to reason, but that did not seem to be in the cards for me. Not when he was like this.

The room was pitch black as my eyes strained to adjust to the lack of light. I stumbled backward again as I tried to put as much distance as possible between Kaston and myself. But I didn't see the desk until it was too late. I slammed into it and the pain that radiated through my knees was excruciating, I bit down on my lip to stifle a scream but a whimper escaped anyway.

I needed to get away from him.

As my eyes adjusted to the darkness, I could make out the shapes of bookshelves lining the walls, their spines barely visible in the gloom. I knew I was trapped and the panic started to set in as Kaston stalked closer. Even in the dark I could see the fury in his eyes. He lunged toward me and I dodged to the side to avoid him- my hand brushing against the cold metal of a paperweight on the desk as I did so. My fingers curled around it, hoping it would be enough to fend him off. But he was too quick, and he knocked it out of my hand with a sharp twist of his wrist.

The sound of things shattering and hitting the floor echoed through me as he cleared the top of it. His fingers gripping my arm as I struggled against him. The coldness of the wood hit my exposed back as he pinned me down on top of it. I couldn't stop fight him, struggling against him with all the strength I had left in me. His breath was hot on my face as he leaned in close. His voice was a low growl in the darkness. "If you scream, if you make any noise, you'll wish you hadn't."

I could see the fury in his eyes as he pulled away to look down at me, my heart was pounding so hard I thought it might burst from my chest. I felt for anything I could use to defend myself, my fingers groping wildly over the empty desk to smash into his head. But Kaston had cleared it of anything that could be used as a weapon.

The edge of my dress was pushed up as he lifted my legs and forced himself between them. I watched his hand go for the buttons of his trousers- freeing himself before yanking me to the edge, his grip on my thighs bruising. I had enough freedom to push him off as adrenaline coursed through my veins. With as much force as I could put behind it, I shoved my feet into his chest. It was enough to send him staggering backwards, allowing me enough time to get up and try running for the door.

But not enough.

His arms found my waist before lifting me up as he carried me back toward the desk and bent me over. A scream lodged in my throat as the air in my lungs forced out. My face hit the top of the dark wood- no matter how much I struggled, he was still stronger. Pushing me into the desk as the hem of my skirt was yanked up again. Exposing me to him as he yanked at my undergarments.

No.

Tears welled up in my eyes as a sob escaped my lips, the realization hitting me hard. He was really going to do this, right here and now, mere yards away from the crowd of Nobles and his own family. Panic surged through me, and I fought the urge to scream out for help, to alert everyone to what was about to happen. But his threat, coupled with the shock of the situation, paralyzed me- like a sharp knife slicing through my resolve to fight him. My eyes darted around the room, desperate for a way out, but there was no escape. I was trapped, and he knew it.

"Stop," I whispered, my voice barely audible over the pounding of my own heart. But he didn't listen, didn't care. He had all the power, and he knew it. And in that moment, I knew that I was truly alone, trapped in a nightmare with no way out. I was losing. This man was going to take me against my will if I stopped struggling, and I would not stop.

Ever.

Bucking up against him, doing my best to get some traction to get my arms under me, *anything* to push him off. But before I could, he was shoving me back down again.

"Stop fighting this." he snarled.

I felt his weight then, pinning me down as he whispered in my ear. The tears that had I had been able to hold back finally fell down over my face as he spoke, "I want you, and no one else will have you. You're mine. The more you fight me, the more you'll have to endure." The bite to my ear had me yelping in pain. I felt him then. Having lined himself up at my entrance.

"Kaston, please don't. Please."

The tears streamed down my face in a hot trail as I pleaded with him, my voice trembling with each word. But he didn't seem to care, not about my fear, my tears, or me. I couldn't see his face, but I could hear the snort of contempt as he spoke.

"Oh Serra," he said, his voice dripping with arrogance. "Relax and enjoy it. You liked it once, remember? I know I did."

His words made me sick to my stomach. How could he be so callous, so cruel? He didn't care, all that mattered to him was his own pleasure and his own twisted desires. I struggled to breathe as his weight pressed down on me again, his hot breath on my neck sent shivers down my spine. I tried to push him away again, to push him off of me, but his grip was too strong. My mind raced as I searched for a way out of this nightmare, but I was helpless against him.

My heart raced in my chest, and my breathing quickened as I waited for what was about to happen. His hand moved between my legs, and I felt a surge of panic. I closed my eyes, unable to bear the thought of him violating me in this manner. My body went numb, my senses disconnecting from the world around me as I waited for him to take me- to claim me as his own once more.

But it never came.

A thud in the back of my mind and a growl of displeasure ripped through the room. I heard the knocks then, pulling me from my stupor. The pressure of his grip subsided slightly as Kaston bellowed, "What?!"

Caine's voice flitted through the door- firm but calm. "Kaston, mother and father are looking for you."

"I'll be just a moment, Caine!"

"*Now* Kaston." I could hear the dark tone in Caine's own voice.

The groan of frustration that rippled through Kaston as he pushed off me, stuffing himself back in his trousers. He gripped my hair in his fingers, the force causing my back to arch against him, "Not at word, Serra. Or the next time it'll be far worse for you."

His grip loosen as he took a step back, giving me space to stand upright. I watched as he strode towards the door and wrenched it open with a forceful tug. Caine was standing there on the other side, his eyes shining. His gaze followed his brother as he barged past him before finally settling on me. My mask had been lost somewhere during the struggle and my hair was tangled and unkempt. My dress was now in disarray and a bruise had started to form on my arm.

I saw the sadness in Caine's eyes, and it triggered a fresh wave of tears. Caine beckoned for me to follow him as he picked up my mask off the floor. "It's going to be alright. Do not let them see you cry, Serra. Do not show them weakness. Kaston is a monster."

He placed the mask back on my face after wiping away my tears, straightened out my dress and fixed my hair. A small act of kindness after the terror I had just gone through. His fingers found mine as he squeezed a small smile spreading across his face. He placed my hand in the crook of his arm, before escorting me back to the ballroom.

He was quiet as he spoke, "Strength is our guild. Without it, we're weak, we are fragile. To show strength, means you are not without fear. But we do not let it rule us. Do not let the fear win out."

I learned something in that moment as his words settled in around me, something I should have learned before. Something that caused my blood to go cold. I did not have the strength or skill set to defend myself from anymore of Kaston's advances. I was at his mercy, I was his victim. His pursuit would continue until he got what he wanted and he was not the type to be told no.

I stared up into Caine's eyes, the golden brown color that he shared with his brother. I did not feel scared and I did not want to flee. This man, this man who shared Kaston's blood, was nothing like his brother. In his presence, I felt safe. His eyes sparkled as he smiled down at me again, leaving me wondering how far the apple had fallen from the tree with Kaston.

CHAPTER
Ten

Serra

A CROWD HAD FORMED in front of a small group of people. Lord and Lady Conwell stood at the center with Kaston flanked between them. Lady Conwell wore a beaming smile of pride, while Lord Conwell looked as though he was already bored and yearned to disappear into a glass of brandy. However, it was the young woman standing next to Kaston that caught my attention.

She was the same one I had seen with him the other day, and I could only guess who she was, Cressida. Despite her petite frame, she stood confidently beside him, her blonde hair and blue eyes shining. What struck me was that none of them were wearing masks, and it appeared that a new theme was starting to emerge. Those who wore masks lingered in groups, whispering behind their ornate disguises.

While those who did not- stayed close to their respective partners or hovered near the edges of the ballroom, scanning the room with interest. The atmosphere was charged with anticipation and expectation, and it was clear that something more than just a simple social gathering was taking place.

Lady Conwell was cunning, she clearly had crafted a matchmaking ball with every intention of bringing together couples who would be advantageous to each other's social and financial status. The idea made me ill, was this her plan the whole time? I still wasn't sure why she had picked me to begin with. Why choose me at all in the first place? The feeling of being watched returned as I stood there and pondered what she was up to. I could feel the eyes on me as I scanned the room looking for whoever it was. But it wasn't until my eyes snagged on Kaston again that I felt small.

His own eyes had scanned the crowd a couple of times before finding me and locked onto mine. I could feel the way they simmered with rage, could feel the lethal air that came off of him having found me standing next to Caine. His eyes burned brighter seeing my hand in Caine's arm.

I caught the smug look on his brother's face at Kaston's displeasure. Only realizing now this was a competition for them. And I was the object they fought over. The fury and violence that radiated off Kaston had me pulling my hand free. Caine picked my hand up and tucked it back into the crook of his arm. Rubbing his thumb along the top to steady my shaking.

"Stand up to him, Serra." He whispered.

"I did. And look where it found me."

"He does not own you." He looked down at me then, his eyes soft behind his mask. "Kaston is selfish and jealous. Always has been. Mother dotes upon him because he's the baby. He's spoiled; she created the monster that lives inside him."

"If I fight him, he'll just take whatever he wants anyway. It'll only be worse for me if I do."

"Only you hold the power of what people are allowed to do to you. You hold the power of what they hold against you. You. No one else." His words echoed inside my head. A remnant of words, from a distant, long forgotten memory, a vision.

A trigger.

As the young boy stood before the throne of gold, the man with a coronet of gilded laurel leaves on his head spoke with a stern tone, his voice echoing through the room. The boy's eyes widened as he listened to the man's chiding words. Meanwhile, a younger girl looked down at her feet, feeling ashamed of her actions and blushed in embarrassment.

"She was only following along, Sire. It is not her fault," the boy defended, speaking up for her.

"You hold the power of what people are allowed to do to you, boy," the man replied, his tone unchanged. "She is well aware of the consequences. She knows others can and will hold power against her, and you for that matter."

Feeling remorseful, the girl's voice was quiet and meek as she spoke, "I'm sorry."

The man's expression softened as he turned to the girl, "No need to be sorry, child. You have learned your lesson, and that is enough."

Then, he turned his gaze to the boy and said, "Protect her, she is yours. And you are hers. You are stronger together than you are apart."

The boy and the girl responded with a respectful bow, saying in unison, "Yes, sir."

Lady Conwell's voice echoed through the room, pulling the vision from my mind. Bringing me back to my body- blinking rapidly to clear my head. I had no idea where the vision came from or who they were, what it meant. It was not one of *my* memories. Her voice cut through the hum of chatter, drawing everyone's attention to her. "Oh it is so good of you to join us here tonight. Not only as we celebrate the arrival of Spring but for this very special occasion."

Her words were met with polite applause, but my attention was drawn to the couple standing at the front of the room. Cressida slipped her hand into the crook of Kaston's arm, a loving and tender gesture that he all but ignored. Her smile as she beamed up at him gave the impression that she was head over heels in love with him. That he was good and loving. How the veil had been pulled over her eyes.

As Lady Conwell continued her speech, the murmurs in the room grew louder. "Yes, yes we are here to celebrate the betrothal of our dear son. Our youngest boy, Kaston, to the lovely Lady Cressida Finkley." A round of applause went up around me and Caine, but I barely heard it. My grip on his arm tightened, his presence grounding me.

The hurt still hit me hard, like a punch to the gut. I had loved Kaston once. I had wanted him to be mine. So this news, this announcement of their betrothal was still very painful. Even after Kaston's declaration of keeping me for himself. It still caused my heart to ache as I watched them. I should have expected this. It should not bother me the way it does.

"Are you okay?"

I heard Caine's voice float around inside my head. My gaze left Kaston to look up at him, the concern in his own eyes behind his mask. A small smile spread across my lips as I nodded my head, but my voice betrayed me. A squeak as I replied. "Yes, I'm fine."

Caine slowly pulled his eyes away from my face to look at his brother. Accepting the congratulations, with Cressida on his arm beaming. "There was more to what I saw in the study wasn't there?"

I shook my head, Kaston's threat rang in my ears. "No." I lied.

He squeezed my fingers before letting go of my hand. "Would you like a drink Serra?"

"Please."

Caine nodded before he slipped away silently. I lost sight of him as the crowd moved around me. The masks glittering in the light from the chandeliers above. I had no idea who anyone was. No one here that I knew. I was not one of them. A stark reminder of where my position was. A soft melody embraced me as the music played.

Out of the corner of my eye I saw . . . no, I felt . . . someone watching me again. I spun in place to see who, but there was no one there. An even stranger feeling that darkness watched me, waited for me to acknowledge it. Acquainted and calling. Caine reappeared, a goblet in his hand filled with champagne. A small plate of food in the other.

"You should eat."

"I'm not hungry," I offered, taking the goblet from him before downing it in one go. Caine took it back and placed it on a tray as a waiter walked by.

"You're sure? You really should eat something. You've gone pale as a ghost."

"I'm fine." I whispered, my eyes cast down. What I would not give at this moment to disappear.

He sighs, his voice soft, "I have learned in the past that when a woman says 'she's fine' that in reality, she isn't. What's wrong? Something is bothering you."

I stared up at him, I did not know this man. "To be honest Caine, I hardly know you. Sharing my life and its secrets with you? No. Thank you, really, for saving me from your brother but I'm fine. I don't even know why you would care."

He hesitated for a moment before handing the plate to someone else and jamming his hands into his pockets. The silence between us was thick, the tension palpable. I couldn't shake the feeling that I had been too trusting of one Conwell boy already, and I didn't know this man well enough to let my guard down around him.

I turned to make my escape, hoping to find a quiet place to be alone, but he caught my hand before I could slip away. His touch was gentle, almost tentative, as he asked, "Please Serra, will you dance with me?"

His unexpected request caught me off guard, and for a moment, I was too surprised to answer. As I looked around the room, my eyes fell on Kaston, and I felt a pang of sadness in my chest. But before I could dwell on it, Caine's hand on mine drew my attention back to him.

"He's busy with Cressida." His fingers squeezed mine as he said, "I care, because Kaston likes to throw tantrums. I like to see him get flustered and angry. I care because I've seen you before. But I did not know your name. I care because.. . . Truthfully? I can see the pain in your eyes. He hurt you. I will not ask you what he did. That is your secret, but please give me the chance to show you that not all of us are evil."

I hesitated for a moment, unsure if I should accept his offer. But before I could make a decision I found myself nodding once. He took my hand and led me to the dance floor, where couples had already paired up. The music was lively, and I soon found myself caught up in the rhythm, moving in time with Caine.

As we danced, I felt a smile spread across my face. It was a brief moment of happiness, a reprieve from the struggles of my life. Caine led me through the steps, his eyes focused on me as he twirled me out and pulled me back in.

In that moment, I caught sight of Kaston watching us from across the room. His eyes were filled with madness and loathing, directed at his brother. I felt my neck grow warm under his gaze, and I knew that I was nothing more than a plaything in their twisted rivalry. As he pulled me back in, catching my hand again. I tried to excuse myself once more from his presence.

"Stay."

"I will not be used," I hissed under my breath. "Not between the two of you. I do not know you and you do not know me. Nor do I trust you."

Too trusting, too trusting of this man. Pulling away from him, my steps were quick as I headed towards the doors, my mind set on escape. But it was cut short as a hand reached out and grabbed my own- the grip tight and unyielding- before yanking me backwards into a hard chest. I looked up at the face of the man who had pulled me back into the dance. My stomach dropped as his eyes met mine.

I could feel the anger emanating from him as he spoke. "I warned you once," he growled in my ear. "Stay away from Caine."

The music swelled around us, the dancers twirled and spun in a blur of colors and movement. My heart raced as I tried to pull away, but his grip only tightened. "If you cannot listen, Serra," he continued, his voice low and menacing, "then you leave me no other choice. . ."

"Is this another game for you, Kaston? See how far you can go this time? You'll lose. You cannot have everything."

He snickered, "My dear, I don't need to lose. I've already won. It's as easy as laying a false rumor about you, keeping other men away. You see, men are simple love, we don't want spoiled goods. We don't want what someone has already had. You though, I've already had a taste of you. I've taken you myself, you so freely offered it to me last time. And I've rather enjoyed myself, so to me you are mine, and always have been. Having you again. . . well Serra, that makes me a very lucky man."

A lucky man.

I did not know in what world he thought that I would just bow down before him. The thought that lingered in his mind that he had some claim on me. But I knew that Kaston was not going to let me go.

Not here, not ever.

A spoiled child with a bad temper, throwing a tantrum until he got what he wanted. And *I* was what he wanted, *I* was what he was after. I was not going to play his game, I was done with this man. I tried to yank my hands from his grip, to get away, but he held tight.

"Let go, Kaston."

He stared at me, his expression was lethal as he pulled me closer to him. He did not say a word, not as we spun about the room with the dancers. Not as I looked for Cressida, Caine, Lady Conwell, anyone to save me. They had disappeared in the swarm of people. Leaving me here with him.

Oh, do I wish someone would save me from this man.

His breath was hot in my ear, his scent invaded my nose as every one of my senses screamed. Kaston's hand on my lower back caused the skin there to burn under his touch. His fingers squeezed my hand, hard. "You will let me in tonight. You hear me? Enough of this. There is no more room for you to fight me. You will yield."

I could not see his face, but I knew his eyes simmered with anger, the promise of violence if I did not comply. The feeling I'd felt earlier returned. The feeling of being watched. The hair along my arms stood on end, my neck and ears warmed under a hot wave of unease. The feeling made my mouth go dry. A voice echoed behind me, smooth as honey. Carnal and caressing.

"My turn."

Kaston's muscles tensed as the intruder stopped behind me. "Shove off."

The man let out a low growl, deep and minacious, the vibrations of it radiated. I could feel it deep within my chest as my heart pounded. It however caused Kaston to stop, his eyes going wide as he was forced to retreat back to Cressida. I watched him weave his way through the people and dancers. Her face was warm and welcoming as he approached, but her eyes found mine; a promise as she glared. The threat in them and I felt all too relieved at his departure.

"Are you enjoying the party, Serra?"

The sound of his voice caused another shiver to run down my spine. I turned to look up at my rescuer. His face remained obscured by a black mask. But his eyes were visible, one almost like ice and one green as emerald. His white-blonde hair fell around his face. His lips pulled back in a smile to reveal two sharp canines. My instincts told me to run. To get away.

Involuntarily, I searched for Caine, for safety.

I don't know why I did so, not after dismissing myself so rudely. But the newcomer's eyes caught my attention again, his eyes were. . . familiar. I'd seen them before. Like a ghost haunting my mind. I'd seen him before, the gentleman from the tavern. He pulled me into a dance, the warmth of his hands in mine. The heat that radiated off of him was comforting. As if I'd known him my whole life. The nagging feeling that would not let its grip on me go.

How did I know this man, who was he?

It only took a few short seconds for something to trigger. His scent was the key to unlock what I had forgotten. For the memory to surface from a time in a garden. My garden, weeks ago. A Fae male standing before me in a cloud of smoke and shadows. White blonde hair and mismatched eyes. His smile grew as understanding dawned on me, as the lapse in my memory filled. Another break opening up the floodgates that were already weak, allowing it to surge forward.

"*You.*"

"Yes?"

"*You*, I remember you."

He twirled around, his hold on me forced me to go with him. The faces of those around us spun by, his eyes found mine. Holding them as he asked, "Oh? Have we met before?"

I glared at him, my strange dance partner. "Yes."

"Hmm, I do not recall such a meeting. Are you sure?"

Now I was getting irritated. Questioning myself, my own memory. Questioning. . . if it had actually happened. "I'm sure."

"What else do you remember then, Princess?"

What else did I remember? What else was there, there was something, something important. It was a couple more turns around the ballroom before something caught my attention. Something in the back of my mind screaming at me. a voice I did not realize was there- it was not my own.

Yes. . . yes that's right. Fear me, love me, do as I say. You know what it is that you seek.

"I-I remember you stole something from me."

His smile turned wicked as his eyes flashed. "Is that so?"

"Yes." I hissed back at him.

"And just what would that be?" He leaned in close enough that my heart began to race wildly. His scent washes over me again, calming every tense nerve and muscle. Smoke, citrus and evergreen. His breath was warm on my ear, sending fireworks through my body.

I'd forgotten how to speak, what it was I sought.

"I-I don't know."

"Well, then how can you be so sure? You accuse so easily."

"I just am."

"Are you now?" He was toying with me, this strange male. I knew him, but I could not place him.

"Hmmm. . ." He spun me before he pulled me back to him, his hand grazed my lower back. The touch sent a burning fire up and down my spine. A pleasurable sensation, unlike the one Kaston left, his hand soft and light as it grounded me. But even as his fingers traced up my spine, he went on whispering in my ear, "if you are so certain, if you are so sure of yourself that we've met before. If you are convinced that I have stolen from you, then humor me won't you?"

I stared back at him, hesitant to even continue this conversation. I nodded, my lips pursed. "Fine."

The rumble in his chest was deep, a growl that forced itself up before he asked, "Play a game with me?"

"A game?"

"Yes, a game Princess."

"Don't call me that."

He chuckled but it was soft, light even, "A game. To retrieve what it is you accuse me of taking from you." His eyes darkened under his mask. I felt my face heat as my heart continued to thunder away in my chest.

Screaming, yelling, telling me to say no.

To walk away. To *run away*.

His grin turned feral as I finally realized who he was.

What he was.

He was the Goblin King.

"What did you do?" I seethed, trying to pull from his grasp, but he held fast.

His laugh was low, the sound came from deep within his chest, "Come with me. Play my game and find out."

"Why? Why would I do that?"

Another spin, his hand found mine as he placed it on his shoulder, pulling me closer so he could whisper in my ear. "You could stay. By all means deny my request. But. . ." He glanced toward Kaston who wore a mask that promised bloodshed for being crossed. "I wouldn't. Lest you find yourself in unwanted situations. *Again.*"

The Goblin King's eyes simmered with mischief as he gazed down at me, waiting for me to rebuke. I peeked over at Kaston. In the mindset he was in, he was far too dangerous to even consider being alone with. Especially in my own home. And after his intimidation, I did not want him to touch me.

Let alone hurt me again.

"And if I go with you?" I only toyed with the idea; he was not the only one who could play word games.

His smile widened, allowing me another glimpse of his canines. "Why Serra, is that a yes?"

"No. Why should I trust you? I apparently trusted you once already. Shame on me for doing so."

"I only did what you asked of me."

"And what was that exactly?" I could play his game. Whatever it was he took from me had to be important to him. Whatever it was, it still belonged to me.

It was mine.

He laughed again, the sound vibrated, capturing a sliver of my heart. "You're cunning Princess. Do you accept my offer or not? I do not have all night, and by the glare of your sweetheart, neither do you."

I saw Kaston disappear into the crowd. "He's not my sweetheart."

"Ah. But that was not the impression I got. And I assume, not the impression anyone else here got. The exchanged glances between brothers and the seething look of his betrothed would suggest otherwise." The Goblin King spoke, step after step he kept in turn with the notes. Even when the music picked up another song. Throwing us into it with ease. "You've captured the attention of more than one man in this room, Serra."

His expression was smoldering, even behind his mask. His lip peaked as partners changed, the conversation around us lingered slightly. More and more eyes found their way to us. He was not going to let me go until he had an answer. I caught sight of Lady Conwell, a stiff smile on her lips. Had she intended for this to happen? The humiliation I showed her as her guest, vying for both of her son's attentions. One newly engaged and the other? Caine was known to be a bachelor, uninterested in marriage. No doubt a rumor would spread, people would talk after this. I had yet to speak to her, to give her my thanks.

I wasn't sure I wanted to at this point.

I noticed then, Caine standing beside her. His eyes as he watched me- the tightening of his fingers, the white knuckles. His face questioning. Somehow, somewhere, I had captured the attention of Lord Caine Conwell. I had somehow regained the attention of Lord Kaston Conwell. Attention I did not want from either of them. I had a feeling that the feud would escalate if I did not leave and leave immediately. A lingering feeling of another feud caused my eyebrows to pull together. Another feud between brothers, a much older feud.

My gaze wandered around the opulent ballroom, taking in every detail- the vibrant colors of the decorations, the ornate chandeliers casting a warm glow, and the musicians playing their instruments. As my eyes met those of a few guests, I quickly averted my gaze, feeling self-conscious. But when I looked back up at the Goblin King, I couldn't help the question that formed in my mind. What was he playing at? The whole situation was so bewildering, it left me feeling disoriented and unsure.

Yet he waited.

Even after we had stopped moving, he waited for me to answer. The curious looks and hushed whispers pricked at the back of my mind. I had trusted him once- for some reason, to offer *something* to him. And he was giving me a chance to get it back. Whatever it had been, I had enough certainty then to give it to him.

I could be making a big mistake.

I could come to regret this later.

Everything in me told me not to do it, not to go with him. But as much as it screamed at me, the curiosity I had, the questions that formed would not go away if I did not go. There was only one way I could see out of this, one way to find the answers I sought.

"Okay," I said, "I'll play your game. As long as you return what you took."

He did not hesitate.

His smile widened into a grin as he hugged me closer to him. Both eyes shining with devilry and satisfaction. In a rush of smoke and shadow we disappeared. The screams of terror, the sound of glass shattering and shouts for help as the room vanished, along with all the guests. Caine, Kaston, Cressida, the Conwell's, everybody disappeared.

His body was hard, firm but warm as we whipped through space. The feeling of nausea took over my stomach. Caine had been right, I should have eaten something. I had to squeeze my eyes shut to stop the contents of my stomach from coming up. The world continued to spin, even as he spoke to me again.

"You can open your eyes."

We were on solid ground again.

The world had stopped spinning, but my stomach had not. The urge to empty it took over as the Goblin King let me go. He stepped back from me, keeping his distance as it emptied on the ground.

The champagne had been a bad idea.

He watched over me with disgust, his mask gone from his face revealing his features, the sharpness of his jaw and high cheekbones. I straightened my posture, taking a moment to survey the area around us.

It wasn't until a few seconds had passed that I recognized our location. Dread washed over me, but I couldn't help but ask the question as fear coursed through my body, "Where are we?"

"The Ebony Woods." He said it with such ease, as if he wasn't bothered and was unafraid of what lived within these trees.

"W-what? Why are we here?" I could not stop the panic that coated my words. Not as my heart continued to race in my chest, not as my body began to tremble and shake.

"You have to pass through the Ebony Woods, Princess. The game has started. You have four days to find your way to the castle. Make it there- alive. And I will give back what I've stolen." He was not cruel, but he was not kind as he spoke. A hint of indifference coated his words.

"And if I don't?"

"Then you die and I keep what I took."

I blinked once, twice. Making sure that I had heard him correctly. I pulled my own mask from my face and tossed it to the ground. "Die?"

"Stay on your guard. Make it to the castle in four days, Serra. That is all the time you have, all the time I can give you." He turned away from me, about to disappear.

"Wait. What do you mean I die? How am I supposed to know the way?" I asked, watching him turn back to face me again. His eyes narrowed as he regarded me, his lip peaked as a smile formed. For some reason, he found this humorous.

I sure didn't.

"As I said, if you can make it to the castle beyond the Ebony Wood, cross the Realm to get there I promise to return what I took from you. You have my word. I am nothing but bound to it. I assure you." He said turning away from me again.

The Goblin King's words swirled around me as he disappeared, darkness and shadow engulfed him first before a light flared.

"*I'll be seeing you again, Serra.*"

A raven took off above the trees, its black feathers gleamed in the moonlight. Abandoning where he'd once stood- leaving me alone in the Ebony Woods. Surrounded by the black barked trees and the sounds of the wind as it whistled through the brush and leaves.

Calling. "*Serra...*"

His game has started. I had four days. . .

And I had to stay alive

PART II

GOBLIN KINGS AND
WICKED THINGS

V.A. HAUGEN

CHAPTER
Eleven

Serra

T HE WIND WHISTLED THROUGH the trees causing them to
creak and groan. I was left in the Ebony Woods, with no
direction from the Goblin King on which way to go. Fear crept over
me as I imagined getting lost and never finding my way out, leaving
the Goblin King to claim victory and keep whatever he had stolen. It
was well past midnight and the darkness of the forest only added to
my unease.

The Ebony Woods were a sight to behold though even in the dark.
With the dark bark glistening in the moonlight and the white leaves
glowing in its beams. Although brighter than I had anticipated, the
forest was still dark enough to limit my visibility to just a hundred
yards in any direction. And I couldn't help but wonder what creatures
were watching me from the shadows.

The mist and fog spread across the ground, and the sounds of nocturnal animals filled the air, seemingly indifferent to my presence. I knew that my home and Rothnia were to the southeast beyond the Glenmer Mountains which bordered the Ebony Woods.

The barrier between the Lands and the Realms.

The Castle, the only one on our tiny continent- the only one that I had seen was located in Inirea. It was not a place I wanted to go. Not really and it was not because of the warning I had seen as a young girl.

I remembered the old map, once hanging in another tavern that sat at the edge of the shipping docks. Nona and I had stopped in once to deliver a basket of vegetables to the cook- a bargain she had made for some extra coin. The map was faded and worn, but it showed Rothnia and the Adrid Seas, Elliner to the south, and all the way up to the Duval Sea to the northeast.

The map showed all the cities and villages- from the human settlements, to the abandoned isles in the far north. Inirea was nestled on the edge of our landmass, to the northeast of Rothnia. On the edge of the Banheim Strait- the body of water that separated the two northern continents.

It had been crossed out by someone with a scribbling across it that read; *Do Not Tread Here.* The problem was I had no idea where the Goblin King brought me. How far north, south, or even east or west. For someone who had been raised with the tales of the Lost Fae and the Goblin King, this was truly terrifying. What had I gotten myself into?

Inirea was certainly not where I wanted to go.

But if I lingered too long, who knew what was going to jump out and eat me alive. A low whistle and a soft breeze blew past me, the same call I always heard ringing. *"Come home."*

A chill ran down my spine.

I did not know my way back, I could not go home. My lids fluttered closed, my ears listened to the world around me, trying to pick up where it was coming from. But I could not pinpoint it, it sounded all around me swirling and changing direction. Behind me and in front of me all at once. I had to pick a direction, it was my only choice.

Straight, I'll go straight. The direction ahead of me.

As I picked up my skirt, I tried to step forward but something made me hesitate. Something was telling me *no, don't go that way*. I felt a small pull, telling me to go in another direction. I turned toward my right, the sensation eased- as if that was the direction I *should* be going in. Without hesitation, I followed the tug as I slipped into the trees.

A S I WALKED THROUGH the seemingly endless forest, my surroundings became increasingly monotonous. Every tree, exposed root, and rock looked identical, stretching out before me for what felt like hours. My dress caught on the rough bark, the knotted roots, and the dense underbrush, causing the hem to tear and snag.

To make matters worse, something cold and slimy slithered across the tops of my feet, hidden from view by the thick mist. My heart raced as I dared not contemplate what could have caused the sensation. I quickened my pace, desperate to get away from whatever was lurking in the shadows.

But it was a short reprieve.

Suddenly, I felt eyes on me- watching me from every direction. The tiny, mischievous laughter of invisible creatures echoed through the forest, growing louder and more intense with every step I took. The fear and panic grew within me which caused me to trip and stumble several times as I ran. The unseen creatures seemed to be playing a game with me; leading me further and further into the darkness.

I had lost track of time and direction, with exhaustion and hopelessness beginning to set in. With every step the forest seemed to become denser and there was no sign of progress or any indication that I was making my way towards my destination. In frustration, I kicked a nearby tree letting out a growl of exasperation. I felt completely defeated, having all but given up hope of finding my way out of the woods. The realization hit me that I had foolishly thought I could outsmart the Goblin King, but that's when I saw it.

A small flicker of light in the darkness that surrounded me. . . A lantern floated ahead as it bobbed up and down in the dark. A small sliver of hope bloomed in my chest as I raced for it. Even as it moved away from me.

"Hello!"

Nothing.

I called again. "Hello!?"

As I drew closer to the source of the light, I could make out the figure that was holding the lantern. As the light flickered, its glow revealing a faun standing tall on his hooves. I had to pause for a moment, he wore a green and yellow plaid vest, the colors faded with age and a worn scarf wrapped around his waist. His fur was of rich golden honey, soft and inviting, but his hooves were black as the night sky. A hand-stitched shoulder bag hung loosely across his torso adorned with several colorful patches.

The most striking feature of the faun, however, were his horns. They resembled those of a ram, curling down around the sides of his face in a magnificent display of strength and beauty. His curly hair cascaded down around his large ears.

I couldn't help but feel a sense of wonder and awe at the sight of the faun. It was as if he had stepped out of a fairytale, a creature of myth and legend long thought to be extinct. I knew that no one had seen a faun in decades and that their stories had been lost to time, told only to children as nursery rhymes. Yet here he stood before me, real and alive, a testament to the magical world that I had only ever dreamed of.

"Excuse me." I tried again. He still didn't hear me. "*Excuse me?!*"

Startled at my approach, his hand flew over his heart, "Oh."

"I'm sorry." I apologized quickly. He eyed me cautiously, mortals did not venture into the Ebony Woods, so I was probably just as much of a shock to him as he was to me. "Can you tell me which way it is to the castle?"

"The castle? Why on earth would you want to go there?"

"I'm afraid I have to." I replied. "Could you just point me in the right direction?"

He looked me up and down- the tears in my dress and sleeves, the mess of my hair, "It's that way." He replied pointing towards the south, "But you won't find it a welcoming place. I suggest you don't go at all in fact. There's darkness there."

"Darkness?"

"Oh- oh dear," he exclaimed, "Forget I said anything."

"Wait!" I called after him but he'd disappeared into the trees. The lantern light went out as the dark surrounded him.

I huffed in frustration as I realized I was alone yet again.

As my eyes scanned the direction the faun had pointed in, I could feel the pull- the same tug that had led me to him, drawing me towards it. This could only mean one thing- the Goblin King had left me stranded further away from Rothnia than I had expected. I couldn't afford to waste any more time, I had to make it to the castle as soon as possible.

As I pushed forward, the trees seemed to stretch endlessly, their thick foliage almost forming a barrier that was closing in on me. The air grew heavy with a sense of foreboding as I walked farther into the Ebony Woods, the darkness seeming to engulf me with every step. The trees were so close together that their branches intertwined, creating an almost impenetrable canopy overhead that barely allowed any light to filter through.

Despite the oppressive atmosphere, I forced myself to keep moving forward. Every step felt like a struggle, my feet sinking into the soft ground with each step, the rustling of leaves echoing around me. The silence was almost deafening, punctuated only by the occasional chitter or scurrying of animals through the underbrush.

Despite the feeling that crept up my spine, I could not turn back. Something compelled me to continue, to press on through the endless trees and the darkness. It was a pull, a tug that seemed to come from deep within me. Even though I couldn't place my finger on why I was doing this, why it was so important to reach the castle, I knew that I had to keep moving forward. It didn't matter what the Goblin King had taken from me; I was determined to get it back.

I knew deep down that this was all part of my fate, and strangely enough the Goblin King felt part of it too. Our paths intertwined and destined to cross. He was lethal predator, but he was familiar to me, and I could not place why. There was a something between us that I couldn't explain, as if he had always been a part of me. It was like the connection of an old friend who had gone their separate way, but never lost touch. Whatever it was, whatever he was, whatever he had meant.

I would find out.

His words from the garden echoed in my head, the memory unlocked. The confusion lingered but the truth a bit clearer.

'I have been watching you for a long while. Do you think that your wishes went unanswered? That I did not hear them?'

What did he mean by it?

My mind raced with questions and doubts as I stepped over the fallen tree. Had every wish I ever made been granted? Had every dream I had, given to me? But I couldn't dwell on those thoughts for too long. Something was wrong. This place didn't seem right. It wasn't what I had expected, not what I had asked for. I had dreamed of a knight, but got Kaston. I had dreamed of the Goblin King, but this wasn't what I had in mind.

But maybe it had been.

Something told me that it was true. Something told me that indeed my wishes had been heard. That I had been heard. He'd been biding his time, he said, but for what? What was he waiting for? Why did he appear to me now? For decades I had dreamed about him, wished for him, and now he shows? What game was he truly playing at? What were his true motivations?

Whatever they were, I would find out. My mind raced with determination, fueled by the burning desire to uncover the truth. I had to find out what he took from me and why. As I trudged through the forest, stepping over fallen trees, the anger in my chest grew with every step.

My life had never been easy, but it was mine. Nona was my only companion, the only person I had ever truly relied on. We kept to ourselves, barely interacting with anyone outside of our small circle. Bern was one of the few people Nona knew well, but there was something about her that didn't sit right with me.

Memories of Nona flooded my mind, and I couldn't help but dwell on them. I remembered how she would watch me play as a child, her eyes always lingering on me with a hint of concern. I recalled her hushed whispers to herself, and the cautious way she went about her business in Rothnia. But most of all, I remembered her fear of the Fae and the Goblin King, and the stories she would tell me of the missing children.

As I thought back on these things, I couldn't help but feel that something was still missing. The answers I sought were not yet within my grasp. The stories of the missing children didn't make sense to me. They went missing, yes, but as I grew older, so did the children that were taken. There was a piece missing from this puzzle, and I was determined to find it.

"Oh Nona, what have you not told me?"

Silence was the only response to my question as I continued to push my way through the thick foliage. The mist that had enveloped me dissipated as I clambered over fallen logs and crawled under low-hanging branches. I weaved my way around stubborn bushes, tugging at my dress when it caught on their thorns. With every step, the cool air of the night seeped into my bones, and my weariness became more and more palpable.

Yet, despite my exhaustion, I refused to stop. I trudged on, determined to press forward through the mysterious and eerie Ebony Wood. The moon's glowing orb rose higher and higher into the sky as the night wore on, a constant companion on my journey. I knew that eventually, the night would give way to the dawn, and the sky would transform. The colors of morning staining the night sky in pinks, oranges, and blues.

I didn't mind the day, but it was the night that I looked forward to. Sunset was my favorite time of day. Watching as the sun would go down, painting the sky in its evening colors. The stars started their twinkling dance in the dark. Night was when the world called to me. And I never knew why. Only that it felt like it was an old friend and would embrace me in a hug that felt familiar.

But I could not go out at night, thanks to Nona.

I knew I wasn't supposed to be out there, but the urge was too strong to ignore. Carefully, I would drape a blanket over my shoulders, wincing at the sound of the rustling fabric and tiptoe past her sleeping form; trying to make myself as small and quiet as possible. Finally, slipping out and into the night air, the cool breeze brushing against my skin.

The weight of her superstitions lifted off my shoulders as I laid under the stars in the grass. The twinkling lights above me seemed to dance in the sky, and I felt at peace. Sometimes, I'd meet Kaston and we would sneak off into the night together. The nights were comforting-calm and relaxing. The moon was our companion, casting a soft glow over everything, and the stars were my true friends.

Just as the sun would start its dance across the sky, the trees around me started to thin. The world opened up again as I continued forward before finally giving way. The edge of the Ebony Wood yielded to a world far larger than the one I was accustomed to. Aeris was bigger than the place I had been raised. The walls stretched, opening up to show me all that it was. My breath caught as I stepped out of the tree line the world dropped away. Perched on the edge of a cliff, I spied the land laid out before me.

The Fae Realms.

While stories of the Fae changed over time, coming and going with the mercenaries, sailors, and storytellers, one thing never changed. The tales of the Lost Fae. Even Nona had dappled in the story once or twice. Remembering now, that they had disappeared. The Fae of this continent disappeared into fairytales and myths, told to children at night before bed with all the other lore of our world. But no one knows why. No one knows what happened to them or where they went.

We had shared this world with them. Mortals and Fae had once been friendly, but for decades we occupied the landmass alone. I had my suspicions, based on Nona's story of the Goblin King. And before me now, I knew what it was that everyone was talking about. The land was far from thriving.

The world before me was as dry as the desert of Elliner. The trees had lost more than half of their leaves. Rivers and lake beds had dried up and were caked in mud. The hills and prairies dried and dusty, tumbleweeds rolled across them as the wind blew. The Fae Realm was indeed dying. Anything past this part of the Ebony Wood was barren. The colors muted as the world struggled.

As I surveyed the desolate landscape before me, my heart ached with a deep sense of sadness. It was as if life had been drained from the land, leaving only a shadow of what it once was. My mind wandered, conjuring up images of what the land had once looked like. In my mind's eye, flashes of greens and blues fluttered around, each one a poignant reminder of what had been lost.

I glimpsed fields of flowers in all colors, taking up hillside after hillside, their petals dancing in the gentle breeze. Warm lakes and flowing rivers that fed the land and its inhabitants, providing sustenance for all. Miles and miles of tall prairie grass stretched across the ground, creating a carpet of green as far as the eye could see. And beyond the prairie, forests sprung up from the fertile land below, teeming with life.

But now, as I gazed out at the barren wasteland that lay before me, I felt a deep sense of sorrow. The once-lush landscape had been stripped of its vitality, leaving behind a lifeless expanse of dirt and dust. The animals that once roamed the land had disappeared, their homes destroyed by the destruction of the natural world. The circle of life had been broken, and I felt helpless to mend it.

A thriving land.

This had once been a land rich in color and life. A single tear fell down my cheek as I looked out over the horizon. The pull in my chest told me to keep going, that I had to. My eyes grazed over the barren landscape. Just there to the southeast- barely on the horizon far off in the distance- I saw the outline of a castle. So small one would have missed it. But the land held on there, the dull shades of green stood out against the vast land before it.

There was so much between me and the castle, it would take days to get there, especially on foot. But I would not let that deter me. I would get to the castle and confront the Goblin King.

The edge of the cliff loomed as I looked down. Although it was not a long way down, it still was a long way to fall if I lost my grip. It was enough that it caused my head to spin as the world dropped away before me. The height suddenly became more and more terrifying to me. There was no other way down though- at least not for miles.

I did not have that kind of time either. The sooner I reached the castle, the better. The sooner I got there, the sooner I could go home. I would have to scale the side of the rock to reach the bottom. If I did fall, the trees at the base would not cushion me at all. The lack of leaves and the rocks that scattered the ground were a recipe for injury.

Possibly even death. . . Fantastic.

As I stood there, looking down at the steep cliff face in front of me, I knew that my dress and slippers would be a hindrance to my descent. The tattered hem would surely snag on the rough edges of the rock, and my slippers would offer no traction. With a heavy sigh, I hesitantly slipped off my slippers and tossed them over the edge, watching as they disappeared from sight.

With one final huff of breath I began my descent, gripping the edge of the rock firmly with both hands and lowering myself down. As my legs swung over the edge, I felt my heart pounding in my chest. With the tips of my toes, I could feel a small lip in the cliff face, and I shifted my weight to it cautiously. Suddenly, the rock shifted beneath my feet, causing my breath to catch in my throat. I closed my eyes tightly and whispered, "Please don't fall, please." Slowly, I opened my eyes and checked again to make sure the rock wouldn't shift again.

Firm.

The rock was firm and did not budge. I was able to breathe again but my heartbeat increased in tempo as I worked my way down the side. Slowly testing each spot carefully before putting any weight on the rock face. My fingers screamed with each ticking second it took me to get to the bottom. I had been lucky so far, but my luck was about to run out. The rock under my foot suddenly gave way, my hand slipped from a ledge as I plunged.

A scream lodged in my throat.

My body slammed against the jagged rock, my limbs flailing as I desperately sought anything to stop my fall. Pain seared through my fingers, arms, and legs as they scraped against the rough surface. In my peripheral vision, I caught sight of a tree branch jutting out from the side. I reached out for it, the tips of my fingers barely brushing against it. The branch seemed so close yet so far away. With a burst of energy, I propelled myself towards it, my fingers finally clasping tightly around it.

Relief washed over me as I clung to the branch, my heart pounding in my chest. But the pain persisted, my hands throbbing with every beat. Blood dripped from my fingertips, staining the rock below. I gazed down, watching as the rocks tumbled down the cliff, their echoes piercing the silence.

Surveying the immediate area, I searched for anything else to grab onto, but the branch began to bend under my weight. Panic surged through me as I realized the ground was closer than I thought. I had fallen farther than I had anticipated.

My options were limited.

I could either climb down the rest of the way and risk another rockslide or take a leap of faith. Every inch of my body ached, my feet scraped up from the rough terrain, my hands barely clinging on. Blood streamed down the side of my face, the warmth of it a stark contrast to the cool air. I knew I had hit my head against the stone at some point.

My dress was in tatters, the silk organza sleeves and overlay completely shredded. The hem was ripped in several locations, the once-beautiful fabric now in ruin. But in that moment, I didn't care about the dress. I dangled from the side of the cliff, battered and bruised, my grip slipping as I struggled to hang on.

Yes. I thought ironically to myself as I hung from the edge of the cliff, my fingers screaming as I tried to hold on desperately. *This was exactly how I had planned to die.*

This did not bode well for me, for how the rest of this would go. I could sense the foreshadowing in this, the outcome and fate as if it were mocking me. There was so much ground to cover between here and the castle and I would die right here. So early into this.

Foolish.

I was so foolish for accepting his offer. What had I agreed to? What was I *thinking*? I hadn't been. I *hadn't* been thinking. I had been so desperate to escape from Kaston, from the Conwell's, from the stares and hushed whispers. From the masquerade ball. That I had not considered how dangerous this would be. I had been so desperate to get answers. And now I was paying the price.

My eyes widened in terror as the branch creaked and groaned under my weight. Sweat and blood mixed on my palms, making it nearly impossible to keep my grip. I could feel my fingers slipping, inch by inch, and my heart pounded in my chest. "Oh no," I gasped, as the branch gave way again, now almost vertical.

My mind raced as I desperately searched for a solution. I couldn't hold on much longer, but the ground was too far below for me to survive the fall. My only choice was to take a leap of faith and hope for the best.

I closed my eyes and took a deep breath, trying to steady myself for the jump. The wind whipped past me, making my hair fly in all directions. With one final burst of courage, I let go of the branch and plummeted towards the trees below.

The world spun around me as I fell, and for a moment, I felt weightless. Even as I crashed through the branches and trees below.

CHAPTER
Twelve

The Goblin King

PERCHED HIGH ABOVE THE trees, I surveyed the landscape below, my wings tucked in closely- my black feathers glistening in the warm sun. The wind blew through me, sending shivers down my spine while the fresh air caressed my senses, invigorating me with a sense of freedom that I savored with every passing moment.

From this vantage point, I could see everything- from the smallest creatures scurrying about to the grandest landmarks looming in the distance. In this form I was free. They were moments of pure bliss, a time when I could soar freely without any hindrance or restraint, and I relished it with all my being.

Despite the peacefulness of my surroundings, my mind couldn't help but dwell on the girl who had fallen down the cliff. She was lucky to have survived the fall, but it was her recklessness that had caused her to end up in that situation in the first place.

Watching her from my vantage point, I couldn't help but feel a twinge of anger and frustration and even a hint of guilt course through my veins. It caused my feathers to ruffle in agitation. Although she had not needed my help to survive the fall, I couldn't help but feel that I should have done something more to prevent it from happening in the first place.

Perhaps I could have warned her of the danger or guided her to a safer path. But as much as I wanted to blame her for her recklessness, I knew deep down that it was not entirely her fault. She was new to this world, and she had much to learn about the dangers that lurked around every corner.

It wasn't that I didn't want to help her. I had even assisted her in landing safely on the ground, albeit just a little bit. But it was the fact that she had put herself in danger that irritated me. Why couldn't she just be more careful? Why did she have to be so careless and reckless?

Despite my initial urge to save her, I *had* held back, knowing that it was not my place to interfere in her journey. But even as I watched her from afar I couldn't shake off the feeling that I needed her to stay alive. If she kept getting herself into life-threatening situations it would be a long and arduous journey, one that I doubted I could keep up with at this rate. She already looked battered and bruised, her clothes torn and her skin covered in scrapes and bruises.

And she had barely started her journey.

Watching her as she walked through the dead trees, a shiver ran through me, sending another ripple through my feathers. I promised myself that I would not intervene again unless it was absolutely necessary. I would watch over her from a distance, keeping a close eye on her every move, but I would not interfere unless her life was in danger.

It was a difficult decision to make, but I knew that it was for the best. Even so, I couldn't leave her entirely on her own. I would have to keep a closer watch on her. Even if it meant sacrificing my own rest and comfort. The past few days had drained me, both physically and emotionally, and I worried about the amount of magic I had expended and the cost of using it. But I knew that I could not falter, not when there was more at stake.

Maybe I could send Hendrix.

Hendrix could watch over her. If she got herself in any other life-threatening situations at least he would be there. While I questioned his loyalty, and I did not wholly trust Hendrix- he would have to do. But it was my nature not to trust many beings to begin with.

However. . . it would give me the time I needed to rest and recharge. Time was not on our side, though. I'd been patient, or at least patient enough.

The well where the power I was blessed with rippled, as if to say it too would like to rest and recharge. That it needed time to regain some strength as well. The shadows curling and twirling around the source as if protecting it. We were not one without the other. I needed it as much as it relied on me to breathe life into it. So being this drained of energy was extremely dangerous. If it went out completely, I could not fathom the outcome.

Her yell reached my ears, a chuckle lodged in my chest as her words settled in around me.

"Oh if you only knew Princess. Little do you know how merciful I'd truly been in my drop-off location. You're lucky I had not left you where I had originally planned."

I'd had every intention of dropping her off farther away, but at the last moment though something had prevented me from doing so, a change of heart. I certainly would not be falling for that again though. If she was going to be this ungrateful then I would not be so courteous in the future.

But, something made me hesitate. Something told me that it was cruel to say such a thing. Maybe one more time, for her sake. She certainly could not continue in that awful dress, in the scraps that remained on her.

They offered little coverage and while it had been stunning on her back in the Mortal Lands, now it just looked. . . degrading. The thoughts were intrusive as I'd watched her dance with those mortal men. How radiant she looked, it was then that her wish reached me. Her call to save her.

For years I'd heard them, for years I'd responded- granting them to her. But last night. . . last night was different. She'd been scared, terrified. I don't know what compelled me, what pushed me toward her. I could not stop myself not as I danced with her around the room. I wanted her then.

I shook my head, ridding myself of the thoughts. One should not think such things. Now was not the time. I would do her this one favor, even if she was angry at me. It did not bother me in the slightest.

She had four days, and time was of the essence. She needed to do this. Her encounter earlier in the Ebony Woods had proven every suspicion I had correct. The faun had offered a minimal distraction, a test to see if she could accept guidance from others when faced with the will to give up. A chance to see how well she could perceive the things around her and judging by the outcome, she would be able to succeed in this task. If she didn't let her stubbornness get in the way first that is.

And she certainly was stubborn.

The persistence she had, the fight and will she carried; a trait I found thoroughly amusing. Her frustrations with me would only fuel my own in return though. I'd been told I was stubborn and strong willed. A mind of my own even since I was young. And I could be headstrong too. An eye for an eye. If she could hold onto it, it would be useful.

For all of us.

This game with her would be rewarding. If she could manage the trek to the castle without actually dying or any more run-ins with death itself, then there was some kind of hope. I scoffed to myself.

Hope.

Not something I wanted to have, not something I'd carried with me, not for a very long time. To have hope was to have false ideals of one's reality in my not so humble opinion. Hope was the reason I was in this mess in the first place. Hope was a curse, and I'd abandoned all hope long before now.

In the earlier days before the curse, it had taught me that having hope for things was only going to lead to disillusionment. Hope was a myth, a dream. At least to me. I didn't have dreams, not in the ones that would have made me happy. Or brought joy, or even. . . love.

I was more a cynical being, it was part of my nature, who I was. I learned a long time ago to never get attached to someone, because attachments lead to expectations and expectations lead to disappointment. But this pull- like my heart, my soul, was saying something. This pull I had toward her, the need to save her, to help her through this and to get her to the castle. To protect her, it certainly wasn't something I'd foreseen either.

This was a dangerous game we were playing. This did not bode well with me. This did not bode well with me at all.

CHAPTER
Thirteen

Serra

AS I MADE CONTACT with the ground, my body absorbed the full brunt of the fall. My bones rattled and my muscles tensed, screaming in agony. My head throbbed as it hit the hard ground, causing my vision to blur and spin. I couldn't believe I had survived that fall. The journey down was rough, the branches and rocks I hit on the way down only made things worse. Letting go and free-falling was the hardest part. Despite the fall not being too far, the pain was excruciating.

I took a moment to assess myself, relieved to find that nothing seemed to be broken. I was grateful to be in one piece, but I was definitely scraped up. The exposed flesh on my arms and legs bled, and small bits of rock had embedded themselves in my skin. The scrapes were painful, but they would hopefully heal without leaving scars. As I gingerly rose to my feet, my body ached all over.

A sharp intake of breath escaped my lips as I brushed off the dirt and rocks that had embedded themselves into my skin. I knew it could have been worse, but the discomfort was still unbearable. My feet and fingers had taken the worst of the fall, the dried blood and dirt caked onto my skin and nails would need to be washed off, but the cuts on the bottoms of my feet and toes would make this journey a difficult one.

From the base of the cliff, the trees looked like withered skeletons, reaching their bony branches towards the sky in a desperate plea for life. The once lush foliage had shriveled and turned brown, leaving the forest floor blanketed in a sea of dead leaves. There was no sign of life, no rustling of leaves, nor chirping of birds. It was as if the forest was holding its breath, waiting for something to bring it back to life. But what could possibly revive this desolate land? I made my way through the petrified forest, the path was dry and rocky, making each step feel like a struggle. The forest was a graveyard of what it used to be, and it was evident that this place had seen better days.

As I continued on the path, I stole one last glance back at the cliff and the barren trees. The landscape was a haunting reminder of the fragility of life and the impermanence of everything we know.

However, my attention was soon drawn to a rustling in a nearby bush. A jackrabbit darted out, startled by my presence. It was a relief to see that there was still some life in this desolate place, but my heart ached for the creature. I knew that its options for food and water were scarce, and it was only a matter of time before it would become prey for a larger animal. As I neared the edge of the tree line, the path forked into two directions, one leading to the north and the other to the south. I couldn't help but wonder which way to go.

"Now which way?" I said to no one in particular.

As I stood there. gazing at the enormous mountains looming to the south, I couldn't help but feel a sense of dread creeping up my spine. Gwendier, the tallest peak, seemed to pierce the sky, reminding me of my insignificance in the grand scheme of things. However, I had no other choice but to make my way towards the castle, no matter how daunting the journey may be. The open plains to the north looked more inviting, but my destination lay to the southeast.

My frustration bubbled up and spilled over as I shouted out into the desolate landscape, "Why did you have to make this so difficult for me?" The sound of my voice echoed back at me, hollow and empty, as if mocking my predicament. But I had to keep moving forward, even if it meant traversing the rough and rocky path that lay ahead.

With a heavy sigh, I set out towards the south, my slippers crunching on the dry, rocky ground. Each step sent jolts of pain up my legs, but I pushed on, determined to reach my destination. The open expanses of land seemed endless, and I couldn't help but wonder if I would ever make it to the castle.

This was unfair.

Goblin Kings and their tricks. He was a beast, an evil male. Cruel, insensitive, and loathsome. He was many more things, but I couldn't dwell on those at the moment. But it would seem however that my mind had not listened, it decided to focus on him.

Solely him.

There was something about him that I couldn't figure out, something that bothered me about him. It was like my mind was screaming at me to figure it out- to understand. And truthfully, I could not deny that he had an air about him that had my attention. I could not deny that I *was* intrigued by him. I could not deny that he made my body react in a way that was new and exciting. A simple touch had caused my skin to tingle, my heart to race and my core to heat. And while he made me feel those things, he was also alluring, confident, and... well he was handsome.

I could not deny that either, nor had it been lost on me. Not at all, but he was Fae. And above all else, he was aggravating. I should not, could not, allow these feelings or thoughts to run their course. I was already stupid enough to make a deal with him, I was not stupid enough to fall for him. I would be playing a lethal game if I did, I would be playing with fire and I would get burned.

As his face filtered through my head, his cruel but still handsome smile taunted me. For the briefest of moments, it distract me from the gravel path ahead. I lost my footing, and my feet skittered out from under me as I began to slip down the hill. The ground grew steeper, and I found myself struggling to keep my balance on the loose rocks and gravel beneath me. With every step, my feet threatened to slide out from under me, until finally, they did. I tumbled down the hill, feeling each rock and stone dig into my skin, the impact jarring me with each successive bounce.

When I finally came to a stop, I was bruised and battered, but thankfully not seriously injured. My thoughts went back to cursing him. Back to cursing *at* him. A string of unsavory words formed on my tongue as I righted myself. "Fucking prick."

"I never imagined such foul language coming from someone like you."

The voice caused me to jump. Whirling around to find the owner. I hadn't seen him, hadn't noticed his arrival. My blood boiled as my eyes found him. I was so angry that I could not form any coherent sentences. So angry, that all I wanted to do was lash out at him. His eyes gleamed as his grin grew, his canines on display.

"Hello again, Serra."

"If you are here to taunt me then I want nothing to do with you." I had nothing nice to say to him anyway.

"Oh? What have I done?"

"You know exactly what you did."

He watched me for a moment, his features smug as he crossed his arms, "Is that so? Well why don't you elaborate for me then?"

His question caught me off guard. "You really expect me to make it to the castle in four days? That's bullshit and you know it."

"Well, I guess you better hurry. You are never going to get there with that mindset."

Oh, oh he was infuriating. I snarled at him, "fucking *prick*."

"I do find that foul mouth of yours rather," He paused, "*fascinating.*"

"Go away."

The Goblin King glanced down at me, his cloak fluttered in the breeze. His hair loose as his eyes danced, the words echoed themselves inside my head again. Cunning, cruel, alluring, and aggravating. "If I did not believe you could do it, then I would not have asked you to."

My head tilted, I couldn't stop myself, couldn't stop the question that bothered me, "did you mean it? That I would die if I failed?"

He tensed at my question, hesitated only a moment before saying, "Yes."

"Why?"

The Goblin King closed the distance between us, only to stop a breath away. My eyes found his, forced to look up into his face as he towered over me. "Here is what you have to understand, Serra, there are forces outside my circle who would be more than willing to kill you. Forces that want you dead. You dying would be a bad idea. So I suggest that you don't."

"What is that supposed to mean-" I would not allow myself to be afraid of him. He had no power over me, or at least that's what I would have told myself. Even as he spoke about others who would see me dead. "Do you want me dead?"

His sharp gaze pierced through me, and his lip twitched with a hint of amusement as he assessed my disheveled appearance. He didn't respond to my question, instead his eyes trailed down to the tattered remnants of the once luxurious silk fabric clinging to my body.

"A bit indecent, aren't you?" he remarked dryly, causing my face to flush with embarrassment. Ideally wearing the dress Kaston had given me was not the best choice, but I hadn't had a chance to change before he'd whisked me away.

The male's infuriating demeanor only made me more irritable. I couldn't stand his arrogance and indifference to my discomfort. I muttered a string of curses under my breath as I pushed past him, desperate to distance myself from his presence. However, his voice stopped me in my tracks.

"I came to offer you something more appropriate to wear, but it seems you are more interested in hurling insults than listening to what I have to say." His words echoed, causing me to turn back to him.

"Why bother?" I retorted, my tone laced with bitterness. "Why are you even here?" I looked into his eyes, searching for any hint of a sincere answer. For a moment, I thought I saw a flicker of something in them- but it was gone as quickly as it had come, replaced by the familiar coldness that always seemed to surround him. My cheeks heated up, embarrassed by my outburst, but also frustrated that he seemed so apathetic.

I crossed my arms over my chest, trying to hide the tattered remains of the silk dress. I would have preferred to strip it off and burn it, but I had no other clothes to wear. He seemed to enjoy seeing me in this state, helpless and exposed.

He shrugged, his eyes scanning my torn outfit. "You are more than welcome to carry on wearing that," he said, pointing to the pale blue shreds. "but I cannot imagine it being very comfortable." His voice was laced with a hint of amusement, as if he found all of this amusing.

I gritted my teeth, resisting the urge to lash out at him. Instead asking, "why are you being so gracious right now?"

His whole body tensed. "I'm not."

My eyes narrowed, "are you not? Why offer me something else to wear at all then, how is that not an act of kindness?"

The Goblin King faltered, his resolve cracking. "You mistake motive for kindness. Let me remind you, let me be perfectly clear, Serra. I am not kind, nor am I willing to bend for anyone, least of all for you."

I should have been hurt, his words should have made me crumble and shrink away but I couldn't help but smirk at him. Not as a dangerous thought entered my head. It could have come forth from a many number of things. My own impulse or lack of sleep but with as much courage as I could muster I swaggered up to him, cocking my head to the side as I said, "No? But you offer something anyway. I wonder though. . . Is this dress too revealing for you now?"

Oh, was I playing a dangerous game.

What had been left of it barely covered anything. Exposing more skin now than it had last night. I ran a hand down the front, across my décolletage and over the curve of my breasts. My heart thundered away in my chest as his eyes followed the movement. He did not move, he did not hesitate.

He watched unabashedly. His eyes tracked my hand as it ran down the front and over my navel. I should have felt embarrassed but oddly in that moment I felt powerful. As if I had a hold over him, his attention solely on me.

"Quite the contrary, Princess." his voice was hoarse, I'd affected him. Nevertheless, a hint of cold indifference laced his next sentence. "It truly is not for my welfare that I offered you a change of dress."

And just like that it was gone. Any courage I had, melted away as his eyes flicked up away from me. Vicious, abhorrent, and insensitive. He silently stepped around me not caring to utter another word and walked away, disappearing into a cloud of smoke before soaring up into the welcoming blue sky and white clouds.

I muttered under my breath, "Prick."

My scowl deepened as I watched him soar away, but as I turned back to face the spot where he had been, my anger dissipated when I saw a neatly folded pile of fabrics. It took a moment for me to realize that he had left me a change of clothes after all.

My curiosity was piqued as I stepped forward to examine the pile. The fabrics were soft to the touch and I couldn't help but wonder where he had obtained such fine garments. As my fingers brushed against the chemise, I couldn't resist the urge to pick it up and examine it closer. My gaze was drawn back up to the sky as I watched him soar high above, leaving me behind. A sense of longing washed over me as I watched him disappear into the horizon. But my attention was soon brought back to the chemise as a small smile spread across my face.

Holding it in my fingers, the linen chemise felt familiar and comfortable as I slipped it over my head, discarding the last bits of the silk dress. The navy skirt was soft and luxurious, its hem embroidered with forest animals and mushrooms. Little foxes and rabbits graced the hem in a beautiful display of fine and neat stitching. Each animal and mushroom was so delicately crafted that they seemed to come to life, almost as if they could hop or scurry off the hem at any moment. I pulled on the corseted bodice next, lacing it up as I had done many times before, it hugged me comfortably.

The navy blue color was so rich that it reminded me of the darkest depths of the ocean. and the forest green and white lace of the bodice perfectly complemented it. It was the nicest set of clothing I had ever worn, even more meaningful than the silk dress that Kaston had gifted me.

I felt like a completely different person in this dress. No longer was I clad in uncomfortable, revealing silk. For a moment, I forgot about the irritating man who had left me this clothing, lost in my own thoughts and admiration of the garment.

"Why did he have to be so insufferable?" I muttered to myself as I looked down at the skirt. Despite my irritation with him, I couldn't deny that the man had a certain charm about him. Maybe it was his confidence or the way he effortlessly commanded your attention. Or maybe it was the fact that he had left me with this beautiful dress, showing that perhaps there was more to him than just his prickly exterior.

Shaking my head to clear my thoughts, I set off down the path, the soft swish of the embroidered skirt against my legs a soothing sound. While I was still very angry with the Goblin King, the clothing he'd left for me felt like more than just a nice gesture. It was as if he knew me better than I knew myself. I glanced up into the sky again, in the direction he had flown off in, but he was gone, having disappeared into the clouds.

M Y FEET HAD BEEN moving for what seemed like an eternity, taking me deeper into the unknown terrain. My feet ached, and my throat was parched from the dry, dusty air. Despite this, I continued on, driven by the knowledge that I was getting closer to my destination with every step I took. The sun had been a constant companion, rising higher and higher in the sky, its heat bearing down on my skin.

The landscape had been ever-changing, first leading me through a maze of trees and barren rock, then opening up to a vast expanse of prairies and dried river beds. Mud caked their banks, and the grasses were dry and brittle, rustling in the wind. It had been a challenging hike, and by mid-morning, I was already feeling the fatigue in my bones.

Every step was a struggle. and I couldn't ignore the hunger pangs gnawing at my stomach anymore. The thought of food made me dizzy with desire, and my mouth watered at the idea of a hot meal. The day continued on, time unbothered as I grew more and more tired. I yearned for a place to rest- even if it was just for a moment, but I couldn't find any shelter from the scorching sun.

My lack of knowledge about this unfamiliar land made me nervous, and the feeling of being watched only heightened my unease. Although I couldn't see anyone, I had a strong sense of being followed, and the rustling grass hinted that I wasn't alone. But the wind was blowing so fiercely that I couldn't discern whether it was an animal or a person.

As I walked on, the landscape continued to change around me, transforming from the open prairies to small, wooded forests. The sun, unrelenting in its journey, casting long shadows over the trees and rocks. Despite my aching body and numb mind, I pushed on, driven by the knowledge that the castle was waiting for me.

With each step though, the weight of exhaustion seemed to grow heavier, threatening to bring me to my knees. I longed to collapse at the base of one of the trees, to rest and gather my strength. But just as I had made up my mind to do so, the sound of an angry chitter caught my attention.

Curious, I followed the sound until a flurry of movement caught my eye. A reddish honey-colored squirrel with a white underbelly darted from one branch to another, its tufted ears perked up in alarm. But where a tail should be, there was nothing. Cut short as it twitched in annoyance. He was unlike any of the squirrels back in Rothnia. Chittering away as nuts were pushed out of a burrow in the trunk. I could not stop the laugh that escaped my lips as I watched.

Such an interesting sight to behold honestly. He turned on me at the sound, "It isn't very nice to laugh while others are in distress!"

It took me a moment to gather my bearings, still shocked at the possibilities, I couldn't believe what I'd just heard. It spoke again, "Well don't just stand there, be on your way!"

Carefully, I stepped toward the little creature, trying my best not to spook him. "Who are you?"

He scoffs, "Who are you?"

"Serra."

"Hmm." He shoved another handful of nuts into the hole before they came flying back out at him.

"What's your name?" I asked.

"Jesper." he replied gruffly.

"And what are you doing?"

Exasperated, "What does it look like?"

"Well," I paused, assessing what I was looking at, "to me it looks like you are trying to shove nuts into a tree."

"Yes, thank you for your obvious observation." he huffed, "The problem is, the sprite that has decided to make it its home, keeps shoving them out."

"Perhaps, you could find another spot?" I offered.

He chittered, his ears and tail twitched as he said. "Nonsense! I found this first, it's mine!"

Oh, he was a selfish little beast. "Would you like some help?"

"No. I do not need help from someone like you."

Stunned, I replied, "What do you mean someone like me?"

"A round ear," he said as he shoved yet another handful into the hole. The ringing of the sprite inside echoed, as if it was laughing at him as the nuts came back out again.

"A round ear?" My hand instinctively went to my own ear, brushing the top of it with my fingers.

Jesper turned to look at me, his beady black eyes scrutinizing as he scanned my face, "As I said, a round ear."

"That isn't very nice."

Observing him, I could tell he had grown frustrated with his current task. He rested his hands on the branch before him and addressed me, "Girl, do you even know where you are? What are you doing here anyway?"

With reluctance, I replied to his inquiry, "Yes, I do. I have to reach the castle."

He sat up abruptly. "The castle?"

"Yes."

"Why?"

It was a challenge not to reveal to him that I had made a deal with the Goblin King. "I just do, and I have four days to do it. Can you help me or not?"

"Hmm, that's not a place I'd go, but," Jesper leaned his chin on his claw, contemplating before he said, "I can, for a price."

"What would that be?"

"Twenty acorn nuts," he replied firmly.

"Twenty?" The number seemed high, considering the trees in the area were all but dying. I wasn't certain where I could find that many.

"Yes."

"That seems a bit steep. Where can I find twenty acorn nuts?"

He shrugged his furry shoulders before resuming his work. "No idea. That's for you to figure out."

"To find that many, I'd have to travel back to the Mortal Lands.

There are no trees here that could produce that many acorns, especially in their current condition."

"That's too bad. Good luck on your journey," he replied, disinterested.

"Can't you at least take me part of the way? I can travel the rest on my own." I was exhausted and needed a place to rest. Anywhere with shelter would suffice.

"I'm afraid not. Times are tough, and one must be prepared. Twenty nuts," he said, tossing another nut into the hole of the tree. It immediately flew back and hit him on the head.

I suppressed a chuckle as he brushed his fur and peered into the hole. "Will you at least help me find a place to rest?"

Jesper turned to face me. "I'll tell you what, I'll take you as far as the rock caves, but no further. Will you leave me alone then? You can help me collect whatever nuts you can carry along the way."

I nodded in agreement. "Deal."

CHAPTER
Fourteen

Serra

ANY NORMAL PERSON have figured out by now that they should not make deals with anyone on this side of the Ebony Woods. I, however, had yet to learn that lesson. Jesper had taken off ahead of me as quickly as he could. Only to stop and wait until I was in his sights again before he scurried on. It took more energy and effort to keep up with him than I had used all day.

The pockets in the navy skirt started to feel heavy the farther we traveled; the weight of the gathered nuts bringing them down. Before long though, we had reached the edge of a large rock face. Here the land was divided by a large river that had dried out- a small amount of water sat at the bottom, turning the banks to mud. There was no way across the deep embankment without slipping and sliding and no way back out again.

The mud made the climb impossible. But Jesper had led me away from the river. Taking me along its edge, sandwiched between the rock and the looming bottom of the river.

"Um, do we have to climb?" I asked.

I was not in any shape to do such a thing. I was done with cliffs and rock climbing for a while. If not for the remainder of my mortal life.

Jesper whirled on me, I could see the whites of his beady black eyes, "Are you crazy? No. There's an entrance to a cave just there that you can use to cross the Dried River. It runs down under the rocks."

"A cave?"

"More like a passage." he said, holding his tiny paws out. I dug around in my pockets and pulled out the nuts I had gathered before handing them to him.

He would not be able to carry all of them back. "What are you going to do with all of these?"

As he stuffed some of the nuts into his cheeks and grabbed as many as he could, "Store them. What else?"

"There's no way you can carry all of them at once."

"Just leave them there next to the rock. I will come back for them."

I placed the remaining nuts in a neat pile and turned to thank him for his help, but he had already vanished without a trace. As I looked up, the sky was awash with brilliant shades of amber, gold, and red. Painting a stunning canvas against the once bright blue sky. The white, billowing clouds reflected hues of pink and violet as the sun began to set.

Realizing that I needed to find a place to sleep soon, I scanned my surroundings, aware of the potential danger lurking in the night. Hoping to find a sheltered alcove beyond the cave entrance, I knew it was best not to take any chances with any creatures that might roam around after dark.

The sudden chill in the air made me shiver as the wind picked up and blew through my hair. I was grateful for the skills Nona had taught me, including how to build a fire to keep warm on chilly nights like this. As I looked for dried kindle and sticks, I reflected on how crucial it was for my survival to have acquired these skills through my schooling. Finally, with enough materials to keep me warm, I turned towards the cave entrance. Ready to seek refuge for the night.

With each step, the echoes of my footsteps bounced off the cave walls as I made my way into the depths of the cave. The darkness enveloped me, and I paused to let my eyes adjust to the dim light. The drip of water from the cave ceiling mixed with the sound of my footsteps, making it clear that it was much colder inside the cave than outside. However, I knew that staying outside was not an option.

As I ventured further in the darkness seemed to deepen and the musty, damp smell of the cave wasn't entirely welcoming. Anything could be lurking in the shadows and I wouldn't know until it was too late. But I continued down the long passageway anyway. Despite the heavy and stale air that surrounded me. The farther I went, the more I questioned my decision to enter.

What if I got lost?

What if I stumbled upon a creature that would end my life and leave only my bones behind? My heart raced as I imagined the unknown beast tearing into my flesh with its teeth and claws.

"Oh Serra, you do have a vivid imagination, don't you?" I said to myself the words echoing off the stone walls, mingling with the sound of the water that dripped. It was the same sentence Nona had said to me once as a little girl. After one of my many playtime games and adventures. Sadness grasped ahold of my heart as tears sprung to my eyes. I missed her so much. so many things in my life recently had changed. So many things that did not entirely make any sense to me. But the loss of her, Kaston's threats and pursuing attraction, Caine's attention, the Goblin King, and his game.

All of it was so much.

My legs shook uncontrollably as I leaned against the rough stone wall for support. The weight of my entire existence felt like an unbearable burden, crushing down on me with unrelenting force. It was as if the entire world was against me, and I was alone in this struggle. The materials I had been clutching slipped from my trembling hands, clattering to the ground as I collapsed onto the cold, damp stone.

Tears streamed down my cheeks, mixing with the water that had gathered on the ground. I had fought so hard to keep it all together, to keep my composure, but now it felt like all the walls I had built around myself had crumbled down. The realization dawned on me that it was not my own doing that had caused this pain. He had done something to me, something that had shattered my spirit and broken me down to my very core.

His words replayed in my head.

I only did what you asked of me.

What had I asked of him? What did I ask him to do, what had changed to find myself here? Question after question formed in my head as I cried. The release I needed from everything in the last weeks. Slowly my sobs eased as I was able to piece myself back together. I had to finish this, so I could go home. When I was finally ready I gathered the sticks, the dried brush and piled them together in a formation to start a fire.

Searching the ground around me for a pair of rocks that could start a spark, my tears rolled off my chin. When my fingers found a pare I struck them together and failed. A couple more frustrated strikes and nothing. A growl ripped itself from my lips as I tried again and failed. Taking a deep breath I tried one more time, this time the sparks flew to the bundle at my feet. Setting the rocks to the side a wave of relief went through me. Carefully picking up the dried bundle in my hands and slowly blowing across the embers to ignite it, the small flame danced along as I set it under the tower. Willing it to light the branches. It would have to do in the dampness of this cave.

I SAT THERE IN SILENCE for a while as the flicker of the flames caused my eyes to become heavy. Exhaustion had finally caught up with me and took over. My eyelids drooped as sleep called me. My consciousness slipped away as I fell down into a slumber. The sound of crickets and night owls echoed off the cave walls. The lull of their call grounding me, visions of rainbows and blooming flower groves welcomed me with open arms. The smell of fresh honey and morning dew hung in the air, invigorating my senses. Rain and sun, the world before me flickered in and out, ever-changing as I dreamt. But through it all, a lingering feeling that I was not alone in this world.

That I was being watched.

I jolted awake, gasping for breath. My surroundings were familiar; the room, the bed, the house- all mine, back in Rothnia. It took a moment for me to realize that it had all been a dream. I let out a deep sigh of relief and sank back into my soft pillows. But as I looked around, I couldn't shake off this unsettling feeling. Something was not right, even though everything appeared to be in its place.

An ache bloomed in my chest, my heart longed for someone, pulled at me. I sat back up, my eyes scanning the room for what it was I searched for, what it was I was missing. In the shadows at the foot of my bed stood the Goblin King. His mismatched eyes glinted in the darkness as he watched me, a sly smile playing at his lips. Had he been there the whole time, silently observing me as I slept? My stomach twisted with unease, but at the same time, a fluttering sensation bloomed within me.

Without a second thought, I reached out to him, pulling him towards me. His lips met mine, his hands gripping my waist tightly. It was electrifying, a mixture of fear and desire coursed through me as our bodies pressed together. My own fingers found themselves wrapped in his hair, tangling in the soft strands. Our kiss deepened as he lay me back down atop my sheets- positioning himself above me.

My fingers trembled slightly as they reached for the buttons of his shirt, unfastening them one by one, feeling the warmth of his skin beneath my touch. His muscles rippled as he moved to allow me to slip the shirt off his shoulders, exposing his muscled chest. My hands traced their way down his arms, marveling at their strength and power. He broke our kiss and pulled the shirt off, discarding it on the floor with a thud. Our lips found each other again, hunger and desire fueling our passion.

A soft demand for more as he traced a line of kisses along my jaw and found the sweet spot behind my ear. Long tender kisses down the column of my neck caused my toes to curl. The gasp that came from me had my body arching off the bed as he nipped and sucked- placing an affectionate kiss to the hurt there. His hand grazed my side as it pulled at the lacing of my bodice. His fingers were quick and fluid as the bodice came loose, releasing the tightness around my breasts. Palming one gently, his thumb caressing as it peaked.

I craved his taste, he was intoxicating.

My hunger for him intensified, a fire ignited within me as his lips touched mine. I craved more, my hands gripping his face to pull him closer, deepening the kiss. His tongue brushed against my bottom lip, asking for permission which I eagerly granted. But my desire was not sated without hesitation, my hands moved to his trousers, unbuttoning and pulling at them with a fierce urgency. I wanted to feel all of him, to be consumed by him. I flipped him over effortlessly, straddling him as I continued to undress him. My hands explored his body, tracing every muscle and curve.

Nothing would satisfy me until I had all of him.

His eyes watched me, full of desire and curiosity.

A smirk formed on his lips as I pulled him free. Grasping him in my hand, stroking him gently. I watched as his eyes rolled back- a gasping breath escaped from between his teeth. My name on his lips, uttered softly as I worked him slowly. My core heated as I watched the Goblin King come undone under me. my hand squeezing him as he growled- the sound shattering and unadulterated. Reaching for me, pulling me back to him as he places a kiss upon my lips.

Demanding and fervently.

In a matter of seconds, his hand was on my hip, flipping me onto my back on the bed. The sheets bunched beneath me as his gaze locked onto mine. My body hummed with a need for more, for something deeper than just his touch and taste. The heat between my legs throbbed with desire, begging for his attention. I arched my back, silently urging him to take me, to give me what I craved.

I wanted him.

I wanted him to take me, I wanted to come undone, to shatter under him. To feel a pleasure that left me breathless and wishing for more. Even now with him above me, his hooded gaze as he stared down. There were no words, no thoughts, just the feeling of his fingers on my skin. His breath on my face, his smell as it swirled around me. My skirt rode up as his hand ran along my leg. His feather-light touch against the bare skin of my thigh, his fingers had found their way to the wetness between my legs. His smoldering gaze, his grin wicked as if he could read my mind.

Honestly, I could lay here all night long, until the morning sun peaked its way through the window pane; in pleasure and ecstasy. Sharing in it with this fae male. I was his at this moment. I was his to take, to taste, to have.

"Serra."

His voice echoed as my room dropped away. The image swirled as my consciousness pulled itself back, waking me up.

I was back in the alcove.

The fire flickered lightly as the embers snapped. Sitting up, my head pounded. A sudden weight pressing down on me. The consequence of what I had just dreamt. And it had been just that. It had been a dream, a vivid one too. My face heated from it; it felt so real. My skin prickled, his touch, his lips on my skin all of it had felt real. My fingers brushed my lips, relished in the memory of his touch. I couldn't believe how quickly he had taken control, how easily he had made me submit to him.

Even in my dreams.

As I raised my head, a sudden flicker of movement drew my attention. Across from me, on the other side of the crackling fire, a striking red fox with black ears and legs sat, its white belly fur glowing in the dancing light. Its sharp gaze was fixed on me, tracking my every move as its tail swished back and forth.

Had I made its home my resting place?

Suddenly, something strange happened; the fox began to change before my eyes, transforming from a furry animal to a flesh-and-bone creature. The fox was no longer a fox but a tall, striking figure with pointed ears and arched brows. His high cheekbones and sharp jawline caught my attention, as did his dark brown tousled hair and hazel eyes. A sense of familiarity washed over me, but as I looked closer, I realized that this was no human - he was Fae.

And I knew him.

"Corey?"

CHAPTER
Fifteen

Serra

H E CLEARED HIS THROAT as he bowed before me, "Actually, my name is Hendrix. It's a pleasure to officially meet you, Serra."

I was speechless.

The Rusty Goat's barkeep was Fae. The Fae male that stood before me in fact. Corey was not a mortal. Corey was Hendrix, Hendrix was Corey. I stammered as I struggled to form a coherent sentence.

"I-I don't understand." My groggy mind struggled to comprehend what was happening as the figure before me spoke urgently. I could feel the worry that came from him, the thickness of it as he stood there in the dark.

"There is a lot to say, to explain to you. But we don't have the time," he said, his intense gaze darting in every direction.

It took a moment for my disoriented mind to wake up and process what he was saying. He seemed afraid to be there, and I had barely stood up before he kicked the embers of the fire out, scattering its remains across the stone floor. Frantically, he motioned for me to follow him down a path. "We should not linger here," he warned.

"Why?"

"These caves are not safe, many dark and otherworldly beings dwell within and the magic that lives here is older than anyone who lives. These caves thrive on your deepest desires. It's its way of pulling you in and keeping you trapped here."

Deepest desires?

I didn't desire to have the Goblin King take me, did I? Yes, I was attracted to him, I could not help myself either. I was drawn to him, all of it out of my own self-control. My voice cracked as I asked Hendrix what he meant.

"T-the what?"

He lifted his gaze to meet mine, his eyes betraying a deep weariness. It was clear that he was carefully choosing his words. "The Caves of Desire," he began, "have a certain allure for those seeking to escape their own reality, to revel in the magic and false experiences it provides. But respectfully, that is until the creatures and inhabitants that dwell within find you."

As he spoke, I could sense a hint of fear in his voice. I felt the blood drain from my face. Jesper tricked me, the wicked little beast tricked me. Hendrix spoke again, "You made it farther inside than I had anticipated. It was a struggle to find you."

"Find me?" I asked, my voice rising an octave, "why would you need to find me? Have you been following me?"

I could feel the knot in my stomach as it tightened, waiting of him to answer me.

"Ah. Well. . ." he hesitated as he rubbed the back of his neck, avoiding any eye contact with me. With a sudden huff of air he replies, "Yes." There was a flicker of amusement in his eyes as he finally met my own gaze again.

I knew the rustle in the prairie grass was not my imagination. I had been right, I was being followed. At least he was honest, I could appreciate that. "How long have you been following me?"

"Not long. I lost you when you took off after the squirrel."

The mention of Jesper sent a wave of anger through me; the next time I saw him I would have to have a talk with him. But the thought of the Goblin King and his hands on my skin came to mind again. My cheeks flushed with embarrassment and indignation at the thought. I cleared my throat trying to focus on the present moment, and glanced around before looking back at Hendrix. I watched him closely as he finished scattering the remains of my poor little fire.

"Why were you following me anyway?" I asked, glaring at him. My question had come out sharper than I had intended but I couldn't help the bit of suspicion in my tone as I spoke.

"I'll tell you," he said, his voice low but I could hear the underlying tone of urgency as he held out his hand for me to follow him. "But we have to be on our way. We cannot stay here, we have to move. *Now*, Serra."

I could tell he was uncomfortable. His eyes dart around even in the darkness of the caves. I couldn't help but follow after him, slipping deeper into the unknown.

As we made our way through the winding paths of the cave, the shadows and darkness closed in around us, and the sound of dripping water followed us, like an eerie accompaniment to our journey. It was a maze in here, with paths that broke off in different directions at random locations. I would have certainly gotten lost on my own. The smaller inhabitants skittered away into the dark as we passed, far less intimidating than Hendrix had said.

The silence was thick, heavy, palpable as it stretched between us as Hendrix avoided my gaze. Annoyed, I turned to him. "Why *were* you following me?"

Hendrix hesitated, clearly I'd made him uncomfortable with my directness. But he replied, the words slipping from his lips easily, "I wanted to make sure you were okay."

"Were you sent to follow me?" This certainly reeked of the Goblin King. As immoral as he was, would he send someone after me? He had not offered to help me, nor give me assistance. Hendrix didn't answer again so I tried another question. "What are you doing here in the Fae Realms? Why aren't you in Rothnia?"

He glanced back at me as he said, "My home is on this side of the Ebony Woods, Serra. I wouldn't have stayed in Rothnia long. I wouldn't have been welcome indefinitely."

Not really the answer I was expecting, but I inquired anyway hoping he would indulge, "Why not?"

He sighed, "Because I'm Fae. We aren't exactly popular."

I mean he wasn't wrong, many feared the Fae for what they were capable of. What they could do, who they were. Even Nona had feared them. The stories of the Lost Fae were widely known.

"Why were you in Rothnia?"

He didn't answer.

Instead, he avoided the question again. Okay, if this was how he wanted to travel, then I could play along. "What do I call you? I know you first as Corey, but your real name is Hendrix?"

He smiled softly at me, "Hendrix will do just fine."

Hendrix was only the second Fae I had ever met, and he was not like the Goblin King. But two Fae in a span of a few weeks had me a little on edge. I could not lay all my trust in him, having worked beside him or not. That would be foolish; he was still lethal. Another question came to mind as we walked along the dark.

"How did you hide your ears? While in Rothnia I mean."

Hendrix paused for a moment, his gaze fixed on me. "The Fae can glamour themselves." He said, "Appear as we want others to see us. I was able to do a simple glamour of my ears to hide the tips. But it's weak, easy magic. It's as simple as thinking. It takes far more energy to transform entirely, to weave that kind of magic. And you have to have incredible strength and magic to do that. It's an older magic, and even fewer carry it. There are some who hold infinite power, so much that they are considered royalty. There's only one I know who can."

"Who is that?"

He smiled softly, the slightest tug at the corners of his lips but did not answer. I couldn't help the unease that he was hiding something. He had secrets too it seemed. If it took more energy-more power- to transform entirely, how was he able to transform from a furry animal to flesh and bone? Was he stronger than he let on? Just another set of unanswered questions on my growing list of curiosities.

"But you were just a fox."

"I inherited that trait from my father," Hendrix turned to look at me again. I couldn't help but notice how handsome he was as Fae, even in the dimly lit passageway of rock and stone. His hazel eyes sparkled and his smile revealed a set of canines that could pierce skin. It made me pause and feel a fluttering sensation in my stomach as his gaze locked onto mine. "Actually, many of my family members share the same trait."

"Are all of you able to transform into foxes?"

"Not all of us, no," he chuckled, but then seemed to hesitate as if debating whether to say more. Finally, he spoke up again, "There are two distinct lines in my family. One follows a certain path, while the other follows a different path. It's always a gamble when a new offspring is born, as you never know which line they'll follow. But this is just within my own family. There are countless other Fae families with their own unique lineages."

I watched him with an odd mix of curiosity and wonder, his cheeks seemed to flush slightly under my gaze. He rubbed the back of his neck as he said, "My line went the less desired route."

My interest piqued at his words. I wanted to know more. I had so many questions. So many thoughts ran through my head at the endless possibilities in this world. I'd never heard that Fae could shape-shift or about any who could control ancient magic. It had me wondering, "What are the differences between lines? What line did you take after?"

"I-" He paused, his hand flew up to stop me from speaking the words that had danced on my tongue lost as he glanced back behind him, listening to whatever it was that caught his attention.

I couldn't hear anything, but he was Fae and I had no doubt he heard something that my ears had yet to pick up. But as he stood perfectly still my unease increased. I'd forgotten that Fae were still predators. Their unnatural stillness, keen sense of smell and hearing things long before others could. But it did not take long before my own ears finally picked up what he'd heard.

The noise was jarring and grating, causing a prickle that made my skin crawl as if someone were grinding two rocks together. The friction between them was enough to set my nerves on edge, and the sound grew in volume the longer we stood there.

Hendrix's face paled, *"Run."*

His urgent words sent a surge of panic through me. The way he grabbed my hand and pulled me along only made it worse. We ran down the path we had been traveling with the sound behind us growing louder and more chaotic. The noises seemed to overlap with each other, creating a discordant symphony of grinding and scraping.

As we darted through the rocky path, the sound behind us was a strange mix of grinds and hums. I couldn't make out what it was but it sounded like the buzzing of bees more than anything else. It was an eerie and unsettling sound that added to the panic I felt as we weaved around larger rocks and turned corners, trying to put as much distance between us and whatever *they* were.

I had to yell to be heard as I asked him, *"What is that?"*

His grip on my hand tightened as he shouted back at me, "Rock trolls. They are not kind or forgiving if you find yourself in their hive. They will rip you limb from limb."

Rock trolls? *Rock trolls?*

Oh, he had to be kidding me!

This place was going to give me a heart-attack. Fauns, talking squirrels, Fae that can change into animals, caves that prey on your deepest desires, rock trolls, what else lived *here?*

"Faster! You'll never see another sunrise if they get hold of you, because there will be nothing left," he shouted, his grip on my hand tightening. He pulled me closer to him, urging me to run as fast as I could. I still had not fully recovered from my lack of sleep, stumbling over fallen rocks as I hurled myself forward. Hendrix grabbed my arm to keep me from falling, and I gave him a grateful smile as he righted me again. His response was quick, and it made my heart race.

"Will they devour us?" I asked with fear in my voice.

"No," he replied, "But they're lethal. They don't tolerate any interference with their hive. They don't care if you're friend or foe. If you disturb their hive, you better know your way out. They may be small, but they are dangerous."

A small cry left my lips as another fork in the path appeared ahead of us.

"Left Serra, go left!" Hendrix bellowed. He'd stopped, placing himself between the rock trolls and me.

A barrier. I couldn't let him do this.

"What are you doing?" I asked frantically, turning to him and grabbing his arm. "If they're really that deadly, why are we stopping?"

"Just trust me, go."

I only hesitated for a brief moment, unsure I wanted to leave him. I'd spent many weeks with this male back in Rothnia. While I did not know him and had not gotten to know him as Corey I was not going to leave him behind. "I can't leave you."

"Serra, go. You have to trust me." He glanced backward as the sound of the rock trolls as their cries increased, gaining ground on us. "Go. Take the path to the left and it will get you out of here. Once out, keep going. They will not follow you. They are cave dwellers and will stay within its bounds."

"Hendrix," It hurt me to leave him, a pang of guilt surged through me. I could not place why it bothered me to leave him, but it did. He smiled softly at me again, his eyes once having been full of fear now danced with determination.

"I'll be okay. Go."

I knew if I stayed I would not fair well against the rock trolls. And I had a task to complete. A deal with the Goblin King to fulfill. Without any more hesitation I took off down the path, the one to the left as he had said. Leaving him standing there between myself and the trolls. I wished that he would be okay, that they would not kill him.

I RAN AS FAST as I could, as fast as my legs could have gone, anyway. Any rest I had gained from sleep had been expelled at this point. But the farther I ran, the farther away I got from the Rock Trolls. At least it's what I told myself, any distance between me and them was welcome. I did not know what Hendrix would do or if he would even survive. But he gave me a fighting chance to get away, and for that I was grateful.

If I saw him again, I would have to convey my thanks, because without him. . . I'd certainly have perished.

The darkness of the cave started to give way as a light bloomed ahead, lighting the path before me. Relief flooded me as I rushed forward, a small cry escaped as I ran for it. The cave entrance loomed before me as I barreled forward and out. My feet carried me as I ran into something- right into a hard object.

Right into a solid chest.

Right into the Goblin King's arms.

I had not seen him standing there, I had not noticed over my fear and sheer will to get away.

His voice was quiet as he asked, "What have you done now?"

The moon above sparkled, night still blanketed the world under its dark sheet while the stars danced across the sky-twinkling and laughing as the world slumbered. The way the light hit him though had my stomach flipping, the thoughts of him and the way he touched me from my dream caused my cheeks to flush. He was wearing the white cotton shirt from my dream; unbuttoned halfway down his front, the bottom of it tucked into the top of his trousers.

His hair was tousled like he had been pulled from sleep. The bags under his eyes told me he had. He wore no cloak or jacket, it was as if he had sprung from bed at a moment's notice. The muscles of his arms tensed under the sleeves of his shirt, flexing as they held onto me.

"Serra?"

His face contorted into an expression that was hard to read, a mix of irritation and concern, but which one was dominant, I couldn't tell. My mind wanted to believe that he cared about my safety, but I knew that was ridiculous. He was probably more bothered by the fact that I had disrupted his sleep. I struggled to speak, my breaths coming in ragged gasps as I tried to regain my composure.

"Trolls. . . chasing. . .ran. . . away."

The sound that escaped from between his lips had me stepping away from him, I couldn't tell if he was exasperated by this inconvenience or annoyed by having to be here, by our encounter yet again. Ripped from slumber just as I had been.

Good. I thought glowering at him, my voice finding more solid ground, "I did not purposely ask for this. I did not ask to be chased by a hive of murderous Rock Trolls that want to pull my limbs from my sockets, thank you very much!"

He eyed me cautiously, his eyes narrowing. I really would not be here running for my life if it wasn't for this vexing male before me and his stupid game. As I glared at him, the overwhelming urge to lash out surfaced once again. My fists curled and my nails dug into the palms of my hands. Taking a deep breath, I steadied myself and suppressed the rage that bubbled up inside me. I knew I couldn't succumb to anger or violent outbursts, not now and not in front of him, especially with the threat still looming behind me in the caves.

"How did you get away? Very few survive the Caves of Desire let alone the hive of Rock Trolls that live within its dwellings. Or any of the other demonic and unworldly inhabitants, why were you in them in the first place? What could you possibly have been thinking? It's a surprise you were not lured away, or enslaved." His voice pulled my attention back.

My blood ran cold as he spoke, the idea that there were other *things* that lived within had every nerve in my body going numb. I tried to swallow- tried to push down the lump in my throat and ease the feeling in my chest. But I found it far too difficult to do as I watched the male before me.

As I caught my breath, I watched the Goblin King pace to the edge of the cave entrance, his expression etched with concern. Despite the looming darkness outside, I found it less intimidating than what I had just fled from.

Even in his presence.

"I just wanted to sleep." I whispered.

"There are safer places for that." He responded, not bothering to look at me.

I couldn't help but wonder if this had been a set-up, if he was working with Jesper to lure me inside. Hopeful that I would come to an end at the hands of another creature, and in turn keeping what belonged to me. My fear had subsided slightly, replaced by a mix of anger and sadness. How could he accuse me of not being careful? I had escaped the trolls and made it this far. But then again, he couldn't know that, could he?

We had barely spoken to each other, and even then, it had been brief. For a moment I let the thought simmer, anger building in my chest as it replaced the fear, but the feeling did not last long. I felt the blood drain from my face as I thought of Hendrix.

His name a whisper on my lips.

The Goblin King whirled on me. His eyes found mine as he asked, "Hendrix is inside?"

I nodded softly, my voice meek, "He allowed me the time I needed to get away. Got me through the labyrinth of stone and rock."

I was fairly certain without Hendrix I would not have escaped. I was unsure of the look he wore, it was a cross between fury and concern. Unknown if he was angry at me or feared for what could have happened. He mumbled something to himself, his eyes cast down. After a moment the Goblin King spoke again. His words were firmer than any other time we had encountered each other.

"You should not linger here, Serra. Keep going." He turned back toward the cave, the sound of the trolls did not reach us but the fright they had left me with had me grabbing his arm.

"What are you doing?"

He glanced over at me, his eyes flickered with another unknown emotion. But there was a warning in them, so I yanked my hand back. Another wave of dread washed over me, the Goblin King's voice rang as he spoke, his words caused a cold chill to run down my spine.

"If you do not keep going, something far more dangerous could find its way out of those caves."

The tension in the air was thick and palpable as the Goblin King's warning echoed through my mind. I couldn't shake the feeling of dread that settled in my gut as I stared at him, unsure of what to do or say. His words had cut through me like a knife, and I couldn't help but wonder what he meant by 'something far more dangerous.' I knew I couldn't stay here any longer, but at the same time, I didn't want to leave without knowing more.

I asked softly, my voice barely above a whisper. "What did you mean by that? What's in the caves?"

He turned to face me again, his eyes dark and unreadable. "Things that are better left undisturbed," he said cryptically. "Trust me, Serra. You don't want to know."

I couldn't help but feel frustrated at his response. How could I trust him when he was withholding something from me? But at the same time, I couldn't deny the sense of danger that lurked in the air. I knew I needed to leave, to keep moving forward and away from whatever he meant. I glanced back at the cave, my thoughts consumed by the danger within. Suddenly, a hand grabbed my arm, causing me to jump in surprise. I turned to face the Goblin King, who was now standing beside me.

"Not everything stays in the dark. You are neither safe nor protected here from what lives within. Do not say I did not warn you. Three days left, Serra."

His hand still rested on my arm, and I felt a warmth spread through me at his touch. It was a feeling I had denied ever existed, but now it was impossible to ignore. I opened my mouth to speak, to say something to him, but the words caught in my throat. I knew what I wanted to say, but I couldn't bring myself to say it.

With a deep breath, I turned and started walking away, my mind racing with thoughts and questions. But as I walked, I couldn't shake the feeling of regret that settled in my heart. Regret for leaving Hendrix behind, regret for not pushing the Goblin King for more answers, and regret for not being strong enough to do this on my own.

CHAPTER
Sixteen

Serra

THE FEAR THAT HAD gripped me after the Goblin King's words was a suffocating weight on my senses. It sliced through me like a steel blade, leaving me feeling vulnerable and exposed. The thought of something far scarier lurking within the dark depths of those caves was enough to send shivers down my spine. I knew I had to keep moving, to put as much distance between myself and that eerie cave entrance as possible. There were only three days left to reach the castle, and I couldn't afford to waste any time. I wouldn't stick around long enough to see if Hendrix or the Goblin King would make it out alive.

With adrenaline pumping through my veins, I darted down the hillside and into the darkness. My heart was racing, and my legs were carrying me as fast as they could. I couldn't shake the feeling of concern that had lodged itself firmly in my chest. Despite my better judgment, I glanced back at the cave entrance once. It remained dark and ominous, as if concealing something sinister within its depths.

It wasn't until I reached the edge of a trickling waterfall that I allowed myself to stop. Or what remained of the waterfall, it was closer to a small babbling brook that cascaded over rocks, rather than a cascade of water. The rocks were no taller than me, and the water dribbled down in a slow, steady stream. I was grateful for the water, which was enough to clean the dirt off my hands and face and remove the crusted blood from my nails from the cliff. I took a long drink, cupping my hands to catch the water and bringing it to my lips.

The water was oddly sweet and crisp, and I drank until my stomach was no longer grumbling. But the lack of food around the glen was disconcerting. I had not seen one berry bush, fruit tree, edible grass, or herbs. Everything around me was dead or dying. My stomach grumbled in protest, but the cool water from the fall would have to be enough for now. At least until I found something that was edible and not dead.

When I had my fill, I glanced around the glen. It was quiet, and the only sounds were the trickle of the water and my own breathing. The absence of crickets and owls was unsettling, so unlike the nights in Rothnia, where their chirping and hooting had been a comforting lullaby that put me to sleep. Here, in this strange and desolate place, I felt alone and vulnerable. Even the cool water couldn't wash away the fear that lingered deep within me.

My heart raced with the memory of my nightmares, the same ones that had plagued me every night. Every night, I woke up drenched in sweat, gasping for air. The fear never left me, and it followed me wherever I went. Even now, as I sat by the babbling brook, the sound of the water couldn't drown out the sound of my racing heart.

The memories of fire, heat, and shouts caused me to shudder

involuntarily. It was a nightmare that visited me every night, a relentless reminder of the horrors I had heard. But last night, for the first time in what felt like forever, the nightmare had not surfaced. I had been granted a moment of peace, a brief respite from the terrors that plagued me. The dream of the Goblin King had been a strange relief, an unexpected diversion from my usual torment. I couldn't help but wonder about the motive behind leading me to the Caves of Desire. Was it Jesper's doing, or was it something more sinister? A chill ran down my spine as I considered the possibility that the furry creature may have been working with the Goblin King all along.

As I sat there, sleep called to me once again. The gentle lullaby of the water hitting the rocks, the cool breeze that kissed my face, and the sense of safety that enveloped me were all too enticing to ignore. The glen I found myself in was a peaceful haven, tucked away in an alcove of paper birch trees and rock. From the top of the cliff at the edge of the Ebony Woods, the land had looked barren and lifeless. But down on the ground, it was a different story. The land was complex, as if under a spell or enchantment that made it seem like it was trying to keep people away.

Despite its dying state, the land still seemed to be fighting for survival. It was a small victory in a world full of chaos and destruction. And as I closed my eyes, letting the sound of the water and the cool breeze lull me to sleep, I couldn't help but hope that the land would continue to fight and thrive, even in the face of overwhelming darkness.

I heard the cries in my head as I drifted off to sleep. The image surged forward, unable to stop it from playing. A darkened room, lit only by moonlight, the fire in the hearth having gone out long ago, but the ashes gave off a rich glow. Everything starts coming clearer, the drapery and wood of a four-poster bed, the moon outside casting its soft glow on the blankets and rug.

The cries echo in my head again.

The cry of a woman rang again through the halls as the maids and nurses scurried past her door. It had been left open a crack, so she could call for them if the nightmares plagued her. The nightmares that always visited her in the dark. The ones that had her rushing from her bed into that of her parents.

But on that night, the screams and cries of her mother echoed down to her instead. Something wasn't right, something was wrong with her. Someone had peaked in once to check on her, but she had pretended to be asleep. Pulling the door shut behind them as they left. Her mother's cries echoed again as a set of feet ran past her door, she couldn't take it anymore.

Sliding from under the sheets she went to the door and pulled it open. The hallway was a flurry of motion. Nurses running back and forth, soiled and clean towels passed between them, looks of pure distress and panic. Their faces were stained with tears.

A man with long dark hair stood in the hall, watching. Dressed in a dark suit and black cloak. He was not someone she was fond of, this man scared her. This man was a stranger to her, but she knew what he could do. His dark eyes found her as the door to her room creaked open. He left his post as he approached her.

"Go back to bed." His voice was chilling.

Her voice was quiet as she spoke, "But momma..."

"Your mother is fine. Go back to bed."

She did as she was told, climbing back into bed as the man watched her. His voice sent a wave of terror down her, a feral grin on his lips as he said, "Good night young princess."

Closing her door, washing her room in a blanket of darkness, the hoot of an owl outside her window drew her attention. Sleep barely held its grip on her as the agonizing screams and sobs of her mother echoed down the hall. By morning the news would circulate that the new babe had not survived.

My gasping breaths pulled me back to consciousness, my chest heaving as I struggled to draw in enough air. The dream had been all too vivid, the cries of the woman still echoing in my mind- her despair and agony piercing my heart. The little girl in the dream had been so young, yet aware of the horror unfolding before her. The weight of her fear and sadness settled heavily in my chest, mingling with my own emotions until it was hard to distinguish between them.

I rubbed my bleary eyes, trying to shake off the fog of sleep and make sense of it all, but it was no use. The glen around me was peaceful, the birch trees swaying gently in the cool breeze, the water trickling in a soothing melody. Dawn was approaching, but it brought no relief to my restless soul.

I couldn't remember the last time I felt truly rested. The last two dreams had left me feeling drained and unsettled, but I had to keep going. There was a path before me, and I had to face whatever lay ahead.

I leaned over the water, cupping my hands to drink from the falls and ease the dryness in my throat. When I had my fill, I rose to my feet, ready to move forward. But a sudden sound shattered the stillness, a branch snapping in the darkness beyond. My instincts screamed at me to run or fight, but I stood frozen, waiting to see what would emerge from the rustling grass. Was danger lurking in the shadows, waiting to strike?

The Goblin King did say far worse things could make their way from the caves, that I was not safe here. Had something slipped past him and gotten out? Had it found me as I rested? My heart was going to explode from my chest as the grass rustled again. "Who's there?"

The grass rustled once more, a creature unlike any I had ever seen emerged before me. It was enormous, with the front half resembling an eagle, complete with sharp-clawed legs. The back half, however, was that of a standard mare with a dark coal-colored coat. What truly caught my attention were its wings, which were folded closely to its body. The massive wings were tipped in silver, reflecting the moon beams back at me.

The creature was beautiful and majestic, with beady black eyes that watched me intently. In my sleepy haze, I had not noticed it before, it's dark coat allowing it to blend in with the surroundings. I had heard tales of such creatures from the storytellers in Rothnia, but I never thought I would encounter one myself. They were said to be solitary creatures, living their lives alone in packs and avoiding any contact with humans or other creatures.

The hippogriff looked at me from across the water, tilting its head as it sensed the air around it. I held my breath, afraid to make any sudden movements that might startle or provoke it.

I wondered if I had unknowingly stumbled upon its den or home. The events of the past twenty-four hours had been unimaginable, but encountering a hippogriff was by far the most absurd. The creature took a deep drink from the water that cascaded down the fall, its eyes never leaving me as it watched and considered me. The words in my head repeated itself.

Don't move, don't move… don't move.

As it finished drinking, the hippogriff stood up. However, it did not immediately leave. Instead it remained motionless- watching me intently as it took another slow step forward. My heart pounded in my chest, and I wondered if the creature could hear it. I feared the worst as it pushed its beak against my ribs, causing the air to escape my lungs and leaving me gasping for breath. This was it, this was the end, this creature was about to attack me with its sharp claws and leave me disemboweled on the ground.

In that moment of terror, I closed my eyes. I did not want to see its sharp claws coming for me. But the hippogriff did not move. My eyes flew open, I was surprised to find that the hippogriff was still standing before me. Its head loomed above mine, and its eyes were a mesmerizing blend of darkness and swirling colors that resembled the vastness of the cosmos. I couldn't help but feel awestruck and captivated by the creature's beauty

Despite my fear, I couldn't help but wonder if this was how the hippogriff usually hunted, by drawing its prey in with its captivating presence before attacking them. As I braced myself for the inevitable, the creature did something unexpected. It bowed to me, its proud form lowering itself before me as if I were its master. I knew this was not the norm for such creatures, and I couldn't help but wonder what the Goblin King's game was.

As the shock of the moment overtook me, I found myself frozen in place, unable to reciprocate the creature's gesture. But it didn't seem to mind, and instead it gave my hair a sniff before it nudged me with its beak again, causing me to stumble back. Without thinking, I reached out to catch myself and found my hands gripping onto it. Up close, I could see its face clearly, including its dark eyes.

We stared at each other as it allowed me to steady myself, slowly my hands found themselves stroking its feathers. They were so soft, the ones around its face felt like velvet. It closed its eyes as I found the spot on its head that made it lean into me. Carefully nuzzling against my arms, its head pushing itself into my chest. Despite my heart still beating wildly, I no longer felt the same level of fear that had I had earlier.

After a moment, the hippogriff pulled away bowing once more before making its way out of the glen. As it disappeared from view, I couldn't help but feel a sense of longing to have more encounters like this with such a beautiful creature. I shook my head to steady myself, to clear the thoughts.

It had been surreal, this could not be happening.

Two days ago, I never would have believed I would find myself here, in a moon-lit glen petting the face of a hippogriff. Having been chased from a labyrinth of cave passageways by trolls that gathered together in a hive like bees. Rescued by a Fae male who was not only able to transform from a fox but was someone I knew.

Nor would I believe I had been led there by a bobtail squirrel that could talk, demanding nuts for whatever reason in the first place. All following a deal I made to play a game, with a creature far more dangerous.

The Goblin King.

Honestly, I probably would have laughed at you and told you that you were crazy. But here I was, and it was happening.

CHAPTER
Seventeen

Serra

AFTER LEAVING THE GLEN, I took a moment to collect myself and regain my composure. By the time I felt ready to continue my journey, the sun had just started to rise, casting a warm glow across the landscape. I noticed that the terrain had transformed once again, with the birch trees giving way to a vast expanse of prairie grass that stretched out before me. The path meandered up and down hills, weaving in and out, promising another long day ahead.

Even with the challenges that lay ahead, I felt a renewed sense of energy, having finally been able to rest a little. I hoped that today would be less eventful than the day before, with no more falls down cliffs or close calls with trolls. Ideally, I just wanted a peaceful day with nothing to distract me. I'd come so far already and it was too late to turn back now.

As I walked, I couldn't help but think about how much I missed home. I had never been away from Rothnia for an extended period of time, and I had certainly never left my cottage for more than a day. Nona had always been there to look after me and ensure that I never wandered too far. But now that I was on my own, I was starting to realize just how much I craved the comfort and familiarity of my own home.

My thoughts drifted the farther I went, lingering on my own disappearance. What would others think, would they know? What if I never made it back home? Would anyone notice or care?

Were there people who would question it? I mean, look at Imogen. Her disappearance had not gone unnoticed or unquestioned. They had opened an investigation for her. But she worked for a prolific family, her absence had been felt. It had been noticed.

But would anyone care with mine?

Would they question it as they had hers?

I thought about Bern, what he had said on that night he had walked me home. I really had not thought this through, taking the Goblin King's deal. The display in the ballroom of the Conwell Manor would raise alarms, sure. It would cause rumors and whispers, or the Conwell's would mute the situation and it would all be hearsay, hushed.

But would it be enough for someone to look into it?

Oh… he really has made a mess of things, hasn't he?

My heart sank as I thought about the worry that must be consuming Bern at this very moment. He had always been a kind and protective figure in my life, and I knew he would be beside himself with concern if I failed to show up for my shift at the tavern the following night. He had already been worried about my safety, walking me home after my evening shifts and double-checking the deadbolt on my cottage before leaving.

Now, on top of his own troubles, he had to worry about my disappearance as well. The weight of it all made my urgency to complete my journey and return home even more pressing.

I'd been so lost in thought, I failed to notice the small creature following me at first. It wasn't until he hopped from one side of the path to the other, his red fur a blur as he did so, that I became aware of his presence. Despite my worries, I couldn't help but smile at the sight of him. He was stalking me, following my every move. I continued walking, and the little creature trailed behind me.

After a few paces, I ducked into the tall grass beside the path and counted to see if he would notice.

One.

Two.

Three.

I heard the rustle again as he jumped out. At the same time, I jumped from my own hiding spot. A laugh on my lips as the poor little thing halted, its mouth open in a silent scream, ears flat against its head. Its tail had gone full, its whole body going into a defensive position.

"Well, it serves you right." I grinned as it righted itself. The laugh lodged in my throat as his fur finally relaxed, "Hendrix."

The fox transformed back into the fae male that he was. Brushing the dirt off his lapel and trousers. His hair was even more tousled than it had been last night, but his hazel eyes shone brightly. I knew foxes were clever and devilish little things, always playing and looking for trouble. But I had not considered that Hendrix's personality would so closely resemble one.

"That was not very nice, Serra."

"Why were you following me again?"

"I wanted to make sure you were okay," he said, shoving his hands into his pockets. The wind blew through his hair, causing the already messy locks to tangle some more.

"What happened to you?" I asked.

He did not answer. he just stared at me. He shrugged, hands hidden away in his pockets. As the silence stretched between us- becoming more and more uncomfortable- I was beginning to think that he was never going to. But when he finally did open his mouth, it was not an answer, at least not to my question.

"Are you okay? I mean you obviously got out and away but, are you okay?"

I wasn't sure how to answer him.

Was I okay?

I couldn't be sure, not after everything that has happened over the last twelve hours. Shuffling my feet in the dirt, not really sure how to answer his question. Do I avoid it? He didn't answer mine.

"I. . . I guess so?"

"You guess so?" he huffed. "Serra, we were chased by a hive of rock trolls through the labyrinth of passageways within the Caves of Desire. And you guess you're okay? I find that hard to believe."

Hendrix paused for a moment, studying me closely, "I have been following you now for well over an hour and I could tell by the look on your face that something is wrong."

"I mean, I don't really know how to answer that, Hendrix. So much has happened in the last twenty-four hours that I don't really know." I said, my voice faltering slightly. My hands would not stop there fidgeting as we started walking. "I was just thinking about how everyone is going to take my disappearance. You know that girl, Imogen?"

His brows furrowed in recognition, "Yes. The ones the guards back in Rothnia were asking about?"

I nodded.

"Yes, her. Well. . ." I started, I was still unsure if he was entirely trustworthy. Unsure if I should even say anything. It would open a whole bag of cow shit I was not ready, nor prepared to deal with. But I had to tell someone.

"Well, the night she went missing, she stopped by my cottage. She had a box with her, from. . . him."

"From whom?"

"Kaston."

"Conwell?"

"Yes, it was the dress I was wearing, before the Goblin King whisked me away from the Conwell's Ball. But that's not what I am trying to say." I was hesitant. I did not want him or anyone to think that I had anything to do with her disappearance. Only that I was concerned for her. Afraid that something bad had happened to her, by Kaston's hands.

"What is it, Serra?" Hendrix urged, concern in his eyes.

"She had a bruise. On the side of her face. Kaston had asked me to meet him in the Ebony Woods. I fear. . . I fear he may have harmed her when I ignored his request." The weight of it finally released itself off my shoulders as the words settled around us. Hendrix hesitated, watching me with weary eyes.

"Do you think. . . do you think he could be the one behind it? I should have said something, I should have spoken up when I had the chance. This is my fault." I whispered, my voice had gotten quiet. I was afraid Kaston would be near, overhearing everything I said.

He did not immediately answer.

I had no idea if he knew the Conwell's or if he knew their sons. Or if he even knew anything for that matter. But her disappearance had not been a coincidence. It weighed far too heavily on my shoulders, knowing what Kaston was capable of- having been a victim myself. When he started walking again- he took my hand. The action had finally stopped them from fidgeting, before tucking it into the crook of his arm. Only now had I noticed how good he smelled.

Good Gods. . . did he smell good!

Like sea salt and leather, with hints of crisp winter snow. I did not recall him smelling as such back in Rothnia. But being around the smells of the tavern, it was hard enough to disconcert ale from vomit. Or sweat from stew. Let alone how he had smelled amongst the other patrons. His voice echoed as my mind committed his smell to memory.

"Serra, you had nothing to do with her disappearance. You hear me? Absolutely nothing." He sounded so sure, but I could not help as his words soothed my worry, my concerns. Maybe I was overthinking it, maybe my first initial thoughts were right, she was safe and had indeed run off with someone.

For some reason though, I believed him.

We walked in silence for a while, the words said between us hung around refusing to be let go. But neither of us spoke of it again, instead allowing the sounds and noises of the critters close by to infiltrate and drown out the conversation entirely.

When the sun had reached high noon, Hendrix had urged that we stop. Taking a moment to rest before continuing. The dialogue never lingered long between us as we lounged in the grass, not as we talked about his short time in Rothnia. Hendrix's curiosity about the mortal world only seemed to grow. He asked about the strange quirks and rituals of the people in Rothnia, the bustling harbor with its comings and goings of sailors, and the stark division between the rich and the poor. I shared what I knew, recounting what I had seen and heard over the years. But it wasn't just about the world around us. He also asked me about myself, what I was like as a child, and what it was like growing up in Rothnia.

I hesitated when it came to sharing about the Goblin King and Kaston. I wasn't sure if I could trust Hendrix, but something in the way he listened to me made me feel safe. So I told him about Nona and all the little wonders she had shown me. I shared stories of the animals in the forest, the flowers that bloomed in the spring, and the stars that lit up the night sky. Through it all, he listened with rapt attention, as if every word was a treasure to be cherished.

But when it came to talking about the Caves and how he had escaped the rock trolls, Hendrix was tight-lipped. Even when I asked if he had encountered the Goblin King, he managed to redirect the conversation to other topics. I couldn't help but wonder why he was so reluctant to talk about it. Was he ashamed of needing to be saved? Or was there something more to the story that he didn't want to reveal?

Despite my best efforts to get him to open up, Hendrix remained elusive. It was as if he had mastered the art of redirection, skillfully moving the conversation away from anything he didn't want to talk about. It made sense now why he had landed a job at the Rusty Goat. His ability to steer the conversation in any direction he wanted was truly impressive. Though. . . it wasn't until I had brought up the creature I ran into after the caves that his attention peaked, his face an unreadable expression. His words tumbled out in a wave of disbelief.

"Wait, you saw a hippogriff?"

"I think so? I'm unsure, I've never seen one before. But I have heard stories." The wind blew a gust across the plains, the bundle of grasses we had decided to rest in moving in it. The sound was a soft hum.

"You're sure that's what you saw?"

He placed a hand on my shoulder, as if I would sprint away in trepidation. I would not be running anywhere, not unless I had to.

"Yes?" I hesitated, was he finally losing it? Was the sun too much for him? Was all the talk about the caves catching up to him now?

"I need you to be sure, Serra."

"Large creature with massive wings, half eagle, half horse? I would believe it to be so, why?" I wasn't sure why he was so insistent, why he was pushy as to what exactly I had seen. He considered for a moment, before answering my question. One of few that he had deigned to.

"They disappeared eighteen years ago. For it to be here now would be. . ." He paused. His eyes grew as he looked at me.

"What?" Oh, I did not like that look. "What is it, Hendrix?"

"I have to go." He stood abruptly, his eyes had lost their luster. "Keep going. But I really have to go."

"Go where?" I yelled after him. "Hendrix!"

I'd gotten to my feet to chase after him but he had changed back to his fox form. His tail swished back and forth before he disappeared between the tall grass. I huffed in exasperation, he'd left behind me yet again.

D ESPITE HENDRIX'S ABRUPT DEPARTURE, I trudged along for another couple of hours on my own, hoping to make some progress before the sun set completely. I was grateful for the temporary respite from trouble, or perhaps trouble simply hadn't found me yet. The prairie stretched on as far as the eye could see, with the grass swaying gently in the dry, scratchy wind that provided little relief out in the open. The wind picked up bits of dirt and dust, whipping them into my face.

As I approached the distant castle, it felt like I had barely covered any ground at all, despite my best efforts. My legs were starting to feel like lead, my feet ached, and I desperately longed for some sleep. It reminded me of the harvest season before last, when I worked alongside

Nona. We had planted an excess of crops to help a family who had lost everything in a tragic event, barely escaping with their lives. As they slowly rebuilt their lives, Nona provided them with the nourishment they needed. It was just one example of the many selfless acts she performed for others.

She did that a lot.

Nona had a heart of gold and went out of her way to help those in need. If anyone sought her out for assistance, she never hesitated to provide help, whether it was salves for scrapes or tonics for colds. Unfortunately, some superstitious villagers believed that she was an enchantress, which caused many to fear her and avoid her. But those who didn't fear her quickly learned that she was the epitome of kindness and selflessness.

Despite the rumors and accusations leveled against her, Nona never spoke ill of anyone or held grudges. She was a beacon of light in my world, always ready to lend a helping hand to those in need. I couldn't recall ever hearing her utter a harsh word about anyone, and I doubted she had a mean bone in her body.

Even after. . .

No. I would not think about him.

Not now, not ever again. But fear still wove its way over my nerves. I could not imagine what he would have to say once I was back. I would not imagine it, no!

My mind was made up.

I would stand my ground, stand up to him. He had no more power over me than anyone else did. I was my own person, I would not cower before him in terror or allow him to continue his ill-fated pursuit. But the thoughts of Kaston did not leave me, they lingered like a vulture over a dead carcass. However, my mind questioned how much of this had been by his own fruition and how much of it had been influenced.

I so desperately wanted to believe that was not the real him.

Another face flashed before me, his mismatched eyes, his scent, his white blonde hair. My heart fluttered again as I remembered the way he held me at the Conwell's ball. The warmth of his hand on my skin, the intense gaze as the people around us all melted away. The melody played in my head, the feel of his strong arms as he whirled me across the marble floor.

Lost for a moment in the memory.

It flickered in and out as it morphed into another. This one was not one I recognized. This one was not mine. She was there again, the little girl, but she was in the arms of the same man I'd seen before. The one with the coronet of laurel leaves upon his brows. His strong hands held hers as her feet rested atop his.

Their laughs echoed through the room.

The room was dark, with wood paneled walls lit with a warm glow from the fire and sconces. Covered in paintings of centuries long past. The lush deep burgundy carpet under her feet muffled, deafening her giggle as she smiled. He held onto her, her little feet atop his as they danced. Their laughter reached the far corners of the room.

The smile he had, matched hers as he showed her the proper steps.

The music was a tune they all knew well. A tune they shared with her every night. In the corner a woman sat in a large settee; her white cotton dress puddled around her feet, watching the pair. A soft smile on her lips as she embroidered, the needle going in and out of the white satin. They did not speak, they did not need to.

She could feel the love from them, from the pair of them. She was their world, and soon they would be joined by another. Soon the three would become four. The excitement she had felt earlier that day had continued as the time wore on. The fire crackled in the hearth, the flames dancing along the logs. The music had hit its crescendo and as it came to an end she bowed to him.

The little girl ran to the woman, tugging her hand as she led her back to the man with the laurel crown. Taking her in his arms, she restarted the music for them. As she watched them dance across the room, her heart burst with joy and love. The warmth of love and happiness shared within the stone walls of their home never seemed to end. Nothing could be better than this, nothing could separate them.

Not ever.

When the memory faded, the image wavered before fading to black, it left me alone in the tall grass. My heart aching, wishing to know who they were. Why I was having these visions. What the purpose was behind them. Was I supposed to see them, supposed to help them?

Who were they?

The biggest question that hounded me over and over. The question burned like a hot knife. If I wanted any answers I would have to ask. But who? Who would know? I glanced up at the castle again. It was at least another day's journey away. It was then that it occurred to me. The Goblin King would know. He had to know who they were. With a renewed sense of purpose I made a dash for the castle. Going as far as I could before I lost my breath. I needed to cover as much ground now as I could, I needed answers.

CHAPTER
Eighteen

The Goblin King

IN THE RIPPLING WATER of the seeing well, I caught a glimpse of her determined face as she made a beeline towards the castle. Her lithe figure moved with a purpose that hinted at her strength and determination. I couldn't help but feel a sense of awe as I watched her, a small smile tugging at my lips.

She was truly something else.

As the sun began its descent, the stained glass windows bathed the room in a kaleidoscope of colors. Time was of the essence; she had only two days left to complete the task. If she succeeded and everything went according to plan, I would finally be free. Free to seek the revenge that had been burning within me for so long.

Suddenly, the sound of footsteps on the stairs broke my reverie, and my heart leaped to my throat. I was no longer alone. The door slammed open, and Hendrix barged in, his presence shattering every sense of calm and serenity I had cultivated.

Tossed out the window.

Hopefully followed by Hendrix as he tried to speak to me. If he didn't stop huffing soon. . . his failure to catch his breath was grading on my patience. Whatever it was that he had to say must have been important enough for him to run all the way here. Despite being Fae, the curse limited far more than just access to power, to the magic, to the veins of it that flowed through the land. The power of healing was limited to all of us.

Lesser Fae and immortals could not access any of the Realm's magic, not while it was cursed. What power I could access had little to do with the curse. It was part of who I was, just like Hendrix. While we both could transform, we were restricted in what power and magic we could pull. I learned early on that if I sacrificed a little bit of myself, I could pull more. Weaving spells and webs in this game.

Hendrix, however, was a *special* case. I eyed him carefully as he finally tried to speak.

"She. . . she saw. . ." He paused as he took in another lung full of air. "She saw a hippogriff."

There it was.

Her face vanished from the well as I turned toward him. My eyes found Hendrix, crouched over clutching at his side. I could feel my heart race as the words settled within me. The anxiety and irritation coursed through my body. If she saw the hippogriff, then the magic of the curse was weakening. It was all beginning to crumble. The Realm was waking up, the magic was flowing ever so slightly again.

Finally.

There was a small sense of relief, everything I had worked so hard for was coming to fruition. But I should have known, calculated this possibility. I should have guessed this would happen. Of course the hippogriff would have found her, known exactly who she was. It would come back, especially if she was here. A chill ran down my spine, time truly was of the essence at this point.

"It approached her, sir" Hendrix said, this time with more steadiness to his words. He was no longer bent over, or panting, or taking in large amounts of air. Good, because it was really starting to irritate me. It took an enormous amount of effort not to actually toss him from the window. Nor fling my shadows at him for causing this disturbance, the only semblance of peace having been shattered by him bursting in without consideration.

By his mere presence.

"It's her, isn't it?" His words hung in the air.

I couldn't stop my reflex to roll my eyes but would not answer him, it was not any of his business.

Of course he would have figured it out, why wouldn't he have? Hendrix had spent more than enough time with her back in the Mortal Lands to put it together. But he never would have, had I not sent him there in the first place. Although he had proven himself useful, until now.

He was going to thwart this whole thing. Everything that had been designed right down to the tiniest detail to get her here, even going so far as to alter the miscalculations, and he was going to spoil it. Years' worth of careful planning.

"That is none of your business, Hendrix." I replied, far more irritated with him than I cared to admit. Irate with him really, I hated this male, and I did not want to be in his company. "You knew what your orders were. Keep her from death. Not to pry into her life or her past."

At least he had the common sense to remain quiet. Not daring to say another word as I glanced back at the seeing well. Her face re-emerged. She had covered a good distance. But she was going to wear herself thin.

"Sir, if I may be so bold?"

"No, you may not." I snapped, my eyes locked on her.

"But, if it really is her. . ."

"I'm warning you now, Hendrix."

He really had the audacity to presume such a notion. Of course it's her. Why wouldn't it be her? I no longer had the time I thought we did, forcing my hands. I had no other choice. But I would neither confirm nor deny it, I'd keep this to myself. But I knew Hendrix- he was smart, despite the unfortunate circumstances they found themselves in. And if he was smart. . . he would keep his mouth shut.

"Sir, I really must protest."

"Silence!"

Hendrix went still as my demand bounced around the room. He'd crossed a line, he knew as well as anyone where he needed to remain. Where his station was.

"I do not care what you have to say at this time. I do not care if you *feel* for the girl, if you worry for her. You know what is to be done. You know it has to be done. I didn't ask for you, I did not ask for your company. I do not want you here any more than you want to be here, let me make that perfectly clear." the shadows slipped from my fingers, twirling around the tips before leaking into the room.

It felt good, finally releasing them again. Even if I was angry. The power that dwelled within flickered in happiness. Everything I'd done, every bit of magic and power I had used before had a price. And if it was not for this stupid curse, I would have torn the world apart already. This bloody, unforgiving *curse.*

The anger rose, letting it linger, letting it consume me, the shadows rippling around us. The room darkened, the last of the sun snuffing out as my mood turned murderous.

This was Fate's fault.

Fate was cunning, it was poisonous. And it was messing with me. Fate was its own master and this was punishment, I *knew* it was. It was punishment for my choices, for my involvement in her own threads. For altering the path. . . for using her for my own gains. Fate knew how to play this game better than I ever could. It knew what I wanted, what I was after, and would throw every curve ball at me as I tried to reach the end.

But Fate forgot one thing.

I was death and darkness.

I was nightmare and shadow.

I was the dark to her light.

I was the master of my own game.

Fate was cruel.

Fate was unforgiving, and Fate had no power here. Not over me. I would win in the end, and I would have full access to the powers I had been blessed with. Magic would be unrestricted to me. And nobody, not the sisters, not the Immortal Gods, not even death, nothing would be able to stop me.

Because of who I was, who I *truly* was.

And I should be feared.

CHAPTER
Nineteen

Serra

MY DECISION TO RUN was a hasty one, and now my sides throbbed with each breath I took. I gasped for air, hoping to fill my lungs with enough oxygen to continue running. I grasped at my aching sides, but the pain only intensified. As I stumbled forward, the world around me began to change again. The endless prairie grasses slowly gave way to a lush forest, but it was not a daunting and ominous place. Instead, the trees and foliage intertwined in a captivating display of natural harmony. The enchanting beauty that enveloped me was nothing short of mesmerizing.

The trees intertwined with vines and moss, radiating a faint ethereal light. The air was heavy with the sweet and earthy scent of magic that emanated from the wood. It was unlike anything I had ever felt before; a powerful force that commanded respect.

The forest exuded an air of mystique, yet the sounds of the

prairie still lingered faintly in the distance. I could hear the chirping of crickets and the rustling of the breeze, but they were no match for the rustling of leaves and the creaking of branches in the wind. The forest was alive, with a pulsing heartbeat that resonated through the trees and the dirt beneath my feet. I felt the ancient magic in the air, a power born with the forest itself.

The serenity of the area was reminiscent of home, of the peaceful nights I spent in Rothnia. As I breathed in the cool night air, I was filled with a refreshing calmness that carried the scent of enchanted flora- hinting at the mystical world surrounding me. The sky above was a canvas of indigo, with the last remnants of sunset still visible on the horizon, casting a warm orange glow on everything. The clouds were low, as if they were perched on the horizon, creating an ethereal effect. The stars were starting to emerge, sparkling like diamonds in the dark.

The humidity had yet to set itself upon our continent, making the nights comfortable. Inirea and the Fae Realms were in that odd transition just as Rothnia was. Where winter had yielded to spring, and spring would soon yield to summer. While last night had felt cold, tonight felt marvelous. A cool spring breeze caressed my face, fluttering in my hair as it said hello. So unlike the wind that had whipped at me for most the day, as if it was angry.

The castle sat off in the distance, waiting and taunting me with itself. The sun was sinking down behind it, casting it all in an eerie darkness. It would take me another full day to reach it.

Tomorrow. . .

Tomorrow I will get my answers and end this madness. End this game of his, I would be triumphant. He would have to answer my questions and return what was rightfully mine.

Return me to Rothnia.

Despite being out of breath and my legs about to give out from under me, I did cover quite a bit of ground by sprinting. Knowing full well that I was racing against the clock, I was racing against the sun. Every hour I lingered, every second I wasted, counted against me. The longer I stayed here, the longer it took me, the more people would notice my absence, my disappearance. Not that it mattered, I had been invisible for most of my life. But did I want to remain invisible?

Did I want to remain on the outskirts, in the dark?

No. I did not want to be that girl anymore. I did not want to be just a nobody, someone else's victim. Maybe coming here had helped, maybe coming here was the right choice. Even if it felt like it wasn't.

Closing my eyes and taking in the sounds of the world around me, the smell. Listening closely to what was around me. This was peaceful. My eyes fluttered open to watch the last of the sun's rays. The bright orange disk was dipping lower and lower. Even as it finally sunk below the horizon, its rays flaring across the sky. The moon shone brilliantly as it said good night, taking over for the time being.

A timed dance between them.

I filled my lungs with more of the night air. The moment passed as I looked at the scenery around me. The trees beckoned to me once more, their branches sparkling with thousands of tiny fireflies. Swarms of them crowded the entrance as I peaked in. Swirling back and forth in a dance to music with little notes. Against my better judgment, I took a step forward. Only glancing back once to the world behind me, these woods did not seem dangerous.

In fact they were lovely and inviting.

The trees towered above me, their branches stretching out like skeletal fingers, casting eerie shadows on the ground. The air was thick with the scent of pine and damp earth, and I could hear the rustling of leaves and the scurrying of small animals in the underbrush. But the fireflies lit the path before me, weaving in and out of the trunks. The branches above sparkled like the night sky.

As I wandered, a soft hum sounded as if it emitted from the trees themselves. A song of such happiness, as if they were content here. In here, I felt safe. Cocooned in the trees as if they wanted to protect me. The fireflies danced around again, swirling around me as I pushed forward.

The path that I had been walking on finally opened up to a breathtaking sight. In front of me was a dark cenote nestled in a grotto, its still waters reflecting the night sky and the faint light of fireflies that floated around it. The water had risen to the rocky ledge's brim, displaying a brilliant shade of bright blue and crystal-clear clarity.

The sight of the cenote made me forget about my tiredness. I couldn't help but be awed by the serene beauty of the place, and yet a sense of eeriness lingered in the air. The cenote stretched out beyond the point where I stood, disappearing under rocks and greenery. It was an odd sensation being here, standing before this body of water that held so much mystery and history.

As I stood there, I couldn't help but feel as though time was slowing down, giving me the chance to take in everything around me. The longer I lingered, the farther I traveled, the more memories surfaced, some of which I had long forgotten. The veil of forgetfulness had lifted with each passing day, and this moment was no different.

Standing before the waters of the cenote, a particular memory came to mind. It was a legend that I had heard as a child, a fairytale story about another cenote similar to the one that I had just come across. I remembered hearing it from an old storyteller in the center of Rothnia while waiting for Nona to finish her appointment.

In the story, the cenote was said to be the gateway to the

Underground, home of the Death God. It was said to be so deep that the water appeared black, and no one had ever been able to find it. No one had seen it for centuries. The story had always fascinated me, and being in this cenote made it feel as though I was one step closer to that magical world.

As I gazed at the water, memories flooded back to me. The story of the cenote as the gateway to the Underground. I remembered asking Nona about it, but she brushed it off as a farce, a made-up story. I believed her, as I believed many of the things she told me. Her stories had come true, just like the warning she had given me about the Goblin King who had whisked me away at night.

My attention shifted back to the water. The bright moonbeams filtered down through the dense trees, casting an ethereal glow on the serene water. The grotto was aglow with the light of the fireflies that flickered around, making the place seem and feel surreal. I couldn't help but be drawn to the tranquil waters before me, a little piece of paradise amidst all the chaos of my life.

I slipped off one of my slippers and dipped my toes into the water, feeling the warmth emanating from it as if it was heated by a forbidden magic. My muscles ached and yearned for a warm bath to ease the pain and calm my mind. I couldn't resist any longer and stripped down to my chemise, ready to immerse myself in the peaceful waters.

I stepped into the water slowly, testing the depth with cautious movements. The rocky bottom of the cenote felt stable under my feet. Although I wasn't the best swimmer, the warm water embraced me as I waded deeper, submerging me up to my chest. It felt like an old lover's embrace, its warmth filling my lungs before I dipped below the surface.

I swam towards the center of the cenote, my only company being the night sky as I floated weightlessly in the dark grotto. The chirping of crickets and the hum of trees created a soothing melody that filled my soul, making me feel at peace. I closed my eyes, letting the sounds carry me away.

It wasn't until the trees' melody and the crickets' chirping faded away that a sense of unease crept overt me. The alarm bells in my head went off, and I opened my eyes, dipping lower into the water. I scanned the edges of the rock, looking for any sign of what had disturbed my peaceful swim. That's when I saw him- on the edge of the cenote, watching from within the trees. His eyes glowed in the darkness, and the branches seemed to caress his shoulders, as if beckoning him forward.

I felt a tendril of shadow seep from his fingers, twirling around him like a serpent, and I couldn't help but marvel at this magnificent creature. This male I had encountered over and over. My heart raced as I gazed at him, frozen in fear and fascination. The longer I stared, the more the tendrils of darkness seemed to grow, as if taunting me to come closer.

Stepping forward into the light of the moon, into the lights of the fireflies, his gaze never left mine. His long hair pulled back into a bun to reveal the column of his neck. My core heated as I stared. A wave of lust washing over me. The need to have him coursing through my body. I did not want to admit it, but he was a sight to behold. His bare chest stark against his dark trousers.

Every muscle rippled along his arms, his chest, his legs. I felt my cheeks flush as he stopped at the edge, his fingers undoing the tops of his trousers. I wanted to watch, oh did I want to watch as he slipped them off but the voice inside my head screamed at me to look away.

Closing my eyes I turned, waiting for the sound of the water as he splashed into it. Turning around to him again, but he had disappeared.

Spinning around, looking for him, he resurfaced a few feet away. The water dripping off of him. His eyes alight with mischief and need. Slowly he swam toward me, our gazes never leaving each other's. When he was close enough, his hand found mine. It was cold, his fingers intertwining through mine as he pulled me to him. Where I expected warmth, I was met with chills.

His chest was like ice.

"You're cold." My voice came out in a whisper, cracking slightly. The chill of his skin under the palms of my hands caused me to look down, he was naked. The hardness of him pushing against my leg. I was very aware at that moment that my chemise did not cover anything. It was as sheer as gossamer in the water.

My cheeks flushed again.

He cocked his head to the side but did not speak. Instead, lifting my chin to meet his gaze. His lips found mine. It was soft, tender, but it wasn't right. He demanded more, pulling me closer still. Another wave of lust, need, and want coursed through me. Whatever magic this was, it was the worst kind. Temptation, seduction, demand. All together forming a spell over my senses. I couldn't help myself as I wrapped my legs around his waist. His hands found my hips, holding me there.

Oh, this was not good.

I knew this would not be good, what was I *doing*? I had no control over my senses. Over my own body.

The kiss deepened as his tongue forced itself past my lips, my heart slamming away in my chest. A rush of heat coursing through my core. The magic this creature was extruding had a firm grip on me. For as much as I wanted it to stop, I *didn't* at all. I wanted more, more. . . *more*.

His hands pushed my soaked chemise up, my thighs bare to his

226

palms. My breasts peaked from the chill, sensitive against the wet fabric. Even as they brushed along the hard planes of his chest.

A cold chill ran down my spine.

My fear caused more alarms in my head to go off. Part of me knew this was not who I thought it was. That I should be trying to get away. But the other part of me wanted to stay because it wanted more. Drunk on lust, and need, wanting him. All of him. Another wave slammed into me. My fingers found themselves tangled in his bun, pulling it loose as the wet strands fell down past his shoulders.

He broke our kiss briefly to nibble at my neck, his tongue running down the column of my throat as he carried me toward the edge. I would allow him to take me there. Unable to stop him. I would allow him to strip the wet fabric from my skin and taste me from head to toe. Allow his teeth to nib down in any soft and tender spot as he found his way between my legs. I would allow him to enter me, take me hard and fast. Because the magic told me to. Because it would coerce me to.

His lips parted mine again as his tongue entered to mingle with mine. But this was not the Goblin King, this was not the kiss I remembered from the Caves of Desire. But that was just a dream, my mind could have made up any scenario. Maybe he was cold, maybe he had no warmth to him. No, that wasn't true, his touch lit a fire under my skin. His touch caused me to burn, caused everything to burn.

Whatever, *whoever* this was, did no such thing. Not in the way that felt right.

I quickly recoiled from him, feeling a sense of panic wash over me. I desperately wanted to escape from this creature and make my way to the safety of the edge of the cenote where my clothes lay. But his grip on me only grew tighter, his sneer deepening as his sharp teeth were revealed. I shuddered at the thought of those teeth sinking into my flesh. As I struggled against him, I could feel the water around us churning and rippling with our movements. His claws dug into my skin, causing small droplets of blood to fall into the water. I couldn't help but let out a small cry of pain.

Desperation coursed through my veins, my mind raced for a way to defend myself. Without thinking, I raised my fist and punched him square in the face. The impact of my knuckles connecting with his flesh echoed through the night air. He let out a shrill cry, its hands flying up to its nose as it stumbled backwards.

For a moment, I was frozen in shock at what I had just done. I was momentarily stunned by my own actions. I had never hit anyone before. But I couldn't afford to dwell on it. I had to get away. I turned and ran towards the edge of the waters, I was so close, *so close*. Tears stung my eyes as I fled, the fear and adrenaline making it hard to see where I was going.

The sound of rippling water reached my ears, causing me to freeze in place and turn towards the source.

I couldn't believe what I was seeing. The creature that was once before me had transformed into something beyond my worst nightmares. Its eyes, now a chilling yellow and black, seemed to pierce through me. It's fangs elongated, now sharp and menacing as its tongue slithered out like a serpent- flicking through the air with a forked tip. The sight of the creature and its magic held me in a trance-like state. Was it fear or desire that made my body shake uncontrollably? I wasn't sure, but I knew that I had to break free from its hold.

My heart was racing as I gasped for breath- my eyes locked on the creature. It seemed to hesitate for a moment, perhaps considering its next move. I quickly surveyed my surroundings, searching for any possible escape route. The moonlit water was behind me, and the dense woods offered no clear path to safety. The creature was still coming for me, now more grotesque and distorted than before, its movements unpredictable. I knew I had to act fast if I wanted to survive.

Once more, the creature reached out for me with clammy hands that felt as cold as death. But as it did, I couldn't help but notice that something was different. Its form was changing, contorting into a grotesque shape with a sickly green tint. The smooth, pale skin that had once resembled the Goblin King was cracking and falling away, revealing the true monster beneath.

Its eyes, which had previously held a spark of mischief, were now filled with a menacing hunger that made my blood run cold The creature's gaze roamed over my exposed torso, lingering on my heaving chest and the curve of my hips. I tried to pull away, but its grip was too strong, and it continued to push me closer to the water's edge. As I struggled against its hold, I could feel its breath hot against my skin. Its hands roamed over my body, exploring and groping, as if it were trying to claim me as its own.

I shuddered at the thought, trying to break free from its grasp. But the creature's grip only tightened, its fingers digging into my flesh. As I looked into its eyes, I knew that this was not Goblin King I had encountered earlier This was something much darker and more dangerous, and I feared for my life.

My mind went over every creature I had heard about as a child. Every creature that existed that we were warned about. What creature would seduce a woman, what creature had magic strong enough to want a woman to mate with it? My mind raced as I tried to figure it out. My heart raced as I realized the full horror of what I was facing.

It was an Incubus.

The demon's grip tightened around my leg, the tail coiling around me like a snake. Its scaly texture cold against my skin, sending shivers down my spine. I gasped for air, my heart racing as I tried to pull away. But it was too strong, too determined to have me.

As I struggled, I couldn't help but think of the stories I'd heard of demons like this. They were creatures that sought out women in their sleep, taking them as mates to produce offspring. The thought of being trapped with this demon forever, bound to it by some unholy bond, made my stomach turn.

My panic turned to terror as the demon's tail and arms lifted me off the ground and carried me closer to the water's edge. I could feel the cool water lapping at my feet, threatening to swallow me up if I couldn't break free. I fought with all my might, slamming my fists into the demon's face in a desperate attempt to make it release me.

For a moment, I thought I had succeeded as the demon let go of me, giving me a chance to stumble backwards. But before I could get too far, its tail wrapped around my leg again, yanking me back toward it. I could feel its hot breath on my skin, its eyes raking over my body as it contemplated what to do with me next.

The magic that had once held me in its thrall now felt like a curse. It compelled me to comply, to give in to the demon's desires, but I refused to be its slave. I screamed, the sound echoing through the forest as I fought against the demon's hold. My hands clawed at its face, trying to find any weakness I could exploit.

Finally, my palm connected with its nose again, sending a spray of dark blood into the air. The demon sneered, but its grip on me faltered for a moment. That was all the opportunity I needed to break free, to scramble to my feet and reach for my clothes. But the demon was quick, its tail coiling around my leg and flinging me to the ground.

I knew I had to keep fighting, to keep trying to break free, no matter how impossible it seemed. Because if I didn't, this demon would take me and I would be lost forever.

The demon's face loomed over me, and in a split second, I acted on pure instinct. With all the force I could muster, my foot connected with its chest, sending the creature flying backwards into the water. As it emerged from the depths, its disguise had vanished, revealing a hideous sight.

It's true self.

Its skin was a disgusting shade of green and covered in rough scales with writhing tendrils of what I could only assume was hair sprouted from the top of its head. Its nose had shrunk to tiny slits, resembling that of a snake and sharp claws longer than my fingers protruded from its hands. Its teeth, yellowed and menacing, flashed in my direction as its tongue darted in and out. After a moment, it righted itself- its eyes locked on me. I knew there was nowhere for me to run, and that I wouldn't be able to escape fast enough.

I felt the impending doom as it stalked towards me again.

But a tendril of dark shadows snaked across the ground from behind me. As the shadows enveloped the demon, it let out a final, blood-curdling screech. I couldn't believe what I had just witnessed. The power of the Goblin King was beyond anything I had ever imagined.

His shadows, so thick and suffocating, seemed to have a life of their own. They moved with a fluid grace that was both terrifying and awe-inspiring. Gliding over the grass and dirt as they went for the demon. The shadows had snuffed it out as it encapsulated it, blocking its access to me. I was paralyzed, from the depths of the trees the Goblin King stepped forward.

His shadows rolled off of him in a thick dark coat.

I'd never seen anything like this before, never seen what his shadows could do. They were different from the ones I had seen before. They *felt* different, they *were* different. These shadows were lethal, older. I could feel it in my whole being that these shadows were not from here, it made my skin prickle. My heart raced as something deep flickered, something I'd never felt before, calling to them. It hummed in greeting. These shadows were a magic far older than the Fae Realm itself.

The tears pricked at my eyes as my body became my own again. As I regained control of my senses. The magic slipped away back to where it had come from. The disgust finally washed over me at what had just happened. I only glanced back once to where the incubus had been, but it was gone. As the shadows retreated it left the waters of the cenote empty, quiet again.

My voice was hoarse. My scream had ripped it to shreds. "What happened to it?"

His voice was cold as he replied. "Does it matter?"

I shook my head as I stood. I couldn't answer him, I couldn't even look at him. Even if I tried, I knew the tears would stop any words from coming out. I refused to be a hysterical mess in front of him. Standing before him after this encounter was far more embarrassing than anything. He'd saved my life again, whether he wanted me to be or not, I was indebted to him. I opened my mouth to say thank you, but he spoke before the words could form on my tongue.

"It hasn't even been forty-eight hours." He glared. His tone came off even colder than before. "How? How are you such a magnet to things that would otherwise kill you? Or in this instance, try to seduce you?"

Oh, oh this male really was infuriating!

Through all of that I had forgotten how much he managed to get under my skin. How truly angry he could make me.

And I was going to express my thanks?

The unshed tears dried up as I stared at him. His black doublet was unbuttoned, exposing the white shirt he had tucked into the tops of his trousers. The fireflies cast him in a warm glow, far from what the mood felt like with him standing before me.

Icy and dark.

His gaze was calculating as he looked me up from head to toe. I had forgotten I was in my chemise, and I was soaking wet. Leaving nothing for him to imagine. Instinctively, I grabbed my clothes again, covering myself.

"Do you mind?" I snapped back at him, clutching my clothes closely. I'd hoped that maybe, *maybe* he would have some kind of decency to give me privacy.

"No."

I growled in frustration, the sound ripping from my throat. The fucking audacity this. . . this stupid, loathsome male had. Glaring at him as I turned to find a place to dress.

"Fine."

My tone was harsh yes, but he was aggravating. Slipping into the shadows of the trees and dressing quickly his voice carried to me. "What were you thinking, Serra? What did I tell you?"

"Oh, I don't know. I was thinking about how much I really wanted to bathe. To have a moment of *peace*, before running into your annoying ass again." The sarcasm had laced itself into my words before I could stop it.

"Excuse me?"

Once I was dressed again, I stepped back out to see him staring at the water, calculating and scrutinizing it. If he was going to be an ass, I could be one too.

"You heard me."

His eyes found mine, "It wasn't as if I got a moment's peace either. Anyone or anything could have heard that scream and come running. You're lucky it was I who got here first. I did warn you, you are not safe here."

"Oh. . . Oh! I'm *sorry* to be such a bother to you."

His growl reached my ears, the sound of it making me pause. The sound of it caused my body to react in a way I never would have thought. My fingers twitched as I stared at him. As his eyes bore back into mine.

Slowly, so slowly he stepped forward. His steps were careful as he approached. His fingers reached up to brush away the hair that had fallen into my face. Without thinking- without realizing- I'd leaned into his touch. His fingers were warm on my face as his thumb ran along the bottom of my jaw. The hot trail they left in their wake, tracing along the column of my neck. His fingers gripped my chin, forcing me to look at him. I hadn't realized I'd closed my eyes until his gaze bore into me. The intensity of it made me shrink back.

"You do not know what that thing could have done to you. Do you understand that? I don't like to repeat myself so I will only say this once more, you're not safe here. I don't know what more I can do to make you understand that. Do not test my patience or the willingness I have to save you." As he spoke, his grip on my chin tightened.

I winced, but I couldn't look away from his piercing gaze. I could see the concern and frustration etched on his face, and for a moment, I was taken aback. I had never seen him like this before. His voice was commanding, but it was also laced with a tinge of fear.

Fear for me.

I pulled away from his grip, my own anger simmering beneath the surface. "You don't have to save me," I spat back at him. "I never asked for your help."

He narrowed his eyes at me, his jaw clenching tightly. "You might not have asked for it, but that doesn't mean you don't need it. You're reckless and foolish, Serra. You don't understand the dangers that lurk in this world."

I scoffed at his words, rolling my eyes. "Oh please, spare me the lecture. I know how to take care of myself."

He let out a humorless laugh, shaking his head in disbelief. "That doesn't mean you're immune to danger. You may have been lucky so far, doesn't mean that luck will last forever."

I bristled at his words, my own frustration boiling over. "I don't need you to lecture me, I need you to leave me alone. I don't want your help."

He took a step closer to me, his eyes flashing with anger. "You don't understand," he said, his voice low and dangerous. "The creatures that inhabit this world are not like anything you've ever encountered before. They're cunning, they're deadly, and they will stop at nothing to get what they want. And right now, what they want is you."

"And what makes you any different from them?"

He glared at me, "You don't know anything about me," his jaw tightened as he spoke through gritted teeth. "I am not like them. I may be a fae, but I have a conscience. I have morals."

I snorted, unconvinced. "And yet, you seem to be the most dangerous of them all."

His eyes flashed with a mixture of anger and hurt but he didn't deny it. Instead, he leaned in close to me, his voice low and dangerous. "You don't know the half of it."

I instinctively stepped back, my heart pounding in my chest. I couldn't deny the effect he had on me. Even when he was angry, he was still so damn attractive. But I pushed that thought aside, I swallowed before I said, "My life is not your responsibility."

His lip peaked as he glared at me, his tone was harsh as he said, "You're so stubborn. You're vulnerable to all sorts of dangers that you can't even begin to comprehend."

I glared back at him, my own anger flaring up to match his once again. "I can take care of myself."

He stepped even closer, "And what happens when you can't? What happens when you're faced with something that you can't handle? Will you just let yourself get hurt or worse?"

I shook my head, refusing to back down. I didn't want to believe that he was right, didn't want to admit it. I swallowed and forced myself to speak, asking instead, "What was that creature doing here anyway?"

"I don't know." He replied, his gaze shifting to the water once more. "They don't usually wander this far, sticking closely to-"

He glanced back at me, but the look on his face had changed to one of indifference again, "It doesn't matter. You have two days."

Slipping away back into the trees, bathed in darkness, the Goblin King left me next to the waters of the cenote. The soft hum of the trees ringing in my ears again, the fireflies' light flickering as they danced. Leaving me with even more questions than before.

CHAPTER
Twenty

Serra

I HAD MANAGED TO find a place to crawl into to sleep, the roots of a tree creating a natural shelter. Curling and twisting together to form a small hut. The earth was covered in moss and dirt, but it was comfortable. Creating a small sleeping space, the spongy earth smelling like home. I missed home, I missed the garden, the cottage. Even Rothnia and its people.

"Soon you'll be able to go home." I reassured myself. "Soon all of this will be over and you will never have to think about it again. You'll be able to sleep in your own bed, and forget, as if none of this has happened."

There was no point in bothering with any kind of fire tonight, fear of other creatures; one possibly more terrifying than the incubus, finding me. I felt so dirty, far more than I had with Kaston. Even after all of that, this left me with a sour taste. A disgust I could not get rid of even after I had risked bathing again in the waters, in some kind of hope that it would wash some of the feeling off.

But the way its hands and its tail felt on my skin had been burned into my mind. Its cold and clammy skin under my palms, its tongue as it had licked my exposed flesh. A shudder coursed through me as I laid my head down on the mossy earth. Again I had found myself drawn to the Goblin King. Again my body reacted in a way I could not explain. I could not tell what my natural reaction had been and what had been the magic of the incubus.

Sleep invaded my thoughts, allowing them to drift off. My mind was finally able to relax. But one single image, his face, his eyes- they were ingrained in my head even as I fell into slumber. I dreamed of him again. But he was not as I see him now. He was younger, he was thinner. He was not bulked up, so unlike how he was now. So much younger, years younger.

But you could not mistake him.

The dream played in my mind, it was as if I was floating above. Watching the pair as they sat under a large oak tree, in a small courtyard surrounded by stone and green. The sun shone down on the pair as the warmth of it brushed against my own skin.

He lounged in the branch above her, an apple in his hand. He tossed it up a couple of times before catching it. Taking a single bite before tossing it again. She sat at the base of the tree, a book in her hands. She was a mere child, possibly six or seven. Her dark green dress was tucked under her feet, her long dark hair had been braided back out of her face. But it was her bright green eyes; focused on the text of the book.

They sat in silence, refusing to acknowledge each other, he tossed the apple again but failed to catch it this time. It'd fallen far outside his reach on the branch as he stretched for it, almost falling himself. He watched it as it fell toward the earth. Hitting her head- before landing in her lap, the juices staining the pages. While their mouths moved, there were no words that could be understood. She stood up as she held the apple, his face had gone angry as he sat up on the branch before hopping down. He lunged forward and yanked the book from her hands.

The quarrel between them grew as they exchanged words. The apple that had once been clutched in her hand, found its way flying across between them. It soared true, hitting him in the face. The look he gave her was one of loathing, dangling the book in front of her as she reached for it. But he tossed it to the ground, taking the toe of his boot and kicking it across the grass. They watched as it fluttered, the pages falling out and scattering. The book landed in a puddle, and as she watched the words leak away from the pages, the only words that were clear, the only words that were heard. "I hate you." She had turned and ran, tears in her eyes as she left the courtyard. He stood glaring after her, arms crossed.

The image faded away as I felt the warmth of the sun on my face, the sound of songbirds accompanying the morning. For a brief moment my mind wondered if it had all been a dream, that I had never left Rothnia. I was home safely, in my bed. The sound of Nona would trickle in shortly, signaling that it was time to rise. But I awoke to a bed of white flowers, the grass and clover covered in dew and the trees above swishing in the breeze.

My bed of mossy earth and tree roots had cradled me as I slept, keeping me safe. Crawling out of the roots, the flowers spread farther than I had imagined. They had not been there the night before. I was sure of it. Not that I could remember or had seen anyway. But I had been so tired and so ready for sleep that I probably had missed them. I seemed to be doing that a lot lately. My mind was a muddled mess enough already.

But I'd never seen anything like this before, the ground was covered in them. Blanketed in white flowers and green clover, they stretched on and on. The palm of my hand tickled, peeking down as I pulled it back to my chest. A white flower bloomed in the clover before me. Sprouting up toward the sun. I watched it as it grew from the dirt, its petals stretching out to bathe in it. I had never seen something like that before, it was strange.

What the hell was happening? What the fuck was going on?

I felt the sense of despair weighing down on me days ago as I looked out from atop the cliff, my eyes had met a desolate sight. The trees that were brown and lifeless, and the prairies that were barren with colorless grasses swaying in the wind. It was as if the land had lost its soul, and with every passing moment, it had died a little more.

But as I ventured deeper into this strange place, something miraculous happened. The land began to come alive. It was as if an invisible force was breathing life back into the earth. I felt a stirring within me, something unfamiliar and unrecognizable. It was a small spark, a tiny ember, burning bright in the pit of my stomach. No longer was the land dying; it was alive, and it was thriving. It was pulsating with renewed energy.

It was like it had awoken from a deep slumber.

My confusion and lack of understanding only grew as I watched the world around me transform. My own transformation, my time here. I couldn't help but wonder, what had caused this change? What secrets did this place hold? I scanned the area around me once again, taking in the beauty of the forest in the warm glow of the sun's rays. The trees swayed gently in the breeze, their leaves rustling with the sound of magic. Above me, birds chittered and sang, welcoming the dawn of a new day. The beams from the rising sun highlight the dust and magic of the forest, bathing everything in its warm glow.

Sunrise.

I'd slept past sunrise, I hadn't done that in ages, but it was not like I felt refreshed either. I felt far more tired than I had before. It was like each night I slept here, the more and more exhausted I felt, the more I wanted to just rest and never wake up. Maybe this was the Goblin King's way of keeping me at bay. Exhaust me so I never make it.

But I would not, could not let him win. Yes, I knew I was stubborn, I always had been. I acknowledged it. And it would be my stubbornness and my will to prove him wrong that would help me with this, that would get me where I needed to go. A memory from the well in my mind, the ones of Nona sprang forward. Slowly more of her had come to me, more of my life with her.

Somehow I'd forgotten.

There was one time Nona had asked me to wash up. I had just come in from outside, having been on another one of my adventures. I was covered in mud from head to toe, I'd fallen on the banks of the river. And all my efforts to get out clean had gone wrong. By the time I had made it into the cottage most of the mud had crusted in my hair and on my dress.

The climb up the muddy banks and the walk home had exhausted me and all I wanted to do was go to bed. She'd told me, insisted actually, that I needed to take a bath before dinner and I refused. The pout I wore that day would have caused an apple to turn, that's how sour she said my face had been. I remember her voice, the dictation in it as she said. "Child, if you do not wipe that look off your face, and get in that bath now, so help me I will force you into it myself."

I'd crossed my arms across my chest and pushed my lip out farther. But it had no effect on her. She looked at me once more and said, "I will not take that bullheadedness anymore, pout all you want. But you will get in that damn tub. *Now.*"

She pointed to the copper basin with the water she had warmed up for me. The soap and wash cloth sitting on a small table beside it. It wasn't a large tub, taking up much of the floor in front of the fireplace when we did take it out. But it was big enough for us to bathe in. She had started muttering under her breath again about something as she went to retrieve a towel- after I stripped off my dress and climbed into the water. The caked mud on my skirt cracking and falling to the floor. Picking up the washcloth to scrub what mud remained and washing my hair.

I could hear her in the bedroom, muttering something about my father and stubbornness. I'd felt my hopes rise as my heart fluttered, excited to learn more and ask the burning questions that I wanted to know. If I took after him, what he was like, was he kind and considerate. I wanted to know everything about him. Because it was all I had to connect with him. I remembered nothing about him, I knew he died, but I did not know much else.

I wanted to know more about my family I had lost, about all of them, but I was too scared. We never really talked about any of them. Even as I grew older. Nona never said much even when I asked. A small feeling that she knew more than she was telling me always lingered in our conversations. That there was something she wanted to say but could not.

It was only later that evening that I had gathered enough courage to ask as she brushed out my hair, her long knobby fingers working their way through my tangled locks with the bone comb. We had dined on a light supper earlier that evening, mainly root vegetable soup and bread, nestled together in front of the fireplace. The copper bathing tub had been drained and set aside, freeing the space up again. I kept my mouth shut as we ate, not knowing how to ask her about them. She clicked her tongue at the couple spots of mud I had missed behind my ear. "I will tell you about your father another time. Right now, it is time for bed. It is time for you, dear child, to go to sleep."

Nona set the comb down on the nightstand as I crawled into bed. Tucking me in under the blankets and brushing my hair back, before sitting down in the old rocking chair in the corner. As her voice carried through the air, my eyes getting heavier and heavier, she told me another story instead that night.

One I had never heard before.

Thinking back on it now I wish she had told me more about them. More about my father. I wished she had been more open about things, about my life before. I wished. I wished for so many things, and they never happened. I *wished* and here I was. Of all the things that were odd and curious this was by far the most perplexing. Playing the Goblin King's game. Being in the Fae Realm. Racing across the lands to reach the castle in hopes that I could win.

I would.

The forest went on for what felt like forever, and with each step, I discovered something new. The dense foliage created a canopy overhead, casting the forest floor in dappled sunlight. I marveled at the variety of trees that surrounded me. They were of all shapes and sizes, some with gnarled trunks, others with smooth bark that gleamed in the sunlight. The trees were not like the evergreens in Rothnia that I was accustomed to, they were diverse and each one seemed to have its own personality.

The Ebony Woods were a tangle of twisted trees, with branches that seemed to reach out to grab me as I passed. The snag trees were even more peculiar, with branches that were so tangled that they seemed to be in a perpetual embrace as the reached towards the sky. In the glen, there were paper birch trees with bark so thin it appeared to be peeling off in layers. There was this enchanted forest, where the trees seemed to glow with a soft, otherworldly light.

The forest was alive with the sound of birds and insects. I could hear the chirping of crickets, the buzz of bees, and the soft rustling of leaves as the wind swept through the trees.

The forest was full of life, and it was a wonder to behold.

As I walked, my thoughts were consumed by the beauty of the forest. I didn't notice the rock hidden under the mossy brush until it was too late. My toe collided with it, and I went flying forward. It was a natural reaction to brace myself for the fall, to catch myself with my hands outstretched. I expected the pain of the impact to radiate up my limbs, but what happened next was beyond my wildest imaginings.

As my hands touched the ground, little white flowers sprouted from the mossy earth. They appeared to be delicate and fragile, but they stood tall and proud. The moss-grown earth welcomed its new members as they curled up from the dirt toward the beaming sun. The sight was breathtaking, and I couldn't help but stare in wonder.

Curiosity got the better of me as I sat on the ground, surveying the area immediately around me. I placed my hand on the fallen tree trunk that sat closest to where I'd fallen. As I did so, life bloomed where my fingers touched. The white capped mushrooms grew everywhere my fingers had been, leaving behind a trail. It was as if my touch had awakened the forest, and it was responding to me. I snatched my hand back and looked at my fingers, they tingled with a strange energy. I couldn't explain it, but I knew that something magical was happening in this forest.

"Well, that's a bit odd."

Definitely another inquiry to ask about because this was more than just a *little* strange. My lungs heaved a sigh as I stood up, the forest was enchanted. It had nothing to do with me. It had nothing to do with what I was just able to do.

No. That has to be what it was. There was a magic sitting in here that caused that.

Yes. That's right. That's what it was.

Lifting the hem of my skirt I stepped over the fallen log, now covered in mushrooms, they sparkled in the sun as I walked away. Happy that they were in existence, leaving them behind to grow. The sooner I got out of here the better.

I TRAVELED THE PATH alone for another couple of hours inside the forest before it opened up again. The path winding in several directions. Stumped as to which way I should go, I took a moment to ponder everything that has happened since arriving here.

Hendrix, The Goblin King, Jesper, the Rock Trolls, the Hippogriff, the Enchanted Forest with its Incubus, the Caves of Desire. This place was riddled with oddities and strange things. Everything about this place made me feel uncomfortable, but it was also so familiar. Everything here made it feel like I was meant to be here.

A semblance of . . . no.

No, this was not home.

What was I thinking?

My lips erupted into hysterical laughter. If anyone were to stumble upon me now, they would surely deem me insane. But maybe they were right. Perhaps this entire experience was nothing more than a fever dream, a manifestation of my own manic state. Had I contracted some sort of illness that conjured up this entire adventure? It certainly would explain a lot.

Or maybe I had hit my head, slipping into a comatose state that brought forth these wild hallucinations. Maybe Caine and Kaston were nothing but figments of my imagination. Perhaps the Goblin

King and I never shared any meaningful moments. And Nona, she was probably just waiting for me to snap out of it and come back to reality.

The sound of a bird interrupted my thoughts, drawing my gaze up to the cloudless blue sky. I wondered if it ever rained here, unlike the Mortal Lands where it had rained at least once in the last few days. But here, there were no signs of rain clouds. As I watched the dark silhouette of the bird soaring overhead, I knew what and who it was.

Was he here to check my progress again?

Hoping something would stop me from reaching the end? Whatever it was, he was more infuriating now than he had been before. But a small part of me wanted to see him.

A small spark, the ember in the pit of my stomach fluttered to life as I watched him in the skies above. The hope in my chest bloomed that I would get to see him.

Oh Gods. . .

What was *wrong* with me?

"The only reason you are in this position is because of him. You stupid fool, how can you hope like that? You're an idiot Serra."

The words left my mouth as I took the path to the right, the castle remained in the distance. I scoffed at myself as I carried on. The worn path wound its way over the countryside. Around hills, over hills, through more prairies and fields that once hosted wildflowers, past abandoned homes, farms and every so often in the distance, a small cluster of buildings would come into view.

Everything was quiet, there was no one here.

The land was abandoned just as the stories said. Where has everyone gone? What happened to them? What was *really* going on here? I was so caught up in my own thoughts that I did not notice it at first. The small lake and the creature that sat on its edge.

It was larger than I was, capable of pinning me in place. Its paws were as large as dinner plates, its body rippled with muscle under its tan coat. Its wings were tucked tightly to its body, the reddish hue of its mane reflecting in the sunlight. But it did not have the typical face of a lion, no it had a human face. The creature before me was one of myth and legend.

What was it doing here?

I watched the Sphinx as it sat on the outcropping of rocks, its tail swishing back and forth. It was distracted by the fish in the waters before it. The path, *unfortunately*, ran right by it, but maybe. . . if I was quiet enough, *maybe* I could sneak past.

Maybe it would not see or hear me.

But as I took a step forward, luck would not be so kind today. The gravel under my foot crunched, causing my whole body to tense. Its ears peaked up as it turned, its eyes finding mine.

"Halt, who goes there?" The accent in which it spoke was strange. An odd mix of those I had encountered on the docks from Elliner and the villagers of Rothnia.

My heart thundered away in my chest, hoping that it would leave me be, hoping that it would not attack. My words were a tangled mess on my tongue as I tried to speak, only managing to squeak out, "Please, I have to pass."

It ignored me as it moved with a fluid grace to snatch a fish from the glistening waters. Its paw closed around the wriggling thing with lightning speed- it smiled at it for a moment, its sharp teeth glinting in the light. The fish writhed and flopped desperately, its scales shimmering in the sun, as the creature observed it with a curious intensity. Without hesitating it lifted its paw and brought it down sharply. The sound of its razor-sharp claws sinking into the fish's flesh bounced off the rocks as the fish wriggled and twisted- its mouth gaping open and closed as it contemplated its next move.

"Not without my say so you won't." It said after a moment, its eyes scanned over me. They were an odd color of gold, "Why are you here? Are you lost?"

I shook my head, finding my voice this time, "I'm not lost, but I have to get to the castle. So if you could allow me to pass that would be appreciated."

It watched me closely, its eyes narrowing as I worried my lip. It sniffed the air once before asking, "What are you?"

Had it never seen a mortal before?

"A human."

It scoffed. "Highly unlikely. But I will agree to disagree with you, *human*."

My brows furrowed in confusion, maybe it *has* never met a human before and does not know what we are, or what we look like I suppose.

"What is your name?" it asked.

"Serra."

The laugh that came from the beast was a mix of human and lion. A roar with a high pitch of mirth. Its paw slapped the fish again, the mouth gaping open wide.

"Maybe in the Mortal Lands."

"What do you mean?"

It closed its mouth, considering for a moment before saying, "I will give you a chance to pass, *Serra*. But if you cannot solve my riddle, then you will have to turn back, and go around."

Solve his riddle? I do not have the time nor the energy to turn back and start again. "But. . . I have to pass through here. I cannot go back."

It shook its head and said, "Solve my riddle and you can pass. On my honor."

I considered for a moment before I nodded my head. Maybe it

would be easy, I was never really good at riddles. It spoke quickly, pacing the path before me as it abandoned the fish on the edge, it had stopped breathing.

"I am ne'er changing,

Woven into Destiny.

We are sisters, though

You cannot escape me.

Freewill is my Enemy,

But balanced between us.

I will not give up on you,

Even if you delay me.

What am I?"

I felt the groan in the back of my throat, the disheartened feeling as it finished. After everything I had done so far, with how far I had come, a riddle was going to stop me. But I thought over the words, trying to piece them together. I should never have hoped that this would be easy.

Why would it have been?

"Take all the time you need, I am in no hurry." the sphinx said, picking up the fish. It lounged on the rock, the fish in its paws.

It may not have been in a hurry, but I was.

The words of the riddle wove around in my head. I'm never changing, woven into destiny, we're sisters. What did that mean? You cannot escape me, free will is my enemy. But balanced between us?

Well, one could define Freewill as every action and all of its consequences can be individually determined and that the results of those actions is entirely dependent upon the choice that is made by someone. But it is an enemy to what? I will not give up on you, even if you delay me.

What could it be?

I hated riddles, *hated* them, but it did not stop me as I considered this one for a while. Even with the time I sat there thinking about it- honestly, I could have turned around and gone back to the fork in the road by now. I caught sight of the sphinx again, it was sunbathing with its eyes closed. If I didn't know any better, I would've guessed it was sleeping. I wanted to take my chances but I dared not try to sneak past it for fear of the consequences I could possibly incur.

My mind stirred, causing me to ponder deeply. *Consequences.*

The thought of it sent shivers down my spine. Every decision, every action, had an outcome. Although people held the power of free will, they could not outrun their destiny. It was a force that held sway over their lives, whether they liked it or not.

Destiny was woven with. . .

"Fate. The answer is fate." The words came flying from my lips as the sphinx opened an eye. I felt a small sense of pride and relief as it looked at me. A smile spread across my face as I stood there watching.

"Ah. . .very good Serra. There is hope for you. You will do well. Welcome home, Child of Starlight."

I beamed for a second before its words sunk in. The term it used as it stared back at me. Wait. . . what? "I'm sorry, you must be confused."

It stood as it spoke, stepping forward. It took everything in me to not step back in fear. "I am many things, but confused is not one of them."

"I don't understand." That seemed to be the joke here, the theme of this adventure. Let's see how much Serra cannot understand and how crazy it makes her. It was unfair.

"Have you not noticed the world around you? What your presence here is doing?" Its eyes watched my face. When I did not answer it went on. "The land is awakening. It is reviving. It's pulling what it needs from *you*, have you never wondered why the world bloomed around you?

Why the birds, animals, and plants, are attracted to you? Consider it for a moment."

It cocked its head at me, contemplating. "No, I suppose you do not. Curious. I cannot see past. . . that is strange indeed. I see you. I see him. . . But I do not see. . . Ah. . . there."

It laughed at itself, the sound was terrifying.

What did it mean? What did it see?

My words came out shaky, "What do you mean?"

"Hmm. . . it was predicted that you would return. A savior. You're to shine brightly, your fate was foretold. The threads woven long before your birth, but your thread was not woven alone. No, it lies with another- together they are tied. Do not run from your destiny. . . human, but not."

More riddles. "I just want to go home."

It laughed, the sound grated on my bones- it licked its paw once before its eyes searched my face again. "Fate, Serra... Fate is binding, drawn together by the tree sisters, the three goddesses. Each person's destiny is thought of as a thread spun, measured, and cut. You cannot escape what is already laid out for you. But Free will has been and always will be your choice. However, be warned, Fate has a dark way of finding you and fulfilling itself."

As I stumbled backwards, the sphinx's words continued to echo in my head, each one a heavy weight dragging me down. 'Child of Starlight,' 'woven threads,' 'fate.' The world around me spun and swirled, as if it were mocking me, and I struggled to keep my balance.

The sphinx watched me with a calm detachment, its piercing gaze seeming to see right through me. Its voice echoed in my ears, haunting and otherworldly. I felt a sense of dread wash over me, as if I were standing at the edge of a precipice, staring down into an abyss.

"You are life. And he. . . he is death."

PART III

TRUTH, LIES AND WISHES COLLIDE

CHAPTER
Twenty-One

Serra

THE WORDS OF THE sphinx stayed with me as I made my way along the path. '*You are life, and he is death.*' What did that mean? What did any of this mean? There was certainly more here going on than I had the capacity to understand right now. Wrapped up in my own thoughts I had not realized how much ground I had covered until I came upon the site. The smell reached my nose.

A large pond before me stopped any progress I made. It was a far cry from the water in the cenote, even the water by the sphinx. The water here was dark and unwelcoming.

Stagnant and putrid.

The smell that was coming off of it was not pleasant, the smell reminding me of something. A time I had seen my first carcass. The dead animal had been left to decompose on the side of the road as people filtered in and out of the checkpoint outside the city walls. I felt the confusion in my chest at the memory I did not recall being my own. But it was the imagery that followed it that made me stop.

The carriage jostled back and forth. A girl with dark hair that had been braided into a plait around the top of her head, her ears coming to a tapered point, dressed in a royal blue traveling coat sat within. She wrinkled her nose as she pointed, asking what the pile of fur and bones were. "What's that?"

A voice resounded through the lush interior, the velvet muffling much of the vibrations. "It's a dead animal sweetheart. The circle of life will always turn. Death is a natural part of this world. One day you and I will no longer exist in the bodies that we have. One day we will be called away to join our ancestors."

A woman with blonde hair and blue eyes sat next to her. She wore a traveling coat of the darkest red, heavily embroidered in golds as the stitching ran down the length. Her swollen belly a sign that she was with child again. The curtains had been pulled back to allow fresh air in, caressing her face as she peaked out.

It had been a long journey, but they were almost home.

The sounds of the city growing as they got closer. The sound of the horses' hooves as they clopped across the cobblestones. The dirt road long behind them. Excited shouts and cheers rang in her ears, children from the city chased after their carriage as it wound its way up the slopes to the castle. The little girl excitedly waved to them as they smiled and waved back at her. They had finally returned.

It had been a long summer away, and she'd been excited to get back. To see all the new things that were awaiting her inside the stone walls. The carriage came to a halt at the top of a long road before a grand stone structure. Guards on either side of the large doors. The stairs before them laid out as a group of foot men rushed forward to open the carriage door.

Amongst them was a man dressed in rich blues, a beaming smile as he approached. She leapt from the carriage into his arms as he twirled her around in the air before embracing her. A laugh escaped both of them as the woman in red stepped forward before placing a soft kiss on his cheek, a hand resting on her belly.

They were whole again.

The breath I held escaped in a rush. My stomach wanted to heave, but it was empty and nothing but bile would come up. The smells and sounds, the voices of the people echoing in my head. The sight of the city, it was not Rothnia. The smell of the pond filtered back into my nose.

I had to keep going, I had to figure out what was going on. And forward over the pond was the only way. I could not go around. It was too dense- trees, rock, and piles upon piles of debris littered the ground. Large boulders had been piled up to block the remaining paths. Something screamed at me that this was a trap, that I should turn around and go another way, but I really had no other choice.

While every way around had been blocked, a rock and timber footbridge spanned across the length of the murky waters. It certainly was not in the best shape, the years had not been kind to it. The aged bridge creaked as I stepped forward, the timbers sighed under my weight. I prayed it would hold as the waters below taunted me. Forward I stepped, farther and farther out to the middle, the planks of the deck rickety under foot. If I even breathed wrong on it, I feared it would collapse.

One misstep and I could plunge into the dark waters below. A meal to whatever lived beneath its surface. A shutter ran its way through me, the thought of becoming a beast's meal. One more step forward, the timber planks and rocks had given out. Dropping me down into the water below. My scream echoed off the rocks, the frigid waters of the pond hit me as I crashed downwards into it.

The breath in my lungs leaving as I sunk below the surface, the weight of my dress pulling me down. My lungs screamed for air as I struggled for the surface. My vision blurred as I fought against the drag. I was losing, I was going to die by drowning.

I had hoped that I would have lived until I was old and wrinkling, but that did not seem to be how this would end. The burning sensation in my chest gave way as I gasped for air. My airways filled with the muddy pond water. I felt the world slipping away as my consciousness let go, its existence ceasing. All around me, everything went dark. Only one thought repeated itself around in my head.

I wished this was not the way I would die.

A soothing calmness settled itself over me, in my heart. In my mind, the world seemed easier here. A bright light pressed against my eyelids. A warmth heated my face, my body, my soul. My heart. The sun shone brightly as I opened my eyes. An array of colors graced the blue sky as I looked about, blinking in the brightness. Butterflies and birds fluttered around as I took in the sight before me. A grove of lush green grass splattered with wildflowers and trees of various colors. Reds, oranges, yellows and green.

Had I died? Had I really drowned in the pond?

It would have seemed so, I felt so much at ease here, the burdens gone. The heaviness lifted.

A couple of white bunnies hopped around the grass at my feet. Their floppy ears drooped, their noses twitched, pulling loose flowers from the grass as they nibbled on them; the juices staining their chins. I couldn't help but smile. A small nudge at my toe had me glancing down. A young lop bunny with black tipped ears had nudged it. Sitting up on its back legs, its nose twitching in the air, sniffing. Curiosity having gotten the better of it.

"Well, hello."

Bending down to pick it up, glad it did not run away from me out of fear. Its fur was soft as cotton, its whiskers tickled my chin as it sniffed. I was not a threat to it, or its friends. I always had a soft place in my heart for nature. For animals of various sizes. The sphinx's words rang in my head, 'have you never wondered why the world bloomed around you? Why birds, animals, and plants are attracted to you?'

It would seem it had been right. While the little white bunny settled itself in my arms, I glanced around the grove again. The colors in the sky blended and swirled together. It was as if someone had dipped a brush in water and swirled it across the paint, all of the colors mending together. The whole grove smelled of warm summer rain, fresh grass and cut flowers. A soft breeze blew across my face as the tops of the trees swayed.

A song whispering on the wind.

So much peace, I had not felt this at ease, this peaceful in such a long time. If this was what it was like after we died, if this was the afterlife, then I could be happy here. I closed my eyes as I listened to the wind, the melody flowing softly, caressing, and soothing. It was one I had heard before. A long, long time ago. A shiver ran down my spine.

"You are not supposed to be here."

I whirled, my eyes flying open at the voice behind me. But there was no one there, the voice had not a body, nor flesh. Just a shimmer as it moved about. It spoke again. "It is not your time child. You are meant for greater things."

It fluttered around me, speaking with such kindness, but its voice echoed off the tree tops, off the grass. "You have far more to do before your time below is done. Return now. Return and finish what has been prophesied."

The grove was changing. It was morphing. All around me, flower petals and butterflies fluttered, forming a vortex. The white bunnies skittered away, the one I held struggled to get out of my grasp.

"What do you mean?" I asked, setting it back down again. I watched as it bounded away to safety.

"You must return. The state of the world depends on you. Find the match to your soul. Find the other half of you. Life cannot survive without balance, remember what was lost."

The grove wavered as the circle of butterflies and flower petals grew, closing in around me. I felt a pulse in my heart, in my head. It felt like magic, a power as old as time. A sensation of fear, dread and worry accompanied it. And it was pulling at me, forcing me to leave. It was waking me up, I did not want to go. It felt so freeing being here, the heartache, the loneliness, the fear, everything had eased.

I did not want to let it go.

"Look deep within you, Child of Starlight. It is waiting. It is slumbering, wake it up. Remember what was lost, it is the only way." The voice said, its words caressed the inner corners of my mind as it shimmered in the light. I had no idea what it was talking about. What it meant, another pulse had the colors turning to gray, the world shifting back to darkness as my consciousness pulled me back.

"Wake up." it said as it all slipped away from me.

A flutter of movement and a rush of water hit me, I knew then the beasts in the waters had indeed found me. Prepared to make me their next meal. I would not struggle, I could not fight. There was none left in me as I tried desperately to gasp for more air, instead the water invaded. I wanted to go back to the grove, to the safety and serenity. Strong hands gripped under my arms, the sensation of being pulled upward toward the surface, before breaking it.

Lifting me from the depths, the fresh air and cool breeze

caressed my face as I was pulled to shore. My rescuer carried me through the water to the edge. I was back in my body. The world of color had gone, and I was in the nightmare again. I felt the strong arms that held me lay me down carefully, the warm earth beneath my body. The urge to breathe in deep as another pulse of magic coursed through me.

Coughing, expelling the water from my lungs as I lay there on the banks of the pond. Out of breath and ready for sleep. The light of the sun pressed against my closed eyelids. The warmth beat down on me. Maybe I hadn't left the grove, I could open my eyes and still be in a world of color, of calmness and peace. I felt the presence of another, as his scent washed over me, I could not stop my stomach from heaving the water coming up.

I was wrong.

My heart fluttered in my chest as I cracked open my eyes. His eyes and white blond hair came into view. His voice was faint but firm, a hint of relief laced into his words, "You would do well in trying harder to stay alive."

Coughing again, my own voice was hoarse as I spoke. "I do not need your help, nor your advice."

"Ah, but I do believe that you'd be dead if not for me."

I glared at him, standing on wobbly legs. "I would also not be in this situation if not for you either."

"Hmmm." The sound vibrated in his chest as he stared down at me. "You seem to have forgotten what I told you."

"I didn't forget. But there are a lot of things you have yet to tell me. Many things in fact."

"Like what?" He drawled, his arms crossed over his chest. A playful smirk spread across his face. It truly made him far more mysterious than before. I hesitated, the beauty of him, the alluring call. It threw me off, of course when I had the chance to ask him, I faltered. When I have my chance to demand some kind of answers, I lose my ability to speak.

"That's what I thought. You know. . . you should try harder to stay alive. I will not save you next time."

"You're an arrogant prick."

The Goblin King's eyes darkened, his smile stretched as he approached. He towered over me, truly, in this moment my blood ran cold and hot all at the same time. I could see the vein in his neck as it pulsed, "And you are insufferable."

I swallowed, I knew I was playing with fire. Testing the boundaries, seeing how far I could push him. "Is that so?"

"Yes." He hissed. "You have been a thorn in my side. You have tested every nerve I have. My patience stretched thin. And honestly, I'm exhausted."

A smile spread across my face in return. "Then why do you keep showing up? I don't ask for you to save me. You do it on your own."

He hesitates, his lips pursed. But his eyes rove over my face, over my wet hair. I could see the muscle in his jaw flex as his teeth clench. I feel his fingers on my face, instinctively leaning into his touch again. The softness of them on my skin, even as he cups my cheek. I don't know how he does it, why he's able to render me speechless, but in his company I felt safe. I felt whole. I barely register the beating thunder of my own heart, not over his.

But his touch, the warmth of his fingers on my face, the tips brushing back the wet strands of my hair, all of it. A spark flickered deep down, it called to him. And he was standing dangerously close.

This close though, this close to him I could see a shadow of darkness that circled in his irises. I swear. . . they had not been there before. My smile faltered as I reached up, but he stepped away from me, ready to leave. My skin flushed and chilly where his hand had been. I could not contain myself as I reached out and grabbed his arm instead. "Wait."

He paused, glancing down at my hand. "Yes, Princess?"

"Don't call me that."

The gleam in his eyes made my toes curl. Even soaking wet he was handsome. His skin was hot under my palm, despite the frigid waters. His hair was slick, dripping water on his chest. It had been pulled back, half up. The remaining length of it was still hanging down around his shoulders. My fingers flexed on his arm, I noticed then that he only wore trousers. His chiseled chest exposed to the air. Beads of water dripped down his physique.

He looked just as I imagined.

My core heated as indecent thoughts plagued my mind. The dream I had while in the Caves of Desire rushed itself to the front of my thoughts. His toned thighs, his arms ripped with muscle, glistening from the water. It took every ounce I had not to act on my thoughts, to see the dream come to life. I felt my chest tighten as I remembered what it felt like to have his lips on mine. How soft and tender they had been, how demanding they could be as well.

I was vaguely aware that I had been staring. The compulsion to run my hands across his chest and down had my cheeks heating. I'd forgotten what it was I wanted to say. Thank you would have been the right choice. But the distraction prevented words from forming, from escaping past my lips. My tongue was utterly tied. The sound of my heart pounding in my ears, the rush of my blood as the butterflies in my stomach flipped.

A soft growl vibrated through his chest. The sound caused my body to react, to step closer to him. But his demeanor had changed. His body tensed under my hand, surely he could sense my arousal. My eyes flicked to his, but his face was unreadable. His emotions masked as his eyes lacked any kind of feeling, guarded. His breath escaped in a rush; as if he had been holding it, as his nostrils flared. Anything I]d felt left me as he stepped away from my touch.

"Stay *alive*, Serra." The Goblin King turned away from me, his eyes cold and distant once more. The warmth that had been there only moments before was gone, replaced by a sharp edge. I could feel the tension between us, the regret of pushing too far. But I had to know, and had to ask him the question burning in my mind.

"Why do you keep saving me?" I asked, my voice barely audible.

He hesitated but didn't answer right away, instead choosing to stare at me with a piercing gaze over his shoulder. I could see the inner conflict within him, the struggle between duty and desire. Finally, he spoke, his voice low and rough.

"I have my reasons."

"That's not an answer," I replied.

"I don't owe you an answer," he snapped, stepping away from me once more. "You should be grateful that I saved your life."

"I am," I replied, my voice rising. "But that doesn't mean I'm going to stop asking questions."

He whirled on me giving me a long, hard look before speaking again. "Fine. If you must know, it's because I need you."

"Need me?" I repeated, confused.

"Yes," he said, his voice softening slightly. "You have something that I want. Something that I need."

"What is it?" I asked, my curiosity piqued.

"That's not something I can tell you," he replied, his eyes locking onto mine. "All you need to know is that you're safer with me around than without me."

I didn't know what to make of his words, but I knew one thing for sure. The Goblin King was not someone to be trifled with. He was dangerous and unpredictable, but there was also something alluring about him. Something that drew me to him despite my better judgment. As he turned to leave again, I watched him go, wondering what secrets he was keeping.

A rush of air left my lungs as I stared after him.

It felt like a bucket of cold water had been dumped over me. Washing away the heat and feelings that had a firm grip on my senses. He was an odd character. Why was he so concerned about me staying alive? What role did I play in his plans? One would think he'd want me to fail, so he could keep what he'd taken. My touch had caused him to pause, to stop though.

I glanced down at my fingers, before looking up again. Searching for him in the sky above. It had never done so before. Something had changed this time. The Goblin King was a puzzling being, and he had me utterly perplexed. Far more perplexed than the voice in the grove. What did it mean it was waiting?

It was slumbering, what was it?

What balance was it speaking of?

Remember *what*?

What was it talking about?

There were just so many questions that formed in my head, so many *unanswered* questions that forced me to consider that not all was as it seemed here.

CHAPTER
Twenty-Two

Serra

"**W**HAT HAPPENED TO YOU?"

His voice pulled me from my thoughts, whirling to find him watching me with curiosity on his little face. The wicked little bugger stared at me, his black eyes curious. Jesper sat on a stone wall leading into a grouping of hedges.

"What does it look like?"

My words had come out a bit more abrasive than I had intended, but I still haven't forgiven him for what he had done. Glancing back to the far side of the pond, at the foot bridge and all that had remained.

The stone and timbers were gone, lost to the bottom of the pond. The Goblin King had helped me out of the waters and left me on the banks of the other side. Despite the sun, I was freezing. The pond water had soaked me through, shivering slightly in the breeze. My hair and dress were drenched, dripping water on the ground where I stood. I was sure I smelled just as the pond water did, trying hard not to heave again. Twice now I had done so in the Goblin King's presence.

"It looks like you decided to go for a swim. Not the wisest choice, a kelpie makes that pond her home. It's a wonder she didn't decide to eat you for dinner." He chittered, scurrying across the tops of the rocks that made up the wall.

I felt the blood drain from my face, a kelpie?

I glanced back at the dark waters of the murky pond, so sure that I saw dark red eyes staring up at me. I knew from the few books we had that Kelpies were unique and dangerous aquatic creatures, they were considered to be vicious and evil. The folklore around them said they were shape shifting spirits, usually described as a horse-like creature, able to adopt a human form. They were known to lure the unwary to a watery death, dragging you down to the depths of whatever body of water it inhabited.

Yes, it was a good thing she chose not to make me her meal.

Glaring at him, "What do you want Jesper? Are you here to help or not this time? You already tricked me once."

"I did no such thing!"

"You did, the Caves of Desire, Jesper?" I watched him as he wrung his little fingers together. His eyes darted around.

"It was the only way to cross."

"Well, had you at least warned me, I could have made a different choice. But that's beside the point, are you here to help me?"

"It depends, if I will help you again that is."

"On what?"

"On whether or not you have more nuts. I cannot offer you my services if you do not have nuts."

"I do not." I remarked, lacing my words with sarcasm. "Sadly they all fell out and are at the bottom of the pond with the kelpie. You are more than welcome to go retrieve them if you'd like."

His eyes grew wide as he bristled in annoyance. "Certainly not!"

I couldn't help but laugh at him. While I had been mad at him before, he was a funny little creature. Unhelpful, aloof, and maddening, but he was endearing and rather cute. "Did you come here for any other reason, Jesper?"

"Well, I heard the crash and your scream. Decided I would investigate the situation. But you seem to be alright. Although-" He paused, a hand on his furry chin. His bobbed tail twitched as he asked. "I did see the Goblin King rush off rather quickly, would that have anything to do with you?"

"Why would you think that?" I asked, following him into the hedges. With the putrid smell of the kelpie's pond, they were barely alive, mostly roots and branches.

He'd scurried down from the wall and ran ahead, stopping me from stepping on him. "He seemed agitated. What did you do?"

"Nothing. I didn't do anything to him."

"Well you obviously caused him some kind of grief. For him to run off in such a rush." He said, following behind me. I could not stop, I still had ground to cover.

"If you know him so well, you tell me."

He scoffed. His chitter reached my ears as he chased after me. "He's as curious to me as you are, I'm afraid."

I stopped, glancing down at him, "How do you mean?"

"Well, he's the only one like him that I have seen."

My brows furrowed in confusion. What was he talking about? What did he mean?

"Jesper, what is that supposed to even mean? Why does everyone play word games here? Can no one just give me a straight answer?"

His tail twitched again, he did not answer me.

"Jesper." I pushed.

His gaze flicked over before perking up, his ears coming up. The tufts at the ends moved as they did so. "Oh!" He exclaimed before scurrying off. "Look at those gorgeous walnuts!"

"Jesper!" I exclaimed, chasing after him. But he had disappeared from sight. I had no chance of finding him, not here. The scenery had changed as we walked. Tall hedges towered over me, their leaves in different shades of green. The path split before me, forcing me to choose. The path was no longer straight-forward.

I was in a maze.

My first thought was to wonder why there was a hedge maze in the first place. My second thought was to wonder which direction to go in. I had myself turned around, and while I wouldn't say I had a knack for directional navigation, it was something I could manage. But I'd lost sight of the castle, the hedges towering over me prevented me from seeing. However, if I remembered correctly which direction it had been in when I entered, I would be able to stay on the right path.

I think.

As I stood there, shivering in the dampness of my clothes, my mind raced with questions and confusion. I couldn't understand why the Goblin King was so concerned about my well-being. What was it he needed me for? Or did he genuinely cared about me? The more I thought about it, the less sense it made. This was a creature that had taken me from Rothnia, trapped me in his realm, and yet here he was, worried about me staying alive.

But as confusing as his behavior was, I couldn't ignore the way my body had reacted to him. The way his touch had sent a rush of heat through me, the way his proximity had left me breathless. I knew it was wrong, I knew I should be afraid of him, but there was something about him that drew me in. Something I couldn't quite put my finger on.

Even as I stood there lost in thought wondering what way to go, the sun began to move farther across the sky, casting long shadows across the ground. The air grew colder, and my wet clothes clung to my skin. I knew I should move, to keep going where I needed to but there was a pull, a sense of something unfinished that kept me rooted to the spot.

Finally, with a heavy sigh, I turned and began to make my way through the hedges. As I walked, my mind raced with questions, trying to make sense of everything that had happened. But the more I thought about it, the less sense it made. It was as if the Goblin King was deliberately trying to confuse me, to keep me off balance.

But why? What did he want from me? And why did I feel this strange connection to him, despite everything he had done to me?

Lost in thought, I suddenly stumbled over something on the path. I looked down and saw a small object lying in the dirt. It was a ring, a simple silver band with a small green stone set in the center.

I picked it up, turning it over in my hand, wondering where it had come from. And then I saw it, etched on the inside of the band, a single word: *"Remember."*

My heart began to race as I realized what it could mean. Was this message from the Goblin King, a reminder of something important? Or was it from the voice in the grove?

What was I supposed to remember?

I glanced up into the sky again, hoping to see him flying away before looking back down at the ring that I now had in my fingers, a sense of foreboding washed over me. Whatever was coming, it was going to be big. And I had a feeling that there was more left unsaid between us.

O VER THE COURSE OF several hours I took turn after turn, weaving in and out of the hedges. Taking one path after another, I was unsure if I was headed in the right direction, but I would not let it deter me. Very little signaled if I was headed where I needed to go but part of me seemed to know. To remember exactly which direction I was supposed to head in here. The thought flickered in my head of the image I saw the first time.

The one of the woman in white, a smile on her lips. She had surfaced so many times throughout the last several days. Her face was a familiar one. It was as if I knew her, she was something to me, but I did not know what it meant or who she truly was. But her smile, her white dress in the green of the hedges had me pushing forward, as if she was guiding me where I needed to go. Helping me through the hedge maze, helping me get through the labyrinth to the end.

It was on the last turn that everything opened up.

The hedges falling away to reveal an abandoned garden. The fountain at its center was covered in ivy, the marble cracked and the pond dried up. Marble statues placed strategically around the garden in tiny alcoves watched over it, as if they were the unassigned guardians of the place. The flower beds were long shriveled and died, weeds growing in their places.

But despite the space, despite its abandoned state, it was the mausoleum at the end that caught my attention. It loomed before me, built of white stone marble, the chiseled columns of stone held up the roof. It was surrounded by a barricade of evergreen trees. I worried my lip as I stepped forward, passing the statues, the fountain, the weed covered flower beds. The stone of the path before me had cracked over time.

Carefully stepping over the loosened stone, as to not trip. The mausoleum had seen better days as well, the white marble was covered in a layer of grime and dirt. The steps before it had heaved with ground movement. I only paused once, hesitating before putting a foot forward on the only piece of steps you could climb. The structure was modest in size, the entrance tall enough to let in the natural light. My heart jumped as a fluttering of birds flew out, scared of my being there.

The black and white checkered floor was littered in leaves and old flowers. What was this place? Was it a place to grieve? A place one could go to reflect? A resting place? Scanning the interior my eyes landed on a statue. Carved of solid onyx granite. It stood out against the white of the marble walls. The statue was a pair of fae, carved into a lover's embrace. The love on their faces was captured forever in the stone.

I could not pull myself away from them. My eyes latched onto their features. I knew them, I'd seen them before. But I could not place them. Their names were lost to me, their faces haunted me. My brows furrowed, they were the ones that were in the visions. The dreams I had, memories I shared with someone I did not know. The woman in white, the man with the laurel coronet. While I did not know who they were, they felt like home.

They meant something.

TIME TICKED AS I sat there on the stone floor, measured as the sun stretched across the black and white checkered tile.

Staring up at them, I did not want to leave. It was as if I had lost a lifetime with them, unknown to me who they could be, who *they* had been. I knew the answer was there, somewhere, but I could not grasp it.

 It was blocked.

The longer I sat, the more confused I became. Unclear and fuzzy images fluttered past in my head, I could not tell what they were, if they were memories or not. A crack had started to form the longer I waited. The longer I willed them to be free. I wanted to reach for them, to grasp them and never let go. Willing them to clear, but no matter how hard I tried, how long I sat there they never did.

They flashed in and out, over and over.

The few I had the last several days had been the clearest of them but these ones, these ones were deeper. Unreachable. A pain in my head started to throb as I tried and tried to grasp them. It wasn't until my stomach grumbled that I gave up.

Rising from my spot on the floor- having sat there for longer than I should have, the hours had cost me precious time- time that was running out. It took an enormous amount of effort to leave the mausoleum and the statue. But I had to, I was almost there. All of this was almost over. Of course, I knew the only one who would have answers was him. No matter what, he held them. The truth was waiting and I could feel it.

CHAPTER
Twenty-Three

The Goblin King

I COULDN'T BELIEVE IT. I shouldn't have even been there, but there she was, drowning before my very eyes. And I just couldn't let her die. Failure was not an option, not when it came to her. As I paced back and forth on the cold stone floor, the well in front of me revealed her face in the reflection of the rippling water. My heart felt like it was going to burst out of my chest as I watched her sink deeper and deeper, her life slipping away.

Without even thinking, I disappeared into the shadows, shedding my shirt as I dove headfirst into the murky pond. The water was freezing, the stench of decay and algae assaulting my senses. But none of that mattered. All I could see was her, sinking further and further away from me. And I knew I had to save her.

As I swam towards her, my heart pounding with each stroke, the

Kelpie emerged from the depths, its malevolent intentions clear as day. I kicked it in the face, sending it scurrying away. But that was just the beginning of the struggle.

The water weighed down on us both as I reached for her, her body limp in my arms. She had given up, stopped fighting for her life. And I was the only one left to save her. Panic coursed through my veins as I pulled her closer, desperately trying to bring her to the surface. But it wasn't just physical strength that saved her. As I held her close, the well of magic within me pulsed with an energy I'd never felt before. It enveloped her, forcing her to wake up, to come back to me. I felt it pulsing all around us, a force so strong it took my breath away.

As she lay on the banks of the pond, her chest rising and falling with each labored breath, I couldn't help but feel overwhelmed. I had never felt so scared, so helpless in my entire life. But then, as if in response to my fear, the magic flared one last time. And she took a deep breath, her eyes flickering open. She coughed and sputtered, I recoiled in horror. I had saved her again, against my own better judgment. I had warned her that I wouldn't be there for her every time, but my actions proved otherwise. I wanted to leave her there, alone and vulnerable, but something kept me rooted to the spot. The relief I felt was overwhelming, almost suffocating.

I had not meant to be so cruel, to push her away like that. My words had come from a place of frustration and fear. But then, as she reached out to touch me, I saw something. A memory that I couldn't quite place at first. It was a memory that had been lost to me, forgotten under the weight of the curse that affected us all.

It was of us, as children, bickering under the shade of a giant oak tree. I had accidentally dropped my apple, and it hit her on the head before landing in her lap. She called me an idiot and demanded an apology. And in that moment, I remembered.

I'd had every intention to at first until she started yelling at me. Calling me all kinds of names, throwing the apple at me. She had good aim, but it angered me. I'd ripped the book from her hand before tossing it, kicking it into a puddle even. Her last words to me that night were said in anger, '*I hate you.*'

It had been the last night I would see her for a long while.

The memories flooded back like a dam that had finally burst, overpowering and unstoppable. I had been so angry at the time, so fed up with being her constant companion, but now as I watched her face in the well, I felt a pang of nostalgia and longing for those simpler times. But my thoughts were interrupted as I saw her with the squirrel. The same one that had led her to the Caves. That troublesome little beast had been the reason I'd gone to the edge of those caves. How I had been called to her once again. I should have stayed away, kept my distance, but I couldn't bear the thought of her failing, of her *dying*. If she failed, then I would have failed too.

As I paced the stone floor, my heart pounding in my chest, I saw her face reflected back at me in the waters. The memory of that childhood argument, the way she had convinced me to disobey authority, flooded my mind. The anger and hate that I had felt towards her family dissipated in the face of these memories. I couldn't deny the feelings that were stirring inside me. And while the cracks had been forming for almost two decades, this caused a tsunami of emotions and memories to rush forward. Memories I had forgotten myself.

Memories now have meaning.

Stepping away from the well, I walked to the other side of the room and paused in front of the window. As I gazed out over the horizon, I couldn't help but think that she was out there somewhere, on her way to me. The wind blew through the open window, rustling the curtains of my four poster bed and stirring up the dead leaves scattered about the room. I had been trapped in this castle for far too long, a prisoner in the very place that saw her family's downfall.

More memories, memories that flooded back to me. Memories of the trip from my home to Inirea when I was just six years old, and seeing the magnificent castle for the first time. I remembered meeting her for the first time, a little bundle in her mother's arms. So many forgotten memories of my time with her family, and my time with her, came rushing back to me.

Memories that I had no recollection of having, and that I still questioned if they were truly mine. Among them was the fateful night and the role I played in it. My heart ached as her face flashed before me, so young and innocent at the time. And I had been nothing but an angry boy who wanted nothing more than to see the royal family fall.

Fuck, I was coming undone.

I was a mess, a complete and utter mess, and it was all because of her. Serra. The pull between us was stronger than anything I had ever experienced before. It was a connection that ran so deep, it left me breathless. I had felt it years ago, but had dismissed it as a fleeting feeling. But it had never gone away. It had only grown stronger with time.

And now, fate has woven our lives together in a cruel twist of events. I had asked her to play this game, to take on this role, to risk everything, and I had taken her memories to ensure she played along. How could I have been so blind, so foolish? How could I have not seen the consequences of my actions? How cruel this could be, how fate would play with us like this. How could they do this? How could I do this? Had I known, I would not have done this, I would not have asked her to play this game.

I would have let it be.

The weight of it all bore down on me, a heaviness that settled in my chest. I knew what I had to do now. What I had to sacrifice to make things right. I couldn't let her stay here, not when I knew what fate had in store for her. It would only end in tragedy.

I glanced over at the seeing well, her face reflected back at me. I knew what to do, what I *had* to do now. I summoned what little energy I had left and cast one final spell. Pay for it one last time. The pain shot through me as I sliced my arm with the blade and watched the blood drop into the water. The drops dispersed almost immediately, and I knew I had paid a steep price.

But it was worth it. She couldn't stay here, not when her life was at stake. And as much as it pained me to do so, I knew I had to let her go. It was the only way to keep her safe. I really did not want to know what the price would be this time. I really did not want to have to do this. But I knew one thing, that was for sure.

She could not stay.

CHAPTER
Twenty-Four

Serra

A S I MADE MY way through the towering stone columns, my
footsteps echoed off the polished marble floor. The sound
bounced back at me, reminding me of the emptiness of the space
around me. The scene that awaited me was both beautiful and eerie, as
if it was hiding a dark secret within. A once-grand manor house
perched on top of a hill, overlooking the surrounding land, now stood
in shambles. The windows were shattered, and the balcony that once
stood proudly now lay in ruins. The stonework was weathered, and
the walls were covered in vines and moss. Yet, it was not the
dilapidated building that caught my attention.

Before me lay a vast orchard, stretching out for miles. Rows upon
rows of trees that seemed to go on forever. It was an awe-inspiring
sight, and I couldn't help but feel small in comparison to the massive

expanse before me. Descending the hill, I marveled at the sheer variety of trees in the orchard. Some I recognized, but many were entirely unfamiliar to me. Dozens of different species were all gathered into one place, spread out over acres and acres of land.

There were fruit trees of all kinds, laden with ripe, juicy fruit, as well as nut trees, their branches heavy with almonds, walnuts, and chestnuts. Some trees were covered in delicate, fragrant flowers, while others boasted vibrant leaves of every color imaginable. Silver trees glinted in the sunlight, and gold trees shimmered as if made of the precious metal.

Continuing to walk through the orchard, an enigmatic scent lingered in the air, teasing my senses. A mixture of sweetness and earthiness, with hints of spice and musk, it was familiar yet elusive, and I couldn't quite put my finger on it. Down the rows of trees, I took in the different varieties of fruits and nuts, the scent of peaches, pears, and plums mingling with the sweet aroma of apples. Some trees had leaves infused with a subtle fragrance, adding to the overall atmosphere of the orchard. The scent grew stronger, almost intoxicating, drawing me deeper into the orchard.

It seemed to change with each step I took, revealing new layers and dimensions that left me in awe. But for the life of me, I could not place it. The scent became stronger, almost overwhelming, as I walked deeper into the orchard. I felt like I was on the verge of recognizing it, but it remained elusive.

As I reached out to touch one of the trees, the bark felt rough under my fingertips, and I couldn't help but marvel at the sheer size of it. The trunk was wider than any tree I had ever seen before, and the branches seemed to stretch out endlessly. The leaves rustled in the wind, making a gentle, soothing sound that made me feel at peace.

However, I noticed something strange. Despite the vast size of the orchard, there were no workers tending to the trees. I saw no carts of harvested fruit or tools left leaning against the trunks. It was as if the orchard was thriving all on its own. The more I walked, the more I became entranced by the orchard. The smell of the fruit and the mystery scent had enveloped me, and I couldn't help but feel a sense of peace and contentment. It was as if the orchard was a world of its own, and I was simply a visitor passing through.

I'd only glanced over once and had to look again. What stared back at me caused me to pause. My brows furrowed in confusion as my mind tried to understand what I was seeing. There was a face in the bark of the tree. Its eyes blinked at me as I stared at it, and it back at me.

"It is very rude to stare."

Startled that it spoke, I apologized quickly. "Oh. Oh I do apologize. But. . . I'm just wondering what you are."

The tree quivered as it pushed itself out, its head and torso made of branches. Where hair should be, were twigs and leaves. Its eyes were a radiant violet. Its knobby fingers braced against the tree. But it spoke again, its voice scratchy, "We are the Guardians, moreover, the guardians of the trees. We care for the trees. We protect the trees. But for all we do, the trees are still dying."

"Dying? Why?"

"Because our world is dying. It has been. Although we have been asleep these last decades, darkness has crept into the land. It's killing our trees, killing us. Pulling our life source from within. We could sense change, whispers on the winds even now. It has reached our ears and many of us suspect that it has something to do with you. . . You have caused us to awaken. A stirring, to see the damage."

"Who is responsible? Why are you dying, where did the darkness come from?" I pushed, stepping closer to the guardian.

The bark on its head and arms stood, "I've already said too much. If he were to hear me. . ."

"Who?" I urged.

The creature disappeared into the bark of the tree again. Fading away until there was nothing, "Wait, who?"

Its last words echoed through the orchard.

"Save us."

One more thing on my list of curiosities, one more question, another mystery to solve. Another creature in this dream of impossibilities. I looked around the orchard again. In the trees, in the sky above me, the sun was starting to paint the sky in gold and reds. Another day had gotten away from me. Another day was about to end. Beside me a tree of silver tinkled. The breeze caused the pieces that hung from its branches to clatter. The sound vibrated like a wind chime. I reached out to touch them, to pluck one from the branch.

Holding it within my hand I examined the piece but as I did so it changed. The whole orchard did. The silver had turned to dust under my touch, the gold fizzled out. The fruit withered and burst under my gaze. The smell I could not place earlier was more pronounced. I realized that I had finally recognized the mysterious scent that had eluded me earlier. It was the smell of magic, of something otherworldly and powerful. It was death and decay.

The flowers from a nearby tree drifted on an invisible wind, as if they were raining, caught up in the force. A flurry of them cascaded down in front me. I felt his presence everywhere, his existence grounded me, it wasn't long before my eyes found him.

It was him, it was always him.

The flowers settled down around his feet, his hair fluttered in the breeze that caressed my skin. Kissed my cheeks, said hello as we gazed at each other. His eyes were intense as he stared back. He did not speak to me. We stood in silence for a moment, the butterflies in my stomach causing it to flutter and flip.

"Hello, Princess."

His voice caused a chill to run down my spine again. Why does it keep doing that? My breath lodged itself in my throat as he stood there, leaning against the trunk of a fruit tree. He was resplendent in his choice of dress today. Dressed in a dark green doublet with bright gold stitching. The colors brought out his eyes, his hair. His black trousers were tucked into the tops of the polished boots. Without a cloak, I could see the broadness of his shoulders, the muscle I knew ran down his arms. The muscles in his torso flexed as he righted himself. I could not help but watch.

"Hello." My voice came out as a squeak. I was unsure of what he wanted from me, but at the same time his aura was magnetic, and I found it hard to resist his pull.

"You seem surprised to see me, Princess," he said, his eyes sparkling with amusement.

I nodded, still unable to find my voice. The last time we had met, he had left me confused and unsettled. But now, as I looked at him, all those feelings seemed to fade away, replaced by a sense of longing.

"I. . . I just didn't expect to see you here," I managed to say finally.

He chuckled, his voice deep and rich. "I could say the same for you."

I looked around, taking in the ruined manor house and the piece from the orchard that had turned to dust in my hands. "I was just passing through," I said, gesturing to the landscape. "I didn't mean to disturb anything."

He pushed himself off the tree trunk, taking a step towards me. "You could never disturb anything, Princess. You bring life wherever you go."

A shiver ran down my spine at his words, his voice like velvet against my skin. I wanted to step closer to him, to feel the warmth of his body against mine, but something held me back. I knew I couldn't trust him completely, not yet.

"Why are you here?" I asked, trying to keep my voice steady.

He raised an eyebrow, a smirk playing at the corners of his lips. "Why, to see you, of course. I heard you were in the area and I couldn't resist."

I felt a blush creeping up my neck, but I couldn't help the smile that tugged at the corners of my lips. Despite everything, I was drawn to him, and I couldn't deny it any longer.

"Well, you found me," I said, feeling a sense of unease wash over me.

"I always do," he said softly. "I will always find you."

I knew he was right. No matter how hard I tried, I could never escape him. But right now, at this moment, I don't want to. I wanted to stay here, with him, forever.

My thoughts of him had altered.

Instead, I considered what his existence had been like. What was he going through? What had life been like for him up until now? Had he even been happy, had he ever *loved*? I wanted to ask. The tears pricked behind my eyes. Was he lonely? Was that why he stole away the people from Rothnia? To have company?

He watched; his smoldering gaze holding mine. This male was not easy to read. Part of me wondered why and part of me did not care. I should ask more of my questions, ask them now.

Demand the answers.

But another question danced on my tongue, "why have you really come?"

I did not know it was even possible to render him speechless but he hesitated before answering, "I find myself unable to stay away from you."

"Why?"

His eyes narrowed, regarding me a moment before speaking, "I do not know. In my waking hours, you haunt me. In my sleep, you plague my dreams. You are an intoxication I cannot escape and it has me confused. You. . ."

The Goblin King paused for a moment, his brows pulled together in indecision. "You do not fear me, but yet, you are an enigma."

I watched him for a moment, frozen in front of him, in our place amongst the rotting trees of the orchard. The smell of the decaying fruit drifting on the wind. Before me stood the Goblin King, in all his glory, in all his splendor, and I was the one who confused him? I didn't even know *that* was possible either.

With every encounter I had with him these last days, I was left with more questions than answers. I was left with my mind spiraling down in a world of confusion and wonder. But one thing remained clear to me, one thing I knew was not all was as it seemed in this place. He was not as he seemed. This place. . . it was something different entirely.

He cleared his throat, pulling my wandering mind back to him. "How are you finding this game?" He asked.

But it was his tone that he used, how he spoke to me, it was unreadable. Strained even, like there was a waging war going on inside him. I wanted to answer, I did, but my words had left me again. His question was odd. Was this really a game? Because it did not seem like it was.

Not anymore. I looked at him, perplexed. "What game?"

"The game of wits we've been playing," he clarified. "You and I, trying to understand each other. It's been amusing, has it not?"

I couldn't help but feel a twinge of annoyance at his nonchalant attitude towards our interactions. I shook my head, not wanting to engage in his twisted way of thinking. "I don't find it amusing. And I don't want to play games. I want to know what you're doing. What are you up to? What's really going on?"

The Goblin King's face hardened, his eyes narrowing as he regarded me. "And I have told you before. It is none of your concern."

My fists clenched, my nails digging into my palms, frustration building within me. "How can it not be my concern?"

I remained silent for a moment, contemplating his words. The Goblin King was right. We had been playing a game, a game of wits, and it had been entertaining in its own strange way. But now, it felt like the game had changed. It felt like there was something more at stake, something bigger than just understanding each other.

The Goblin King's expression softened slightly, and he took a step closer to me. "I have my reasons, and they are important to me. I cannot share them with you at this time, but know that I am not your enemy. . ."

I stared at him, unsure of what to believe. His words were reassuring, but his actions spoke otherwise. The rotting orchard surrounding us was evidence of that.

"How can I trust you?" I asked, my voice barely above a whisper.

"You will have to decide that for yourself."

"You want to know what I think?"

He regarded me, waiting for me to explain. I looked up at him, meeting his gaze. "I don't think it's just a game anymore. Something's changed."

He raised an eyebrow, his expression unreadable. "Oh?"

"I don't know what it is," I admitted, "but I feel like there's more going on here."

He studied me for a moment, his gaze intense. "You're right," he finally said. "There is more going on here."

Another shiver ran down my spine at his words. What did that even mean? But before I could ask, he took a step closer, his eyes fixed on mine. I held my ground, feeling the tension between us rise with every passing second. His smoldering gaze held mine, and I couldn't help but feel both curious about him and wary of him at the same time. I didn't know what was going to happen next, but I knew that I needed to be prepared for anything.

"Tell me, what do you think is going on here?" he asked, his voice low and measured.

I hesitated for a moment, trying to put my thoughts into words. "I'm not sure," I said slowly. "But I think there's something wrong with this place. Something. . . unnatural. And I think that you have something to do with it."

He didn't flinch at my accusation. Instead, he studied me intently, as if he was trying to read my mind. "And what makes you think that?" he asked, his voice still calm and steady.

I took a deep breath, trying to gather my thoughts. "I don't know," I said finally. "It's just a feeling I have. Like there's something. . . off about you. And about this place. Like there's something hiding beneath the surface that we can't see."

He nodded slowly, as if he was considering my words. "You're not wrong," he said finally. "There is something going on here. Something that I've been trying to understand, something about you."

I raised an eyebrow, feeling both intrigued and suspicious. "and what is that?" I asked.

"You're different," he said simply.

I felt a knot form in my stomach at his words as I looked up at him, trying to gauge his intentions, but his expression was unreadable.

"Different? How?"

He tilted his head, studying me intently, his voice low and intense. "You don't fear me, you don't cower in my presence. You challenge me. You make me question everything I thought I knew."

I felt a mix of emotions at his words. On the one hand, I was suspicious of his intentions. On the other hand, I was intrigued by him. But the Goblin King was not to be trusted, that much I knew.

"How?" I asked, feeling a mixture of curiosity and apprehension.

"I don't know, but there's something about you that draws me to you. Something that I can't resist."

"I. . ."

I had failed to notice it before, but now my eyes fixated on the apple he held in his hand, its shiny red skin glistening under the sun. The Goblin King noticed my gaze and lifted it up, tempting me with its sight. My stomach grumbled loudly, reminding me of my hunger. It had been almost two days since I had last had anything, and I could feel my energy dwindling.

As he held out the apple to me, memories of a dream from the previous night flashed in my mind. I remembered seeing an apple flying across, but who had she been? Was she someone important to him? The thought pained me, and my heart ached at the possibility of him having another connection, someone who held more value to him than I did.

This was a bit cruel, what he was doing.

He held it out for me to take. I wanted to, oh did I want to, but this *was* a game, right? And I had no idea what his next move would be. He took a step closer to me, the apple outstretched. His boots crunched in the dirt as he took another steady toward me. The expression on his face did not change though, it remained a solid mask of indifference. And I would not cower back; I would not yield.

Another step, another, another...

It didn't take long before he towered over me. So, close I could feel the warmth that came from him, his breath on my skin as he looked down upon my face. With his free hand he grabbed mine and placed the apple he held into it. His touch sent a tingle through my fingers, down my arms, and into my spine. His eyes did not break from my face as I glanced down at the fruit I now held in my own hand. It called to me to take a bite.

My stomach grumbled again.

Bringing the apple to my lips, the skin breaking under my teeth as the juices hit my tongue. It tasted far worse than it should have. It was sour, acidic, and almost rotten. The texture was like mush, my eyes flew to his.

I'd fallen for his trick.

It fell from my hand as the world spun, whatever he had done to it, it had seized every nerve, every muscle. The trees faded as the Goblin King watched, his face twisted in a look of agony and sadness. I could not control my own body, not as it staggered trying to keep its balance. I felt strong arms catch me as I fell forward.

My head spun and whirled, feeling as if I was floating, like everything around me was dancing. I felt his arms around me as I fell. The edges of my vision faded, the pitch-black creeping in. His smell stayed with me, lingered as it caressed the darkness of my mind.

Citrus, smoke, and evergreen...

The air was thick and heavy as I struggled to regain consciousness, the taste of bile and sourness still lingering in my mouth. My eyes fluttered open, taking in the sight of the Goblin King's face, his features remained contorted with concern as he watched over me. My head throbbed, my body felt weak and heavy as

I attempted to move. His arms held me up, keeping me from falling back down as he spoke softly to me.

"You're okay, just rest," he said, his voice filled with a gentleness that I had not yet heard from him. I couldn't help but wonder if this was just another trick, another ploy to gain the upper hand in our game. But as I looked up into his eyes, I saw no trace of malice or deceit.

"What have you done?" I asked weakly, my voice barely above a whisper. He sighed heavily, his expression pained as he sat back on his heels, still holding me in his arms.

"I had to," he explained, his eyes never leaving mine. "You were starting to understand too much, and you aren't ready. Not yet."

Understanding too much? What did he mean? My mind raced with questions, confusion and frustration warring within me. I tried to sit up, but the Goblin King's grip on me tightened, preventing me from moving.

"Just rest, please," he pleaded, his voice laced with a hint of desperation. "I promise to explain everything soon, but for now, just rest."

I couldn't fight against the exhaustion any longer, and as my eyes drooped shut once again, I couldn't help but wonder what other secrets this place held. What other tricks the Goblin King had up his sleeve, and just how far he was willing to go to win this game.

CHAPTER
Twenty-Five

Serra

THE IMAGE SWIRLED AND circled before me; the sound of music echoed in my head. My eyes felt heavy, as if I had fallen into a deep slumber. The sound of laughter and talk smothered me. It took effort to force my eyes open, to awaken from the cradle of sleep, of darkness that lingered. But when I finally did, I'd awoken in a sea of people. I could not recall how I had gotten here. Everything was hazy and covered in a fog.

My hands ran down my front, catching on something. I glanced down, I was not in the green bodice and navy-blue skirt anymore. Instead I wore a gown of gossamer skirts in the deepest blue, almost midnight and a bodice made of lace and crystals. The skirts sparkled as if they had been touched by the stars. Glistening and twinkling as it moved. My hands and arms were covered in dark satin gloves, delicate and soft.

It was beautiful.

Peeking down at my feet, a pair of crystal slippers covered them. Not hard or uncomfortable as one would expect. They were soft and cushioned, like walking on clouds. I saw my reflection in a mirror at the edges of the room. The sea of masked people parting slightly. My hair was curled and styled, the length of it cascading down my back. A pair of pearl combs holding back the bits around my face. My eyes were bright, aware. One deep breath, another.

Another. . .

This was a dream.

Surely it was. The last thing I could remember was the sensation of fainting, and strong arms catching me. I had to still be in the orchard. But the smell of the apples was lost here. Instead, it smelled of bright winter snow and warm chestnuts. Gazing about the room, I realized then where I was.

I was in the very center of a ballroom.

The room around me was bright, shining crystal chandeliers and gossamer gauze cascaded down the walls. Pillars of solid marble in a circle around the hardwood parquet floor. Low tables and sofas piled high with cushions for lounging at the outer edges, dotted the room. Banquet tables filled with decadent sweets and candies. Cakes and cookies. Carved meats and platter after platter of fruits, cheeses, and breads.

A group of people surrounded a table, their laughter and jokes filling the air. Each person held a crystal goblet in their hands as they talked and enjoyed themselves. In the center of the table was a fountain, pouring out a dark purple liquid that flowed over the different layers, splashing and bubbling. The sound of the liquid echoed over the music, adding to the lively atmosphere.

Faerie Wine.

The waiters deftly navigated through the bustling crowd, defying collisions as they balanced trays brimming with goblets of the beverage. Sprites flitted and danced around the room, causing playful havoc and sowing mischief wherever they went. From a raised platform, an orchestra filled the air with a haunting melody that perfectly captured the event's dark and romantic atmosphere.

All of this was reminiscent of another masquerade ball, one I had run away from, one that started all of this, but this one was different. There were no Conwell's, there were no humans, there were no gilded metal masks. This entire crowd was boisterous and loud. No easy-going business conversations. no hushed whispers or proper greetings. The conversation here was filled with taunts and mocking ridicule as it reached my ears, trying to push through them as they closed in. The pointed ears and sharp fangs of those around me told me I was still in Inirea.

Surrounded by Fae.

Where they came from I could not guess. I had only been in the presence of Hendrix and The Goblin King. Jesper had said that he had never seen another, but it did not set my nerves at ease. Not as their laughter reached my ears. Coming from every corner, it was guttural and hollow. The masks were horrifying renditions of animals, ugly and grotesque. The sea of monsters and goblins. This was not for the faint of heart. Designed to give you a fright. A warning not to stay long.

A nightmare.

I continued pushing my way through the crowd bumping into those around me. I needed to get out of here. Something about this place was wrong. Something about this place was cursed.

A hiss sound in my ear as I bump into a female Fae, a taunting flash of her teeth. "Sssssslut."

Another behind me, a male. "Wwwwwhore."

Another, "haaaarlot."

Over and over the whispers and hisses from those surrounding me reached my ears. I could feel the tears pricking behind my eyes. The mockery was more than I could handle. Surly if they knew the truth they wouldn't say such things. Surly they knew I was not, that it was not as it had seemed.

I want out of here.

Desperate to find an escape, the crowd was closing in on me. A group of Fae males had closed in. Taunting and jesting as they rapaciously reached out to grab me, my skirts, my hair. It felt as if they were tugging me in every direction.

But their hands never once touched me.

Their lips pulled back in vicious smiles.

I was startled by a sudden laugh that echoed in my ear. When I turned my head to the right, I saw a fae male wearing a contorted boar mask, while on my left, there was another male donning an oozing bear mask. Behind me, yet another fae, this one in a wolf mask. The crowd was filled with different masks, all adorned with sneering smiles, and they were closing in on me. I pushed past them with all my strength to get away.

As I made my way through the throng again, I sensed that something was in the air. Panic and anxiety washed over me, and I realized that I hadn't touched the food or wine. Suddenly, a flurry of gold flakes rained down on me, and I looked up, feeling someone's eyes watching me. My eyes scanned the ballroom and found him standing there among the crowd of Fae, his gaze locked on me.

There he was, waiting for me. I hadn't realized I had been looking for him, but the anxiety and panic vanished as a soothing calm washed over me. It was as if I had found the missing piece of a puzzle, and everything fell into place. I found peace in his eyes, and I knew I would never forget their colors again. But it was the way my heart called out to him, the way my whole being longed to be in his arms that caused me to pause. It became even more difficult to breathe as I stood there and watched him.

As I made my way towards him, my heart pounded in my chest, threatening to break free from its confines. The crowd parted like the Adrid Sea, as if sensing the electric charge that crackled between us. His eyes never left mine, drawing me in like a moth to a flame. I could feel the intensity of his gaze, the weight of his desire, and I knew I was in trouble.

But I couldn't help myself. I was drawn to him, as if he were a magnet and I was made of metal. As I stood before him, his eyes roamed over my body, taking me in from head to toe. I felt vulnerable, exposed, and yet strangely empowered. It was as if he had the power to strip away all my defenses, to lay me bare, and yet I didn't mind.

Deep breaths Serra.

One.

Two.

Another.

Another.

This beautiful Fae male, the one who haunted my dream, tormented every waking hour, he was going to be my undoing.

CHAPTER
Twenty-Six

The Goblin King

THE ONLY PLACE TO hide from her was the back of the crystal and marble ballroom, just as I'd done before. My eyes tracked her as she made her way through the crowd of masked Fae. Staying far out of sight, lingering in the shadows as they tormented her. I watched as this vicious circle continued to rule over me.

Another deception.

Another prevarication.

How many more could I handle?

How many more lies would I have to give?

It was malicious, what I was doing to her. Using the mortal masquerade like this. What had happened that night, I had not planned for it. I knew long before then what that mortal did. How that man's actions played into this, how he had mistreated her. It weighed heavily on me and I carried it with me now. It was not something I would easily let go of. This was cruel, and I knew it, even for me. More than once I had gone to her rescue, more than once I had saved her life. How could I not though? How could I let her perish? The answer, I couldn't. Not anymore.

I could not keep doing this either. I could not keep this up. I was more than drawn to her. I craved her presence, her touch, her smell. Her scent lingered in my mind, the sweet smell of chamomile and bergamot. The underlying tone of vanilla and that sweet intoxicating scent of spice. It was impossible to forget it.

Even after the first time.

With every fiber of who I thought I was, I longed to be near her, and it was going to be my downfall. Just her being here had caused so much to happen. I'd been waiting for years for this moment, for this time. I felt the magic coming back to me with each new vision and memory she had. And I still could not explain what her touch had done to me.

But the hold the curse had over me?

It was starting to come undone. Each new memory I had lost in all of this, came back the longer she was here. But it only took one memory for the pieces to all fall into place for me. Bringing her back here had been the right choice. But was it for myself, or for her now? I was bound by forces out of my own control.

I- like everyone else, was bound by the curse. But I was *not* bound to keep her here. I was not obliged to follow every order or command.

I was not the beast.

I was not cruel, or malicious, or evil.

I was not what she thought.

While I had freer rein than those around me, the consequences would be severe. The rules had been bent. And I knew what was going to happen if I made this choice. If I acted on what I was thinking. I knew what the right thing to do was. Whether it was going to break me or not.

She just could not stay here.

"Sir?" Hendrix's voice infiltrated my thoughts.

"What?"

His voice pulled me from the inner recesses of my mind, from the dark spiral I was on. Hendrix was standing next to me, wearing a contorted goat mask with antlers furling around his face. It was ugly and nauseating, but this was essential. It was necessary to scare her, as much as it pained me to do so.

"They're getting testy."

"Let them toy with her a moment more."

My eyes flashed back to where Serra was, finding her amongst a large group of Fae males. They'd surrounded her. They were relentless in their jabs and sneers. Even from where I stood, hidden from view by a set of pillars, I could see the hands that tried to reach out and touch. Reaching for her hair, her skirts, anything they could get their hands on, but they never laid a finger on her.

The irritation blossomed in my chest, the feeling grating on my patience. It was nothing like I had ever felt before, the need to whisk her away at that moment should not have materialized. The feeling caused shadows to dance at my fingertips.

"Sir, I-"

"What, Hendrix? You what?" The shadows intensified. Darkening around my hands, my fingers disappearing into them. My irritation was growing with each passing moment, with each second that she was in danger.

He looked away. "Do they know?"

Baring my teeth, my own voice was cold and malicious, it was hard for me to recognize it. Harder enough to recognize the male I was becoming. "They will not touch her; they will not harm her."

"But Sir."

"Go back to the Castle. You are done here." A crude dismissal of him. But he'd done what was ordered, he was no longer needed. Glaring down at Hendrix as he bowed before slipping away into the crowd.

It was time, it was time to end this.

Carefully slipping into the crowd, my presence unknown until then. Those around me finally recognized who I was, they knew better. Kept their eyes down as I passed them, a few brave Fae drunk on wine tried and failed to vie for my attention. But my eyes were set on her.

Always on her.

Only once did I need to bare my teeth. Only once did the growl rumble deep in my chest, a warning to the female whose hands found their way to my chest. Touching me as if she had once been my lover, and she probably had been once upon a time. I don't remember many of their faces. Females put in my path and I had taken advantage of it. Lucky for her though, a male had scooped her up before I could lay a finger on her. A laugh escaping her lips as he did so.

Deceitful and lascivious.

I only paused briefly in my quest to watch the couple, my eyes following them as they wove their way through the crowd to a sofa. The male dropped her amongst the cushions covered in pillows, landing on top of her before engaging in whatever acts they desired. Pulling my attention away, searching for Serra it took all of a few seconds to finally find her again. Her chocolate brown hair catching in the light, her cheeks flush on her skin. It did not take much for me to spot her amongst the drunk and lively throng of Fae at all.

Oh I hated this, I wanted nothing to do with any of it.

But even as she made her way past the males, she was weaving a path toward me. A pull I felt deep in my chest, a lingering feeling that had always been my way of finding her.

The crowd was closing in on her. They had her turned around in the other direction, she was lost in the sea of Fae. Her head turned then, her eyes scanning the crowd. My heart sputtered the moment her eyes found mine. Her bright green eyes were stunning. My blood heated, rushing through me forcing my breath to catch itself in my throat.

She was breathtaking.

The one thing I had sworn would never happen. The only thing I diligently tried to avoid, would not allow himself to feel. The one thing I'd given up on so long ago.

Hope.

Her lips parted as her eyes searched mine. I could hear her heart as it sped up, my ears tuning into her pulse. The bodice of her dress hugged her curves, her breasts. The sharp angles of her décolletage.

What I wouldn't give to kiss the column of her neck. The soft spot behind her ear. To hear her sigh at the tender touch of my fingers as they undressed her or the feel of her lips on my own. The pang in my heart stopped me from stepping forward, what I wouldn't give to hear her laugh again, to smile at me as she had others.

I wanted so desperately to visit the human man who broke her. Took from her, taunted her, assaulted her, bound her with threats and promises. It took everything in me not to go back, to tear him from limb to limb. Show him what real nightmares were, make him suffer in his own darkness.

If only they had known.

No one knew, not one person in her village knew what she was capable of. Of who she was. At that moment, I knew. The truth was ever present, hovering over me this entire time. Fate had played and it had won. Now I would burn the world for her and there was nothing that could stop me. I'd only be denying myself if I did. The one thing I did not want to happen. This beautiful female was going to be my undoing.

And I'd fallen for her.

CHAPTER
Twenty-Seven

Serra

THE CROWD PARTED FOR him. His presence forced them to skitter out of the way as he held my gaze. Slowly, his eyes roved over me, taking in the ballgown, the gloves, the crystal slippers and the twinkle of the skirts as it moved. Before landing on my neck. Sending a shiver down my spine, his gaze was penetrating.

What I wouldn't give to know what he was thinking.

His hair was sleekly pulled back, secured at the nape of his neck, while a dark silver crown of vines and leaves adorned his brow. He exuded an air of darkness and mystery, with his dark polished boots and black trousers. His muscled chest was embraced by a deep ocean blue satin doublet, perfectly tailored to his form. A velvet jacket of the same color, intricately embroidered in silver with delicate swirling vines, completed his ensemble.

The attention to detail extended to the cuffs of his attire, which were adorned with extravagant embroidery. A pair of black diamond cufflinks held them in place, their brilliance capturing the essence of the stars. In every aspect, he appeared magnificent. The same words that had consumed my thoughts for days resurfaced, acknowledging his captivating presence.

Cruel and cunning.

But beautiful and alluring.

My heart raced as I gazed upon this captivating creature before me. Every fiber of my being was drawn to him, an undeniable magnetic pull that defied explanation. There was a sense of familiarity in his presence, a hint of danger lurking beneath it all. The very thought of losing myself in his arms sent shivers down my spine, igniting a fire within me that I couldn't resist. Words seemed inadequate to express the intensity of my desires, but the longing in my eyes and the quickening of my breath spoke volumes. Despite his appearance, he was darkness incarnate.

He was Death.

And it made my heart skip.

As he neared, a trail of shadows and smoke followed him, coiling at his feet like obedient serpents. He stood before me, tall and imposing, with an outstretched hand that seemed to beckon me closer. The tips of his fingers were wreathed in a dark cloud of smoke and shadow, coiling and dancing around them like playful sprites. With each subtle movement, they twisted and turned, as if they had a life of their own. I couldn't help but be drawn in by the hypnotic display, my eyes locked on the mysterious figure before me.

An invitation.

"Dance with me, Serra?" he inquired, his voice a velvety caress that ran along my bones. With a slight bow at the waist, his eyes fixed upon me with an intensity that pierced through my very soul. They glimmered with a mischievous allure, a playful dance of desire that stirred something deep within me.

My breath had caught itself, I could not breathe. The air crackled with anticipation as I considered his request, his gaze urging me to surrender to the allure of the moment. Slowly I place my hand in his, letting him lead me into the center of the room. The musicians picked up the next song. A waltz. The same one we had danced to before.

I felt the heat of his hand through my bodice as he placed it on my lower back. His eyes cut through me as he held my gaze. Never blinking away, never dropping below my neck. My heart thundered in my chest as the music played. Up and down through the notes, the Goblin King led me through the steps.

He never spoke.

He didn't need to. His eyes locked onto mine. This close I could see the dark rings around his irises. A symbol of his shadows, even as they trailed in his wake. We twirled in endless dance steps, his hand on my back as he guided us across the floor. The waltz coming to its crescendo. I didn't want this to end. I prayed and wished that this moment would freeze.

That I could hold on to this Fae male and he onto me.

I would give anything for it.

As we danced, I could feel the heat of his body pressed against mine, his breath hot against my neck. Every move, every step, was a seduction, a promise of things to come. I knew I was in over my head, that this Fae male was going to be my undoing, but I didn't care. I was willing to risk everything for this moment, this feeling, this overwhelming desire that threatened to consume me whole.

The midnight blue gossamer layers of my dress swished around our feet as the next song began. The crystal studded bodice was suddenly too tight as I struggled to breathe. But he doesn't miss a step, he doesn't falter. Guiding me across the floor. The onlookers paused their conversations to watch. Being this close, I could see the way his muscles contracted with each movement, his pulse quickening under my stare.

Still, he pulls me in closer, whispering in my ear, "What is it you want Serra, what do you desire most?"

Shivers run down my back at the caress of his breath on my skin, his closeness. The scent of him washing over me. If I could hold onto this moment, forever, I would. My heart sighed in happiness, my dreams coming true.

My wishes had been granted. My heart was full, at this moment I felt complete. At this moment, I wanted for nothing. The way he made me feel. The way he looked at me, with longing and desire. The love that I had longed for. I realized what it was I truly wanted. Who I wanted. He was the Goblin King and I wanted. . . him.

I wanted him.

I wanted everything.

If anything in my life felt right, it was this. I was so sure of it. "I. . ."

The weight of his hand on my back felt like an anchor, grounding me in the moment. I gazed up into his eyes, once sparkling with mischief, now clouded with sadness. His gaze bore into mine, searching for something that I couldn't name. The shadows at his feet twisted and coiled like restless serpents, a reflection of the uncertainty that gnawed at my heart.

I opened my mouth to answer, to give voice to the truth that lay buried deep within me, but the words caught in my throat. What did I really want? The question echoed in my mind, a taunting reminder of the indecision that had plagued me for so long. I looked up at him, searching for answers in the depths of his piercing gaze, but all I found was a reflection of my own uncertainty.

For a moment, we stood there in silence, the weight of our unspoken desires hanging heavy in the air. The shadows at his feet seemed to grow darker, a mirror of the doubts that clouded my mind. And yet, despite the uncertainty that lay between us, I knew that if anything in my life felt right, it was this.

"You could have everything. I can give you your dreams. I can give you everything you could ask for. I will give you the world if that is what you seek." he mutters, just barely audible. Resting his forehead against mine. I could feel the weight of his words, the weight of the world pressing down on us. His offer was tempting, the idea of having everything I had ever wanted.

But at what cost? What was the price I would have to pay for this? Could I really trust him? Did I want to be tied to the Goblin King for eternity? The questions swirled in my mind, a whirlwind of doubt and fear.

But as I looked into his eyes, I saw something there that made me pause. Something that told me that he truly cared for me. That he was willing to do anything to make me happy. And maybe, just maybe, that was enough for me.

"Everything?" I whispered, my voice barely audible above the din of the ballroom.

"Everything," he repeated, his eyes never leaving mine.

I took a deep breath and closed my eyes, trying to gather my thoughts. When I opened them again, I looked up at him, my decision made.

"Then I want you," I said, my voice strong and sure.

There is a soft tug at the corners of his lips, his reply was easy, "You already have me, Serra,"

My heart fluttered, a feeling of completeness as his words sunk in. His features shifted though sending a wave of hesitation through me.

"I have to tell you something."

"What is it?"

I gazed up into his eyes, sensing the sorrow and turmoil within him. His breaths were shallow and labored, as though he were struggling to contain his inner demons. The pain and guilt etched on his face spoke volumes.

It was clear that he was keeping something from me.

After a moment of silence, he spoke again. "You didn't need to make a wish, Serra," he said, his voice barely above a whisper.

I was taken aback, it was not what I expected him to say. "What do you mean? I don't understand," I asked, my brow furrowed in confusion.

"You didn't need to make a wish for me to come for you. I'd always find you," he confessed.

I was even more puzzled than before, "Come for me? What are you talking about?"

He scanned my face, his gaze shifting between my eyes and the bustling ballroom around us. There was a heaviness in his expression, a burden he carried. After a moment, his eyes returned to mine, filled with both sorrow and determination. A deep breath escaped his lips, carrying his words to me like a gentle breeze that stirred my emotions.

"I'm sorry," he whispered, his voice a delicate thread that tugged at the strings of my heart.

"Sorry for what?" I asked, my confusion growing.

"For everything," he replied, his words fracturing a part of me. We had stopped dancing, and his apology seemed to open a Pandora's box of emotions within me.

"What do you mean?" I asked, my voice trembling.

"When I asked for payment, you offered me your memories, Serra. The reason why you came here and what you were here to retrieve," he explained.

I tried to pull away from him, but his grip on me tightened. "But I never took them. They were not mine to take," he said, his eyes darkening, his lips tightened as if he wanted to say more.

"What did you do?"

"You have to understand that I did not want this, I did not want it to happen like this. It was not supposed to happen like this," he said frantically.

I asked again, "What do you mean, what did you do?"

"Everything that has happened, everything from our time in the garden to now. It was altered, the memories, your reality, your path, all of it was by my hand. I played a game with Fate and I lost."

As I looked at him, I could see the pain etched on his face. It was as if he carried the weight of the world on his shoulders. The Goblin King, the one who had always been so confident and in control, now seemed vulnerable and lost. I felt my world shift beneath me. I tried to pull away from him, but his grip was too strong. My mind was reeling, trying to process what he had just told me.

"How could you do something like that?" I asked, my voice barely above a whisper.

"I had no choice," he replied, his eyes pleading with me to understand.

"Why? Why didn't you just tell me?" I asked, feeling a surge of anger and betrayal.

"I wanted to, believe me. But I couldn't."

"Why would you do it in the first place?" I seethed.

He hesitated before answering, as if searching for the right words. "A lot has happened, Serra. Things that I didn't anticipate. And I had to make a choice."

"What kind of choice?" I pressed.

His gaze flickered away for a moment, as if grappling with the weight of his confession. When his eyes met mine again, they held a mixture of remorse and determination.

"A choice to protect you, to keep you safe from forces that you couldn't even begin to comprehend," he said, his voice tinged with a hint of sorrow. "I told you, there are others outside my circle that wish you harm. To alter the course of events, it was to shield you from that danger. The stakes were high, and I had to act."

I shook my head in disbelief. "But why would you do that to me? Why would you take away my memories?"

"I did it to protect you," he said, his voice barely above a whisper.

"Protect me from what?"

He took a deep breath, steeling himself for what he was about to say. "There are forces at work that even I cannot control. And you, Serra, are at the center of it all."

I felt a shiver run down my spine at his words. "What do you mean?"

"The magic that runs through your veins is powerful. It has drawn the attention of those who would harm you. Beings that would do anything to get their hands on it."

"But. . . what does that have to do with my memories?" I asked, feeling even more confused

"I had to hide them away, deep within your mind. It was the only way to protect you, to keep you safe."

"How?" I asked, trying to make sense of his words.

"A spell for forgetting," he said, and I could see the pain in his eyes.

"Why?" I asked, my voice trembling.

"I had to. It was the only way," he repeated, his grip on me tightening even more. But I could see it in his eyes. He was lying to me.

"Only way for what?!" I demanded, pushing against him with all my strength, but he was too solid, too strong.

"I cannot say," he said, his voice barely audible now.

Another lie. I could feel the tears pricking at the back of my eyes.

"You took away my memories and changed my life. You altered what you should not have. You played a game with me, I was your pawn. You caused more hurt than you ever could have imagined. Why?" I asked, my voice shaking with anger and betrayal.

"I took them away from you for my own agenda," he finally admitted, and I felt a surge of rage and despair wash over me.

He had taken away my memories for his own agenda? What could he have possibly wanted with them?

I stepped back from him, finally free from his grip to put some distance between myself and him. The cold air around us grew irksome. His lack of touch sent an unwelcome shiver through me. I felt like I had been punched in the gut. The Goblin King, the one who had always been there for me in stories and dreams, had been playing his own game all along.

And I was just a pawn in it all.

"You. . . you deceived me," I said, my voice quivered.

He reached out to me, but I pulled away. "Serra, please. You have to understand. I did it to protect you."

"I don't want to hear it," I said, my voice shaking with anger and hurt. "You took away my memories, you changed my life. And for what? For your own selfish reasons?"

He looked at me, his eyes filled with pain. "I never meant to hurt you. You have to believe that."

I shook my head, feeling the tears prick at the back of my eyes. "I don't know what to believe anymore."

"You never had to make a wish," he said softly, his eyes searching mine. "I've always been with you, watching over you, waiting." His words were like a punch to the gut, knocking the breath out of me.

"Waiting for what?" I demanded, my frustration coating my voice. I was tired of all the cryptic messages and half-truths.

"For you to be ready," he replied, and the agony in his expression told me that he was struggling to hold something back.

"Ready for what? What are you talking about?" My irritation was growing with every passing moment. I had no idea what he was trying to say but I was running out of patience.

He glanced around the room- at the figures around us as they began to blur and fade away. "I can see now that it was a mistake. You're not prepared for this, and I have to get you out. I have to get you away from here."

"You're not making any sense," I said, taking a step back from him.

He reached for my hand, his fingers brushing mine. "Come with me."

"No!" I jerked my hand away, the shock of his touch making me recoil. "Don't touch me!"

"Serra, please," he begged, and I could see the desperation in his eyes. The Goblin King was actually pleading with me, and it seemed like he had gone crazy.

"Leave me alone," But the more he spoke, the more my irritation and frustration turned into anger.

"Leave me alone. . ." I said, my voice firm and unwavering. "I don't know what game you're playing, but I'm done with it."

The room around us began to swirl, as if the world was closing in on us. I could feel the darkness creeping in at the edges of my vision. And then, before I knew it, I was falling into it, the Goblin King's desperate cries ringing in my ears as everything began to fade to black. But the room around us began to swirl. The pillars and marble melted away.

"Serra! Wait!" One last desperate cry from the Goblin King as the words he spoke in the ballroom hung over me and I fell down toward the open darkness.

CHAPTER
Twenty-Eight

Serra

THE ROOM WAS DARK.

Bare of any furniture or comforts of any kind. The space was damp, cold. It sent a shiver down my spine. My eyes adjusted to the darkness that surrounded me, seeing where I had ended up. There were no windows, nothing to let in any light. And I couldn't find a door to get out, trapping me inside.

The walls were carved from the earth, smelling of wet dirt and decay. The sound of night-crawlers in the walls had me shrinking back away as I sat on the floor.

I was alone.

I didn't know how long it had been, how long I sat there in the dirt, staring at the carved walls before me. My mind blank, my thoughts lost. My heart was empty for I felt nothing. But time seemed to pass slowly here in the dark. For all I knew, it could have been days or only just minutes. However long it had been, it all blended together even as I sat there. It did not matter anymore, not really. Sitting alone in the darkness as I let it swirl around me in sadness and anguish.

The only real thing that kept me company were the twinkling lights above, having shown up what felt like hours ago. Not really sure where they had come from, or how they came to be, but they were there. Even here, the stars were my friends, keeping me company.

My ball gown had torn, leaving it dirty and in shreds. The crystals on the bodice had lost all of their sparkle, as if they too had given up and no longer wanted to shine. Betrayed by another as well. At some point, I'm not sure when my hair had fallen out. The limp curls cascading down around my shoulders. Falling in front of my face. Pulling my knees to my chest and resting my chin, I stared.

Stared at nothing. My world had been shattered, again. My heart was broken and smashed. Everything I thought I knew was a lie. Everything I believed was also a lie.

He'd lied to me.

And I know I should have known better, I should have seen it coming, but I was a fool. I let my heart lead me thinking one thing, when I should have been listening to my head. Telling me that something was wrong. To play with the Goblin King, to play his game, whatever game this was. . . was a risk in itself.

And I had made a mistake, again.

I had trusted him. I had wanted him. And worse yet, I had fallen for him. My stupid idiot heart had fallen for him. Falling for him had certainly been asking for trouble too. And I played. Oh, I had played his game and I had lost. I had given my heart to someone I didn't even know.

I had held it out to him, thinking it would be repaired. Thinking he would hold it and cherish it. For every encounter it had pieced itself back together. For every moment I was in his presence, it wanted him. I don't know if I would call it love, because love was different for everybody but this. . . it was something. Was it not?

It was familiar. Destined. It felt. . . *right*.

But none of that mattered now.

Everything was different. And I had been a fool. I had played with a being I knew was dangerous. I had risked more than just my life by coming here, by agreeing to play his game. I knew making a deal with him was going to cost me.

And it did.

The tear rolled down my cheek, burning a path as it dripped off my jaw. Brushing it away before laying down in the damp earth. Letting the darkness caress my heart, welcoming its embrace before closing my eyes and drifting off to sleep.

I DIDN'T DREAM, OR at least I don't think I did. The only dream that accompanied me was the nightmares, the same nightmare. Always the same. Fire, shouts, and the sound of steel rang in my ears. It was my only companion in my dark earthen carved room. One that plagued me so many times before, my dreams from the past riddled with it. Often waking up in a fit of sweats. Nona was usually there, to calm me down. But not this time.

Not now.

She was gone.

I was left alone to deal with them on my own. Dozing in and out of consciousness, never really registering where I was. I would wake in another fit of sweats, my hair damp as I rolled over on the ground and went back to sleep. Over and over it seemed, the vicious cycle repeating itself. I never felt rested, it always felt like the energy I had gained was expelled from me almost instantly.

All I really remembered was the smell of the wet earth, the feel of the damp ground and the twinkling lights above before falling back into the safety and familiarity of the darkness. That was, until the nightmares would start again. The events of the ballroom were a long distant memory.

I'm not sure how long it had been. Not sure the last time I had something to eat or even saw the sun. But what did it matter anymore? Really, because did it matter anymore? In this place I was safe, as safe as I could be from those who would harm me. From those who would break me. I was content to stay here forever if it meant I no longer had to feel.

This place was Hell, and it was where I belonged.

I AWOKE WITH A jolt. Suddenly feeling as if I was no longer alone. As if someone watched me in the dark. The feeling of another presence, waiting. "Who's there?" my voice came out hoarse from not using it in some time. How long has it been?

How long have I been down here?

"Why are you crying?" a voice whispered, it was soft but shrill.

I jumped, having not expected an answer. I'd been in here alone for so long I had not realized how quiet the space had been. How my mind had let go of so many thoughts. How the silence had afforded me time to grieve. Grieve for myself, grieve for my parents, my brother. Grieve for my Nona.

My life I had known with her.

How different it would be going back.

"Who's there?" I did not recognize my own voice, not as it quivered. The cords were tight from not being used.

Had I been crying? I don't remember crying, not really. My face felt damp and my eyes were tired. I was so tired. I wanted to lay back down and go to sleep. Sleep sounded so good. But there was a giggle as I felt a light breeze on my face. It was like someone had blown on it, softly as it caressed my cheeks. Only, I realized something had flitted past me instead.

It caused me to sit up, but I was still unable to see the owner of the voice. Even as my eyes adjusted in the dark. "I cannot see you."

A light flickers in front of me. Lighting up the room, my eyes focusing on the figure in front of me.

A sprite.

"Who are you?" I asked, my legs wobbled as I tried to stand. I had been laying in the dirt far too long. My body ached, every muscle screamed from laying on the ground, the lack of movement.

She smiled at me, cocking her head to the side in wonder. I watched the sprite stare at me, taking in my appearance from head to toe. But her face turns to shock as she looks upon my own, her hands flying to her mouth. Her light brightening.

"Oh! It's you!" she finally says.

Dropping her hands and fluttering before my face. Casting a soft glow as she spun around, her hair trailing in her wake. She was rather beautiful, her long hair floated about her face. Her round shape and plump legs, with eyes that twinkled as she smiled at me.

She spoke again, her hands pulling on a strand of my hair. "We've been waiting for you, you know. You shouldn't be here. You've been down here far too long now. You have to go."

"What?" I asked in disbelief.

"You're supposed to be at the castle," the sprite reminded me, her voice musical and light.

"The castle?" I repeated, trying to recall why I was supposed to be there. Trying as hard as I could to shake off the fog that had settled in my mind. It was as if everything in the last several days were being sucked into a black hole, leaving me with nothing but confusion and a sense of urgency.

"He's waiting for you," she sang, twirling around me. Her movements were so graceful, it was almost hypnotizing. I found myself staring at her, captivated by her beauty and her words.

"Who is?" I asked, my confusion growing. My heart skipped a beat. Who was waiting for me? And why was it so important that I get to the castle? The sprite seemed to read my mind, for she landed on my outstretched hand and leaned in close.

"The Prince, of course," she replied with a giggle, her eyes sparkling with mischief. "The one who holds the answers you seek."

The Prince? What Prince? My mind was a blank slate, and I couldn't seem to recall any Prince I knew. I racked my brain, trying to come up with a name, but nothing came to mind.

The sprite seemed to see my confusion as she patiently waited for me to connect the dots. There was no Prince the I knew, not here. Not in Rothnia. But maybe she was talking about another. *The Goblin King.* The name echoed in my mind, triggering a flurry of memories. A ballroom filled with glittering gowns and masks. A handsome man with piercing eyes and a cruel smile.

"Do you mean the Goblin King?" I asked.

Her eyes twinkled with amusement as she giggled again. "No, the Prince," she sang, before darting away into the darkness, leaving me alone with the twinkling lights.

"Wait!" I called out, but she was already gone. I was left standing there, staring at the panel of glass that had appeared in front of me. It looked like a window, and beyond it I could see the outline of a castle.

I hesitated for a moment, unsure of what to do next. Should I trust this sprite and head to the castle? What answers was she talking about? And who was waiting for me there? But all I got in response was a haunting melody that echoed around me, filling the air with a sense of longing and loss. And then, a light appeared, illuminating the panel of glass.

Tentatively, I stepped closer to the mirror, my heart racing with anticipation and fear. I hesitated, unsure if I wanted to see the reflection staring back at me. But I couldn't resist the urge to look after the chaos of the ballroom. Slowly, I lifted my gaze and gasped at the sight before me.

I was a complete disaster.

My hair was a tangled mess, strands sticking out at odd angles. The combs that had once held it back were long gone, and it hung in wild waves around my face. My dress was in tatters, the once-beautiful fabric now torn and dirty. Dirt streaked across my face, and tears had left tracks down my cheeks. I had been crying.

"That certainly will not do," the sprite declared, her tiny voice full of authority I watched in amazement as she waved her hand, I felt the magic she used- the electric current of it palpable on my skin. But as I glanced back in the mirror again I saw I was no longer covered in dirt, my shredded dress gone. Instead, I was clean, my breath caught as I saw what I was wearing.

My new dress was sleek and form-fitting, made of shimmering emerald satin that hugged my curves perfectly. It slithered across my skin as I moved, glistening in the light. The criss-cross of the fabric across my chest, the sleeves that hung off my shoulders, it was beautiful. My hair was now clean, combed, and styled in cascading curls down my back.

"Go on," she urged. "Go find him."

"But what do you mean? What answers, what prince?" I demanded, my uncertainty mounting. The sprite just giggled in response, flitting around me in a blur of light and color.

"Go find him, he's waiting for you."

I didn't know what she meant, but I knew I had to find out. As I approached the mirror again, my eyes fixated on my reflection. The twinkling lights overhead flickered and dimmed, casting a soft glow across the room. A strange urge washed over me, compelling me to reach out and touch the glass. My hand trembled as I drew closer, the tips of my fingers brushing against the cool surface of the mirror.

Suddenly, a loud, piercing sound filled the room, like shattering glass. I recoiled in shock, my heart pounding in my chest. Looking up at the mirror again, I saw that it was now cracked and splintered. My reflection distorted in the fractured surface as it spidered webbed across it. I stumbled backwards, my heart racing. I couldn't shake the feeling that something was going to change.

Without thinking, I stepped closer to it. As I peered into the fractured glass, I saw a figure standing on the other side. It was a male, tall and handsome, with white blonde hair and two mismatched eyes.

"Come to me," he whispered, his voice like velvet. "I have the answers you seek."

I reached out to touch the glass again, but the figure on the other side disappeared. Pieces of glass broke away instead, leaving me alone in the dark with nothing but the sound of my own breathing.

But then I remembered the feeling of being lost and alone, and a sense of urgency washed over me. I took a deep breath and stepped through the opening, leaving behind the earth carved room.

CHAPTER
Twenty-Nine

Serra

AS THE GLASS FELL away, I gasped at the suddenness of it. My hand jerked back as if I had been burned, recoiling from the shards that were now scattered around my feet. I gingerly stepped down from the gilded frame, the crunching sound of the broken glass under my shoes an unpleasant reminder of the shattered mirror.

My heart was racing as I looked around, trying to make sense of what had just happened. The room had changed, somehow. The air was thick with the scent of roses and lavender, and the soft cushions of the settee gave beneath my weight as I sank down onto it. I felt disoriented, as if I had been transported to another place entirely. The feeling of déjà vu washed over me, and I couldn't shake the feeling that I had been here before, that I had experienced this moment in some way.

My mind was racing, trying to make sense of it all.

Was I dreaming?

I'd seen this room before. Before me lay a long corridor. The dark wood panels that made up the walls with the deep burgundy carpet, silencing my steps as I walked. Despite the tall cathedral-high ceilings and exposed beams (now home to the swallows and bats,) they weighed heavily on the space. Taking a couple more steps into the room, uncertainty set me on edge. Glancing back behind me at the frame I had come out of, the mirror was pitch black.

The room I was in, and the room I had come from was dark; No light filtered in, and no sconces had been lit. Casting an eeriness upon everything. It was as if nothing had changed, the space was filled with frames, every inch of the paneled walls.

The same ones from the vision.

Portraits and landscapes, battle scenes and tapestries- hundreds of them. This wasn't just a corridor I realized; it was a gallery. A private one. Dozens of portraits of Fae nobles lined the walls. The room had not been touched in quite some time. Dirt and cobwebs littered the frames, white sheets hung over the furniture in the room. As if it had been covered and no one was expected to be back in some time.

I walked further down the corridor, taking in the details of the portraits. The Fae nobles depicted in the paintings were dressed in elegant clothes, their expressions stoic and unreadable. I wondered who they were and what their stories were, but I had a feeling that I would never know. The silence of the room was oppressive, the only sound being my own footsteps and the occasional flutter of wings from the birds and bats overhead.

As I approached the end of the corridor, I noticed that there was a door, slightly ajar. I pushed it open, revealing a small room that looked like it had once been used as a study. A large mahogany desk dominated the space, with a tall-backed chair behind it. The room was filled with books, stacked haphazardly on every surface. The smell of old leather and paper filled my nostrils.

I walked over to the desk and looked at the papers scattered on top of it. They were old, written in a language that I didn't recognize. There were also ink bottles and quills, as if someone had been using them recently. But who could have been in this room? And why had they left in such a hurry?

As I looked around the room, I noticed a map on the wall. It was old, the colors faded, but it was still legible. It was a map of the fae lands, with different kingdoms and territories marked out. As I studied it, I realized that I recognized some of the names of the places. They were the same ones that I had seen as a little girl. I'd seen this map more than once, each time. . . each time I had been in this study.

There was a feeling like I was suddenly on the brink of a discovery, but I didn't know what it was. The feeling of deja vu that had been with me since I entered the room intensified, and I knew that I had to leave. I carefully closed the door behind me and walked back down the corridor. As I passed by the portraits once again, I couldn't help but feel like I was being watched.

Walking along, my feet muffled on the carpet, the faces stared back at me. My attention waning as a portrait at the end of a long line caught my interest.

The subject looked familiar. A young boy, barely able to stand. A navy-blue dress suit and red sash across his torso. Blonde hair and bright blue eyes. I knew those chubby cheeks. Remembered them.

Aden. My brother.

The brass plaque at the bottom read:

Aden Octavius Marcelle Darthordian

That wasn't right. Aden Octavius Marcelle Darthordian? No, that was wrong. It was my brother in the portrait, but something was off, not just with his name, but with his ears. They were tapered, coming to a delicate soft point. "That's not right."

Confusion and longing battled inside me. Our family name was Harlowe. Not Darthordian

"This has to be some vicious joke." I muttered, catching sight of another painting. Next to the painted portrait was another Fae noble, a name on a brass plaque at the bottom of the frame:

Astraea Irene Linnea Darthordian
Crown Princess, Heir Apparent

Not just a noble. Royalty.

Astraea Irene Linnea Darthordian.

Crown Princess and heir apparent.

Interesting.

The subject in this portrait was a very young girl. She was wearing a gauzy white dress with flowers in her dark hair. A beautiful pink sash at her waist. Her striking green eyes stared back at you. A memory flickered in the back of my mind. Like it was trying to tell me something. Like it wanted me to know.

My breath hitched, my throat constricting.

That was me, painted in the portrait. Only, I was five when it had been done. Mother had wanted my hair left loose and a diadem set atop, but I remembered throwing a fit over flowers in my hair. Flowers I had woven into a crown with Ruthie- mother's ladies' maid.

I desperately wanted them, I had fought her hard. Throwing a tantrum until I got what I wanted. She was beside herself at the end of it and had given in. It wasn't long after it was finished and hung that everything changed. I was a year older at that point.

My eyes scanned the room again. At all the paintings that hung, the space was familiar but foreign. I should not know this room, I had never been here before. The portraits all stared back at me, crushing me with their heavy gazes. I'd been here before, I'd seen this space. But it was occupied by a couple dancing.

"I don't understand."

The large frame at the end captured my attention. Another portrait. This time it was of a gentleman and lady. The woman was seated in a red velvet covered chair, he was positioned slightly behind her, hand resting on her right shoulder. They were both beautiful. Stunning even. While she had bright blonde hair and blue eyes, he had dark brown hair and green eyes. The Name plague was worn, but I could just make out the etching:

His Royal Majesty Elias Marcelle Darthordian

Below the King's name was hers:

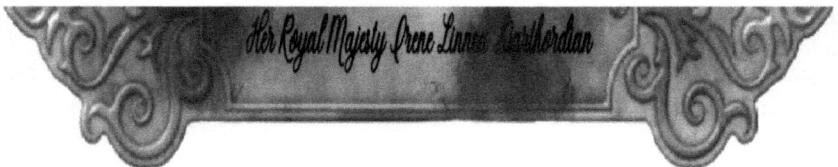

Her Royal Majesty Irene Linnea Darthordian

Elias Marcelle and Irene Linnea Darthordian.

But it was her face in the painting. I knew her face from somewhere. She was the one in the garden, the labyrinth of hedges and trees. A babe in her arms. Her laugh echoed as she called a name. Her white cotton dress stark against the green leaves and tan color of the cobblestones. Her blue eyes were full of life, love, and wonder. Her smile was warm and inviting. The smell of fresh lavender and vanilla assaulted my senses. A familiar smell. Tears welled up in my eyes. My breath came in huge gasps.

The memory washed over me, as if it were my own.

A girl in a green linen dress had a stain on the front, a bear clutched to her chest, as she ran into the room. A streak of tears staining her cheeks. The woman on the stone floor before her lay lifeless, her blonde hair stained red with blood. Her gown no longer white, stained from the wound in her chest. Her once beautiful blue eyes, dead and lifeless, glazed over. The pool of blood was growing ever larger.

A small voice echoed "Momma?"

The girl reached for the hand that lay to the side, the delicate fingers of the woman curled to clutch a necklace. The locket opened, a portrait of the girl and a babe cuddled together and a man resembling the king inside.

She reached out, shaking her mother's arm. Tears and snot dripping from her nose. "Momma." she cried again. "Momma!"

"Astraea? Astraea, we have to go." A voice said behind her, breathless. As if he had run a great distance. Turning her head, a faun stood in the doorway, blade in his hand. Pacing inside, hand outstretched. "We don't have much time. Please."

The vision faded to black as the girl clutched the faun's hand. But before I could gather myself, another replaced it. The faun she had followed, her hand once clutched tightly in his, wielded the blade as he fought the intruders. His voice echoing in my head as he yelled.

"RUN ASTRAEA!"

She did not hesitate. Running in the opposite direction, the direction they were headed was blocked by men in armor black as night. Turn after turn, long corridor after long corridor. She knew where she was going. She had run these halls numerous times. The wood door in front of her at the end of the hall, the one she was after, made her cry.

"Papa!"

Her little legs carried her as fast as she could, "Papa!"

Bursting through the door, the man on the throne leaped up. His sword falling, her tears flowing as he caught her in his arms.

The vision faded again. The portrait coming back into view. The man, the woman. King and Queen. My Mother. My Father. The room spun, my head becoming light as the realization hit. I remembered then. I remembered them. I remembered all of it. Everything. The well opening and overflowing with the memories of my life with them.

The life I had lost, the lives they sacrificed, the chance they gave for me. Spinning around I caught a glimpse of a door at the far end. A door I hoped would take me away from here. Hefting my skirt I marched toward it. The eyes of those in the paintings behind me, watching as I left.

I yanked the door open, and a cloud of dust and ash billowed out. As I stepped into the hallway, my foot caught on something, and I stumbled to the edge of a massive crater in the floor. The hallway had been torn in half, leaving a jagged opening that led to the outside world. The walls were scorched and blackened, and I could see the sky through the gaps in the stone. Turrets and towering stone structures loomed over me, casting long shadows across the ruined hallway. I realized with a jolt that I was standing in a castle, one that had been attacked and destroyed.

My heart raced as I remembered my dreams, the ones that had led me here. This was the castle that the sprite had spoken of, but as I looked around at the devastation, at the destruction that had happened to it. Carefully, I stepped over the missing section of the floor and made my way to the opposite wall, which was half-destroyed, with jagged rocks and broken beams strewn across the ground. It was as if something had exploded from within, tearing the wall apart in a massive blast.

Something large had done the damage.

As I peered down at the desolate wasteland below, memories flooded back of the once-thriving city. Nona had called the Goblin City. But I knew the truth - this was the home of the people of Inirea, my father's kingdom that he had governed and cared for. As a child, I had seen them waving at me from my father's side, but now they were all gone.

Buildings of all sizes lay in ruins, either destroyed by explosions or reduced to charred rubble. The devastation was overwhelming, and it was clear that the attack had started at the heart of the city. I felt a deep sense of sadness and anger as I gazed upon the destruction. Innocent people and their lives had been destroyed. The city was silent, utterly still. Walking closer to the edge of the broken wall, I searched for any sign of life, hoping to see someone, anyone. But the city was empty, as if all of its inhabitants had vanished into thin air. The only sounds were the howling wind and the creaking of the ruined buildings.

I couldn't believe what I was seeing. This was my father's kingdom reduced to nothing but ruins. A kingdom I was supposed to rule someday. But now it was nothing more than a ghost town, a shadow of its former self.

Moving away from the crumbling wall, my only option to avoid falling through the floor and descending to the level below was to approach a set of large wooden doors. Despite being charred by flames, the intricately carved doors loomed over me, featuring a beautiful design of twirling vines and blooming Mandevillas along the outer perimeter. The center of the doors displayed three large circles, with a hippogriff carved at the bottom and an eagle with outstretched wings at the top. The middle circle showcased a special character formed by blended initials, from which I could only make out the letters E and I.

After putting all my weight behind the doors and pushing them open, I entered a massive room. The stone walls were black and crumbling, with a few wooden beams still standing the test of time. Others lay broken and charred on the stone floor, indicating that a fire had once engulfed the space. The roof was long gone, exposing the remains of the room to the elements and the setting sun.

As I scanned the space, my eyes eventually landed on an object at the far end. The wind whistled through the holes in the walls, moving tendrils of hair across my face and neck and causing the skirt of my dress to flutter gently. I felt my breath catch in my throat as our eyes locked, his presence awakening something in me yet again.

The Goblin King.

There he was amongst the charred ruins of the room, lounging in a throne. He wore the same deep ocean blue vest and jacket from the ball. His boots polished and trousers tucked. He looked worse than before, as if he hadn't bothered to change his clothes in some time. The throne he sat in was once gilded gold, marred by whatever had happened here. The room was in utter disrepair and destruction and yet. . . he seemed sad.

He looked so broken. Defeated.

The dark shadows under his eyes stark against his pale skin. His hair was still pulled back at the nape of his neck. His eyes tracked me as I entered the room, never leaving mine.

His smell; caressed every part of me that vibrated with longing. To be held by him. To get lost in his eyes. Touched by him in the most intimate of ways. My name on his lips as I gasped in need and desire.

"Princess." His voice came out scratchy, horse as if he had been screaming. "I have done what you asked."

Startled, I retorted, "You have only done what has been best for yourself, what benefits you."

"I have been generous."

The vision of him and the feeling he roused from me were long gone. My anger pushed me forward, toward the male that sat before me, toward the male I had dreams about, the one who haunted me in my waking hours. To the male who had until recently, held my heart. Marching up to the stone steps of the dais. I could not stop myself, not as I spat at him.

"Generous? What have you done for me that has been generous?"

"Everything!" He leapt from the throne, "Everything I have done, I have done for you! Serra, do you not see it?" His eyes flashed, the raw emotion there.

Stepping back away from him as he descends the step. His strides quickly stop before me. His hair was wild and his eyes dark. "I have done nothing but protect you!"

"Protect me from what? Because it certainly was not from you!"

He flinched. "Everything I have done, I have done because of you."

"What have you done? What have you done because of me? What was so *horrible* you had to protect me from it?" My voice quivered as I spoke.

The Goblin King stared at me. "What is it you want from me? I have done everything you have asked. I have granted you every wish. Every dream. What more do you want?"

Tension crackled in the air as I stood before the Goblin King. I should demand the answers I was owed. My heart thudded heavily in my chest, I needed to know why he had brought me here, to this ruined kingdom, to the place my family had once resided.

"I need the truth," I said firmly, trying to steady my voice. "You owe me that much."

I could see a hint of something softening in his hard features. He seemed to be considering my words, weighing his response carefully before giving a single nod of agreement.

I wanted to ask him about the images that haunted me, the visions of this place that had been plaguing me. But instead, I gestured to the destroyed city around us. "What happened here?" I asked, my eyes sweeping over the ruins of what must have once been a grand throne room.

The Goblin King gazed around the room, lost in thought. "It was a coup," he said finally, his voice low and heavy with emotion.

"A coup?" I repeated, my confusion growing. I had never heard of such a thing happening in a kingdom of fae and immortals.

He let out a heavy sigh, as if trying to decide how much to reveal. "There were those who believed that King Elias and his heirs were not the rightful rulers," he explained his eyes flashing with hatred. "They thought his twin brother, Ezra, should be on the throne."

I felt a chill run down my spine at the mention of Ezra's name. I had never heard of him before, but something about the way the Goblin King spoke his name made me feel uneasy. Something that did not sit right in me.

The Goblin King continued, his pacing bringing him closer to me. "Eighteen years ago, Ezra and his supporters launched a violent attack on the city," he said, his voice growing darker. "They broke through the walls and slaughtered many of the people. By nightfall, they had breached the castle walls."

He stopped then, lost in memory. I could see the pain etched on his face, the weight of what had happened here still heavy on his shoulders. "That was the night the King and Queen were killed," he said, his voice thick. "Their son, the young prince, disappeared, presumed dead. And the princess. . ." He looked at me, his expression unreadable "Well, until now, she was nowhere to be found."

CHAPTER
Thirty

Serra

HE MUST BE BLUFFING. "What?" I asked him, trying to hide my fear.

"You, Serra," he replied, his eyes piercing mine.

I hesitated, unsure of his intentions. I could feel the tension in the room, could feel the magic that simmered in this place. "I don't understand any of this," I said, my voice quivered with each word I said, "You've been mixing truth with lies the whole time, and now you expect me to believe you?"

"Yes," he said simply.

"Why should I?" I demanded. "You've lied to me from the start. What are you protecting me from?"

He hesitated and I knew there was more to the story, more that he wasn't telling me, "The survival of this Realm depends on it," he finally said. "You need to remember."

"Remember what?" I asked, feeling my frustration mounting. "Why am I here?"

"You needed to come back," he replied, his voice softening. "You need to remember."

"I don't understand," I said, my confusion growing. "Why can't you just tell me?"

"Because I can't!" He sighed, his whole body tensed up again. "I cannot tell you. This is your journey, I cannot do it for you. All I can do is guide you."

I felt a surge of anger rising within me, fueling the ember that had been smoldering in my stomach. "Enough with the games," I said, my voice rising. "I need answers, and I need them now."

He sighed heavily, as if struggling with his own internal battle. "I cannot tell you," he said at last. "You have to do this on your own. *Try to remember.*"

I closed my eyes, searching for any memory that could give me a clue. And then it came to me - Luna's face. "Luna was here," I said slowly. "She pulled me from the hiding spot, the fire. . ."

The Goblin King nodded, his expression unreadable. "What else?"

As I spoke, memories began to resurface within me. Visions of a grand castle, filled with nobles and dignitaries dressed in their finest attire. I remembered being there, though I couldn't quite place why. I could hear the murmur of their conversations, though I couldn't quite make out what they were saying.

Then the memory shifted, and I was in a small room, hiding behind a hidden door, the large tapestry that had covered it. The room was engulfed in flames, and I could feel the heat on my skin. I could hear someone calling my name, their voice filled with urgency. And then Luna's face appeared, pulling me from my hiding spot and leading me to safety.

"I remember the fire," I said, my voice barely above a whisper. "I remember Luna saving me. But there's more. . . I just can't-"

The Goblin King nodded, his eyes filled with a mix of relief and apprehension. "Try." he said softly.

I searched my memories once more, digging deeper this time. And then it hit me- the curse. Someone had mentioned a curse, but I couldn't quite remember who or why. "There was something about a curse," I whispered. "I remember someone mentioning it."

The Goblin King's eyes widened in surprise. "Yes, what else?" he asked, his voice urgent.

But my memory was hazy, and I couldn't quite recall any more details. I looked at the Goblin King, hoping for answers, but he remained silent. I could see the weight of the situation pressing down on him, and I knew that there was more to the story than he was willing to tell me. But for now, all I could do was hold onto the memories that had resurfaced, and trust that they would give me the answers I so desperately sought. But I wanted to know something. . .

"Nona?" I asked.

He nodded.

"Who was she?"

He ran a hand through his hair, causing it to become even more disheveled. "Luna was an elf." My mind reeled as the Goblin King revealed more about my past. "She found you, took you to Rothnia. She'd been asked to keep you safe and hidden away from this world. You would have remembered her as Ruthie. She was your mother's lady's maid."

The world spun around me, Luna was Ruthie, my mother's lady's maid, and an elf. It all made sense now- her strange behavior and her fear of the Goblin King. It was because of me. Who I was. Her fear of me finding out whom I truly was. But part of me believed that she told me the stories so that one day I could find out.

But he went on, and it took more from me to understand what he was saying, even as I struggled to separate the truth from the lies. The world spun as the pieces of the puzzle started to fit together. The Goblin King words mingled and swirled around me.

"I found you seventeen years ago," he said. "I went to Luna after, but she banned me from the cottage and cast a spell on the doors and windows, keeping me out. Keeping you safe. I couldn't come to you until she was gone. Her spell broke, she knew who I was."

"How?"

"I don't know. But she was not affected. Only a few escaped and those who did, were killed. Luna got away with you. Many immortals fled past the Ebony Woods. They were lucky. The massacre was. . . horrendous."

"If she was immortal, why did she die?"

"She is a Creature of the Realm. Her life, as is yours, is tied to Inirea. Her passing is due to that tie, the sickness as you call it back in Rothnia. She'd been away too long. Her life was taken from her as the land tried to survive. Any who do not return will eventually die. Any who did not make the crossing back to the Fae Realms before the siege, they passed sooner. Their life sources were weaker. It sought them out, took from them what it needed and it has been for eighteen years. Your return had to happen."

I felt a pang of sadness at the thought of Luna keeping me hidden away from the world for so long. But at the same time, I couldn't shake the feeling that there was more to the story. Why had Luna kept me hidden away? And who was I really?

The sadness I felt at her passing washed over me. The loss of my family and her had taken its hold of my heart once again. I had never really been free of it. I had never really gotten the chance to be.

He'd taken it from me.

Something stirred in me again, something that had surfaced before. The ember that had started to burn- sparked, shining brighter. My emotion, my sadness causing it to flare. The glow of a power not from here. The glow of a power I had no idea I carried. A power that I could feel living within me, swirling and begging to be freed. It was a power that felt foreign yet familiar.

I looked down at my fingers, the tips alight with the magic. Casting the ruins in a soft glow. The Goblin King's face lit up, his eyes wide. The walls around us began to tremble. The ground shook as the stones fell. Fear of them crushing me had the light going out. Confusion and hate, fear and loss. Remembering that the Fae male before me was a liar, an enemy.

No longer would I trust him.

No longer would I play his game.

I refused to play any longer. I was done with him and I was done with the this place. The burning question inside me- the one that had been bothering me. The one that had surfaced after each encounter with him. Who was he? A question fueled by anger and confusion, demanding to be answer. The sprite in my head, *Prince*, echoed in my thoughts.

"Who are you?" I turned to face him, my voice laced with fury. "Who are you really? And don't you dare lie to me again."

He straightened up, his voice firm as he spoke. "My name is Eirsen Arik Faerieth. Prince Eirsen. Heir to the throne of Orndelle."

His name ran in my ears, his identity no longer a mystery. The image came forward almost immediately. The vision clearer than any I had before. I'd seen them before, in a dream under a large oak tree.

But this time, this time it was different. . .

The hallway echoed with the sound of running feet as a girl with chocolate colored hair and bright green eyes darted down it, her pointed ears a reminder of what she was. A voice called out to her from behind, causing her to glance over her shoulder.

"Astraea! Wait for me!"

A boy with white-blond hair and two different-colored eyes rushed after her.

"Hurry up, Eirsen! I want to see the sunset," she urged, her laughter ringing through the halls. She had a good lead, but her stumble on a carpet gave him a chance to catch up.

Bursting past the busy servants, Eirsen called out to her once more. "Astraea!"

"Come on!" she replied, her heart racing with anticipation.

"Princess, you know you're supposed to wait for me," he scolded playfully.

"Quick! The sun is setting. If you don't hurry, we'll miss it!" Astraea urged, urging him on.

He finally caught up with her as they burst onto the balcony, the doors slamming open behind them. They came to a stop at the railing, gazing out at the breathtaking sight before them. The sun was sinking behind the horizon, painting the sky with a riot of pink, orange, and purple hues.

My breath rushes from my lungs. I felt like I had been punched in the gut. Tears threaten at the corners of my eyes again. My voice cracks as I look up at him. "Eirsen."

He'd been my playmate.

My friend.

All this time he had been my friend and companion. The longing in his eyes was unmistakable. That's when it hit me. The realization, the thing I did not want to believe. The truth, what he had done. The pain he had caused me and my family.

The final truth.

He approached me then, his voice strained. "Astraea?"

Cupping my face in his hands, my eyes lock with his. "What else do you remember?"

What I remembered was not worth telling him. Instead, "I don't
  understand."

"You will. Try to remember."

"None of this is real. I'm not fae. I'm a mortal *human* girl with no family. My name is Serra. . ." I whispered to myself, my head spinning. I didn't want to believe him, I didn't want to believe any of this. It had been simpler before, my life had been simpler. Sad yes, with those who had turned on me. Even sadder with the passing of everyone I loved. This was not what I had expected when I had agreed to his deal, this was not what I thought I was after.

This was not what I had asked for, had *wished* for.

It was not what I wanted.

His eyes trace every delicate feature on my face, his thumb caressing my cheek. A tear escapes but he brushes it away before it could fall. "Astraea, you were never just human." He conveys, brushing my hair back and tucking it behind my ear. My soft rounded ear with the lightest touch of his fingers, sends a shiver through me. "You are the heir to the Lost Fae. Your people, they need you. The land needs you."

"No, that's not possible. You're wrong."

His expression softened then, letting me go as I step back from him. "You are. You are the Crowned Princess. You *are* Astraea Irene Linnea Darthordian."

"No!"

My feet faltered as the ground began to quake beneath me, causing a shiver to run down my spine. I surveyed my surroundings, my eyes scanning the throne room. The once stately walls were now scarred with deep cracks, rubble threatening to fall from above at any moment. The sudden realization hit me, and I could no longer hold back the tears. My heart felt heavy, like it was about to crumble along with the castle walls. How could I have been so foolish? How could I not have seen through Nona's stories and the Goblin King's tricks? With a quivering voice, I confronted him, a mix of anger and hurt laced in my words.

"You're lying," I accuse him.

He sighs heavily, acknowledging my words. "For over eighteen years, Inirea has been decaying. It's dying. It needs you."

My fury builds, fueled by his admission. "If it is decaying and dying, it is by your own hand," I seethe, the words spilling out in a torrent of hurt and betrayal. He'd turned against my family and me, betraying us all. My heart aches, and I feel like he's stolen my life and family from me.

"There are greater forces at work here, forces that would harm you. Fae who want you for themselves." He says, "Astraea, please."

But he was a liar- a master at deception and deceit. A crafter of lies and manipulation. It was his specialty, his forte. He could make you believe anything he wanted you to believe, even if it was the furthest thing from the truth. And I fell for it- completely, fully and wholly fell for it. I trusted him with my heart and soul, never once questioning his motives or his true intentions. But now, as the truth slowly reveals itself, I can see him for what he truly is.

And it hurts. All of it hurts so much.

I struggle to process the enormity of his betrayal, a burning light ignites within me, threatening to consume me with its intensity. The memories that had been hidden from me for so long come flooding back, leaving me reeling. I turn on the Goblin King, my anger now in control.

"Why are all these memories coming now? Why did Luna not tell me? Why keep me in the dark?" I spat out my questions, each word infused with anger and frustration.

"It had to be done. When you were taken from Inirea to Rothnia, your memories were blocked. It was to keep you safe. It was to protect you from Ezra," Eirsen repeats, his voice heavy with regret.

The name of the person he's trying to protect me from hits me with a powerful force. Ezra. The thought of him fills me with fear and dread. I try to push the memories of him away, but they come rushing back, unbidden.

I feel like I'm suffocating.

"Stop. Please, stop," I plead, my voice barely above a whisper.

Despite his explanation, doubts nag at me, and I struggle to believe that everything he's telling me is true. My mind races, trying to make sense of the chaos and confusion. The ground continues to tremble beneath my feet, and I realize that everything I thought I knew was a lie. It's too much to bear.

Even with the final truth hanging over my head, I was desperate not to believe it. Everything seemed plausible. It could not have been him, could it? I wanted to believe he hadn't done it. He hadn't played a part in it. It felt like I was shattering. Every part of me splintered into pieces. I could take his confession in the ballroom. I could take his lies, I could take the whispers of the villagers of Rothnia. I could take the perfidy of Kaston. I could believe parts of the lies he had told. I could believe the truths I had learned.

But not this.

My thoughts spiral out of control, and I can feel myself breaking apart. I try to cling to the little truths I've learned along the way, but they're too few and far between. I can't believe that the male who stands before me, the one who has robbed me of everything, could be capable of such betrayal. My heart feels like it's splintering into a million pieces, and I'm powerless to stop it.

I was Fae.

This was my home, my world. But it's all been taken away from me. The one who stands before me, the Goblin King, was the source of all my pain and loss. I feel like I'm drowning in a sea of emotions, unable to escape the devastation that surrounds me.

"Astraea- *Serra*..." Eirsen's hand reached out to me, worry etched on his face, but it was the panic in his eyes that caused me to pause. The ground rumbled again as I felt the last pieces of me break. The last pieces of whom I thought I was, who I knew to be, splintered and scattered inside me. The walls around me trembled as another rumble shook them. The cracks in the stones causing more to fall around us.

"Please..." Eirsen pleaded.

"Take me home," I demanded, glancing back at the throne he had been lounging in- My father's throne. My eyes lingered on the crumbling walls around us, at the charred and broken beams. The once magnificent room, ravaged. Only a distant spark of what I remembered them to be, of what remained of this place.

The look on my father's face as I burst through the door with the sound of steel and muffled voice echoing through my memories. The fear and the longing of the family I'd lost. Tears ran down my face as I remembered, remembered everything. As everything opened up again, released from its cage. I would not tell him that. It was my cross to bear, my burden. Another rumble shook the walls. More stone falling and tumbling. My mother's voice, her laugh. The labyrinth garden at the manor. My father's smile as he chased me through the hedges.

"Serra, please." The desperation in his voice was clear.

"Now!"

I wanted to go home.

My home with Nona. I didn't care if it wasn't where I belonged because this wasn't home, my home was in Rothnia. My home was small, simple, and cozy.

My home, my life there.

The light that had shown itself went out, burying it under a well of darkness- tamping out the ember. I allowed the darkness inside to embrace me, to hold me in comfort as I struggled with everything.

To comprehend all that had happened.

Eirsen's demeanor shifts as something inside him fractured. His eyes that had once been filled with mischief and amusement, now carried sorrow and dejection- dull and empty. Hesitantly, he extends his hand to me once more, silently pleading for my forgiveness. My own hand is slick with sweat as I take his, unsure of what to expect.

As he pulls me close, his familiar scent washes over me, flooding my senses. It's a scent I'll never forget, one that will stay with me from this day forward. A heady mix of smoke, citrus, and evergreen. Despite everything, I can't help but take a deep breath and savor the smell, letting it ground me in the moment.

In a blur of wind, smoke, and shadow, we disappear from the throne room, leaving behind the chaos and destruction. The air whips at my hair and dress as we hurtle through the darkness. I close my eyes, focusing on the one person holding me against him. The only thing that feels real in this surreal moment. His arms warm and secure as he cradles me against the shadows around us. I feel safe here, cocooned in his protective embrace, but deep down, I know that I can never trust him again.

He had played games; he had played *me* and now there was nothing he could do that would allow my already broken heart to mend. He had done that, he had re-broken what had already been repaired. There were so many other things I wanted answers to, lost in the truth of who I was, not having the chance to ask.

It did not matter now. I hadn't realized I was holding my breath until its pushed past my lips. I felt the warmth of the air then. The sounds and scents of home. The cicada's and cricket's chirps flutter along in the breeze. The smell of the air, salt, and fresh grass. Familiarity. He had brought me back to Rothnia. He'd done what I'd asked.

A small voice told me he always would, he always had. No matter what I asked of him, he would do it. I felt the pang of guilt in my chest then, at my words and how I had treated him. He was right, he had only done what I had asked of him. But this was my choice, my own fate. It was up to me to decide now what I wanted to do with the answers I received.

The sun was setting on the horizon, casting the world in shadow as it descended. Eirsen's own shadows faded, shrinking back to where their master pulled them from leaving the two of us standing outside the tiny cottage that I had been raised in, Nona Luna's cottage. The home that had been my only sanctuary, where the memories of our lives together would live on. The tiny windows with the cracked glass remained dark and the crooked chimney was empty of smoke as I surveyed the building, her presence was gone forever.

I turned to say something to him, but he was nowhere to be seen. My heart sank, Eirsen had vanished, leaving me here alone to scan the lane- hoping to see a black raven in the trees. Gone in a moment, a single breath. My hand reached for the wooden gate, the gate I used to run through into Nona's arms, the familiar sound of it as it creaked open.

Home.

I was home.

Epilogue

AS THE BLACK BIRD rustled its feathers, it watched the dark-haired beauty below. The canopy of trees swayed in the wind, filling the air with the scents of the world, a world that was foreign to him. It was her world and hers alone, something they couldn't share.

Eirsen had been sent to keep an eye on her until the time was right. The Haruspex had demanded it, knowing that Ezra was determined to have her. It was only a matter of time before her location would be discovered by his forces, and they didn't have much time left.

Although she had broken part of the curse by regaining her memories and breaking its hold on her, she refused to acknowledge her power, and she refused to acknowledge him. He had seen the look on her face when her power had appeared. All she had to do was grasp it and hold onto it, but she snuffed it out instead.

The curse still held its chokehold on Inirea and its people, and

Astraea-*Serra* was all that remained to save it from ruin and from Ezra. The aftermath of his betrayal had left Eirsen bloody and barely alive. It was a miracle the Haruspex had found him at all.

"*Your lives are entwined, young man.*" The old seer said. "*I have seen it. You are her dionadair, her protector. You two are equals, matched. In life and in power. Infinite.*"

Upon his arrival back at the castle, Ezra had been waiting for him. "Where is she, Eirsen?"

As he turned, he came face to face with the Lord of the Dark Fae, seated upon his throne, gazing down upon him. The Prince of Nightmares, with hair as dark as ink flowing down his back, the embodiment of true Darkness and Decay in Inirea.

"I don't have a clue what you're talking about," Eirsen lied with a feigned air of indifference. The truth was that Ezra was a cruel and ruthless male who wouldn't hesitate to kill you. Eirsen was fully aware of this, but he refused to give in and tell him anything. His attention was caught by the Keepers- eight of them, he counted-standing in their black armor and waiting for their inevitable orders. A fae male in dark armor, as black as the night, stood behind Ezra and the throne, his face concealed by a helm.

"DO NOT LIE TO ME!" Ezra's voice bounced off the decaying stone walls, magnifying. "She was here! You were to bring her to me! You knew your orders!"

"I will no longer be your puppet!" Eirsen bellowed.

He simmered with rage.

For two decades, he had been used and manipulated by Ezra since the day he arrived. It all started when she went missing and he betrayed her people. Every time he failed, he was punished severely, and the anger inside him grew, knowing that the punishment for betrayal was death. But to him, she was everything- the stars, the moon, the world- the very breath he needed to live. She was Life itself, and he was willing to sacrifice everything to save her. Despite her lack of trust in him, he would protect her from harm, for he needed her to survive and help fight this evil.

The years had made him hard and cruel, much like Ezra. At the beginning, he searched for her, forgetting the memories that Ezra's curse had blocked. But now, all the memories had been freed, and he would be free from the male who held his leash. For years, he had played by Ezra's rules and played his game, but no longer. It all started on that fateful day when she turned eight.

That day, everything began to unfold.

She been so young. So innocent. Her beautiful green eyes, full of terror as the boar ran for her. The creature was crafted of pure nightmares. He could *feel* the fear and terror radiating from her. She had displayed who she was. The power that lay in her veins on full display as she eviscerated the boar into nothing. Too soon had she been able to pull from it, too soon had she accessed it. Appearing out of her terror, one of her strongest emotions, to protect her.

When it could have killed her.

He should have taken her then, handed her over. But something had fractured in him- the cracks had started. The fear he had felt that day had never left him. He'd forgotten what it was like to love, to hope. She awoke that part in him.

Those memories he had of her, he cherished now.

He'd gone back every year to check on her. To see if she displayed any more of the power she held. He would do everything he could to save her. His web of lies, his plan forming into what it had become, but he had to do it. He had to protect her from Ezra. Keep her from this world until she's ready. She was hoped for the whole realm. He would sacrifice himself over and over for her.

If it meant she would survive.

He would do it.

She was *his*.

And he was hers. Forever, he would be hers.

If only he had known then what he knew now. That part of him, he realized, would do anything for her. He would reorder time, he would give her every dream, he would do it all for her. And for the last eighteen years he protected her. For eighteen years, he sacrificed another in her place. He took the punishments for failure if it meant keeping her whereabouts secret. And still, he'd lied to her. He'd pushed her, he'd been cruel to her. But everything he did was necessary.

Even though he had forgotten what she meant to him, it was her touch that brought him back to reality and made him see the errors of his ways. He realized that it was not about breaking the curse to free himself, but it was about her and how much she meant to him. He knew he had made mistakes and had to make amends and ask for her forgiveness. He was willing to spend the rest of his life doing so, even if it meant sacrificing everything to protect her from her Uncle.

"No matter. This was your last chance, and after the last girl you brought me. . ." Ezra declared, flicking his hand, "You know what the punishment is for your impertinence and betrayal this time."

Before he could even draw his sword or the power in his veins, the Keepers had pushed him to his knees. A hand in his hair, yanked his head back to stare into Ezra's dark soulless eyes.

"My new invention." Ezra said as the Fae male handed him a syringe. Holding it up, inspecting the cloudy serum inside as it glistened in the evening light. A vicious smile formed on his face. "It'll keep you conscious, but unable to move. Unable to access any magic you have gained, keep you weak."

Ezra scoffed as Eirsen realized what he was saying, "Do not think I did not know Eirsen. Do not think that I didn't know you betrayed me years ago. Don't try to lie to me now when I know what you've been up to. I *know* who you are. I always have, and I know who she is. You cannot protect her forever."

His heart plunged in his chest. No. No he had to have been making a mistake. There was no way, he had been so careful. So aware of the choices he had made, how? How did he know? But it was too late.

Eirsen fought hard against the hands that held him, but he was no match for them. Not as he was held down, the cloudy serum was injected. The effects of Ezra's serum took hold of him immediately. The feeling of lost control, no longer the master of one's own body. A feeling of true drunkenness as it coursed through his system. The source in the pit of his stomach hummed, angry that it couldn't be wielded. Could not defend him.

The first blow came from behind, the pommel of a sword hitting the back of his head, the agony of it. Another came in the form of a kick to his ribs. They were going to beat him to death right here. In the same throne room where Ezra took Elias' life. A couple more blows to his back, his head and his chest sent him spiraling, the edges of his vision blurring and darkening. His head pounding in agony as his heart screamed in grief.

He'd never see her again.

"Enough." Ezra's voice pierced through his foggy daze. The darkness at the edges closing in. "Take him away. Do with him what you will. Drown him, hang him, bury him alive. I don't care, I do not want to see him again. I free you from your oath Eirsen. A deal struck can be unstruck. Not that you will live long enough to enjoy it."

The clanging of heavy armor filled his ears as the Keepers hoisted him up. Darkness crept in at the edges of his vision, but he held on, his mind fixated on her face, her eyes, and her smile. He tried to piece together what had happened, but his memories were fragmented and foggy. They dragged him out of the throne room, out of the city, and left him near the Dead Forest by the Dried River. The serum pulsed through his veins, amplifying the pain of every blow to his head and ribs. Each breath was a struggle, causing sharp stabs of agony in his chest.

But he endured it all, he did this for her.

His vision blurred as the Fae male's cold, blue eyes bore into his own. The blonde-haired male, his helm tucked under his arm and a long sword strapped to his back. Eirsen recognized him immediately.

Ezra's Commander.

Without warning, he kicked Eirsen in the chest, sending him tumbling down the riverbank and leaving him unable to move. As he lay dying, he regretted leaving her vulnerable and alone, with his heart in her hands. She was about to say something, but he couldn't bear it. The thought of leaving her had torn him apart.

But it was the right thing to do.

There was always a right thing to do.

B Y SOME MIRACLE, THE Dried River hadn't flooded for the rainy season, and Eirsen had found himself lying at the bottom, barely alive. His body was battered, bruised, and broken. He couldn't move, couldn't even cry out for help.

But then, through the haze of his pain, he saw her. The Haruspex, with her wild eyes and her tangle of dark hair, hoisted him out of the water and brought him to her hidden home beneath a fallen tree. She tended to his wounds with a gentle touch, her hands working miracles as she nursed him back to health.

As he lay there, weeks passing by, Eirsen's thoughts were consumed by her- Astraea. The dark-haired beauty who had captivated his heart from the moment he laid eyes on her. He thought of her every waking moment, his heart aching to be near her once again. He remembered the day she disappeared, leaving him to face Ezra's wrath alone, and he regretted how he had left her. He wanted nothing more than to rectify his mistakes, to be near her, and to keep her safe.

The Haruspex's words lingered in his mind as he left her home. He would protect her, as was his duty. Keep her safe from the harm he knew would come one day. Even now as the days flooded by he could sense the change in the wind. Could feel it in his bones. They were running out of time.

For several months, he had traveled between the realms. Crossing into the Mortal Lands with the magic he had gained. With the sacrifices he gave to the Immortal Gods. He'd been freed of Ezra's hold over him, his deal broken but he knew that this was not the end.

The sun warmed Eirsen's feathers as he perched on a nearby branch, his inky black feathers standing out starkly against the bright foliage. His gaze shifted, catching sight of her as she weaved her way through the rows of plants- humming a tune to herself as she went about her day. One he knew well. Eirsen's heart swelled with love and longing as he watched her, his eyes fixed on her every move. The gracefulness at which she moved, her scent drifting on the air currents. The sweet smell of chamomile and bergamot. With the underlying tone of vanilla and that sweet scent of spice.

But there was something else there, something he couldn't quite make out. He couldn't quite decipher what it was, but he felt something. A thread of ancient magic, a connection that seemed to tether him to her. It was an electrifying sensation, one that stirred a deep sense of protectiveness within him. He knew without a doubt that he would do whatever it takes to ensure her safety.

The leaves from the trees blew down raining on her in a cascade of reds, oranges, and yellows as autumn descended on the Mortal Lands. For a moment, his heart sputtered in his chest as Astraea looked up, her attention caught by his presence. He spread his wings and lets out a loud *kraa* before taking off from the branch- soaring up into the clear blue sky. He felt a sense of freedom and exhilaration as he flew higher and higher. the wind whipped through his feathers.

Eirsen felt a sense of peace wash over him. He knew that there was much work to be done, but for now, he was content just to watch over her from afar, knowing that she was safe and that they would be reunited again soon. With a final glance back at her, he flew off into the distance, his heart filled with hope and determination.

Until next time, Princess

ACKNOWLEDGMENTS

Oh wow, I can't believe this is it. This is my first published book and I did it. This story has been in my head for going on fifteen years, probably even longer. And because of those who believed in me, I was able to do it. I would not be here today if it wasn't for several people. For you the readers. I want to say thank you. Serra and Eirsen's story will continue.

First off I would like to thank my Mom, because of you I was able to nurture my creativity. Because of you I got to write my stories as a kid and then my fanfiction in later years. Thank you for always being there, and for being my mom and allowing me to do these things and understanding that this is what I am. You never once said that I can't do something, you have always encouraged me to at least try. If I was good or not. You rooted for me since I was very little, you have been my number one cheerleader. The first person to read it in its entirety and pushed me to keep going. I wish dad were here to see this, to hold it in his hands. But I know he has been right there this whole time, guiding me and watching it unfold. I cannot thank the two of you enough.

To my husband, without you, I wouldn't be here either. Allowing me the time to write this while sitting with you or having the time I needed alone to get it done. You listened to me go on and on about things. Talk about what I like and didn't like in the book. Encouraged me to keep writing it. You helped me celebrate each milestone, and you never once complained. You often shared my progress with pride and that alone inspired me to continue. I promised you that I would go on every adventure, be there for whatever life threw at us, thank you for going on this adventure with me. Thank you for dealing with my depressive sadness when something happened that I did not expect. Thank you my love.

My friends and family, thank you for encouraging me with each Facebook post. Thank you for rooting for me and building the confidence to keep going with the progress and every update I shared. You guys mean a lot to me. Grace, thank you, thank you, thank you. You were my hype woman, you got me through the days I could not on my own. Without you, I don't think this story would exist. Thank you for volunteering to be a my first beta reader.

Katie, my partner in crime, my creative best friend and sister. All our time together growing up and creating our own worlds, our own stories. Coloring and designing games, it led to this. My time with you and Mary will never be forgotten. The time I got to spend with your family and mom and dad will always hold a special place in my heart. You were there for so many life-changing moments and the first person I often went to. For that I wish nothing but good things and beautiful opportunities for you, always.

My friends, my lifelong friends, my family. Without you guys I would not be where I am today. Without you, I would not have been able to write this.

357

You guys were with me in the darkest days. You were with me when I needed you all the most and to me that is the greatest gifts. You know who you are. Amber, Eric and Katie, Kristi, Heather, Ashley, Momo, Auntie Wendy, Jeff and Suzanne, Debbie, Cheryl, Danny, Linda, Christy, Lisa, Joe and Dianne, and everyone else because there are so many of you that I could list every person that has made the biggest impact on my life.

Miranda, thank you for indulging me and allowing me to bother you with the promo art. Without you, Serra and Eirsen wouldn't look as they do for others to see them.. They would not be as I would like them to be seen. You helped with that, and I will forever be grateful for it. Thank you!

To my Author group and Bookish Facebook Group... you guys!! You're all so amazing, without your encouragement and kind words I would have given up a long, long time ago. I appreciate you guys for interest and honesty. For being my Beta and ARC readers. My hype team. I would not have gotten the kind of attention I did without you all. Thank you!

My ARC team, thank you guys so much for all that you have done, for being involved and getting to know Serra and Eirsen. Lastly, to Adrienne. Thank you, thank you, thank you so much! There is not enough words in the world for me to express how much I appreciate you and what you have done for this story, for this book!

Daddy, I miss you. I understand now why you pushed me to be better. Why you wanted what was best for me. You knew I was capable of doing it. And I did. The impact you hand on my life will forever be a part of who I am. I love you, and if there was a passage way to wherever you are to see you, I would take it in a heartbeat.

About the Author

As a little girl from a rural town in Minnesota, V.A. Haugen has always loved to tell stories. Her teachers would often take the stories she created and turn them into 'picture books.' From there her imagination expanded, wanting to write her own book one day to share with the world. But before that could happen she dove into the world of fanfiction. Her love of writing never stopped, until one day she took pen to paper and Curse of Lies and Darkness was born.

When she is not writing, she's reading, sewing or working on a DIY project around the house. She currently resides in a small town in rural Iowa with her husband, their three dogs, two cats and a dream that one day her books will make a difference, even if its in one person's life.

If you have a dream, follow it. Do not let it stop you.

-V.A. Haugen

Milton Keynes UK
Ingram Content Group UK Ltd.
UKHW011950210823
427215UK00004B/417